A Tales of Zeaggatha Novel

Trapped:
Scorched by Fear

A.K. Watkins

ISBN: 9798985591521 (Paperback)

PhoenixQuinnPublishing.com

Other Works
by A.K. Watkins

Tales of Zeaggatha Series
Trappped:
Flames for Death
Scorched by Fear

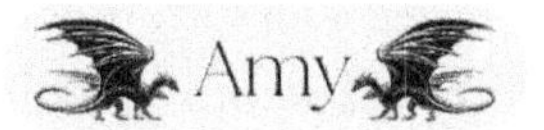

Amy stumbled as the bright flash of light cleared and she reappeared in the Arkhams' basement along with her companions. The eerie glow on the stone walls from the Gate odissipated as it closed behind them.

Lillian immediately rushed forward, her blue eyes wide. "Are you all okay?"

Nolan ripped the helmet from his head, breathing heavily. "No, we're not okay!" He set his helmet on the nearby table and ran his hand through his black hair, slicked back with sweat.

Kila smiled at Lillian, blood still dripping from the small cut above her left eye and matting into the thin brown fur of her face. "Oh, you're so pretty, too. I love your eyes! They're so much prettier than my plain brown ones."

Arkham's eyes narrowed, creasing his face as he looked between Kila and the others. "Was she bitten by a sinspawn?"

Talia's hands fluttered helplessly around Kila. "I'm not sure what to do. I'm basically out of magick and pretty much everyone is injured."

Arkham's eyes ranged across them and a wave of light filled the room, stronger than the one Talia could produce. Immediately, itching replaced the burning in Amy's leg from where the zombies had tried to drag her back into the murky water of the dungeon. She slouched back against the Gate, the fatigue setting in as the adrenaline receded.

Lillian studied each of them, focusing on Talia and Amy. "You two used all of your magick, didn't you?"

Amy's entire body shook. "I used the last of it on a spell against the sinspawn."

Talia shook her head. "I have a little bit left. I was going to use it on whoever needed it the most, but Jax and Nolan managed to kill the last sinspawn."

"You should get some rest. Draining yourself of magick will completely exhaust you." Lillian's gaze drifted down and settled on Amy's shredded pants legs. She gasped. "What happened here?"

Amy glanced down, blinking as a haze settled over her vision. "Uh... I had to swim in a pool with a bunch of zombies. The potion you gave me let me get in okay, but it wore off before I could get out."

Lillian stiffened. "You swam with zombies?"

Amy's eyes didn't want to stay open as she nodded. "Uh... yeah. I had to get a key to shut off a bunch of swinging blades. It was at the bottom of a pool filled with zombies."

Lillian stayed silent for a moment. "We'll talk more after you've gotten some rest. I'll have June draw you a bath. You'll want to clean up really well before going to bed."

Amy's head dropped. "Sounds good."

Jax stepped forward, offering her his shoulder. "Here. Let me help you."

Amy's gaze darted downwards. "What about your leg?"

Jax glanced down at the tear in his own pants. "Actually, it feels fine now."

Lillian knelt next to him, pressing the cloth aside. "What happened to your leg?"

Jax scowled. "A giant bloody zombie rat."

Lillian frowned. "Quaero." Her hand glowed faintly as she rested it near Jax's leg. "As I suspected. The rat passed a bacteria called tularemia into your bloodstream. If left untreated, it attacks your lungs and can do some serious damage. Fortunately for you, I also know how to remove it." She pulled out a tiny bundle of herbs. "Aufero. Now swallow this" Jax blinked, but did as she said, cringing at the taste. "Sorry. It tastes awful, but it will draw the disease to it and then pass harmlessly." While

Amy saw no visible change, Lillian looked pleased as she stood. "Was anyone else bitten or scratched? Or even just *touched* the rats or their blood?"

Nolan shook his head. "I don't think so."

Talia nudged Kila forward. "She was scratched."

Lillian pulled another bundle from her belt pouch. "Aufero." She held it up to Kila. "Alright, Kila, I need you to take this."

Kila smiled and took the offered bundle. "Okay, Lillian. It must be so nice to heal people."

Lillian returned the smile. "It really is. Go ahead and take that for me." She glanced at Arkham. "You'll remove it?"

Arkham waited until Kila had swallowed the bundle before stepping forward. "Do you have any other injuries?"

Kila gazed up at him, eyes wide. "No, sir. Talia did so well and healed me so good. Do you think I could be a healer? It would be so much handier than just being a monkey."

Arkham rested his hand on Kila's head. The same blue light that had enveloped them when their blood had been Awakened surrounded Kila. She stared up at him a moment, then slumped, eyes closed. Arkham reacted quickly and caught her.

Nolan gripped the hilt of his blade. "What the hell did you do?"

Arkham nodded to Lillian and she hurried to the platform. He carefully settled Kila onto the nearby couch, the only furniture in the room besides a small end table and a shelf. "I removed the curse the sinspawn placed on her. Or at least as well as I can. She will probably sleep for a day as it works its way through her body. After that, she will still be extremely prone to envious thoughts, but not as much as if I had let the curse run its course unchecked."

Jax glanced at Amy worriedly as she leaned heavily on him before turning back to Arkham. "What happens if it's left unchecked?"

"It would consume her. She would no longer just wish for things; she would actively try to take them with no regard for who she hurts in the process."

Talia's eyes widened. "But that won't happen now, right? You fixed her?"

Arkham glanced at Kila's sleeping form. "I have done the best I can. As I said, the thoughts will never truly disappear, but she will be more in control of them."

Nolan scowled. "Why didn't you warn us about them? You should have told us that this could happen!"

Arkham's eyes rested on Nolan's hand where it gripped the hilt of his blade. "I did warn you that they forced their sins on their victims. And clearly you would already be trying to avoid getting bitten. What more could I have done?"

The platform lowered toward them again with Lillian and a staff member on it. Nolan's grip tightened before he released his sword and stalked toward it. "I need a drink."

Lillian watched him board the platform and pull the lever before turning back to the group. "Is everything alright?"

Talia sighed and rubbed her face. "He's angry because he feels like we weren't warned enough about what we would be facing."

Lillian frowned, glancing between the lifting platform and Talia. "I wish we could have warned you about everything you may have faced, but the dungeon changes each time and we were afraid of overwhelming you. Certain things appear regularly, like the undead and the sinspawn, but other things—like the trap you faced with the pool of undead—change." Her eyes darted to Amy again, wide with concern. "Honestly, we've only had a few people mention that trap in all the years people have gone into this dungeon. And quite often the one that does the swim doesn't make it out of the pool."

Amy chuckled dryly. "Lucky me, I guess."

"Yes... Very lucky." She glanced over to where the staff member had lifted Kila. "Why don't you head up to bathe? June should have it drawn and ready for you by now."

With Jax's support, Amy started toward the platform.

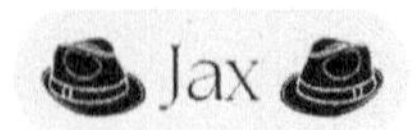

Jax watched Amy closely as they reached their suite. "Are you sure you'll be alright?"

Amy nodded, her damp auburn and black hair escaping its braided confines to fall around her heart-shaped face. "I'm just going to bathe real quick and then head to bed. Forget dinner; I'll just eat a big breakfast in the morning." The slight spattering of freckles stood out against her unusually pale face.

Jax frowned, but let her go. "Alright. Just don't fall asleep in the tub, alright?"

She waved a hand and the door to the washroom closed behind her, leaving him alone in the sitting room. Sighing, he rang the bell to summon the maid who serviced their rooms, June, again.

She appeared in the doorway almost immediately with a curtsy, her blonde hair pulled into a tight bun. "How can I help you, sir?"

Jax waved a hand at the washroom door. "Make sure to check on her in a bit. She's exhausted and I don't want her falling asleep in the tub." He wanted to wait for her himself, but the stench of the undead rot on his clothing and skin drove him to clean up.

June dropped into another curtsy. "Yes, sir."

Jax rubbed his face. "Please. Please, drop the 'sir.' You know I hate it." *I don't think I could ever get used to that. I'm not sure I would want to.*

"Uh, right. Sorry."

Jax waved her away. "I'm going to change and go get some dinner. Could you bring me a basin of water and a cloth? And be sure to check on her soon, okay?"

"Yes, s- Er… right." A deep blush covered her cheeks and Jax shook his head, chuckling as he entered his room.

He carefully removed his fedora and set it on the bed before stripping down. He frowned as he studied the clothing he'd worn into the dungeon. *I doubt even the best tailor in the world can repair these.*

He jumped at a light knock on his door. Swiftly, he pulled on clean pants and pulled it open. June focused on his chest, her golden-brown eyes wide.

Jax glanced down at the scarring and chuckled. "Life of a traveler, right?"

She blinked and refocused on his face, holding out a small basin of steaming water, a rag draped across the side. "Uh. Right, s- uh, never mind. Is there anything else you need?"

"No, that will be all." He closed the door and sighed, the smile falling from his face. He stepped in front of the mirror, studying the scars across his chest and stomach. The silver-white fur helped hide them, but Gallund's knife had cut deep, leaving it thinned in some places. Just over his heart, the thickest patch of scarring stood out amongst his fur. *They're certainly quite the sight.*

Downstairs in the dining hall, he found Nolan back in his regular clothing with two large glasses of ale in front of him. He'd nearly drained the first already, but his plate still appeared to be full. Jax grabbed his own plate of food, settling into a seat across from the other man.

Nolan stabbed a piece of pork chop with his fork. "I hate this damn place."

Jax took a moment to cut a piece of his own pork chop off. "I do, too. At least we survived the first dungeon."

Nolan snorted. "We survived the first one, sure. But it was close. Lady Flame very nearly died in that pool. If she'd been just a few seconds longer, she wouldn't have made it to the edge in time."

Jax shuddered, remembering the sight of the grasping gray-green arms clawing at Amy's legs and her pale face when Talia finally reached her. The blood underneath her… He shook his head. "I know. It never should have been her in that pool."

Nolan raised an eyebrow. "Got a thing for Lady Flame, Fox Boy?"

Jax snorted. "Don't get me wrong, I wouldn't mind the chance to date her, but… no. No, I don't have a 'thing' for her. I care about her. She's my friend, and I didn't like seeing her hurt."

Nolan leaned back in his seat, downing another gulp of ale. "You're going to have to get used to it. If *that* was the 'easiest' dungeon, we're all going to get hurt a lot more."

Jax set his fork on his plate and pressed his palms against his eyes. "I know that. I do. Doesn't mean I have to like it."

Nolan grunted, finishing off the first glass of ale before reaching for the second. "If I didn't want out of this hellhole so bad, I'd walk away right now. But if we're trapped here, what good does that do?"

Jax dropped his hands. "It doesn't." He gestured around them.

"We're stuck here whether we like it or not." He frowned. "Where's Talia?"

Nolan glanced up toward the second floor. "In her room. She said she was going to bathe and then head to bed. Apparently using that much magick is exhausting. That reminds me, why weren't you using that thing you did on Kila in there?"

Jax shrugged, wincing at the reminder of his accidental attack on Kila. "I tried on a few of the zombies, but I mean… they're undead. They don't have minds to attack."

Nolan speared a potato, studying Jax. "Is that how that works?"

Jax nodded. "From what I've been able to tell, I just… overload a person's mind basically. But they have to actually *have* a mind for it to work. So training dummies, plants… undead;" he shrugged again, "it doesn't work on them. They have to have some level of intelligence."

Nolan finished his second glass of ale and stood. "Well let's hope we don't face anything else it doesn't work on." He crossed to the alcohol bar and dug a large bottle of whisky and a couple of shot glasses from beneath it before returning to the table. "Drink?"

Jax eyed the bottle a moment before sighing. "Sure."

Nolan poured them each a shot, then lifted his into the air. "To surviving this hellhole."

Jax chuckled dryly and lifted his own. "To surviving."

They both downed the shots and Jax bit back a cough as the liquid burned his throat on the way down. Nolan poured himself another and then offered the bottle to Jax.

Jax shook his head and shoved the last bite of food in his mouth. "I'm headed to bed. Good night, Nolan."

"Night."

Jax dropped his plate off and headed up to his room. The washroom door stood open and Amy was nowhere to be seen. Relieved, he called June for his own bath and then headed to bed.

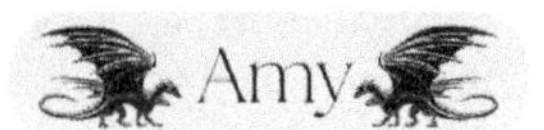

Images of skeletons, zombies, and rats, all engulfed in flames, plagued Amy's sleep. When she finally woke early in the morning, sweat coated her body. Azurys sat nearby and Amy could feel the concern coming from her familiar as she purred reassuringly. Amy sat up and slid her feet from the bed, giving Azurys a grateful scratch before making her way to the washroom to wipe the sweat from her body.

While wiping her body down, a flash of red below her breasts caught her attention and she stilled, studying herself in the mirror. Flames curled around her sides and beneath her breasts in the same reddish ink as her other tattoos, standing out against the paler coral of her skin. She ran her fingers across it. Tutela. She rolled the word over in her mind, but didn't cast the spell, fearing what it would do.

Back in her room, she found several new articles of clothing and a note.

The staff noticed you only had the two outfits so I sent along a few extra that looked like they would fit you. As well as another nightdress.

~Lillian

Amy blinked away tears and pulled one of the tunics from the hanger. It was soft and supple, much nicer than anything she'd worn in a long time. She didn't feel right wearing the clothes, but Lillian had been so kind to her thus far, and she didn't want to offend the sweet woman, so she hesitantly pulled it over her head. She sighed with pleasure as the smooth fabric slid over her skin.

Downstairs, a few staff members sat at one of the tables eating, but otherwise, she had the dining hall to herself.

"Early breakfast?" Amy jumped and turned to see the head Arkham's brother, Fredrikson. His silvery-gray hair fell loosely around his face, the same piercing blue eyes that Arkham and Lillian shared pinning her in place.

Amy shifted in her seat uneasily. "Yes. I was too tired to come eat last night and woke up hungry this morning."

Fredrikson gestured to an empty seat. "Mind if I join you?" Amy hesitated a moment before nodding affirmation. After making his own plate, he sat down across from her. For a while, the only sounds that could be heard were the clanks of forks on plates.

"I hear you all completed the first dungeon last night?"

She glanced up from her food, trying to read his expression. "Yes. It was… difficult, but we managed."

He watched her critically, as if trying to solve a puzzle. "Good to hear. Those dungeons are nothing to mess with."

"Right. So I've heard." She shuddered at the memories of her close call.

He sipped his orange juice, eyes never leaving her. "Your name's Amy, right?"

"Yes… Why?" Amy shifted uneasily in her seat, wondering what he was going for.

"Is that short for something?"

Why does he want to know if Amy is short for anything? She took a sip of her own drink, buying time as she suddenly grew nervous. "Amelia."

He cut off a piece of flatcake, but didn't place it in his mouth yet. "That a family name?"

Unable to read his intentions, Amy picked at a piece of bacon. "Not that I'm aware of."

Suddenly Fredrikson stood, taking his barely touched plate with him. "Pretty name for a pretty girl," he said with a merry laugh, ambling away to join his son Austin at the head family table. "Have a good day!"

Amy blinked in confusion at the abrupt change in attitude from the man. "You… too?" She shook her head and took another bite of her food. *That man is strange. And he knows something he's not saying. I can tell. Why all of the interest in me?*

A light touch on her shoulder caused Amy to jump. Lillian quickly moved into Amy's vision. "Sorry I startled you. How are you this morning?"

Amy relaxed slightly, returning the other woman's smile. "Tired and sore, but otherwise alright. What about you?"

Lillian settled into the seat across from her. "I figured you would be. I thought you'd still be asleep this morning."

Amy chuckled. "I probably should be, but I woke up hungry and couldn't get back to sleep." She gestured toward her plate. "I figured it was already close enough to morning that breakfast might be available."

Lillian nodded toward her uncle and cousin. "We're all early risers. My father eats in his office more than down here, but Austin, Uncle Fredrikson, and I like to eat together."

"I see." Amy bit into a piece of bacon, chewing it slowly to give her time to think. "Last night you said that people didn't normally make it out of the pool…"

Lillian glanced down at her hands, fidgeting with her fingers. "No… no, they don't. I can think of maybe a dozen groups that have dealt with that pool. Don't get me wrong, that dungeon has plenty of traps, but that's one of the deadliest. Usually, they either all try to make it across the path and get knocked into the pool, or just barely get the key to the other side before being pulled under. Or… they just give up. It's one of the few things in that dungeon that can make a group quit."

Amy frowned, running her fingers across one of her legs. The welts had disappeared with the healing, leaving smooth skin with just a few faint white lines in their place. "I almost got pulled back down. I was near the edge and Kila managed to pull me out in time."

Lillian winced. "I'm sorry, Amy. I'm glad you're okay. Can I ask why you were the one that went in, though?"

Amy shrugged. "Jax and Talia aren't great swimmers, Kila was injured by the swinging blades, so she didn't think she *could* swim well, and Nolan was weighed down by all of that armor. I was the logical choice."

Lillian studied her with a raised eyebrow. "Nolan could have taken his armor off."

Amy picked up another piece of bacon, studying it for a moment as she thought over Lillian's words. "Technically, yes. But what would have happened if we'd been attacked while he was trying to put it back on? Or if he'd died in the pool? He was honestly taking most of the hits. Besides," her nose wrinkled, "I don't know about you, but I wouldn't want to be in wet clothes inside that armor."

Lillian chuckled. "Yes, I suppose you're right. That would certainly be unpleasant."

Amy rubbed the back of her neck sheepishly. "The pool wasn't the only thing that nearly got me, either. We came across this giant skeleton and it whacked me in the shoulder with its club." Her fingers trailed to her left shoulder. Arkham's healing had eased the pain in it, but it still ached.

Lillian smiled sympathetically at her. "I'm sorry."

Amy shrugged. "I'll be alright. Just… one question. The stories about being bitten or scratched by a zombie… Are they true?"

Lillian frowned. "You mean that if you're bitten, you turn into one?"

"Jax, Kila, and I were all scratched and I'm pretty sure some of them tried to gnaw on my legs. And Kila was bitten by the sinspawn."

Lillian shook her head. "You don't have to worry. Those are just stories. Zombies are magickally created. The stories came from old necromancers who would reanimate anyone their zombies killed. To outsiders, it looked like it was the zombie's bite that did it."

Amy relaxed slightly. "Thank you, Lillian. That's a relief."

"Of course, dear. I'm sorry you're having to go through all this."

Amy gnawed her lip for a moment, studying her plate. "How long will we have until the next one?"

Lillian sighed, picking at her own food. "Honestly, there's no telling. It could be anywhere from a few days to a few weeks."

Amy chewed on a flatcake, letting the comfortable silence settle between them. "Thank you for the clothes, by the way."

Lillian smiled at her. "I'm glad to see they fit. Your clothes from yesterday will be repaired, but it didn't seem like you had much to spare."

Amy bit her lip, staring down at her plate. "No, I really don't..." Then the first part of Lillian's statement registered and she glanced up at her. "Wait, you said the clothes will be repaired? How? Those pants were shredded!"

Lillian laughed, shaking her head. "We use a tailor that has access to magick. There's a spell that—so long as all of the pieces are present—can repair anything. All of your clothes will be sent to him."

Amy gaped at her. "You mean there's magick for *that*, too?"

Lillian shrugged. "Magick can do most anything if you set your mind to it and use the right combination of spells. But a mending spell is fairly basic."

Amy rubbed her face. "That's... impressive."

Jax entered the mess hall and raised a hand in greeting. "Good morning, Amy," he called across the room. He grabbed a plate and settled into the seat next to her.

Amy grinned. Though she couldn't place it, something looked different about him. "Morning! Did you sleep well?"

"Well enough. Though the undead seemed ill content to leave me be, even in my sleep."

"You, too, huh?"

Jax yawned and leaned back in his seat. "Did you make it to bed okay last night?"

Amy chuckled lightly, face heating. "I uh... actually fell asleep in the tub. June woke me."

Jax snorted. "I figured you would, so I asked her to check on you."

Amy blinked, staring at him. "I suppose that makes sense."

"Was that wrong?" His emerald eyes met hers, his head tilted to the side.

"Well... no. I'm just not used to having people worry about me."

Lillian propped her elbow on the table and leaned against her hand. "Have you not noticed Jax worrying over you constantly since you got here?"

Jax ducked his head and Amy looked between them, mind racing. The way he'd shielded her in town, protesting her doing anything dangerous in the dungeons, made sure she was okay... "Well... yes. I suppose I have." She turned to Jax. "You know you don't have to do that, right?"

He gave her a gentle smile before resting his hand on hers. "Yes, I do. Because we're friends. And friends take care of each other."

Amy stared at him a moment longer before returning the smile. "Yes. Friends. We're friends." Suddenly the difference clicked. "You have another tail!"

Jax grinned and pulled his hand back. "Seems my magick is growing."

"Congrats, Jax!"

Lillian chuckled and picked up her plate. "I'll leave you two to your breakfast. Take a few days to rest. You deserve it."

Amy reached forward. "You don't have to leave! You're welcome to have breakfast with us."

Lillian raised an eyebrow. "Are you sure?"

Jax shrugged. "Why not? Kila's still out, Nolan would never get up this early, and I doubt Talia would mind if she does show up. Far as I'm concerned, you're welcome to sit with us any time."

Lillian set her plate back down and relaxed back into her seat, chewing on a piece of bacon. "I *am* sorry about what happened to Kila. Father was able to mostly remove the curse, but it's not a complete cure. She'll likely struggle with it for the rest of her life."

Jax sighed, poking at an egg with his fork. "These sinspawn… Is this something we're going to have to worry about in every dungeon?"

"Unfortunately, yes. They seem to be the goal. You beat the sinspawn, you beat the dungeon."

Amy gnawed her lip. "What are the other sinspawn like? For the other dungeons?"

Lillian set her fork aside. "Each one is represented by an animal. Of course, you saw Envy's spawn that resemble dogs. Pride's resemble lions, Greed's look like foxes, Lust's look like rabbits, Gluttony's are pigs, Wrath's are dragons, and Sloth's resemble bears." She raised a hand, lifting a finger with each Sin.

Jax raised an eyebrow. "Why those specific animals?"

Lillian shrugged. "I have no idea. But they're all pretty similar to the ones you saw yesterday. They stand on two legs and wield some kind of weapon, but with features that resemble the associated creatures."

Amy picked at her food, thinking over her words. "You said dragons?"

"They only resemble dragons—a twisted version of them." Lillian shook her head, lips pursed. "They aren't actually dragons."

Jax's brow furrowed. "Wait, if no one has made it through Insanity and the sinspawn are only at the end, how do you know what the slothspawn look like?"

"The sinspawn have been around since long before the dungeons. The Generals used them back during the war."

"I see. Where do they come from?" he asked.

"We have no idea. They just always seemed to have a neverending supply." She picked up her plate and stood. "I need to get to work. You two have a good day." She paused next to Amy, her hand resting on her shoulder. "And Amy, you should really rest. Those zombies did a lot of damage to your legs, so give them time to recover, okay?"

"I will." Amy smiled at the older woman.

"Alright. I'll see you later."

Jax tipped his hat. "See you later, Lillian. So what are your plans today?" he asked Amy.

Amy pushed her own plate aside. "Probably going to spend time in the library. That actually reminds me, did you find anything else out about that *Infernal Banishment* book?" she added, her voice low.

Jax shook his head. "Not really. Seems to be much of the same as what we found in *Nightmares of the Abyss*, just related to devils instead of demons, though they seem to be more organized and easier to work with. Did you know that they have descendants like demon-spawn, but they're called devil-spawn?"

"Why am I not surprised?" Amy mused. *If demons and celestials can create half-breeds, why can't devils?* "I need to head to the library. You joining me?"

Jax ate the last bite of eggs on his plate and stood with a grin. "As if I could turn down such a wonderful invitation."

In the library sometime later, Amy still hadn't figured out why a new tattoo had appeared, so she set the book down, leaning back to stare at the ceiling silently. *I have no idea what's going on. My bloodline tattoo is much larger than usual, I have a second one that I can't find any information about… It seems like every time we get an answer, three more questions pop up.*

Movement nearby distracted her and she glanced over. Talia walked down the aisles of the library and approached a section Amy hadn't gone to before. She stared at a book apprehensively before pulling it off the shelf, then turned and brought it to the table Amy was sitting at.

Talia ran her fingers over the title Amy couldn't read. "*Archonic Harmony.*"

Jax approached her other side and looked over Talia's shoulder at the book. "You can read it?"

"It's in the language of celestials, so… yes."

"Archons… Aren't those like demons and devils, but good instead of evil?" Jax asked.

Talia flipped the book open, her eyes ranging across the text. "Yes. They oversee the other good planar outsiders—the angels and atlanti. Just like daemons are supposed to oversee evil planar outsiders. Though unfortunately, they are generally unable to control the demons." Jax and Amy both glanced over at her with furrowed brows and Talia shrugged. "Most of the teachings of the outsiders, especially the good ones, are taught in Arista's temples. It's not uncommon for someone who chooses not to worship a god to worship one of them instead, so we're taught about it as a measure of understanding since we travel for most of our lives."

"So what are you looking at a book about archons for?" Jax asked.

Talia shook her head. "Well, I wasn't intending to look at it. But, you said that the books you found gave off heat? Well, this one did, too. I ignored it for a while, but decided I might as well check."

Amy sat forward, eyes widening. "Wait, you mean this book might be like the other two?"

Talia slowly flipped through until she found the jagged edges of torn pages. She leaned back, leaving the book open. "So that makes three we've found."

Amy's fingers grazed the pendant in her pocket. "Yes, but… Why would he use a book about good outsiders?"

"I have no idea."

Amy's jaw clenched. "I need to get to that bookstore." Jax and Talia glanced at her in surprise. "If we can find out what these pages contained, maybe we can figure out what he did. And if we can figure out what he did, maybe we can figure out where he went. And how to get him back." Her voice lowered. "If he is in that pendant, then maybe figuring out how he got there will help us figure out how to bring him back. I mean, if he was strong enough to defeat the demon lord the first time, maybe he could break the curse that the demon lord placed."

Talia pushed the book away, her brow furrowed. "It makes sense in theory, but I'm not sure about it in practice. Even if we did figure out what he did, how he did it, and how to get him back, who's to say we'd be strong enough to do it? I mean, we've only just started learning magick, do you really think we stand any chance of figuring something of this magnitude out?"

Amy bit her lip, studying the book. "I don't know."

Talia sighed and flipped through the book some more. "It certainly looks like the section missing had to do with spells, same as the others. I'm fairly sure this is like the other two." She flipped the book shut and offered it to Amy. "Do you want it?"

"You hold onto it. You can read it at least. Maybe look it over and see if there's anything that stands out to you? Any lingering magick or anything?"

"Well, alright. I'll see if there's anything I can find," she agreed doubtfully, tucking it into her bag. She settled back into her seat and flipped the book she'd been reading back open.

Jax studied Amy, ears swiveling. "I take it the pendant came back?"

Amy nodded. "It was in my pocket when I woke up the next morning. It won't be that easy to get rid of."

Jax looked as if he wanted to ask something, but shook his head. "Be careful, please."

Amy settled back in her seat, lost in thought. *Why archons? Why devils? It was just a demon lord, though seemingly a powerful one. So why the other outsiders?* She pondered in silence for a while, writing random notes in a notebook and trying to make sense of all the random events happening. In the end, though, she ended up even more lost than she had been before.

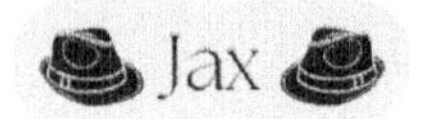

Jax flipped through his book, skimming through the information about the other races that had existed before the fall of magick. *So many races. What happened to them? Where did they go?*

He was pulled from his thoughts as Amy stood and stretched. "Hey, it's lunch. You two coming?"

Jax glanced over at the nearby grandfather clock and set the book back on the shelf before joining her and Talia as they left the library. "Any luck?"

Amy shook her head. "I'm just as confused now as I was when we got in here. Nothing mentions anything about sorcerers getting new tattoos. I think I read in one the first day that said it wasn't unheard of for a sorcerer to become covered in tattoos. But it didn't say how or why. I need to see if that book has any more information on it. It's already in our suite, on the shelf in there, so I'll look at it later."

Talia smiled over at her. "I'm sure you'll figure it out."

Jax squeezed her hand, grateful she didn't immediately pull away. "We know you will."

Amy returned Talia's smile and squeezed his hand back. "I hope so. Maybe I should talk to Gerald about getting into the Wizards' Guild."

Jax tilted his head, tails swishing faster. "Wizards' Guild?"

"Gerald mentioned it. Apparently, I might find a more specialized teacher there." She grinned. "Maybe you'd be able to as well."

Jax bounced on the balls of his feet. "There's a Wizards Guild? Full of magick casters? I want to go."

Amy chuckled and nodded back the way they came. "You can ask Gerald about it."

Jax followed her gaze, desperately wanting to go ask him immediately. "I'll uh… I'll do it after lunch."

Amy grinned and the trio stepped into the dining hall. Nolan sat at a table by himself, picking at a plate of food. They settled into their seats and ate in silence for a moment.

Amy glanced at Jax before straightening. "I'm going to attempt to go into town again after we finish eating."

"You do remember what happened last time, right?" Nolan grumbled.

"We've found three books now. There's got to be *something* to it and if the bookstore has copies of them, maybe we can actually figure out how to break the curse. Without having to go through all the dungeons."

Nolan snorted. "Let's just finish the dungeons and get it over with. Who knows if these books have anything to do with what the guy did? You're probably just wasting your time."

"If I'm wasting my time, so be it. At least I'm trying *something*. If in three hundred years no one has managed to get through the dungeons, why should we be any different?" Amy stood, facing Nolan. "I want to at least try. *Before* anyone dies."

Jax grinned, pleased to see her standing up for herself. "Mind if I tag along?"

Amy nodded stiffly, still meeting Nolan's eye. "That's fine."

Nolan shook his head. "If you die because of one of the Sins, don't come crying to me.

Jax chuckled and stood. "We won't. After all, we'd be dead." He winked at Amy and she quickly covered her mouth, suppressing a laugh.

Talia chuckled and took another bite of food. "Let me know if you find anything. I think I'll check in on Kila."

Amy stepped away from the table, finally breaking eye contact with Nolan. "Alright, sounds good."

The two started out of the manor and toward the town. As they neared the gate, Jax focused on his human form, calling to mind his red hair streaked with black, oval face, and tanned skin. A shiver spread from the base of his tails up to the top of his head. When he opened his eyes, his tails and fur had disappeared.

Amy sighed and pulled her hood up. "I wish I could do that." She paused, biting her lip. "Imitamentum!"

Jax glanced over at the word and gasped. "Amy, look at yourself!" Her coral skin had returned to her usual tan, the blood-red tattoos still dark against it. Her tail and horns had disappeared, the only discernible difference from her original form the streaks of black through her auburn hair.

Jax grinned, bumping his shoulder against hers. "You're human again!"

Amy hesitated, then glanced down at her hands, blinking in surprise. "It worked? It worked!" She grinned and looked up at Jax. "It worked!" she repeated, her green eyes shining brightly.

Jax continued toward the city. "How did you do that?"

Amy shrugged. "I used magick?"

"You don't sound too confident on that."

"I'm not," she admitted with a self-deprecating chuckle.

Jax just rolled his eyes. "You really need to gain some confidence in yourself."

Amy studied her hands again. "Maybe, but… at least things are working out a little better now."

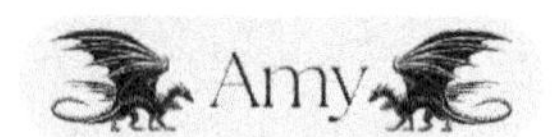

As they walked, Amy looked around cautiously, wary of any empty allies or streets. Much to her relief, their trip was uneventful. After about an hour, they reached Bailey's Bookstore and she and Jax walked in, looking around.

An older gray-haired lady sat behind a desk near the entrance. "Welcome! Can I help you find anything?"

Amy shook her head. "No thank you. We're just browsing." She didn't want to scare the woman by telling her they were looking for books about demons and devils. She waited until the attendant was distracted before turning back to Jax. "You go that way, I'll go this way."

Amy wandered the shelves and found some books that had basic information on the outsiders, but nothing like the ancient tomes they were looking for. In fact, most of the books within the store looked far too new.

The attendant walked up behind her. "You look lost. Are you sure I can't help you find something?"

Amy shook her head again. "I'm just browsing. Do you have any recommendations?" *If nothing else, I might find a new book to read. Though it will probably return here in the morning.*

"Well, I have one that the Arkham boy always bought and read, then returned. He must have read it a dozen times!" She led Amy to a nearby shelf where she pulled a book down and offered it to her. "Is there anything else you need?

"Uh, no thank you." She flipped the book over in her hands and read the cover. "*The Halfling.*" She thumbed through it, pausing at a detailed map of a fantasy world.

"*Yes... I remember that book.*" Recognizing the voice she'd heard before, she reached to touch the pendant in her pocket. "*It's about a sheltered halfing going on an epic quest. I always envied him...*"

Amy smiled, but before she could do anything, the attendant approached her again. "Excuse me, Miss. I'm sorry to bother you again, but there's someone wanting to speak with you in one of our meeting rooms."

Amy frowned but followed the woman into the back of the store. *Maybe I should let Jax know where I'm going.* She backtracked a step, but couldn't see Jax among the rows of books. "Excuse me—" she started to ask the woman to wait, but she was already disappearing down another hallway. *It's fine. It's just a meeting. I won't bother him over something as simple as a meeting.* She hurried forward to catch up, unease settling in her stomach.

When they reached the back, the attendant gestured toward a door, her eyes slightly glazed. "The gentleman is in there." She smiled at Amy and turned back toward the front of the store.

Amy watched her go, brow furrowed. *That was... strange.* She glanced at the door, again debating on whether to get Jax before stepping forward to open the door. As her eyes adjusted to the dimmer light, she looked around at what appeared at first to be an empty room. A table stood in the center with six chairs around it. A second closed door was on the opposite wall. A single figure in familiar white robes with red trim and a low hood stood next to it.

Amy quickly raised her staff and stepped back.

Sloth raised a gloved hand. "Relax," he said in his monotone voice. "If I wanted to kill you, you wouldn't have even made it into the room. I'm simply here for a game." He stepped forward and set a box on the table.

Amy kept her staff raised, but followed the motions of his hands with her eyes. He pulled a chess board out of the box and set it out.

Amy took another slow step toward the door. "What do you want with me?"

Sloth placed the last rook on the board and looked back up at her. "Simply a game of chess. I'll even let you have white."

Amy's eyes darted toward the door. "What's the catch?" *There's enough room between us that I might be able to make it to the door before he can reach me. But Kila said her blade went right through him the first time we met him. What good would getting to the door do? Even if I get Jax, it's unlikely we'd be able to do anything. And what if the other one is nearby?*

Sloth took a seat behind the table, gesturing toward the board. "There's no catch. My brother simply finds you interesting and I wish to see what has caught his eye. Nothing more, nothing less. Your move first."

Amy hesitated a moment longer, then made a decision. *For the time being, it's probably better to give him what he wants, rather than anger him unnecessarily. I can always scream for help if he tries anything.* She stepped forward and studied the pieces in front of her. It had been a while since she played, but she remembered the rules well enough.

Sitting down, she reached forward and moved a pawn, starting the game. "So where's your brother?"

A delicate network of pale blue tattoos spidered down his neck and disappeared beneath his shirt, overlapping and sometimes intertwining with the deep scarring that covered his skin. "Back at our home. He is not aware of our game." He moved his own pawn, then templed his fingers in front of him, watching Amy through red eyes as she made her move. "So, how is it you and your group got here?"

"We were traveling with a caravan. How did you get here?"

He moved another piece, then resumed watching her. "I'm surprised Arkham didn't tell you. We are generals of the demon lord who once ruled this city. We were merely trying to reclaim what was taken from us. Your move."

Amy studied the board a moment, then moved a piece. "Arkham did tell us that. He also told us that you shouldn't be in the city. How are you?"

The game continued. "I have my ways. Ways that I don't quite wish to share with you. You're a spellcaster?"

"Apparently."

"For your appearance, I'm guessing one of blood instead of study. It appears you've discovered how to use it to hide your heritage."

Amy nodded, watching him as he moved his rook across the board. "Yes. The townspeople don't take kindly to demon-spawn, seeing as the last ones they encountered were trying to take over their town. I don't want to draw attention to myself. What about you? What do you do?"

"I suppose it depends on who you ask. Some say I'm a sick and twisted individual. Others may say that I'm a sadistic genius. But I suppose the straightest answer would be that I'm an alchemist." Amy tried not to flinch, but her hand stilled on the piece she'd been about to move before resuming its course. "I'm simply an alchemist who seeks the power of knowledge."

"And your brother?"

"Well, I'm sure you noticed the flaming bulls."

"Yes. But is he like me? Or, as you put it, is he through study?"

"He must study. Though he doesn't tend to use his magick as much as I do. Now, I've told you about myself and my brother. What about you? What about your companions?"

Her eyes narrowed. "Do you not talk amongst yourselves? I'm sure Envy knows our abilities."

"Yes, I suppose they would. I merely wished to see how much you would talk about your friends. But it seems as though you are not stupid enough to release such information. You're wise to be cautious."

"What is your brother's dungeon like?" *Maybe I can get some insight into what's coming.* "We've already fought a bunch of undead. What is his dungeon like?" she added, trying to catch any indication of his thoughts as he moved a piece.

"That would be information I do not wish to share. So I know your abilities. A sorceress. Your monkeyfolk friend appears to have roguish aptitudes. Your two celestial friends are polar opposites. One of them is a natural healer as most of them tend to be and one is a studied arcane caster. And then there's the most interesting of your group. One who's spellcasting is unlike anything I've ever seen. Or at least the way Envy described him."

"So I was right. You do speak among yourselves."

"When need be." He moved another piece, taking another of hers. Several more minutes passed as the game continued until very few of her pieces remained on the board. Finally, he moved his rook into place. "I believe that's Checkmate."

"It appears it is." She stood and backed toward the door.

He started placing pieces back into the box. "Well, this meeting has been entertaining. I never caught your name, however."

Amy's eyes narrowed as she watched him. "Amy."

"And is that your real name?"

"It is the name I've gone by for many years."

"And the name I have gone by for many years is Sloth, however, I still possess my real name: Whittaker. Even if few know it anymore. So tell me, Amy, what is your real name?"

Amy studied him momentarily, fighting with her own instincts of remaining hidden and the logic that she had no reason not to tell him. *Why does he care at all?* Whittaker placed the last piece in the box and raised his eyes to look at her expectantly.

She gnawed her lip, grip tightening on her staff. "Amelia."

Whittaker studied her again. "Well, since you told me the first part of your name, I suppose I can share mine. Whittaker Trace Falks."

Amy stared at him again. *Falks... Falks... Where do I know that name?* "Wait. As in Falks Industries?"

"Hmm. So my company is still alive, then. Interesting."

"*Your* company? Whittaker Falks... *You're* the original creator?" she asked incredulously, her wariness momentarily forgotten. "Falks Industries is the greatest alchemy company in Northern and Southern Sciena! And you're telling me it's *yours*?"

"I suppose it would be hard for a human to believe that," he agreed emotionlessly.

"Hard to believe? Of course it's hard to believe you're here! It's one of the richest companies in the world! Even my father couldn't—" she cut off, realizing what she'd been about to say.

"And what purpose would your father have with my company, young Miss Amelia?"

Amy shook her head bitterly. "It doesn't matter now. He died before he could sign a contract." *Why am I talking to him? It makes no sense. And yet... I feel as if I can trust him. At least in this.*

Whittaker studied her silently for a moment. "My condolences." The words sounded hollow, as if he were just repeating the words proper to the situation. "Now, as you've made quite a fuss over my name, perhaps it is time to learn yours?" Amy frowned. *There's no reason I can't tell him my name. It's not like he'd have any reason to tell the others. Not that it matters.* "What is said in this meeting will never leave this room. This meeting is merely my business, and no one else's."

Amy took another step toward the door, heart pounding. "How do I know I can trust your word?"

"I have nothing to gain from revealing your name."

"And I have nothing to gain from giving it to you."

"Perhaps. But then again, you have nothing to lose, either." His voice remained emotionless and monotone.

Recognizing the truth in his words, Amy raised herself to her full, albeit short, height, regaining the regal features that came with once being a Lady of Zadia. "My name is Amelia Lunsford Pruitt. Does that satisfy your curiosity?"

"Yes. Yes it does. Thank you very much for your time, Miss Pruitt, though I suppose I should just call you Amy." He picked up the box and stepped toward the door.

"Was it really just your brother's interest in me that drew you here?"

He stopped and glanced back at her. "What else could it have been?"

"I don't know, but it seems like an awful lot of effort to go through just because of someone else's curiosity."

"My brother tends to attract unneeded attention. I'm merely making sure he isn't stirring a bees' nest."

Amy's brow furrowed. "Is that not exactly what we are to you? Your enemies?"

"Yes. But at the current moment, you are no more than drones. The rest of your journey will determine whether the drone can raise the swarm or if they will be silenced before they reach the hive." He turned to walk away again. "Do not worry. Once I leave, you will not be followed. Nor will you be disturbed. No one knows of this meeting. And no one will, except for perhaps the companion that was with you here." Amy watched him walk away, eyes narrowed, but made no move to stop him. "Well, then. I bid you farewell young sorceress. And good luck on your journey. You will need it." He opened the door on the other side of the room and stepped out.

Amy stared after him a moment, confused and wondering just what he had wanted and why. And if he'd gotten it.

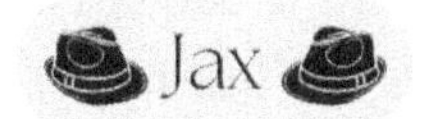

Jax followed the attendant down the hall, his hand gripping Shinzo's hilt. *Why does Sloth have an interest in Amy? And why didn't she say anything to me?* The attendant had explained to Jax that a man in white robes with red trim requested a meeting with Amy. Immediately, his mind went to Sloth.

She stopped in front of a door and gestured toward it. "Here we are."

"Thank you, Miss." The door opened and Amy stepped out, looking perplexed. Relief filled Jax. "There you are! Is everything okay?"

Amy jumped and looked between him and the attendant. "Everything's fine. Just a chess game, apparently." She approached the woman behind him, a barely perceptible shake to her hands as she lifted a small book. Whatever had happened, it clearly unnerved her. "I'd like this book, please."

Jax followed her to the front of the store and watched her hand over a silver coin. "Are you okay?"

"Yes, I'm fine." Once they'd walked away from the attendant, she lowered her voice "Like I said, Sloth just wanted a chess game. What were you doing back there anyway?"

"Well, I finished searching my section and then when I was looking around for you, I noticed you were missing, so I asked the attendant. She said you were in a meeting with a guy wearing white and red robes… I figured you were safe enough as there was no smoke or fire, but I wanted to make sure." He glanced over at her. "So what did he want, anyway?"

Amy flinched at the mention of fire and he furrowed his brow. *Why would mentioning fire bother her?*

She shook her head. "I'm not sure, exactly. Something about his brother's interest in me."

"What do you mean Wrath's interest in you?" Jax whispered. *Drawing interest from the Sins can't be a good thing.*

Amy glanced over. "I'm not sure. And that bothers me. He kept asking questions, pushing me to answer them if I dodged them, but he wouldn't really answer any of mine either. He only really confirmed stuff that I already knew, like that his brother is a spellcaster and that they came here with the demon lord, though he did say that they were 'reclaiming what was taken from them.' It also appears as if they talk amongst themselves. He knew of our abilities, or at least a general idea, which means he had to have spoken with Envy. He was extremely interested in my name for some reason..."

Amy touched something on her chest, but quickly pulled her hand away when she noticed him looking. "Uh, don't worry, though, I didn't give away anything that he could use against us. Or at least, I don't think I did. I refused to answer any questions about you all."

"Well at least you're okay, that's what I'm thankful for," Jax said, though he was still concerned about Wrath's interest in her. He studied the book tightly clutched in her arms as best he could. "What's that? Is it to do with the books?"

Amy held it out to him. "No. Just something the attendant recommended. I couldn't find any of the books I was looking for."

Jax shook his head. "I didn't either." He took the book and read the cover aloud. "*The Halfling.* Looks interesting. Can I borrow it when you're done?"

"Of course."

As they stepped out of the shop, he looked around. "Should we head straight back? It might be a good idea to mention this to Arkham."

Amy frowned and Jax suspected the last thing she wanted to do was tell Arkham about what had happened, not after his clear distrust before. "We should head back. It will be dinner soon."

"We could always get something here in town," he suggested.

Amy shook her head. "I don't want to spend the silver when the food at the manor is free."

"That's true, I suppose." After a moment of walking, he glanced over. "So what was he like?"

"Who?"

"Sloth."

Amy remained silent as they walked and Jax had almost decided she wasn't going to answer when she sighed and shook her head. "I'm not sure. He… he was emotionless and calculating. I'm not the best at chess, it's been years since I played, but it was obvious even to me that he was simply toying with me. He ended the game exactly when he wanted to and no sooner. That and he… I don't know, he was extremely interested in my name, though I'm not sure why."

"What would be important about your name?" Jax asked.

Amy shifted nervously and Jax wondered what she was hiding. Obviously something about her name was important, but he couldn't imagine what it would be. "I'm not sure. I mean, he's been here three hundred years, it's not like he'd know my family anyway."

Jax frowned, glancing over at her. *What is she hiding?* "Either way, you want to head back the way we came or maybe take a more indirect route? Explore a little?"

Amy's eyes lit up as she nodded. "Let's explore a little."

Jax's heart lifted at Amy's enthusiasm. He rarely saw it and quite enjoyed it when he did. As they walked, Jax kept up a steady stream of small talk, grateful that Amy seemed to be opening up to him a little more. They had just started to pass a large, rounded, two-story building when a familiar figure caught his attention. He froze and watched the figure disappear into the building. *It can't be…*

"Jax?" Amy's voice caught his attention and he quickly pulled a drawing from his pocket, looking between it and the building. "Jax, is everything alright?" she repeated and Jax finally turned back to her.

"I swear I just saw my father! I've been traveling for ten years looking for any sign of what happened to him." He looked back and forth between the picture and the building the man had disappeared into, torn. The line into the building already stretched several dozen people long. "What do I do? I can't lose him now!"

Amy smiled reassuringly. "First, we have to get in. Come on."

Jax followed after her, almost in a daze. As they bypassed the line, they were blocked by a large man with skin as black as night. Jax's gaze trailed up the man, completely in shock at his size. He had to be almost two feet taller than them and three—maybe even four—times their weight with ropes of muscle lining his biceps. "Get back in line," he rumbled, not even looking at them.

"S-sorry to bother you, but we're actually looking for someone. We just saw him enter," Amy stammered, her bravado from before gone.

He finally looked down at them, one eyebrow raised. "There's a lot of people who come in and out of here, Girly. I'll need more than that to go on."

Amy hesitated, glancing back at Jax. "Well, I don't actually know him. Jax?" He jumped and focused on her, then the man in front of them. "Jax, what does he look like? Or his name?"

Jax absently held out the sketch.

The bouncer took it and studied it for a moment. "Oh, Shane!" Immediately his demeanor lightened. "Yeah, that's Shane. He just went in. It's a gold to enter."

Amy's face fell as she looked over at Jax. "Go on in. I don't have a gold coin." She glanced back at the man. "What is this place, anyway?"

"Fighting Pits. Bare-handed only, no weapons or spells. It gives fighters a chance to let off some steam."

"I see."

The man studied her. "You're one of the new group aren't you?" he asked and Amy nodded. "Have you been through a dungeon yet?"

"We just completed Death yesterday," Jax said, shuddering. *We've only completed one dungeon so far and I'm already dreading the next one. How could we hope to make it through all seven?*

The man grinned and gestured towards the door. "Then I'll give you a discount. Four silver each. The name's Kraven, by the way."

Amy hesitated, but Jax just dug into his bag, handing over his silvers. "I'm too close now." Amy dug in her bag, lingering a moment before passing them over. Jax could see her reluctance and made a mental note to pay her back later.

"Thank you, Kraven. I'm Amy."

"I'm Jax. Jax Silvers." Jax didn't pay any attention to their surroundings after Kraven waved them inside. He focused on a man leaned against a wall, intently watching a fight. "That's him. Could he have really been trapped here the whole time?" He turned to Amy helplessly. "What am I supposed to do? I never thought I'd actually find him."

"Go." Amy nudged him gently. "You've come all this way, go talk to him."

Jax hesitated, glancing back at her. "Are you sure you'll be okay? Those two Sins seem to be very interested in you. Are you sure you should be alone?"

"I'll be fine. Go!" She pointed toward a group of tables by a bar. "I'll go wait over there." Jax gave her one last conflicted look before starting toward the man.

Jax leaned against the wall about five feet away from his father, shifting his gaze between him and the fight he was watching. A white-haired man faced off against two others, quite efficiently holding his own. When the bell rang, the three fighters were pulled back to their corners and Jax approached his father. "So, who do you got your gold on?"

His father only half looked over as he gestured at the white-haired man. "Chouza. He's the one there with the white hair. But don't let that fool you, he's young and strong still. Almost undefeated." He studied Jax more intently, his eyes narrowed. "Hey, do I know you?"

Jax fidgeted nervously with a coin. "Well, that depends on how far back your memory goes," he hedged, watching as the fight resumed.

His father continued to study him, and when he spoke, his voice had lowered. "What's your name, boy?"

Jax took a deep breath before turning to meet Shane's eye. "Jax... Jax Silvers, and you're Shane Silvers, correct?"

Shane's eyes widened and he took a half-step away. "Jax? But... What are you doing here? What about your mother?"

Jax continued to fiddle with his coin. "After Mother died, I started traveling. As for why I'm here, I was with a caravan and then some of us got separated and trapped here. We're under the Arkhams' employ, going through the dungeons. We just got through Death yesterday."

Shane sighed. "Your mother… she's… gone?"

Jax nodded, looking down at the coin in his hand. "Yes. She died ten years ago, give or take a few months." That wasn't entirely true. Jax knew exactly what day his mother had drawn her last breath. He'd been there with her. It was a memory he would never be able to forget.

"I see... Well that's…" His voice cracked slightly. "Well shit." His eyes were sad as he looked back toward the new fight taking place in the pit.

Jax stayed quiet for a moment, watching the fight like Shane. "So, is this where you've been for the last twenty years?"

Shane kept his eyes on the ring. "Well, technically I've only been here about fifteen years."

Jax finally turned to face him. "Ah, so only for the last fifteen years. What about the five before that?"

Shane shook his head. "Like I told your mother, if I didn't leave when I did, something bad was going to happen."

"Bad like what? You never told us anything. We never *got* anything. You literally just disappeared. As far as I knew, you just left one day and never came back. The only reason I knew what you looked like was because of this." He pulled the drawing out of his pocket and held it up. "This picture is what I've had for the last twenty years. For the last ten years, I've been going from town to town, all the way from Xarxus to here in Koven. I've been poking and prodding, not diligently mind you, but I've been looking for the answer to that one question. That one simple answer is all I want. What were you running from that you felt like you had to protect us from?"

Shane sighed and brought his hand up to cover his face. "Come on. Follow me."

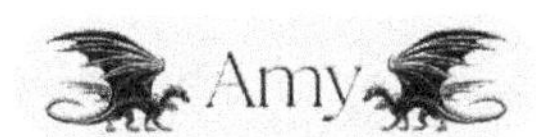

Amy watched Jax walk away with a soft smile. *Hopefully, he finds what he was looking for.* Then she shook her head and looked around again, focusing more on the events around her. Two of the rings were occupied: One with a white-haired man fighting two other men, the other with two women. She circled the outer edge of the room toward the seating area by the bar. It would give her a good view of Jax, but she wouldn't have to pay too much attention to the fights.

There was a light chuckle behind her. "I love this place." Amy's stomach dropped. She recognized that voice. Cautiously she looked behind her at what appeared to be an empty wall. Then the air shimmered and the red-skinned demon-spawn Wrath appeared. He leaned back against the wall, smirking as he watched the fight. His dark pants and leather jacket blended well with the shadows.

His red eyes darted to her and he winked. "I love coming here. Seeing humans senselessly beating on each other is the highlight of my day." Amy's eyes narrowed with suspicion. "I'm surprised I don't see your other friend here. The cocky celestial?" he goaded. "What about you, Spitfire? You getting in the ring?"

She kept one eye on the nine-section whip strapped to his hip, his tail wrapped around his waist just above it. "Fighting isn't really my thing."

"Shame. Maybe next time." He grinned at her and she shuddered.

"How did you recognize me?"

"Come now, that red hair and tattoo combo would be hard to miss, even disguised as you are. Nice use of magick, by the way. So tell me, what can I do for you? I can see the wheels turning in your head."

Amy frowned. *I have to get better at hiding what I'm thinking. Maybe if I can get him talking, I can figure more out about him and gain an advantage in his dungeon. Better to start small. This would also be a good opportunity to find out if it really is the Falks Industries creators.* "Sure. What's your name? Not Wrath, your *real* name."

"Ooh, looks like we're getting personal." He chuckled again, then smirked. "Fine. If you want to know, tell me your name first."

"Amy."

Wrath shrugged. "Eh. I like Spitfire better. A deal's a deal I suppose. I'm Bradley."

So it is him. There's no way there could be a second Bradley and Whittaker Falks who lived three hundred years ago.

His gaze lifted to behind her and his smirk widened. "Shame. Seems we're about to be interrupted before we get to the good stuff." Amy followed his gaze to see the white-haired man from the first ring heading her way, the people around him clapping him on the shoulder in congratulations. "See you around, Spitfire."

Amy whirled around to tell Wrath to wait, but he'd already disappeared. She scowled and turned back to find herself entirely too close to a very bare, very muscled, chest. "You alright, miss?" the chest asked.

Amy forced her eyes up, trying not to focus on the sheen of sweat glistening on tanned skin. He was clearly waiting for an answer, but Amy found herself distracted by his deep blue eyes.

"Miss?" His voice pulled her from her shock.

She realized her mouth had been gaping open and closed it with a snap, her face heating. "I'm fine."

"You sure? You seemed as if you were looking for something." Amy took a step back, fighting the urge to find out if the muscles were as hard as they looked. Instead, she focused on his face. White, shoulder-length hair framed a young face and she guessed he couldn't be older than his mid-twenties.

"I'm fine. Just waiting for a friend." She took another step back. *Why am I so desperate to touch him?*

He cocked his head, studying her. "I won't bite." He chuckled, but when she didn't answer, he mellowed. "Hey, are you sure you're alright?"

Amy blinked, trying to focus. "I'm fine, just waiting for a friend," she repeated. She dragged her eyes away from his face, searching the area where she'd last seen Jax. "Who has disappeared." She tensed, her gaze darting around the room.

The man followed her gaze. "Who were you looking for?"

"My friend Jax. He was with a man named Shane. They were near that wall over there."

"Shane Silvers? Yeah, he was watching my fight. Probably bet on me. If he's not there, he's probably in one of the meeting rooms." He shrugged. "They're open to the public."

Amy hesitated, looking around. "Well... I'm sure he's fine, then."

"Hey, it's almost dinner. Are you hungry?"

Amy hesitated. "A little."

The man gestured at the counter. "Well, if you want, we got a bar. Could I buy you something?"

Amy gnawed her lip, unsure of his motives. "Um, I'm fine, but thanks."

He shrugged. "Alright. Would you like me to take you to your friend at least? You look a bit lost."

Amy gulped, glancing at his bare chest again before looking away quickly. "I'd appreciate that."

"Should I put a shirt on first?" he asked, the amusement back in his voice.

"Yes, please."

He chuckled and started past her to a door she hadn't even noticed. "I'll be right back."

Amy relaxed slightly as he disappeared through the doorway, though her stomach growled. The trek back to the manor would take another hour and she had almost decided to take his offer when he stepped back out.

"I'm Chouza, by the way. Chouza Zhang." *Chouza. The name suits him.* "Come on, the meeting areas are back here." His fingers grazed her back to direct her through the crowd. Amy lurched away from the light touch, twisting away from him as panic welled inside her. "Easy! Easy!" He held his hands up in front of him in a placating gesture. Amy tried to take calming breaths, but the crowd seemed to be closing in around her and had the opposite effect as her eyes whirled, looking for somewhere to escape. "This way." Chouza led her around the outside of the crowd to another doorway and into an empty hallway.

Amy darted inside and sank to the floor, burying her head between her knees as she tried to snap herself out of the approaching panic attack. Chouza was silent and Amy assumed he'd left. *Of course he would. Who would want to be near someone who panicked at the slightest touch?*

Several minutes passed until she was breathing normally again, though her heart still raced. She leaned her head back and spotted Chouza leaning against the wall across from her. He silently offered her a glass of water and Amy took it gratefully.

"Thanks. Sorry about that."

Chouza shrugged. "It's fine. I shouldn't have touched you without permission." His deep voice was gentle as he watched her. "Are you okay now? That was quite a panic attack."

Amy nodded. "I'm fine. That was a milder one and I was able to get out of the situation quickly."

"*That* was a milder one?" Chouza asked, eyes wide with what seemed like concern. Amy nodded again and looked away. "If that was a milder one, I'd hate to see a serious one."

Amy's face heated and she looked down at her hands cradling the cup. Suddenly, the coral tint of her skin clicked and she glanced back up at Chouza. "Oh. Oh, no!" She gasped, scrambling to her feet. "I'm sorry! Please, I swear I'm not one of the Sins! Imitamentum!"

He watched impassively as her disguise returned and shrugged. "Five of the Sins are male, I've heard tales of Lust and you clearly aren't her, nor do you sound like Envy. While it's possible you can disguise your voice using magick as well, the fact that you lost the disguise in the first place makes me think that you're just a newbie who still hasn't mastered her magick. Am I right?" When she didn't answer, just staring at him in shock, he shrugged again. "I may not be the smartest person in the room, but I am observant. You're clearly not a Sin."

Amy rubbed her arm, shining nervously on her feet. "I'm not. That's just what my blood Awoke as." She looked away. "Arkham wasn't too happy about it."

"I can imagine not." His voice softened. "It's alright, though. Your secret's safe with me."

"Thanks." She took a deep breath. "I'm Amy, by the way."

A smile lit his face. "It's nice to meet you, Amy."

"You, too. So uh, how long was my disguise down?"

"Don't worry. The door closed before it became too obvious. You should be fine."

"Thanks, Chouza. I owe you one." Chouza grinned and Amy approached the door, taking another deep breath before knocking.

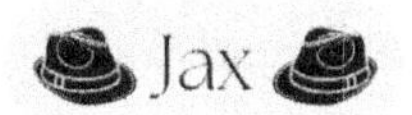

Shane led Jax into one of the back rooms of the Pits and closed the door behind him. "I want it to be known. I didn't want to leave. I didn't. But... The best I can put this is... things from my past didn't want to die."

"So, what? Did you have debts to pay off? Did someone have a hit on you? That still doesn't explain what you were protecting us from!" All of his pent up pain and anger suddenly bubbled up to the surface. "You abandoned us! We barely survived! I was *alone* when my mother died!" he yelled. "Thirteen years old! I was *thirteen* and I was alone! What could be more important than that?"

Shane flinched and looked away. "When I was younger, actually close to your age now, maybe a little younger, I went into the mercenary business. I... did jobs that paid well and did whatever I was paid to do. I was honestly pretty good at it. One of my jobs went awry. The group I had been hired with decided they weren't being paid enough by our employer, so they decided to switch sides. The two brothers decided they wanted an even share and one extra person was more than they wanted to pay for, so they didn't mention it to me. They had our employer killed and placed the blame on me. I was able to get out and had been on the run for about five years when I met your mom. We settled down, had you, and I thought my life was perfect.

"A few months shy of your third birthday, I heard rumors that, apparently, I still had a hit on my head and there was a group of bounty hunters hired specifically to find me. So, I left. Because if they found out I had a family, they could use leverage against me... You both probably would have been dead. Or worse."

Jax's head reeled as his father told his story. "So they betrayed you..."

Shane nodded. "Since they pointed the blame at me, the family put a hit on my head, saying I had killed the head of their family. After I left you and your mother, I dodged their bounty hunters for about five years, then one day I was just going on a normal path and all of a sudden I found myself in the woods. I looked around, ran across a merchant who didn't know what he was doing, and found the town. I went under the Arkham's employ for a while, hoping to escape here and eventually make it back to you and your mother once it was safe."

Jax's eyes widened. "By yourself?"

Shane chuckled. "Oh no, kid. I wasn't dumb enough to go against these seven deadly dungeons alone. I asked around town to see if I could find anyone who wanted a second attempt at them. We got through three of the dungeons before two of them died and the other decided he couldn't do it anymore. And I've been here ever since. So for the last... fifteen years I guess. Time's kind of hard to judge in this place in case you haven't noticed.'

Jax shook his head. "What do you mean? I assume that the time loop would make things interesting, but what do you mean time is hard to judge passing? It's still night and day, right?"

"Well, yeah, kind of." Shane scratched his head, thinking. "When the day passes and it's the exact same day as before, it gets hard to judge how many have passed."

"Wait wait wait. What was it Arkham said? They were trapped in an... eternal loop? Arkham said that the days were repeating, but he didn't really elaborate on that."

"Well, let me put it this way. If there is a cat walking down the road and it stops to take a shit, the next day, it'll do it again and the one from the day before will be missing."

Jax's jaw dropped. "The days repeat themselves literally?"

Shane shrugged. "That's the best I can explain it. Magick's not really my thing. I'm good at street smarts and knowing how to hit things in just the right place to make it hurt. Magick was not one of the things I studied."

"Well, that's where we're different." Jax grinned and touched a pencil on the table, focusing his magick to make it glow. "I happen to have a bit of magick."

"Huh. Would you look at that? My son's a magician." He chuckled. "Who would have figured?" A knock on the door interrupted him. "Who is it?"

"Ummm. It's Amy. I'm looking for Jax?"

Jax glanced at Shane, then hurried to the door. "Hey, Amy. Is everything alright?"

She shifted uneasily and her eyes darted past him to his father. "Yes. I didn't see you and I was getting hungry. I was just about to head back to the manor."

Shane raised an eyebrow when he saw her, but didn't comment. Then he looked past them and grinned. "Chouza! I hope you know you just won me ten gold!" The white-haired man from the ring stood behind Amy, at least a foot taller than her.

"You betting on me again?" Chouza asked, returning the grin. Amy's jaw dropped and Jax blinked. Ten *gold? The people here are living easy if that's what they're betting.*

"Of course. After all, you're almost a sure bet."

Chouza chuckled and reached past Amy to shake Jax's hand. "I'm Chouza. You must be part of Amy's group. What's your business with Shane here?"

Jax glanced at Shane, who nodded, and Jax turned back to Chouza. "He's my father."

Chouza burst out laughing, much to everyone's shock. Amy jumped and took a half-step away from the boisterous noise. "Looks like Jason owes Kraven five gold."

Jax and Shane looked at each other and Shane raised an eyebrow. "And what about me having a son means Kraven gets five gold?"

"Come on, you have to know the guys take bets on which of your stories are true. You having a wife and son was too much for them to pass up. Last I heard, they were trying to figure out how to prove if it was true or not, though I guess you solved that for them."

Jax frowned. "Yes, well, I'm not quite sure that's a good thing."

Chouza's smile faded. "No. Being trapped here definitely isn't a good thing."

Amy shook her head. "Anyway, I was about to head back to the manor. Are you coming?"

Jax hesitated, looking between Shane and Amy. He wanted to spend time with his father, but hated to leave Amy alone with the Sins' interest in her. "I suppose I should."

"If you want to stay, then go ahead. I can head back on my own."

Jax gingerly touched her hand. "Are you sure that's a good idea?"

"If you need someone to take her back to the manor, I could do it," Chouza offered.

Amy bristled, her cheeks reddening. "I don't need to be *taken* anywhere. I can go by myself."

Jax's brow furrowed. "Amy…"

Chouza dipped his head. "My apologies. I didn't mean to offend you. I merely meant that if you needed or wanted someone to walk back with, I'd be happy to do it."

Amy gnawed her lip, her tense posture easing slightly. "Are you sure you don't mind?"

Chouza shrugged. "I don't have any other fights today and I was probably just going to head home. Maybe go get dinner at a tavern. Just let me get my kid."

Amy stared up at him. "Your kid?"

Chouza nodded and a fond smile appeared on his lips. "Yeah. Her normal babysitter couldn't take her today so she's in the onsight daycare."

Jax raised an eyebrow. "The Pits has its own childcare?"

Shane rested a hand on Jax's shoulder. "You have to remember, the people that fight here are all people who were either born within Lorencost or wandered in like you. Some of them lost their partner to those dungeons, in one way or another." His eyes flicked to Chouza and the other man winced. "This is often their main source of income, so Kraven made sure that their kids had a place to stay while they worked."

"That was kind of him." Jax pictured the large man outside the door with a new respect. He clearly cared about his employees if he set up childcare for them just so that they could work.

"Kraven takes care of his people," Chouza agreed. He shrugged. "So if you're fine with that, we'd be happy to walk with you back to the manor."

Amy glanced at Jax and he shrugged. "Alright."

Jax quickly grabbed her hand and lowered his voice. "Just be careful, okay?" Obviously, his father liked Chouza, but he didn't know what to think of him yet.

"I will. It was nice to meet you!" Amy called to Shane as she and Chouza left.

"You as well," Shane answered. Jax waved and as the door shut, Shane raised an eyebrow. "Who is she?"

"She's one of my companions that I came into the town with."

"You seem quite fond of her."

"Yes well, Amy is… interesting. I feel as if she needs someone to look out for her."

"I see. So tell me, how did you end up here?"

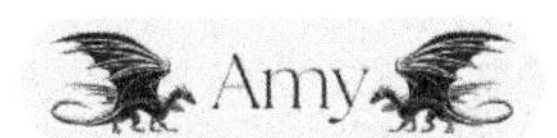

Chouza led Amy further down the hall where she could hear the squeals and giggles of children. Chouza opened a door to an older woman sitting on the floor surrounded by chubby-cheeked toddlers while a younger woman gently rocked a tiny baby.

The kids looked over at the door opening and a small brown-haired girl with almond eyes jumped to her feet. "Papa!" She froze and glanced at the teacher still sitting on the floor. "May I go, Miss Heidi?"

Miss Heidi smiled and nodded. "Have a good day, Kimi. You should bring her more often, Chouza. We love having her."

The girl ran to Chouza and jumped into his arms. He picked her up and squeezed her lightly before settling her onto his shoulders. "I might. Glinda's getting a bit up there in age and Kimiko is a lot. Plus, it does her good to be around other kids."

"Well, you know where to find us."

Amy pulled back to allow Chouza to step out of the room, ducking to keep from hitting the little girl's head on the frame. She studied Amy with wide eyes. "Papa, who's she?"

Chouza squeezed his daughter's leg and led Amy further down the hall. "Her name is Amy. She works for the Arkhams like Papa used to. Amy, this is Kimiko. Most everyone else calls her Kimi for short."

"Oh. It's nice to meet you, Kimi."

"It's nice to meet you, too!" She grinned at Amy, but focused back on Chouza quickly. "Miss Heidi said I know my colors really well."

"That's wonderful, Baby."

Amy watched the two interact silently, awed by how the large man clearly adored the tiny child that couldn't have been more than three or four. She couldn't help but wonder what had happened to her mother, since Shane's words seemed to have been directed toward Chouza's own situation.

Chouza opened the door at the end of the hall and stepped outside into a narrow path that led to an alleyway. It blended well with the wall of the building, creating a nicely hidden entrance.

Amy sighed in relief as they exited the stuffy building. "Thank you."

"Any time. This way." He led her down the alley and out onto the main street. "Let me tell Kraven I'm headed out and then we can go. Sound good?" Amy nodded and watched him walk over to the much larger man. They exchanged a few words before Chouza rejoined her. "Kraven likes for us to let them know when we leave so they know not to accept any requests. Most of our fights are scheduled, but occasionally, there will be requests from the audience for certain fighters. If they're both at the Pits and agreeable, then it works out. Otherwise, it'll be scheduled for a later day."

Fighting for sport seems… brutal. Why does anyone want to do that? And where does betting come in? She glanced over at him again, mesmerized by the way his mouth moved when he talked.

"Everything okay?" Chouza's words pulled her from her daydream.

"What?"

"I asked if you'd seen the reset yet and you didn't answer. Is everything okay?"

"The what?"

He glanced down at her. "The reset every morning. All the original residents live their day in reverse for a bit."

Amy gaped at him. "You mean it literally happens in reverse? The day doesn't just start over?"

Chouza shook his head. "I guess that answers that question."

"It's funny!" Kimi chimed. "Papa, can I walk?"

"Of course, Baby." He lifted her off of his shoulders and settled her back onto the ground. At that level, Amy realized she wasn't actually all that tiny, she just appeared so in proportion to the much larger man. Her head came up to Amy's midsection and Chouza's hip.

Amy bit her lip for a moment. "So when does the reset happen?"

"Just as the sun rises"

"I'll have to check it out!"

Chouza grinned and they lapsed into companionable silence as Kimi's chatter filled the air. It was an odd feeling for Amy. She was perfectly content to walk along with Chouza and Kimi, something that had taken Jax months of travel to accomplish. Even once she found herself back in familiar streets, she didn't comment, letting them walk her all the way back to the manor.

Chouza stopped just outside the gate. "I guess this is where we leave you."

"Right." Her eyes traveled up the path toward the manor hidden behind the treeline. She didn't want to go back to where Nolan and Kila were. It was just going to be more of a headache. But she was hungry and that meant going to the dining hall.

Chouza cleared his throat. "Hey, I've lived here for quite a few years. If you'd like someone to show you around sometime, Kimiko and I would be happy to."

Amy blinked. *Why is he being so nice?* "Really?"

"Of course. I mean, Obviously I don't know where everything is, the city's pretty big, but I'd be happy to show you around what I know."

Kimi tugged on Chouza's hand excitedly. "Can we go to the park, too?"

"Yes, Kimiko, we can go to the park tomorrow if Ms. Amy doesn't mind."

Amy stared at him a moment. *It would be nice…* "Are you sure you don't mind?" It seemed strange for someone to go out of their way to help her for no real reason that she could see.

Chouza shrugged. "I don't have a fight scheduled tomorrow." Amy gnawed her lip, trying to decide if it was some kind of trick. "You can say no if you want. It won't offend me."

Amy hesitated, looking for any sign of reluctance from him, but Chouza just offered her a small smile. And she *wanted* to spend more time with him. Plus something about Kimi just fascinated Amy. "A-alright."

Her stomach flip-flopped at his breathtaking grin. "Great! What time would you want to meet tomorrow?"

Amy shrugged. "Whenever would be good for you."

"How about around ten, then? That gives us time to have breakfast and get dressed." He leaned closer and lowered his voice. "It takes her forever to get dressed in the morning."

Amy chuckled. "That sounds good."

"Okay. Then we'll see you here in the morning."

"I'll see you in the morning."

Kimi yawned and stretched her arms up to Chouza. "Carry me, Papa?"

"Of course, Baby." He picked her up and she settled her head on his shoulder. "Tell Ms. Amy bye-bye."

The little girl waved at her and Amy couldn't help but smile. "Bye, Ms. Amy."

"Bye, Kimi." When she glanced back, Chouza was watching her. He waved and she flushed, embarrassed to be caught looking. But even still, she couldn't deny the flutter in her chest.

Kila and Nolan were disappearing down the back hallway when Amy stepped into the entryway. Talia was a few steps behind them, but stopped when she saw Amy.

"Where are you headed?" the older woman asked Amy.

"The dining hall."

"Did you have any success at that book store?"

Amy shook her head. "They didn't have them. I did find a new book to read, though, assuming it doesn't go back." She pulled the book from her bag. Azurys chose that moment to peel from her tattoo form on Amy's stomach, slinking from beneath her shirt toward the stairs. Talia raised an eyebrow and Amy just shrugged. "What about them?" She nodded to the forms heading out of the manor.

Talia sighed. "Training. Kila woke up just after lunch and said some… not so nice things to Nolan. Now they're both angry with each other, but insist that they need to train to be more ready for the next dungeon, so I'm going to just go make sure they don't actually kill each other. Hopefully," she added with a hint of uncertainty to her voice.

"I'm sure it will be fine."

The other woman smiled, then hurried after the two that had already disappeared down the hallway.

Inside the dining hall, cooks started pulling the trays of food back into the kitchen. More staff sat around a few of the tables, joking amongst themselves. As soon as she walked in, they quieted, eyeing her suspiciously. Even though she'd grown used to the looks, they still made her uncomfortable, and she hurried forward to gather a plate of food.

Not wanting to sit in the uneasy silence of the dining hall, she took her plate up to her suite, settling down at the table in the sitting room. As she ate, she pulled the book she'd gotten from the bookstore out, opening it to the first page and letting herself get lost in the story.

She had just finished eating when Jax walked in. He sighed in relief and closed the door behind him. "Oh good, you made it back."

Amy glanced up, jarred out of the world of *The Halfling*. "Uh, yeah. Chouza and Kimi walked me right to the front gate." His name sent a thrill of pleasure through her.

"I'm glad. I'll admit, I was rather worried that something would happen."

Amy shook her head. "Everything was peaceful. Did you eat already?"

Jax dropped into the seat near her. "My father and I got some food from the bar at the Fighting Pits."

"Okay." She glanced at the clock, frowning. "I think I'm about to head to bed. I wanted to get up early enough to— Oh! Chouza told me about something you might be interested in!" she exclaimed, cutting herself off mid-sentence. Jax raised an eyebrow. "Apparently the reset that happens everyday? It doesn't just restart, it goes in reverse!"

Jax's eyes widened. "Wait, what?"

Amy nodded enthusiastically and quickly repeated what Chouza had told her before. "I was going to see it tomorrow." She hesitated. *Friends invite friends to do things that the friend would like, right?* "Would you… want to come?"

Jax studied her face a moment. "If you're sure you don't mind."

Amy smiled, relieved that she hadn't misjudged. "Of course not!"

Jax grinned. "Alright. You said it happens at sunrise?"

Amy leaned towards him. "Chouza said it happens every day just as the sun rises. I'll meet you by the front door about fifteen minutes before that?" she offered.

"I'll see you then," he agreed. "Good night, Amy."

"Good night." She rinsed the plate from her dinner in the washroom before leaving it on the table and heading into her room. Azurys merely twitched her ears in greeting when Amy walked in. Amy gently scratched her ears before changing into the new night dress Lillian had the staff leave and settling into the bed.

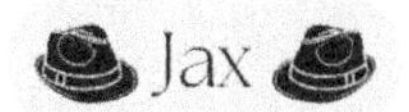

By the time Jax came down the stairs the next morning, Amy was already waiting by the front door. "And here I thought I was an early riser."

Amy grinned and took another bite of the apple in her hand. "I'll admit. I was a bit excited."

Jax chuckled and shook his head. "I can't say I blame you. Do I have time to get a quick breakfast of my own?"

Amy shrugged. "Of course."

Once Jax grabbed his own apple, the two entered the city. They had just made it into the city proper when the few people near them slowed and stopped. Jax watched in awe as people began to move in reverse, their pace increasing until they were racing past them and the streets grew crowded. He grinned at Amy and the two ran to a nearby building, climbing up to perch on the rooftop for a better view. Nearby a merchant laid all his things back out and sat down on a blanket; a cat spat a mouse back out; a woman sitting at a table outside a diner pulled a fork full of food from her mouth.

"It's amazing," Amy breathed.

"Indeed," Jax agreed, his own eyes wide. *To think such a thing exists…*

After a few minutes, Amy glanced over at him. "Want to get a closer look?" Jax nodded and they slipped back down into the street. People raced around them, their forms blurred and indistinct. "It's eerie," she whispered.

He grinned at her. "It really is." He started to call out a warning as a person neared her, but the person fazed right through. "What just happened?"

Amy shivered and rubbed her arms. "I have no idea, but it was unpleasant."

Jax extended a hand in front of a person racing by, quickly yanking it back as a chill went through him. "Interesting… It's as if they've turned into ghosts."

Amy knelt in front of a person sitting on a rug, watching as they twitched and moved quickly without getting up. "Hard to believe this happens every morning."

"Indeed." The people's movements slowed. "Does that mean it's over?"

Amy blinked and looked around. "It would appear so. A full day condensed to no more than half an hour…" The streets were almost empty again as people returned to their usual routine. Most of the townsfolk were only just waking up; only the earliest risers were out.

"Shall we head back or did you have something else in mind?"

"We should head back. I want to get a little reading in before I meet Chouza this morning."

Jax raised an eyebrow. "You're meeting Chouza today?"

Amy smiled shyly. "He offered to show me around the town a little bit. I figured it was a good idea to find out where some things were so that we didn't have another incident like the bookstore." Her cheeks gained a rosy tint.

Jax suppressed a chuckle. "I see."

"You're welcome to come."

Jax silently mulled over what she had said. Part of him suspected that Chouza simply wanted to spend more time with Amy. And from the blush on Amy's cheeks, he imagined she did, too. *Interesting…* "I'll pass this time," he said. "I think I want to try and look for more information on my magick."

Amy frowned. "I could stay and help if you need me to…"

He chuckled and waved a hand. "No, no. You go ahead."

"If you're sure…"

"Quite sure."

Amy's smile was small and hesitant, but Jax was pleased by it nonetheless. He still wondered what had happened to her that caused her to be so reserved around people, but he was honored that she had told him about her plans for the day and even more so that she had invited him, even if he was slightly jealous of Chouza.

They slowly made their way back toward the manor and Jax glanced over. "So what did Arkham say about your encounter with Sloth yesterday?"

Amy bit her lip and looked down. "I… didn't tell him."

"You didn't tell him? Amy, this isn't something we can just ignore!" Amy cringed and shrank away from him. Guilt flooded him and he immediately realized how harsh he had sounded. "If you don't want to tell him, I can understand why. I'll stand by you if that's your decision, but I really think he should know."

Amy shook her head and Jax was once again struck by how small she looked. "No, you're right. He does need to know. The Sins being in his city is something he needs to be aware of."

"Would you like me to go with you?"

"You don't have to." The empty words carried little weight.

"I don't mind. I know Arkham still frightens you." Amy gave a small nod but didn't look at him. Jax almost kicked himself for bringing up something that had upset her after seeing her in such a good mood.

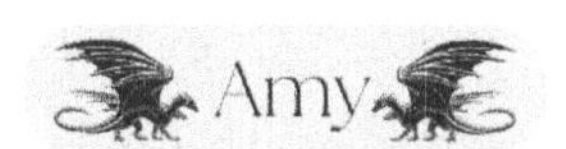

When Amy and Jax returned to the manor, Amy immediately set a path to Arkham's office. Jax was right, Arkham needed to know about her encounter with Whittaker… and Bradley… But she was loath to admit that she had seen Bradley as well. *It's probably safe to just mention Whittaker. That will let Arkham know that the Sins were out again, without drawing even more attention to the fact that they were interested in me.*

Arkham's eyes narrowed when she knocked on the doorframe. "Amy? Jax? What can I help you with?"

Amy fidgeted nervously and glanced at Jax who gave her an encouraging nod. "I ran into Sloth in town again yesterday," she said quietly.

"What? Where?"

"Jax and I went to a bookstore in town—"

"Which bookstore?"

"Bailey's Bookstore. It's in the Southeast district?"

Arkham's eyes softened. "I'm aware of it. It was one of my son's favorite places, especially after my wife died."

Amy gulped. "Well, like I said, Jax and I were there and we had split up. The attendant found me and said that someone wanted a meeting with me so I followed her and it was Sloth."

"Are you alright?"

Amy shrugged. "He didn't try to hurt me or even threaten me; he just wanted a chess game."

"A chess game?" Arkham's suspicion dripped from his words.

"Yes. He was asking a lot of questions, using the game as an excuse to keep me there."

"What kind of questions? What did you tell him?" Amy shifted nervously and Arkham's suspicious expression eased. "I am not asking because I think you betrayed us. I am asking because Sloth is capable of getting answers in ways we do not anticipate. I am not so much interested in what you told him so much as what you *said*."

Amy hesitated a moment longer but nodded. "He asked about our abilities and I didn't answer, just said that Envy would know. Then he started talking about our abilities, which I guess means that they do talk amongst themselves. He said that he was just seeing if I would talk about my teammates and how much I would give away. Then said that it was good that I wouldn't." Amy found herself rambling, trying to make sense of the meeting herself.

Arkham's fingers stroked his beard. "That is concerning."

Amy blinked and Jax raised an eyebrow. "What is concerning, Sir?" he asked.

"Until now we have had no way of knowing for sure if the Sins were able to communicate amongst themselves or if they were trapped in their individual dungeons. If he knew of your abilities, that implies that they do indeed have access to each other. What else did he ask?"

"Umm..." she thought back. "He wanted to know how we got here. I didn't see any harm in that so I just said that we were traveling with a caravan and got trapped here. Was that wrong?"

Arkham thought for a moment before shaking his head. "No, I do not think that was wrong. Was there anything else?"

Amy hesitated a moment longer. "He... wanted to know my name."

"Your name? Why would he be interested in your name?"

"I'm... not sure. It's not as if he would have any reason to know of my family."

"What *is* your family name?" Arkham asked.

Amy glanced nervously at Jax. He would know of her family. If she admitted who she was in front of him, he would know. He watched her curiously and Amy realized she trusted him not to spread the information. He would keep her secret.

She took a deep breath and faced Arkham again. "Pruitt. My family's name is Pruitt."

Arkham frowned, thinking. "The name does not sound familiar."

Amy shook her head. "That doesn't surprise me."

Arkham looked between them again. "Was there anything else?"

Amy shook her head again, deciding to keep Whittaker's name to herself. For some reason, the fact that he had trusted her with it made her want to keep it a secret. She wasn't even sure why. "Once he got my name, he said goodbye and left," she said with a shrug. "He said I wouldn't be followed and no one but who I told would know of our meeting."

Arkham gazed down at his hands and Amy could almost see the thoughts going through his mind. "He didn't try to recruit me or anything! Or even threaten me!"

Arkham glanced back up at her and gave her a small smile. "I believe you, Amy. Is there anything else?" Amy and Jax glanced at each other and then shook their heads. "Very well. You are dismissed. I will send some of my men into town to see if they can find any trace of Sloth."

"Yes, Sir." With that, the pair left the room.

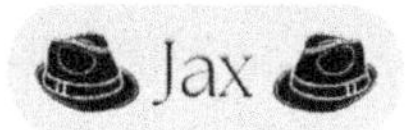

Jax mulled over the conversation between Amy and Arkham as they left the office, noticing Amy glancing at him nervously. "Pruitt, huh?" he finally asked as they made their way down the stairs. It had taken him a bit to remember why the name was familiar. And what Amy was probably short for.

"Yeah."

"It wouldn't happen to be *Amelia* Pruitt would it?"

Amy hesitated, then nodded. "Yeah."

"Forgive me for saying, but everyone thought you were dead."

Amy ducked her head. "I know. And I preferred it that way. If they thought I was dead, they wouldn't look for me."

Jax frowned. "Amy… What happened? Why did you leave?"

Amy looked away, but Jax could see her blinking rapidly to try and fight back tears. "It doesn't matter. My family is dead, so what does it matter?"

Jax didn't press it. "It does seem strange that Sloth would be interested in your name, though. I mean, the Pruitts weren't exactly around that long ago."

Amy sniffed and shook her head. "No. The Pruitt trading company was created by my grandfather. There's no way it was around that long ago." She paused, then grinned over at him, the smile not quite reaching her eyes. "I did find out his name, too, though. You'll never believe it."

"Oh?"

She glanced around quickly, then leaned in. "Whittaker Falks."

Jax blinked, again trying to place the name. *Falks*… "Wait… You don't mean Falks as in the *biggest* alchemy company in Northern *and* Southern Scienna?"

Amy waited until a staff member had passed before continuing. "He and his brother are the creators of the company."

Jax stared at her in shock. "How did the creators of the biggest alchemy company in the world become connected to a demon lord?"

Amy shook her head. "I have no idea."

"And even more curiously, what is their interest in you?" Jax added, glancing at her in concern. He grinned. "I mean, I know you're a princess and all, but it's not like they know that."

His smile fell as Amy looked away. "I'm not a princess, Jax."

"I know. But still. What's their interest?"

"I have no idea. It's funny, though. Fredrikson was interested in my name, too."

"He was?"

Amy's brow furrowed as she paused on the steps for a moment before continuing. Jax wordlessly followed her to Fredrikson's office.

When they arrived at the open door, Amy knocked lightly on the frame. "Sir Fredrikson?"

Fredrikson looked up from his book. "Amy, Jax? Can I help you?"

Amy hesitated and glanced at Jax. "Well… I was wondering if I could ask you something."

Fredrikson set the book aside and waved them in. "Sure."

Jax followed Amy into the room and pulled it shut behind him. Amy nodded thanks to him before refocusing on Fredrikson. "We ran into Sloth in town again."

Frerikson's eyes narrowed and he sat forward. "Are you alright?"

"We're fine. But he was extremely interested in my name. And me." She stepped forward, her eyes narrowed. "What would be Sloth's interest in me?"

"I'm not sure."

"He wanted to know my name. And you did, too. What is so important about my name?"

Fredrikson studied her silently. "Well… Perhaps he thinks there's a relation between the two of you."

Amy immediately stepped back, shock covering her face. "What are you saying? You think I'm related to them just because I'm a demon-spawn?"

Fredrikson shrugged. "It's certainly a possibility."

Amy shook her head and yanked the door open before fleeing through it. Jax glared at Fredrikson before following her. Amy hurried out the front door and he could see her wiping at her face. "Amy! Amy, please wait!"

She stopped and kept her back to him. "What is it, Jax?"

Jax's heart broke at the pain in her voice. "I just wanted to make sure you were okay." He stepped closer.

She still didn't turn to look at him. "I'm fine. But I need to go. I'm supposed to meet Chouza soon."

"You know I support you, right? I'll be your friend no matter what your blood Awoke as."

Amy finally turned to him with a small smile. "I know. And I really appreciate it."

Jax reached for her, but let his hand drop as she walked away. *Why would Fredrikson say such a thing? Surely he's smart enough to realize that just because her blood Awoke as demon-spawn doesn't mean that she's related to those monsters. And from the way Arkham talked about Sloth, he certainly wouldn't jump to that conclusion. So what was Fredrikson's goal with that statement? Just to antagonize Amy? But why? He doesn't seem like the type to be cruel just to be cruel. What was his goal?*

He sighed and shook his head. *So many questions and so few answers.*

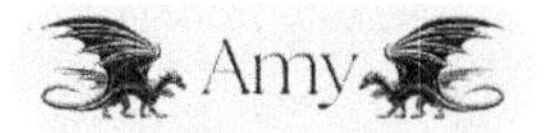

By the time Amy reached the gate, it was almost time to meet Chouza. Fredrikson's words still echoed in her mind. *Is that what he thinks of me? Is that what they all think of me? Do they think I'm like the Sins? Am I like the Sins?* Amy shook the thought away. Lillian had been nothing but kind to her. And while she rarely talked to Austin, he had at least been cordial. Arkham himself was still suspicious of her, clearly, but he was tolerant and his suspicions seemed to have been easing.

A few minutes later, she saw Chouza and Kimi approaching. He grinned when he saw her and waved. Amy returned the wave and couldn't help but feel her mood lifting. "Good morning."

"Good morning."

"Good morning, Ms. Amy!" Kimi's hair had been pulled back into a neat ponytail, a pretty blue ribbon that matched her dress tied into a bow around it.

"Hi, Kimi. How are you this morning?"

"Papa made us flatcakes!"

"That sounds yummy." Amy smiled up at Chouza, amused by Kimi's chatter.

Chouza chuckled and squeezed her hand. "You haven't been waiting too long, have you?"

Amy shook her head. "Just a few minutes."

"That's good." He gestured for her to follow him and she stepped forward, falling easily into step next to him. "Did you sleep well?"

Amy shrugged. "Well enough."

Kimi slipped between them and reached out to take Amy's hand as well. Amy stiffened, but didn't pull away. Chouza glanced over and frowned. "Kimiko, we don't touch other people without permission. You know that."

"Sorry, Papa. I forgot! I wanted you and Ms. Amy to swing me!"

Amy glanced down at the girl, melting at the pleading look in her eyes. "It's alright. What do I do?"

"She just wants us to swing her back and forth while we're walking. But she's heavy so I wouldn't blame you if you don't want to."

"Pleeeease, Ms. Amy?"

Amy hesitated, then chuckled as Kimi poked her bottom lip out. "Alright, Kimi."

"Yay!"

Chouza shook his head. "How you get everyone to do what you want is beyond me, child." He glanced over at Amy. "Ready?"

Amy hesitantly nodded and Kimi dropped her weight, allowing Amy and Chouza to swing her forward. They took a few steps and swung her again, Kimi giggling all the while.

Gradually, the neatly paved streets gave way to cobbled paths as they left the North District and entered the Northwest District. The Temple of Naroe towered over most of the other buildings in the district, large stained glass windows reflecting the morning light.

"Lorencost was built in a circle," Chouza explained as they walked. "With the mountains to the north, it provided an easily defensible position. The demons coming from the Rift were forced to funnel through that narrow pass and the soldiers here were able to easily guard it. The walls around the outer edges helped prevent any demons from making their way around. There are four gates that enter the city at each of the cardinal directions: Most people come through the South Gate from Koven, but occasionally, people get pulled from Kush and come through the East Gate. The Crane estate is through the West Gate and the pass to the Rift is through the North Gate.

"The North District is mostly residential with a few high-class taverns in it. It was where the upper class lived back before the curse.

You saw the Pits yesterday. They're in the Northeast District. A lot of us live over there and in the East District. It had a lot of damage from the war, so few of the original citizens went back there. Over the years, generations of travelers have repaired the damages and even built new homes and apartments."

"That's where we live!" Kimi volunteered.

Chouza chuckled. "Yes, we live in an apartment complex in the Northeast District. Anyway, you'll find travelers all over the city, but that's where the highest concentration is. The Southeast District has a lot of the original businesses, as well as many of the old residences. It's pretty heavily mixed, though. You're just as likely to come across one of us as you are one of the original residents.

"The South District is fairly mixed as well, though there's very few travelers' residences there. Many of them have set up stalls in the Traders' Market there, but it was pretty densely populated after the war and most of us tend to stick together."

Amy listened silently as Chouza explained what he knew about the history of the city, her eyes alternating between watching Kimi and studying their surroundings. The further south they worked, the more uneven the streets became and the dingier the buildings.

"In the Northwest and West district, you'll find many of the temples. Most, in fact. I think there might be one or two over in the East district, but those were added by travelers after they realized their god didn't have a temple here in town already. The West district is also the largest merchant district, with a mix of original shops and travelers' shops. In fact, we're almost there if you'd like to take a look around."

Amy shrugged. "I'm just along for the tour."

Chouza seemed to debate with himself for a moment, before nodding. "I can show you the difference between shops."

"What do you mean?"

"Well, I assume one of the Arkhams told you that if you buy something from an original resident, it goes back to them during the reset, right?" He paused and waited for Amy to nod before continuing. "Well, to kind of reduce the inconvenience of that, travelers mark their shops so that the rest of us know whatever we get there is safe."

"Oh. And that works?"

Chouza indicated a simple star painted in green paint above the door frame of a building. "It does. See that star above the door? It doesn't detract from the way things look, but it marks it as an obvious traveler's shop."

Kimi tugged on Chouza's hand. "Hey, Papa! Can we visit the toy store?"

Chouza glanced at Amy questioningly and she shrugged, Kimi's hand still resting comfortably in hers. Chouza sighed. "Alright, Kimiko."

Kimi squealed and pulled her hands free, running down the street.

Amy chuckled and rubbed at her hand, surprised at how empty it felt after Kimi's had been gripped in it. "She's got a lot of energy."

"Yes, she does. It's exhausting," Chouza admitted, but his smile betrayed the warmth he felt for his daughter.

Kimi stopped at a door and waited impatiently for them, bouncing on the balls of her feet. Chouza chuckled, but Amy's eye had been drawn by a different shop further down the street. Bright pencils and chalks were displayed in the front window along with sketchbooks.

She glanced at Chouza, then back at the shop. "I'll catch up with you."

Chouza's brow furrowed, but he didn't question her, instead hurrying to catch up with Kimi inside the toy store. Amy approached the other shop, her breath catching when she saw 'Art Supplies' etched on the sign with a green star next to it. She took a breath and stepped in, turning in a circle to take in as much of the shop as she could. Different pencils, crayons, chalk, paints, and papers lined the shelves. Another section shelved clay, and yet another had canvases and wood for framing items.

"Welcome, can I help you find anything?"

Amy jumped and turned to the counter where a young man was carefully laying out a line of pencils to be boxed together. "Uh, no. I've never actually seen an entire shop devoted solely to art supplies."

He chuckled. "Yes, it's not a very prosperous business, but around here that's not such a bad thing. I make enough to support my family."

"I see." She carefully picked up one of the boxes of colored pencils, heart pounding. "How much would a set of pencils and a sketchbook be?"

"Pencils are a silver for a box of 10 and three silver for a box of fifty. Sketchbooks vary by the size and paper quality." He walked from behind the counter and over to the sketchbooks. "These smaller ones are two silver, the larger ones are five."

An easel nearby drew Amy's attention and she brushed her fingers across the intricately carved wood. In her heart, she knew she wouldn't be able to afford it, but it called to her in a way she couldn't resist. "And how much is this?"

"Three gold. My father hand carved every piece of that and I only have three. It works with these canvases here." He gestured to thin canvases on a nearby shelf. "It's meant for portraits."

Her suspicions confirmed, Amy sighed. "And how much for the canvases?"

"A silver a piece."

Amy gnawed her lip as she counted out the coins in her purse. After spending the four silver to get into the Pits the day before and the one at the bookstore, she only had six silver left. Her eyes were drawn to the larger book and the set of fifty pencils.

The bell over the door chimed as Chouza and Kimi walked in. "Pleeease can I have the pony?" Kimi begged Chouza.

"You already have that exact toy pony at home, Kimiko. I'm not going to get you a second one."

"But I don't know where it is!"

"It should be in your toybox."

Kimi pouted, but her eyes widened when she saw Amy. "Ms. Amy! Are you buying crayons?"

Amy glanced questioningly at Chouza and he chuckled. "This is where we come to get Kimiko her art supplies. She loves to color."

"Oh. Um, no, I wasn't actually getting crayons. I was looking at his drawing supplies." She set the box of fifty down and grabbed a box of charcoal drawing pencils. "I'll just take this and the smaller book, please." *I can always come back later and get them after we get paid again. After all, we'll probably be here a while.*

The shopkeeper quickly wrote the numbers down in a book behind the counter. Amy passed the coins over before Chouza set the box of fifty pencils and a small box of crayons on the counter.

"I'll take these, please."

Amy took her things and stepped outside with a sigh. *It would have been nice to get some colored pencils again. I miss drawing.*

Chouza followed her out, Kimi bouncing along happily as she held the crayons. "I can't wait to get home and color again!" she squealed.

Amy couldn't help the small smile as she watched the girl's excitement. Chouza stepped up next to her and offered her the box of pencils. "Here."

Amy took the box and stared at it a moment before looking at Chouza. "What's this?"

"You clearly wanted this and I figured you probably haven't been here long enough to have a decent store of gold yet."

Amy gaped at him, then shook her head, trying to pass the pencils back. "I can't! You have Kimi to support, I can't take your money!"

Chouza chuckled and pressed it back toward her. "I've already bought them. What am I going to do with colored pencils? Besides, you're helping keep my kid entertained. That's worth a few silvers." He shrugged. "The Pits pay well. Trust me, Kimiko and I don't want for coins. Please, let me treat you."

Amy hesitantly glanced at the box again, unable to deny the swell of excitement. "Thank you."

"My pleasure."

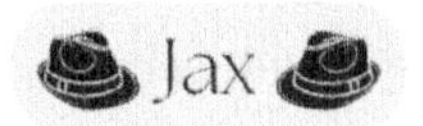

Jax sighed when he walked into the dining hall and immediately heard Nolan and Kila arguing. *Maybe I should have gone with Amy. Hopefully she's okay.* His gaze trailed toward the city, wondering about her date with Chouza. She had seemed so happy when she told him about it, and he hoped that her not being back yet was a good sign.

"You ass, I told you I don't want your training! There's a perfectly capable teacher here."

Nolan glared at Kila. "And I've told you before that I'm better than any of them."

Kila huffed and crossed her arms. "And yet she's beaten you every time you've 'trained' with her."

"No, I've let her win."

"You are an ass and a liar. And you have a superiority complex. Get lost." She turned her back to him.

Talia rubbed her face as Jax sat across from her. "I take it this has been going on for a while?" he asked.

Talia nodded. "Pretty much since they got up this morning. They went out to train and of course Lucile offered to train them. Nolan challenged her and well… You see the result."

Jax frowned and shook his head. "I envy Amy right now."

Nolan glanced over with a raised eyebrow. "Where is Lady Flame, anyway?"

"One of the men from the Fighting Pits is showing her around town so that maybe we can get a better lay of the land." He carefully refrained from mentioning her excitement or the fact that he suspected Chouza had invited her on a date.

Kila's tail twitched as she straightened. "Fighting Pits?"

Jax wrapped a noodle around his fork. "Yeah. Apparently there's Fighting Pits over in the Northeast district."

Nolan grinned. "I don't suppose you remember how to get there, do you Jax?"

Jax raised an eyebrow. "I do."

Kila grinned. "So then, show us!"

Jax crossed his arms and sat back. "What if I don't want to?"

Nolan's eyes narrowed. "Technically I outrank you…" He let the threat trail off, but Jax knew exactly what he meant. Nolan could technically order Jax to show him.

Jax snorted. "Nolan, you're as aware as I am that none of us outrank the other here. We're all just trying to survive. So don't pull that crap." Nolan growled, but Jax continued before he could interject. "But I will show you where the Fighting Pits are. I'd been planning on going again today anyway. Turns out my father is there."

Talia cocked her head, studying him curiously. "Your father?"

"Long story, but yeah. Apparently he's been here for about fifteen years." Jax wasn't entirely sure whether he fully believed what his father said, but he did want to at least give him a chance.

"That's nice that you've found him."

"Yeah, yeah. That's great and all, but are you going to show us how to get there?" Kila interrupted.

Jax rolled his eyes and gestured to his plate with his fork. "Let me eat first."

"Fine." Kila sat back with her arms crossed, tail twitching.

Jax took his time eating, giving Talia time to do the same. Nolan and Kila were both either already done or had no interest in eating.

Eventually, he stood and Kila jumped to her feet. "Are we going now?"

Jax set his plate aside. "Let's go."

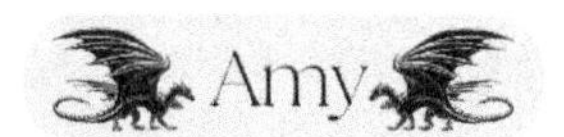

Amy's eyes trailed across the tavern Chouza had insisted on bringing her to. The blue walls were decorated with beautiful tapestries and the dark wood left the room dimly lit and cozy. Two gray-skinned, white-haired, humanoid people that Chouza had called shinkuhata worked behind the bar.

Kimi bounced excitedly in her chair, looking around them with a grin. "Do I get ice cream?"

"If you eat your food," Chouza promised.

"I will!"

Amy's brow furrowed. "Ice cream?"

Chouza shrugged. "Think of sweetened, super-cooled milk. I don't know exactly the process, but that's the closest I can get."

Amy blinked, frowning. "Okay…"

"They have lots of flavors!" Kimi held her little hand up and started counting with her fingers. "They have vanilla and strawberry and chocolate…" She licked her lips and Amy chuckled.

"I take it you like chocolate?"

Chouza tucked a lock of Kimi's hair behind her ear. "Yes, chocolate is a big treat for both of us."

Amy tried to remember the last time she'd had chocolate but couldn't. It had been when her family was still alive, and she could only barely remembered the slightly bitter taste.

"I love chocolate!" Kimi added.

By the time their food arrived, Kimi was chattering away again, barely taking a breath between sentences. The waiter set three plates in front of them and Amy eyed Chouza's curiously. Some had some kind of pink meat covering white rice and others had rice wrapped in what looked like a dark green film, with a different meat in the center. Next to it was a bowl of pinkish-orange sauce.

Chouza chuckled when he noticed her look. "It's sushi."

"Sushi?"

Kimi's nose wrinkled. "Papa likes it, but I don't! It's slimy!"

Chouza chuckled. "It's not slimy, Kimiko, the texture is just different from what you like."

She 'harrumphed' and dug into her own bowl of chicken sitting on a bed of rice and veggies. "Well, I don't want any, Papa."

"That's fine, Kimiko. You don't have to." He chuckled and gestured to it with his chopsticks. "Would you like to try one?"

Amy picked up her own chopsticks, fumbling with them for a moment before getting them settled in her hand. It had been a long time since she'd used them and it pleased her that, while clumsy, she still remembered how.

"Are you sure?"

Chouza slid his plate closer to her. "Go ahead." Amy carefully reached forward and picked up one of the pieces of pink meat covering the rice, surprised when it didn't just fall apart when she lifted it. Chouza tapped the container of sauce with his chopstick. "Flip it over and dip it in there. It's better with that."

Amy did as he suggested, then took a careful bite of the roll. She agreed with Kimi's assessment of it being slimy and her nose wrinkled. She set it aside and shook her head. "I think I'll pass. What is it, anyway?"

Chouza chuckled and shook his head. "More for me. The meat is raw fish and this is seaweed," he explained, tapping the green film around the other rolls. The sauce is sakura sauce."

"Oh. Well, that's.... Interesting."

Chouza shrugged and dipped a piece in the sauce before biting into it. "It's not for everyone. But it's a fairly traditional dish of Calionisia, one of the nations in Aelish, so my mother used to make it. I was thrilled when I found out the Black Ring served it."

Amy refocused on her own chicken and rice, marveling at the strong flavors. "This place is amazing."

Chouza finished his mouthful of food before nodding. "It's one of my favorite places. The Black Ring Serpent was opened by the shinku that were here even before the curse hit. They attempted the dungeons, so their memories remain intact. Kraven and I come here all the time."

Amy's brow furrowed. "What do you mean their memories are intact?"

"I'm sure Arkham mentioned that if one of the original residents attempted the dungeons, they became like the Arkhams themselves; never aging, but seeing the passage of time?" Amy nodded and Chouza gestured subtly to the two shinku behind the bar. "Those two were soldiers who attempted the dungeons. Once they quit, they came back here and continued their lives as usual. Now they've hired a few travelers to work for them and they've grown in popularity, but the tavern itself is the same as it was three hundred years ago."

Amy studied the man and woman with more appreciation. "Thank you again for bringing me. I've learned a lot."

Chouza glanced at Kimi poking a carrot suspiciously. "Kimiko, eat your veggies."

"But Papa, I don't want to."

"No ice cream unless you eat your veggies."

Kimi's lip pooched out and she picked up the carrot. "Alright."

Amy picked up her own carrot. "On the count of three?" she offered. Kimi beamed and held hers up. "Alright. One. Two. Three!" She popped the carrot in her mouth and Kimi did the same, her face scrunching up.

Chouza rolled his eyes and watched them with a smile. "Trust me,

Amy. Showing you around today has been anything but a hardship," he said, his eyes soft as he watched Kimi pick up a piece of broccoli.

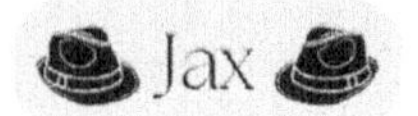

Jax covered his face with one hand as Nolan got his ass handed to him in the ring. Shane raised an eyebrow and glanced over. "One of your group, I take it?"

Jax groaned and dropped his hand. "Can I get away with saying no?"

Shane chuckled and watched as Nolan's match ended. "Unfortunately, I think you have to claim him. Is that the best he can do?"

Jax sighed, but shook his head. "He's actually a fairly competent fighter when he's not drunk off his ass and has a weapon."

"He's drunk?"

"He always is. The only time I've seen him not totally wasted was in the dungeon. And then he was actually pretty damn good."

Shane frowned as Nolan stalked over to the sign-up table and demanded another match. "He's rather… insistent isn't he?"

Jax snorted and crossed his arms. "That's one word for it, I suppose."

Talia kept her head lowered and Jax glanced over. It had surprised him when she'd joined them. "You alright, Talia?"

Talia shook her head. "He's embarrassing."

Jax silently agreed with her as Nolan argued with the people at the table. He slammed a few more silver onto the table and stood watching the next match. "I guess he got his way."

"Of course he did. They're making easy money off of him," Shane explained. "Each match has a sign-up fee that they use to match bets with. If you win, you get a portion of what was bet on you. If you lose, they pocket the money. At least at his level."

Talia leaned forward to look around Jax at Shane. "His level?"

Shane shrugged. "You have your rookies like him that pay to fight and then get rewards for wins, then you've got paid fighters like Chouza who get paid per match regardless and then get a bonus if they win, and then you've got the VIPs who get paid a salary, no matter how many fights they participate in."

Jax's eyes narrowed. "VIPs?"

Shane nodded. "They're the best of the best. They've worked their way up to where they are and only fight on request or for special exhibition matches that Kraven sets up about once a month. You just missed the last one."

"What's an exhibition match?"

"Basically a tournament showing off all of the best fighters. Usually one of the tier two fighters gets a chance to become a VIP during it. Chouza only barely missed out this last one. He was one win short of qualifying." At Jax's confused look, Shane elaborated. "To qualify to become a VIP, you have to participate in forty matches in a month and win at least thirty-five of them."

"But he didn't have enough wins?"

"Didn't have enough matches, technically. He's got thirty-four wins out of thirty-eight matches."

Jax raised an eyebrow. "That's… impressive. All of that in hand-to-hand?"

Shane took a long drink. "He is impressive. That match you saw yesterday was a request and didn't count toward his total, unfortunately They have to be ono-on-one."

"This is quite the system."

Shane's eyes trailed past them and he offered a hand to a man with short, neatly groomed blond hair. "Vallun! Good to see you!"

The man he called Vallun shook his hand. "Good to see you as well, Shane. Out here betting as usual?"

Shane snorted and gestured to the ring Kila stood in, facing off against another woman about her size. "Not much to bet on. Jax, this is my boss, Vallun. Vallun, this is my son, Jax."

Vallun raised an eyebrow and studied Jax more intently. "I've heard a lot about you. It's nice to finally meet you."

Jax tipped his hat, then indicated Talia. "You as well. This is Talia. She's our healer."

Vallun took her hand, bowing low to kiss the back. "It's a pleasure to meet such a lovely lady."

Talia's cheeks colored as she giggled lightly. "It's nice to meet you as well."

Vallun straightened and released her hand. "I must say, this doesn't seem like the kind of place someone like you would frequent."

Talia shook her head. "I'm just here to make sure my teammates don't get killed."

Vallun chuckled and watched as Kila forced the other girl from the ring, winning the match. "Not bad. Fighting isn't for everyone, but it is kind of you to be here for your friends."

"Why do you come to watch?" Talia asked him.

"There's not much else to do in this city. I can make a handful of silver off of the fights here and there and it gives me an idea of the new people coming into town. Everyone seems to find their way here eventually."

Talia nodded and watched as the next fighters took the ring. "Do I really stand out here? I've noticed the stares in the streets, but I didn't think it would be so bad here."

"You do. Your blood is Awakened which means you're attempting the dungeons. Many people have an interest in that. Plus, if I may say, you're quite beautiful."

Talia flushed again, dipping her head. "I guess I do sort of glow."

Jax bit back a chuckle as Vallun flirted with Talia. Shane raised an eyebrow and gestured toward his usual spot on the wall and with a quick glance at Talia and Vallun, Jax followed him. "Looks like he's taken an interest in her."

"It would seem so. She could definitely do worse than Vallun. He's the leader of the Thieves' Guild and has a reputation as a gentleman."

Jax leaned against the wall next to him, watching as Vallun pulled a seat out for Talia and sat next to her. "Thieves' Guild? Didn't you say he's your boss?"

Shane waved a hand. "Don't worry, it's just a name. They dropped actual thievery years ago. Now it's more like a messenger guild."

"Oh." He watched as Nolan entered the ring, wincing as his opponent leapt forward and knocked him out with a single blow. "That had to hurt."

Two men with a stretcher carefully lifted Nolan and removed him from the ring. Talia started to stand, but with a few words from Vallun lowered herself down again, glancing between him and the door to the back rooms. Kila walked over and dropped into a seat next to them, chatting to Talia animatedly.

Jax shook his head. "Nolan's going to be insufferable later."

"That bad, huh?"

Jax sighed and shrugged. "He's convinced he's the best fighter there is, but not only did he just get beaten twice here, the trainer back at the Arkhams' place has beaten him many times."

"He's going to be trouble," Shane warned.

"I'm aware. I just hope he learns before it becomes an issue."

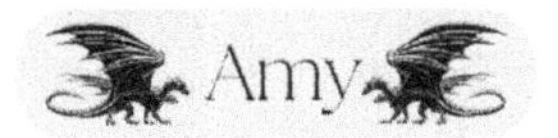

Three bowls of mounded ice cream sat in front of Amy, Chouza, and Kimi. Kimi squealed and grabbed her spoon, digging into the brown ice cream as Chouza lifted his own spoon. "Dig in."

Amy hesitantly dipped her spoon into her own chocolate ice cream, surprised at the chill it sent through her. Immediately the creamy goodness coated her tongue and she sighed in pleasure. She shoveled several more spoonfuls into her mouth before Chouza's chuckle stopped her.

"Take it easy, Amy. If you eat too fast it will give you a brain freeze."

Amy frowned. "What's a brain freeze?"

"It's when your head hurts because you ate too much ice cream too fast!" Kimi explained.

Amy eyed the ice cream suspiciously, wondering how something so delicious could cause pain. Chouza's laugh startled her and she stared at him wide-eyed. "It's alright, Amy. It isn't going to attack you. Just don't eat it too fast."

"Oh. Okay." She continued eating at a slower pace. Across from her, Chouza and Kimi did the same. As usual, Kimi's chatter filled the air between bites.

Once they were done, Chouza set the coins to pay for their meal on the table and led Kimi and Amy out. Amy ducked her head, her cheeks heating. "Thank you for the meal."

"Happy to. Everyone should experience the Black Ring at least once. It's a right of passage." He winked at her and Amy's heart raced.

Kimi yawned and tugged on Chouza's hand. "Papa, I'm sleepy."

"I know, Baby. It's about your nap time, isn't it?" Kimi nodded and rubbed her eyes with her free hand. Chouza picked her up and she leaned her head against his shoulder. "How about we go to the park later?"

"But I want to go *now*," she whined.

"We'll go after you get up from your nap, okay?"

She let out another small sound of protest but tucked her head into Chouza's neck. "Promise?"

"I promise."

"Okay, Papa." Kimi's eyes fluttered shut and it didn't take long before her breathing evened out.

Amy smiled at the small girl before turning back to Chouza. "I can find my own way back to the manor."

He shook his head. "I'll walk you back."

Amy fell into step next to him, occasionally glancing at the small bit of Kimi's face she could see. "How old is she?"

"She'll be four in a little over a month."

"She's precious."

Chouza smiled adoringly at his daughter. "Thank you."

"Her mother…?" Amy didn't want to pry, but he seemed so kind and the girl was still so young that she couldn't help her curiosity.

Chouza's face hardened and his gaze went straight ahead of them.

"She died in one of the dungeons when Kimiko was just a few weeks old."

"I'm sorry. I shouldn't have asked."

"It's alright. It's a natural question. Single dads aren't exactly common." He gave a dry chuckle. "If you'd have told me four years ago that I'd be raising a daughter alone, I'd have called you crazy. But now I wouldn't give her up for the world."

Amy's heart ached at the pain on his face. "You seem to be doing a really good job at it."

Chouza's arms tightening around Kimi slightly. "Thank you. That means a lot. I've tried to do my best for her."

"I think you have."

"So, tell me more about your group. I met Jax yesterday, but I don't know anything about any of your abilities."

Amy hesitated, wondering if it was some kind of trap. *No… No, he's a good person. I can feel it.* "Well, I'm apparently a draconic sorceress. I use fire spells. Jax uses something called psychic magick."

"Psychic magick? I don't know much about magick, but I know I've never heard of that."

Amy shrugged. "Apparently it's pretty rare. Anyway, there's us, Nolan, Talia, and Kila."

"What do they do?"

"Talia's our healer. She's a cleric of Arista. Kila is good with traps and uses daggers. Nolan is a soldier in a tin can."

Chouza chuckled and glanced over. "A soldier in a tin can?"

Amy shrugged. "He's the apprentice blacksmith to the King of Zadia. He trained his soldiers for him. And what else would you describe that giant metal armor as?" She shuddered. "It's a tin can that you can move in. Barely."

"I suppose that's one way to describe it."

The streets evened out as they left the northwest district behind and the houses grew in size. Birds chirped, a dog chased a cat just down the street. It just felt so… normal. "It feels strange to think that such a peaceful place is cursed."

Chouza sighed. "It does." He glanced at her for a moment before taking a breath. "You said you have two fighters?"

Amy shrugged. "Nolan's our main fighter, I guess. Jax and Kila are pretty good with their weapons, but Nolan's really the one that does the most damage."

"Have you considered looking into getting someone to join you?"

Amy frowned, thinking carefully over his words. "I guess not. The way Arkham talked, it was us or no one."

Chouza nodded. "In a way it is. Most of us want nothing to do with those dungeons. Not after what we've witnessed. What they've taken from us." He rested his head on Kimi's for a moment before continuing. "But some of us do want another chance. There's always a few who want a second go."

"It sounds like you're saying you want to."

"Kimiko will never see life outside this city if this curse isn't broken. She'll never see rain. Never see snow. Never see the true night sky. Have you noticed that?" he asked and Amy shook her head. "The stars are exactly the same every night. The same as they were three hundred years ago. Kimiko will never get the chance to see what the outside world has to offer as long as we're trapped here. I want to know that I did everything I could to give her that chance."

"But what if something were to happen to you? What if she were to lose her mother *and* her father?"

Chouza didn't answer for a moment as they walked, waiting until the Arkhams' gate came into view. "I know it's a risk. It's a huge risk. But… I can't let Khiran's loss be for nothing. I can't let her daughter grow up under the curse that claimed her life." His voice cracked slightly and he cleared his throat. "Like I said, it might be something to consider. Having another good fighter on your team would better your chances."

Amy stopped outside the gate. "It probably wouldn't hurt," she admitted. "I nearly died in that dungeon and it's supposed to be the easiest. I'll… I'll talk to the others. But I think you should consider whether growing up here is truly worse than growing up without your parents."

"Trust me, I have. I have no intention of leaving her without her father. But it's a risk I have to take."

Amy sighed and pressed the gate open. "I'll talk to the others. Thank you again for today, Chouza. For everything." She tightened her grip on the sketch book and pencils in her hand. "I really enjoyed myself."

"I did, too. Maybe we can do it again soon. After all, we never even made it to the west district or the park."

"I'd like that."

"Tomorrow I have a match, but maybe the next day?"

Amy's stomach fluttered as she nodded. "I'll see you the day after tomorrow, then."

Kimi shifted and Chouza kissed her head. "Tell Ms. Amy bye bye."

"Bye bye," Kimi mumbled before falling asleep again.

Chouza chuckled and shook his head. "Bye, Amy. I'll see you in a couple days."

"Bye, Chouza, Kimi."

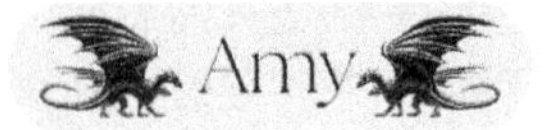

Amy pulled her eyes from the people flowing around her to grin at Jax. "To think this happens every morning."

Jax matched her grin before leaning a little further over the rooftop they were standing on. "My father wasn't kidding. Look!"

Amy followed his gaze and watched a cat walking backward toward what appeared to be— "Ew! Jax, no!" Jax cracked up and Amy's face heated. "That is disgusting."

"Of course. But it made you smile."

Amy's cheeks heated even more as she shook her head. "You're incorrigible."

"Perhaps. But you wouldn't have me any other way, now would you?"

Amy rolled her eyes and bumped her shoulder against his. "No. No, I wouldn't."

He grinned and the two lapsed into silence as they watched the people reversing around them. The night before, he had returned and found her drawing a picture of Chouza and Kimi. It had been nice to finally be able to draw again and she had happily shown her work to him.

"Unnerving isn't it?" a voice behind her asked. Amy jumped and glanced over her shoulder at a young brunette man, not much older than her. Jax's hand went to his rapier, eyes narrowed.

Amy blinked, relaxing as she studied the man's human features. "Unnerving? No! It's really cool!" She returned her gaze to the street, keeping him in her peripheral. She didn't like that he'd been able to sneak up on her. Jax relaxed as well, releasing the hilt of his rapier.

"You must be new. It's cool the first dozen times. Growing up here, not so much," he said, voice bitter.

"Growing up here?"

"I was born here after my parents failed the dungeons. The name's Roxuh, by the way." He offered a hand to Amy, then Jax.

Amy shook it, then pulled back. "Amy."

"Jax. So you've lived here all your life, then?"

Roxuh nodded. "Yeah. My dad attempted the dungeons thirty years ago, my mom twenty-eight. After she failed, it wasn't too long before they met. My older sister and I were born here and live every day hoping someone breaks that stupid curse so that we can actually see something besides this town."

"Have you attempted them?" Amy asked.

Roxuh shook his head. "Nah. I'm not much of a fighter. I work for a local guild keeping an eye out for people entering the town, running messages, that sort of thing." He shrugged. "It pays well and I get to meet all kinds of people."

Jax cocked his head. "Part of the Thieves' Guild?"

Amy's eyes narrowed, but Roxuh titled his head. "How'd you know?"

"My father works for them as well."

Roxuh's gaze flicked between Amy and Jax. "Your father? I thought you'd just entered?"

"Long story, but yes. My father is Shane Silvers. He's been here for about fifteen years. Amy and I only entered a few days ago."

"Shane's your father? Huh. Well, it's nice to meet you."

"Were you the one that saw us enter town?" Amy asked.

He shook his head again. "I wasn't on duty that day. You came in the South Gate so that was probably Kiv."

Amy nodded, looking back at the people below them. Her nose wrinkled in disgust as she watched a dog spitting food back out onto the ground. Roxuh chuckled. "Told you it was unnerving."

"Still cool. So this happens every morning?"

"Every morning at the exact same time. Never fails, never changes," he agreed bitterly.

"That must get hard." She studied the blurred images of the people passing around them again. *It* is *cool, but after a while, it probably would get old.*

Roxuh leaned against the nearby chimney. "So did you two decide not to do the dungeons, then?" She glanced at him in surprise. "Well, you're still human. If you were attempting the dungeons, you'd be a nonhuman."

Amy shook her head. "We're going through them. We finished Death two days ago."

"So why are you human still?"

Amy sighed. "I'm just… disguised. I don't like the attention not being human brings."

Jax's form shimmered and he returned to a silver fox. "I just like not standing out. Being in the Arkhams' employ draws a lot of attention."

"A foxfolk, then." Roxuh refocused on Amy. "Are you the same?"

Amy shifted uncomfortably, looking away. "Could we please just not talk about it?" Roxuh looked surprised, but shrugged. "So what else is there to do in this town?"

Roxuh grinned. "Well, there's the Fighting Pits if you're into that sort of thing. There's lots of taverns, some owned by previous travelers so you could actually have someone to talk to about it. Oh, and there's the Wizards' Guild."

"Wizards' Guild?" She straightened. "Gerald mentioned that before the dungeon. He was supposed to take us there."

"Yeah. They have a huge library full of magickal texts, merchant streets with magickal items, even their own inns and taverns. And no one in there is affected by the curse because the ones that built it originally either died or attempted the dungeons early on! It's entirely run by adventurers now."

Amy's jaw dropped and Jax's ears pricked forward. "Could you show us where it is? Amy's a sorceress and having someone to maybe help me learn *my* magick would be amazing!"

Roxuh nodded. "Sure, come with me!" He jumped down from the building, barely missing one of the backward-walking people flying past.

Amy watched him from the corner of her eyes as they followed him.

"So you said you're a member of the Thieves' Guild?" Her hand reflexively reached for her coin purse and he laughed.

"Relax, I'm not going to steal your gold. We're called the Thieves' Guild because that's what it was back before the town was cursed, but now with the old members being trapped in the loop or dead and the new members being travelers and their kids that are stuck here, we made an agreement for no more thievery. It made things entirely too dangerous for us. Well, the people almost three hundred years ago made the agreement. Our generation just follows it."

"So if you aren't part of *this* guild, then how do you know about it?"

"My father was a member. He used to take me when I was a kid."

Jax glanced over at him. "Used to?"

Roxuh frowned and looked away. "Yeah. He stopped going recently. I think he's missing the freedom of being able to roam. He never meant to settle down."

"Oh." Relief that the 'used to' only referenced him quitting and not dying filled Amy. "So what made you join the Thieves' Guild instead?"

Roxuh grinned again. "Because this is more fun," he told her, holding up her coin purse. Amy looked down at her side, then back up at him incredulously, reaching out to snatch it from his hand. "Don't worry, I didn't actually take anything. I just like showing off." He chuckled, then shrugged again. "Honestly, I didn't develop blood magick and I had no patience for studied magick, so I didn't really have a place there. Though I still know how to get in."

Amy gnawed her lip and kept Jax between them, not quite sure what to think of the stranger.

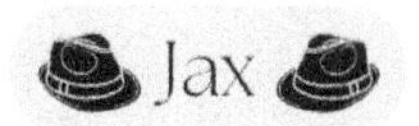

Eventually, Roxuh led them down an alleyway and Jax glanced around nervously. In the streets, people were still going about their days in reverse, but the alley was empty, ending in a dead end.

"Are you sure this is the right way?" Amy asked. Jax's eyes narrowed as he studied the alleyway around them, noting the easy hiding places for an ambush.

"It is." Seeing their nervousness, he raised a hand. "I swear I have nothing nefarious planned. It's just with all the knowledge that the Guild possesses, they tend to keep it well hidden and hard to get into." He reached the end of the alley and ran his hands over the brick. "Here." He ran his finger along the crease between bricks, down, left, down, right, up, left, up, left. Jax followed the pattern carefully, trying to learn it through observation.

Roxuh circled back to the beginning and stepped back. Nothing happened for a moment and just as Jax started to think the man was crazy, there was a click and the bricks sank into the ground, leaving a large, open archway. Roxuh grinned at their awed expressions and gestured broadly. "Welcome to the Wizards' Guild."

Jax and Amy cautiously approached, following him through the archway and stopping to watch the bricks lift back into place behind them. "How does it do that?" Amy asked in a breathless voice.

"Magick. They needed a way for even non magickal members to go in and out, so they made it to where if you knew the code, you could manually access the Guild." He shrugged. "I memorized it since my dad preferred it."

"Oh." Her jaw dropped when she finally saw the inside of the guild.

Jax followed her gaze and his eyes widened. The streets were still quiet, but people were beginning to move about, much more naturally than what was happening outside the wall. Merchants set up stalls, barely sparing the new arrivals a glance as they passed. Children played in a nearby alley, kicking a ball back and forth as a cat sat nearby with its tail over its paws. Azurys appeared from Amy's tattoo and trotted over to greet it.

Roxuh raised an eyebrow at Azurys's appearance. "Where'd he come from?"

"*She* can turn into a tattoo. She favors circling around my navel," Amy explained, emphasizing the 'she'. "Can't all familiars do that?"

"I guess. I'm not a wizard so I have no idea."

As they walked, a large building appeared in front of them, towering over the surrounding landscape. The domed towers naturally drew his eye upwards.

"What's that?"

"That is the Wizards' Library. It stands at the center of the Guild. A wall circles the entire Guild and everything is built between it and the library."

Amy gaped up at it. "*That's* a library?"

Jax's eyes widened. "*Why* didn't we get Gerald to bring us here earlier?"

"Because I didn't realize it would be this impressive."

Two stone soldiers, each at least ten feet tall, stood on either side of the double doors to enter the library, dual swords crossed in front of them. As Amy walked forward, Roxuh threw an arm in front of her. "You don't want to do that." His voice turned gravely as he said three words in a language Jax couldn't translate. "I'm not sure what they mean, but it's a code to enter the library. If you don't speak it before you enter, those soldiers tear you to shreds."

Amy froze at his words. "Knowledge is power," she whispered.

Jax glanced at her. "What?"

"It means, 'knowledge is power,' which I find quite fitting." She grinned at him.

"You understood it?"

Roxuh shrugged. "Either way, I got you in. Have fun!" With that, he gave them a wave and took off back the way they had come at a jog. Jax watched him go with a raised eyebrow, then followed Amy into the library.

As he pushed open the massive double doors, Jax's jaw dropped. Behind a large desk, a circular staircase rose up story after story. While the building had appeared about four stories from the outside, it truly stretched closer to a dozen, with rows of bookshelves extending in every direction.

"This place is amazing."

"Who are you, and how did you get in here?" a woman asked, voice dripping with animosity.

Jax looked back at the desk in front of them, shocked to find a child— no, a gnome, standing on it with a dagger in her hand. The gnome stood eye to eye with them thanks to the height of the desk, her bright blue hair seemingly defying gravity.

"I'm sorry. A man named Roxuh showed us—" Amy started to explain. "Oh no."

Jax's stomach dropped as he realized where the gnome's animosity had come from. Amy's disguise had disappeared, leaving her in her full demon-spawn form. He'd switched back to human before they'd followed Roxuh, but his disguise hadn't fallen.

The gnome bared her teeth, raising the dagger a little higher. "Don't move. Who are you?" she demanded again.

Jax growled and reached for his rapier, but Amy blocked him with one arm before raising both hands in surrender. "My name's Amy! My companions and I entered the town a few days ago. We work for Arkham and just completed Death two days ago. Please, I don't want to hurt anyone. My blood Awoke as this—this *demon-spawn*," she spat the word in disgust, "but I'm not like them! Please, I'm just looking for help. I can leave if you'd rather."

The gnome hesitated, watching her, then jumped down from the desk. "Gerald mentioned you." The dagger disappeared into a hidden pocket and the gnome gestured for Amy and Jax to follow her. Once on the floor, the little gnome rose barely to his hip. "Follow me."

After a minute of walking, she stopped and knocked on a closed door. "Yes?" a man's voice called through.

"It's Kukuri. I've got someone you need to meet. She says she was shown here by Roxuh and needs help."

"I'm here, too," Jax muttered, hand still resting on the hilt of his rapier. Amy squeezed his hand lightly, giving him a reassuring smile. He relaxed slightly, but didn't release his blade. He didn't like that people automatically assumed the worst simply because of a heritage she didn't even know she had.

After a moment, the door opened and an older man stepped through. His hair and beard were solid gray and wrinkles creased his face, though they did nothing to detract from how brightly his blue eyes shone.

"Kukuri? What's going on?"

Kukuri glared at Amy, teeth bared slightly. "She's the demon-spawn

Gerald told us about."

"Yes, yes, clearly. But it's not as if she's one of the Sins. You and I both know that. If she's here seeking help, then the least we can do is hear her out."

Kukuri sighed. "Sorry Balthazar. It's just that I've never heard of Arkham Awakening a demon-spawn before."

Amy cleared her throat and shifted uneasily. "That's because he hasn't. Though he had much the same reaction as you did when he saw what I'd become." Her eyes darted to Kukuri.

Kukuri huffed and stalked off, leaving Jax and Amy with the man she'd called Balthazar.

He grimaced and shook his head. "Sorry about that. Kukuri's last experience with demon-spawn was the war and then the dungeons so she has a very dark impression of them."

"Understandable."

"My name is Balthazar. I run the Wizards' Guild."

"I'm Amy."

Jax offered a hand. "And I'm Jax Silvers."

"Any relation to Shane Silvers?"

Jax blinked, mouth falling open. "Uh, yeah, actually. He's my father. How do you know him?"

Balthazar chuckled. "Come on in." He led them into his cluttered office and Jax's eyes widened. Every inch of usable space had *something* on it. A large cork board dominated one wall, a chalkboard the second, a giant desk piled high with books and papers filled the corner between them, filing cabinets lined the third wall, and bookshelves filled to the brim with books and scrolls ran the length of the fourth wall. Even the floor had boxes with piles of papers and books on it.

Balthazar took a seat behind the desk and gestured for Jax and Amy to take the two across from him. "I run a census every year to keep up with new travelers. The Thieves' Guild helps with that, so by extension, so does your father."

"Oh." He glanced back at the door, frowning. "I thought Arkham changed people back once they stopped going through the dungeons?"

"He does."

"But Kukuri...

"Kukuri was already a gnome."

Jax rubbed his face, utterly confused. "I thought gnomes disappeared hundreds of years ago, along with most of the magick?"

"Out there they did. But she was here already."

"So she's an original resident?

Amy sat forward. "Like the shinkuhata that run the Black Ring?"

Balthazar nodded. "Yes, exactly like them."

Jax glanced at her in surprise. "The shinku-whata?"

"The Shinkuhata. Chouza took me to a place called the Black Ring Serpent for lunch yesterday and it's run by two shinkuhata. They attempted the dungeons three hundred years ago and are like the Arkhams now."

Jax stared at Amy, slightly hurt that she hadn't shared the information sooner. "I see. What are shinkuhata?"

Balthazar stood and pulled a book from one of the shelves, opening it in front of Jax to an image of a gray-skinned humanoid with white hair. "They are a race of humanoids much like the rest of us. They originated in one of the nations of Aelish, but a few families made it over to Sciena before the curse hit three hundred years ago."

Jax studied the image critically. "From Aelish, eh? I suppose that makes sense as to why I haven't seen anything about them then." He glanced at Amy, eyes narrowing. "Sir? Why did Amy's disguise fall, but mine didn't?"

"I presume you're a foxfolk?" Jax nodded and Balthazar lifted a hand. "Well, that's why. You are not disguising yourself, but switching between two forms that are equally a part of you. Amy's disguise was simply magick hiding what she is. There's anti-illusion spells placed on the inside of the building. We have to make sure those that come here are who they say they are."

Amy rubbed her arms, gaze falling. "Oh. So my disguise just doesn't work in here?"

Balthazar waved a hand dismissively. "It's alright, no one will bother you. What can I help you two with?"

Amy glanced at Jax before taking a deep breath. "Um, we were hoping someone could help us learn how to use our magick a little better. Gerald didn't seem certain that I was a draconic sorceress and Jax's magick is seemingly unknown."

"Sentio." Balthazar studied Amy a moment, then shook his head. "No, you're certainly a Dragon-Blood." He opened a drawer of a filing cabinet and flipped through before pulling out a folder and copying something onto another page. "Fortunately Inzo is still taking on students so I'll send a runner to him and see if he'd be willing to take you on. Return here this afternoon and I'll have him meet you then."

Amy blinked. "That's it? It's that easy?"

"Of course. We all help the current adventuring party as much as possible." He glanced at Jax, studying him critically. "You, however, are a bit more difficult. I know of no one who wields your type of magick within this city."

Jax sighed, his shoulders dropping. "I was afraid of that."

"That does not, however, mean that we can't help you. If you return with Amy, I'll see if I can scrounge up any books for you. If nothing else, perhaps one of our arcane teachers can nudge you in the right direction."

Jax relaxed slightly, grateful that he'd found someone to help him at last. "Thank you, Sir."

Balthazar settled back into his seat and linked his fingers in front of him. "Is that all you needed?"

"I— Well, yes. Though I have so many questions!" Jax stammered.

"That's natural. I'll answer what I can."

"How does the library look big on the outside, but *huge* on the inside? Where did all these books come from?"

"Do you have more information on blood magick? What about familiars?" Amy added.

"Do you have any more information on the dungeons? Did you go through them?" Jax continued.

Balthazar chuckled. "Slow down. The library is magickal. There's not enough room to add onto it horizontally, so my predecessors added onto it magickally using scrolls they found stored here. As for the books, people have brought them in with them, some travelers have written down their accounts of what happens in the dungeons, some of the rooms contain scrolls that previous magi have scribed. As for information on blood magick, yes there's a whole section on that, familiars as well. And I believe I already answered your question about the dungeons."

Amy's eyes shone as she sat back in her seat. "This place is amazing. I can't believe there's so much magick that still exists and the outside world has no way to access it, or even know it's here."

"Yes. Well hopefully once this curse is broken, magick can be returned to the world. Now if there's a pause in your questions, I'd like to ask you some of my own."

Amy's eyes narrowed, but she nodded. "What do you want to know?" Jax took her hand and squeezed it gently.

Balthazar pulled out two clipboards and held one out to each of them. "Would you mind filling these out for me?"

Amy took hers and began reading. "What's this?"

Rows of text lined the form, with blank spaces next to them to be filled in. *Name: Age: Spouse: Children: Awakened Form: Location: Abilities:.*

"I keep a record of every adventurer who enters. It allows for later parties to seek help if necessary," Balthazar explained. "On that same note, how many of you are there?"

Jax barely glanced up from the clipboard. "Five."

"And what are they?"

"Us, two Celestials, and a monkey-folk."

He pulled out a few more forms. "Would you take these to the others and see if they'll fill them out? And make sure to let me know if anyone quits or dies so that I can update them, please." Amy flinched at the callous way he talked about their companions dying and Balthazar shook his head. "It's likely to happen. You saw how difficult Death was. And that's the easiest."

"I know. Doesn't make it any easier to think about them dying, though." Jax squeezed her hand again, setting his own clipboard aside. The image of Amy's pale face rose unbidden into his mind and he shoved it away. He hated the idea of any of his companions dying, but his stomach clenched when he imagined her death.

"Go. Return here just after lunch and your teacher will be waiting." Balthazar stood and Jax and Amy followed suit. "Oh, one more thing." He pulled two round coins from within a drawer, offering one to Amy and the other to Jax.

"What's this?" Amy asked as she studied it. An image of the library dominated one side of the silver-coin sized disc and sharp text with very little variation in height or width lined the other.

"It's an entrance disk. It's inscribed with magick that interacts with the magick of the walls around the guild. If you press that disk to any wall surrounding the guild it will part and let you in. Beware it doesn't fall into the wrong hands, however."

Jax studied his coin critically before flipping it to the side with the writing. "What is this language and what does it say? Roxuh used it to get us into the library, too."

"Grant thee entrance to all of life's knowledge," Amy translated.

Balthazar nodded approvingly to Amy. "It's the language of dragons."

Amy's brow furrowed. "How do I know it then? I've never learned it."

"You are a Dragon-Blood. Speaking their language is as natural to you as breathing."

Jax studied the disc before pocketing it. "So why do you use it for the library? And the guild? I'm assuming not everyone here is a Dragon-Blood?"

Balthazar shook his head. "Of course not. But dragons were the pinnacle of magick, the strongest creatures known to roam the lands, second only to the gods themselves. When people began to learn magick, they adopted their language as its official… face? I suppose that is the right word."

"But it isn't the language of magick," Amy argued. "I don't understand the things I'm saying when I cast spells, but I do understand the dragon language."

"No. Unfortunately we don't know the language of magick. Either the knowledge was lost millennia ago or it was never a full language to begin with. Is that it?"

"I suppose so. For now at least."

Balthazar nodded and opened the door for them. It wasn't until they'd walked away and the door had shut that Jax realized Balthazar never answered his question about whether he himself had gone through the dungeons. Or how he had known that they had already completed Death.

He shook his head. "That was… enlightening."

"Yes… Jax, something is bothering me."

Jax raised an eyebrow and glanced over. "What's that?"

"He said the knowledge for the language of magick was lost millennia ago, but I don't think that's true."

"What do you mean?"

Amy paused, her hand tucking into her pocket. "Lillian said that all of Devon's notes are written in what he called Nixian. She said he called it the language of magick."

"Wait, you think Devon actually knew the language of magick?"

"I think he did, yes. Lillian told me that no magick could translate his notes because only a select few were *allowed* to learn it. That the language itself is protected by magick." She bit her lip. "And I think it's the same language scribed on his pendant."

Jax rubbed his chin, eyes narrowed. "So then his mother knew the language, too?"

"It would appear so. I think it's time I talk to Lillian."

"Are you sure?"

Amy fiddled with the pendant a moment before nodding. "Lillian has been nothing but kind and understanding to me. If anyone would answer me without judging, it's her."

"If you're certain. Do you want me there?"

Amy shook her head. "I like Lillian."

As they approached the front of the library, Jax spotted Kukuri sitting on a high stool behind the desk. She swiveled to scowl at Amy as they approached. "I'm guessing Balthazar grilled you on all things related to your group?" she asked Jax, pointedly not looking at Amy again.

Jax glanced at Amy and sighed before nodding and holding up the papers Balthazar had given them. "He gave us these to fill out as well."

Kukuri shrugged. "It's part of his census. Every year he has the Thieves' Guild figure out how many people stand outside of the curse, either by entering the town or children born to those travelers. It helps us know who is where in case of an emergency or if a group needs a new member."

"Does that happen a lot?" Amy asked nervously. Jax's heart squeezed again at the thought of her dying and the others simply replacing her.

Kukuri's eyes narrowed, but to Jax's relief, she still answered. "A lot, actually. Usually, if someone dies or quits, a group will attempt to find a new member to keep going. Rarely do they come back a second time, though. If they lose a second member, they have usually lost the will to keep going and return to their human forms, making a life here in the town. I've seen it happen more times than I can count."

"That's sad."

"It is. But it's the way of life here, unfortunately. It's that or lose innocent people, and that's one thing we all agree can't happen. Fortunately there's enough travelers and their descendents here to prevent someone unawares from being sucked in. Usually if the Gate has opened and no adventurers have appeared, they send word to Gorum and he lets us know so we can rally a group to send through, even if it's just through the one dungeon. Most of them don't want to go for another full attempt."

Jax cocked his head. "Who's Gorum?"

"He was my teammate when we went through the dungeons. He owns a tavern here in town."

"Oh."

"You said you've gone through Death, right?" Kukuri asked.

Jax nodded. "Yes. We just finished it a couple of days ago."

"How did you fare?"

Amy frowned. "We all survived." Her fingers reached up to touch her shoulder where the giant had hit her. "It was certainly painful, though." Jax winced in sympathy. His own leg still ached sometimes, even with the magickal healing he'd received.

"The dungeons are hard. The fact that you all survived is a blessing.

Just remember that."

Jax followed Amy's gaze to where Azurys was sniffing around a bookshelf. The cat rocked back and forth on her haunches.

Kukuri raced forward and scooped Azurys up. "No, little cat. That is not for eating!"

Jax looked to where Azurys had been heading, noting a bluebird sitting on the top of the bookshelves. "Is that a familiar?"

"Not just *a* familiar— *my* familiar. And I would appreciate it if you would keep your pet away from him." Kukuri held the squirming cat out to them.

Amy glared at Kukuri as she took Azurys from her and smoothed her ruffled fur. "She's not my pet. She's *my* familiar."

Kukuri tilted her head, the animosity gone from her gaze. "How? Dragon-Bloods don't have familiars."

Amy's grip tightened on Azurys. "She's definitely my familiar. She appeared when my blood was Awoken. Lady Arkham had one, too." Jax glanced at her in surprise. She hadn't told him that.

"Lady Arkham? As in Madam Lillian?"

Amy shook her head. "No. Ms. Lillian's mother, Lord Arkham's wife."

"I'd known that Lady Arkham was a Dragon-Blood, but there was no mention of her having a familiar. Where did you find that out?"

"Lillian told me herself when she met Azurys. I suppose having another cat around reminded her of her mother's."

Kukuri studied her with pursed lips. "Huh. Well, besides the two of you, I've never heard of a Dragon-Blood having a familiar. I guess there's a first for everything, though!"

"Right… I'll see you this afternoon, then." She hesitated at the door. "One more thing? Where is the line that allows me to put my disguise back up?"

Kukuri waved a hand at her. "You'll have to go back out the doors. You can't cast the spell inside. It won't work."

"Oh. And the statues outside? Roxuh said something about them needing that phrase. Does it need to be said when leaving, too?"

Kukuri chuckled. "No, just when entering. I'll see you later Jax.

Amy."

They each bid her goodbye and stepped out onto the streets, eyeing the statues on either side suspiciously.

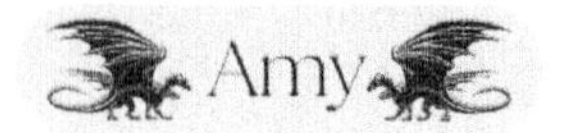

Amy and Jax settled into their seats at the manor across from Talia and Nolan. Amy's brow furrowed as she turned to the healer. "Where's Kila?"

"On a date. With the blacksmith," Nolan muttered, finishing off another mug of ale. Two empty glasses and a half-empty bottle sat in front of him. He poured another glass as she watched.

Amy looked between them, confused. "The blacksmith?"

Talia leaned toward her, keeping her voice low. "He means Austin. They got into another huge fight last night after they got back from the Pits and Austin comforted her, then asked her if she'd have lunch with him today." She shrugged. "They left just before you arrived and Nolan has been moping ever since."

"Oh." Unsure how else to respond, Amy fell silent.

Talia watched Jax scarfing down his food with a raised eyebrow. "Hungry?"

Jax shook his head. "Amy and I found this place called the Wizards' Guild. We're supposed to go back after lunch and the head guy said he'd have teachers for us."

"Wizards' Guild?"

Amy nodded. "It's protected by a wall and you need a password to get into the library. It's huge." She grinned, her tail twitching behind her. "It's about the size of the manor on the outside, but it's absolutely huge on the inside. What should be four stories is actually closer to about twelve. And books and scrolls line every inch of it."

Talia chuckled. "It sounds like you're both excited to go back."

Amy completely forgot about her food for a moment. "If I can find someone who understands magick really well, I might be able to master mine better. And then I'll be more of an asset in the next dungeon."

"You did fairly well in the last one. Better than me."

"Talia, you saved my life. Twice. And you healed all of us at least once. I think you did pretty well."

Talia flushed and glanced down at her plate. "I suppose you're right."

Nolan huffed and downed another glass of ale before shoving it away. "I'm going back to the Pits," he grumbled, swaying as he stood up.

"You're drunk," Talia pointed out unnecessarily.

"I'm just fine." Nolan stumbled toward the door, catching himself on one of the tables.

Amy, Talia, and Jax watched him in concern. Talia sighed and stood quickly. "I think I'm going to keep an eye on him. I'll see you tonight?"

Amy nodded and took their plates over to the bar, giving Lillian a smile and wave before following Jax out.

Azurys trotted along beside her as they walked, head and tail high. Amy felt a sense of unease spread through the little cat as she stopped, ears swiveling. She lifted her nose to scent the air.

Amy followed her gaze. "What is it, Azurys?" She thought she saw a shadow move, but she had no way to be sure.

Jax's hand went to his rapier, his eyes darting around them. "Everything alright?"

"I'm not sure. Azurys saw something that she didn't like, but I didn't see anything."

"Do you think we should head back to the manor?"

Azurys sniffed the air again before her raised hackles lowered and she rubbed against Amy's legs. "No… Let's just keep moving."

Jax released his rapier as they continued on. "What was that all about?"

Amy shook her head. "I'm not sure. She saw something that bothered her, but I'm not sure what. I'll feel better when we're in the safety of the Wizards' Guild."

Eventually, Amy found the same alleyway Roxuh had shown them and pulled the disk Balthazar had given her from her belt pouch. "Here goes nothing," she muttered, pressing it to the wall. Nothing happened for a moment before she heard a click and the bricks lowered, once more forming an archway.

Jax grinned. "I'm never going to get tired of that."

Amy hummed in agreement. Outside the library, she stopped. "Knowledge is power." She eyed the statues on either side, relieved when neither of them moved.

They stepped through and Kukuri looked up from her desk, eyes narrowing when she spotted them. "Welcome back." She gestured down the hall. "Inzo is in the training room. I'll show you the way," She hopped down from her stool behind the desk and led Amy and Jax back down the hallway.

Amy hurried after her, startled at how quickly the much smaller person could walk. "You have a training room?"

Kukri nodded. "Well of course we do. After all, this is where young Wizards' go to learn how to cast spells. We have to have *somewhere* that they can practice."

Of course there's somewhere for the wizards to learn, as if wizards were just commonplace. Which, I guess here, they are.

Amy remained quiet as they passed the room they had met with Balthazar in that morning before stopping in front of a large doorway. Different training equipment lined an expansive room with high ceilings. Straw and cloth dummies filled one area to her right, to her left were small stones stacked against a wall, and the back wall was lined with high ledges. A few benches sat along one wal for pupils to sit on. On one such bench, an older blond man sat.

He stood as they entered and examined Amy and Jax with a critical eye. A deep blue cloak covered his form, his clothing distinctly Kushen in style, with loose fitting pants cuffed at the ankles and a long, pale blue tunic with long sleeves. "This is her?" he asked, his accent thick.

Amy was nervous under his gaze, knowing that her demon-spawn heritage would probably make him leery of her.

Kukuri nodded. "Yep! This is Amy! And this is Jax. You three have fun!" With that, the little gnome exited the room, leaving Amy and Jax alone with their new teacher. He resumed studying her.

Jax immediately stepped forward, holding out a hand. "As she said, my name is Jax. Jax Silvers. You're an instructor?"

Inzo shook his hand with a smile. "I am. Though I must admit, I have never heard of your style of magick. I will need to take more time to figure out how to help you. So I will start with her." His gaze shifted to Amy and Jax's ears drooped as he stepped back. "Do not worry, Jax. I will help you. But I can only help one of you at a time. Since I don't know how to help you yet, why don't you go explore the library? I am sure there is much here that would interest you."

Jax's ears perked slightly. "Right. Okay, sir." He squeezed Amy's hand on his way past. "I'll see you later."

"Yeah. See you later."

Inzo's eyes focused back on Amy, his head cocked as he studied her.

"Hi. Um… Like Kukuri said, I'm Amy."

Inzo immediately switched to the same growling language she had used to grant them entrance to the library. "Yes, yes. I know who you are. And I am Inzo. You will call me Master Inzo. All right Little Dragon, let's get started. First off, let's see what you can do. Telekinesis is one of the basic skills that many spellcasters can master, so let's start there." He led her over to a pile of small stones. "Lift one with a spell, and then move it over to that stool and set it down."

Gerald had tried to get her to do the same thing, but she still couldn't. Amy stumbled over the transition in languages for a moment. "I-I don't know how."

Inzo studied her again. "All right, how about levitation?"

Amy shook her head again. "Sorry, sir."

Inzo frowned. "Okay how about you just tell me what you can do?"

"Well, I can disguise myself using magic, and I can conjure fire."

Inzo circled her, rubbing his chin. "So you're a red Dragon-Blood, then." Amy tried to answer, but his words were a statement and not a question. "Very well." He nodded toward one of the training dummies. "Light it on fire."

Relieved to find something she could do, she raised her hand.

"Ignis!" she commanded, desperate to prove herself to her new teacher. Flames poured from her palm, stronger even than the one she had produced within the dungeon. When it cleared, the dummy was little more than charred remains on the floor.

Inzo hummed approval behind her. "Impressive control for one so new. So tell me, Little Dragon, what is it you want to learn?"

Amy didn't even have to think about it. "I want to be able to cast spells without hurting my allies. Is that possible?"

Inzo pursed his lips. "Quite possible, though it does require quite precise control of your magick. A lofty goal for your first lesson."

Amy gulped. "I don't want to hurt my friends if they get caught within range of my spells. Is this something you can teach me?"

Inzo stepped forward. "Of course I can, Little Dragon, though it will take much practice. Do not expect to master it quickly."

Relief filled Amy. "I understand, I just want to learn."

"Very well, when you cast your spells, do you ever notice that you can visualize the magickal energy leaving your reserve?"

Amy thought back to when she had cast her fire spell for the first time. And then again in the dungeon. He was right: when she pictured her magick pool to cast spells, she could see the magickal energy flowing through her own body. And when it left, it encircled the effect of the spell.

"I see that it does. Very well, what you must do is this: when you picture the magickal energy leaving your body you also have to picture it warping around your allies. Form a protective bubble around them with your magick while casting the spell, and command the flames to avoid the bubble. Are you ready to try?"

Amy refocused on the training dummies. She stepped forward and raised her hand, once more picturing her magick pool, as well as a bubble around the training dummy. "Ignis!" When the flames cleared, the dummy was nothing more than a crisp on the ground. She frowned and turned back to Inzo. "I don't know what I did wrong. I did what you said."

Inzo shook his head. "I told you, this is not something you will master quickly. Let's continue."

For the next several hours, Amy destroyed training dummy after training dummy, not once successfully avoiding them. As her magickal energy began to drain low she stood panting, frustrated, and dejected.

"That is enough for today," Inzo said as another training dummy stood in cinders on the ground.

Amy shook her head. "No! I need to figure this out." She continued spell after spell until finally the last of her magickal energy disappeared. She suspected she had just enough to retain her disguise until she got back to the manor, but that would be it.

"That is enough!"

"Yes, Master." Amy instinctively dropped to the deferential title for him and lowered her head. "Can we resume tomorrow?"

"Wearing yourself so thin won't be good for you. This takes patience and practice. Frustrating yourself with failure won't help you learn any faster. I will teach Jax tomorrow."

"I have to protect my friends! My fire is dangerous! I can't let them be hurt because I can't control it!"

The passion and desperation in her voice must have given Inzo pause as he studied her contemplatively. "No. I will teach Jax tomorrow. You come the day after."

Amy deflated and gave the older man a bow. "Yes, Master."

"This was a good session today. Do not be discouraged just because you haven't seen any success yet."

Amy sank onto one of the benches for a moment. "Thank you, Master." She studied him out of the corner of her eye. In the hours they'd been training together, he'd made no comment on her heritage, nor even seemed bothered by it. *Is he as unfazed as Chouza by what I am?*

Noticing her watching him, he raised an eyebrow. "Something on your mind, Little Dragon?"

Amy flushed and looked away, choosing her words carefully. "I was just wondering why my being a demon-spawn didn't seem to bother you."

"You have had unpleasant experiences thus far?"

Amy's hand rose to her throat to the small indention where Arkham's blade had pierced her skin. "Too many people equate demon-spawn with the Sin Generals."

Inzo studied her, as if choosing his words as carefully as she had hers. "Did you know that a sorcerer's powers can arise from many sources?" The change in subject startled her, but she nodded, remembering reading that in one of the books she had gotten from the Arkhams' library. "Well, one of the possible bloodlines for a sorcerer is demonic."

Disappointment filled Amy. "You mean I could be a demonic sorceress, not a draconic one?"

"Oh no, you are most definitely a Dragon-Blood. You see, while there is demon blood in your body, it merely gave you a few minor physical alterations, granting you the ability to see in the dark, a tail, horns. But your *power*—what makes you who you are—comes from dragons. Yes there is demon blood in you, but there is also dragon blood, and it is stronger." He tapped the tattoo on the back of her hand. "You may be a demon-spawn, but you are first and foremost a Dragon-Blood."

"So I have the blood of two different powerful beings in me?"

"Yes. You will be quite powerful when you have fully mastered your abilities, far more powerful than me, I suspect."

Amy hadn't considered just how strong she could potentially get, but that knowledge cemented her determination to master the ability to manipulate her magick around her allies. "Thank you, Master." She glanced down at her hands, remembering one of the other things Gerald had tried to get her to do. "Why don't I have claws? The instructor at the academy said I should."

Inzo 'tched' and shook his head. "Foolish. He does not know enough about Dragon-Bloods to presume to try and teach one. Yes, claws are one of the abilities that we gain, and usually fairly early, but it varies by dragon. My dragon gave me mine first." He held up a hand and Amy watched in fascination as his nails elongated into sharp claws and his forearm covered in brilliant blue scales. "Some rare Dragon-Bloods only get them after they get their dragon form."

"Dragon form?" A shiver of excitement coursed through her body.

Inzo lowered his hand and the scales receded back into his pale skin. "One day, you will unlock what is called your dragon form. You will be able to use your magick to turn into a full dragon, temporarily of course. But you have much to learn before you reach that point." He stood and Amy scrambled to follow. "I will see you day after tomorrow, Little Dragon. Rest well." With that, he left the training hall, leaving her to contemplate his words.

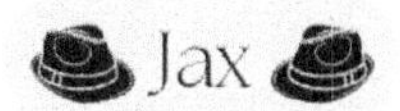

Jax had made his way up to the sixth floor when Amy found him several hours later. There, he'd found a few books about psychic magick, reading through them while he waited for Amy. She practically had to drag him from the library and only her promise that he would be returning for his own lesson with Inzo had convinced him to set the books aside and follow her out.

He filled her silence with information about psychic magick as they walked through the quiet streets, explaining how he needed no words or focuses to cast his spells. It was inherent to him, not a studied art, lending itself well to their current situation.

Jax frowned as her steps slowed. "Are you alright?"

"I just used up a lot of magick today."

Jax's eyes sharpened as he scanned their surroundings uneasily. He followed Amy's gaze to where Azurys had been sniffing at some garbage and noticed her tensed, staring down an alleyway with her hackles raised.

Amy gripped his hand. "Keep moving," she whispered.

Their pace quickened as they hurried along, Azurys racing beside them. They didn't slow until they'd reentered the manor grounds and Azurys trotted calmly next to them again.

Jax glanced behind them. "I think we're safe."

"Probably." Amy stumbled with obvious exhaustion and Jax quickly caught her as her disguise fell away.

"What *was* that?"

"I'm not sure, but it's not the first time it's happened. Azurys notices something and gets nervous, but we leave with no incident." She shuddered and Jax frowned, linking her arm through his for support.

"Are you okay?"

Amy nodded. "Just a theory I hope is wrong."

He studied her, but didn't press when she failed to elaborate. They entered the manor unchallenged past Fredrikson's closed study door. Jax hesitated at the foot of the stairs. "Do you want food or bed?"

Amy glanced between the stairs and the dining hall before sighing. "Food."

Jax helped her to the empty dining hall and, ignoring her protests, fixed each of them a plate of fruit and cheese. Settling across from her, he let her take a few bites of food before continuing their conversation.

"So back to what I was saying before— rough session?"

Amy shrugged. "I didn't manage to do anything I was trying to learn."

"You'll get it. After all, you're an awesome spellcaster. I'm sure it just takes time." He gave her his usual roguish grin and she chuckled.

"I hope so."

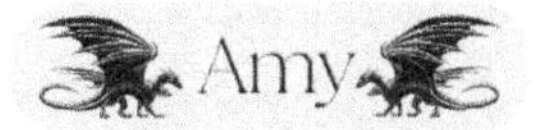

At lunch the next day, Amy poked at her food uneasily. Once everyone had settled into their seats and started eating, she cleared her throat.

"I have something to say." Everyone looked at her in surprise and Amy took a deep breath. "I think we should consider adding a new person to the group."

Nolan grunted. "We're fine as we are."

Kila rolled her eyes. "Hardly."

"Got a problem?"

"Enough," Amy interrupted, her frustration peaking. "We got our butts kicked in the last dungeon. We need more fighting power. I propose we add another trained fighter to the group." Her mind strayed to Chouza's face, but she pushed the image away. "Balthazar has a list of people who want to attempt the dungeons again. If everyone agrees, I can talk to him this evening and he can find someone for us."

Kila glared at Amy. "What makes you think that would help?"

Amy's skin prickled, but she ignored the rising panic. "I think having someone else who can handle a weapon efficiently would be to our benefit. Talia and I are no good with weapons. We should round out our group."

Jax brushed his fingers across the back of Amy's hand. "I agree. We need someone else who can hit hard. It takes Kila and I way too much time to take out an enemy. We need someone else like Nolan."

Nolan raised an eyebrow. "Okay, fine. You two agree. What about you Talia? Do you think we need help?"

Talia hesitated, twisting at her fingers. "I think… I think we do, yes. If for no other reason than to make sure Amy and I aren't right at the front."

Nolan scowled and refused to look over at Kila. "Fine, Lady Flame. Talk to this Balthazar. Find us a suitable teammate."

Amy sighed in relief as the attention turned from her. Jax grinned at her. "Good call."

"I hope so. Chouza actually suggested it, but he's right. We need help. Nolan's the only one who's had formal training. We need someone else who can fight."

Jax carefully reached for her hand. "You're right. And you did well speaking up."

Amy forced a smile, even as her heart continued to pound and her hands were slick with sweat. *I won't let my fear control me.*

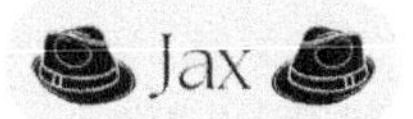

Jax left Amy in the lobby of the library and approached the training room where Inzo waited. Despite his excitement, his heart raced in his chest and his nerves were on edge.

Inzo looked up from the journal he was writing in. "Ah. Young Jax. It is good to see you again."

"Hello... Master... Inzo." He hesitated over the 'Master,' but decided it was probably best to use the honorific Amy used for the teacher. It felt strange rolling off his tongue, but Inzo nodded approvingly.

"Good. I have been researching more on what your magick seems to be. Come, sit." He motioned to a bench and Jax followed him. "Based on what I have read, it seems you have a magick pool, not unlike an arcane or divine caster's. You simply activate yours differently."

Jax's ears twitched. "That's what I've found as well."

"Good, good. So then there is no reason I cannot teach you the same as I am Amy. First off, what are you capable of already?"

Jax hesitated, glancing at the training dummies on the other side of the room. "I can use my magick to summon weapons and attack living creature's minds."

Inzo waved him forward. "Show me the first, please?"

Jax stood and called to mind the image of his rapier Shinzo, picturing the weight and the way the grip felt in his hand. Immediately, his hand tightened around the solid form and his eyes opened.

Inzo stood and circled Jax, studying the rapier appreciatively. "Not a word spoken, yet a spell was cast. You are quite interesting, young Jax. And what happens if you release it?"

Jax opened his hand and let the rapier fall. The moment it left his skin, it vanished. "I can't give them to anyone either. But if I can imagine it, I can conjure it."

"Fascinating. And the other thing you said? Attacking someone's mind?"

Jax shrugged. "From what I can tell, I use my memories and my thoughts to overload their minds. I can't exactly demonstrate, though."

Inzo nodded. "No, you can not demonstrate that. Let's move on. See those stones over there?" He gestured toward a pile of stones nearby. "I want you to move them with only a spell. Then place them on the stool there."

Jax focused on the rocks, again imagining what it would feel like to pick them up and move them. One of the stones shifted, but didn't lift and Jax blinked, losing focus.

"Very good. So it is within your capacity. I suppose telepathy and telekinesis go hand in hand. Keep trying."

Jax focused on the rock again, once more imagining it lifting into the air. Slowly, it hovered, wobbling about a foot in the air. Jax gasped as he felt the immediate drain on his magick and the stone dropped again.

"You're doing wonderfully! One more try!"

Jax repeated the process, raising the rock and shifting it to just above the stool. Once it hovered over it, he lost hold and it landed with a thud. Jax dropped to a knee, panting. "Why does this take so much more than my weapon summoning?"

"I suspect it is much like our Dragon-Blood abilities. Our blood-related abilities come naturally and drain our magick very little. Other spells, however, take their toll. Your weapon-summoning is part of your natural abilities, but telekinesis is not. Thus it takes more magick and concentration. It will get easier with time."

Jax stood, taking a breath. "That makes sense. Thank you, Master Inzo."

"Of course. I am happy to teach you everything I can, even if that is not as much as I would like. Now, let us continue."

Once Jax disappeared into the training room with Master Inzo, Amy made her way to Balthazar's office, heistating only a moment before knocking.

"Come in!" Balthazar's gruff voice called through the door.

Amy peeked inside, her eyes ranging across the cluttered office. "H-hi. Do you have a minute?"

Balthazar waved her forward. "Of course. What can I do for you?"

"You mentioned before that we can come to you for new members, right?" Her heart clenched when she thought of losing a member, but she stubbornly suppressed it.

Balthazar nodded and gestured for her to take one of the seats across from him. "I can. Are one of your members quitting?"

"No, I was just hoping to get some extra fighting power. We have Nolan, but he's only one person." She carefully refrained from mentioning his drunken state, not wanting to give Balthazar the wrong idea. "And Jax and Kila are good, but they aren't as strong at combat as Nolan. Talia and I… Well, let's just say we're better in the middle."

"I see. So someone from the Pits would probably be a good choice then." He rubbed his beard between his thumb and forefinger.

"It was actually one of them that mentioned it. And asked if he could join us."

Balthazar raised an eyebrow. "I see." He stood and made his way across the room, once more pulling a drawer from the filing cabinet. He flipped through a few folders before pulling one and setting it on the desk in front of her.

Amy leaned forward. *Ranking of Request — Pits*

"Are these the fighters?"

Balthazar opened the folder. *High Priority* lined the top of the first page above a list of names. "Do you see the fighter's name on here?"

Amy quickly scanned it and shook her head. "No. He's not there."

He flipped to the next page labeled *Medium Priority.* About a third of the way down, Amy spotted Chouza's name.

"There." She pointed to it and Balthazar spun the page to read it.

"Chouza Zhang. Hmm. Normally, we would focus the high priority unless the group specifically chooses someone else. Is that what you're doing?"

Amy gnawed her lip. "What's the difference?"

Balthazar flipped the folder to the third page. *Low Priority.* Even more names than the first two pages lined it. "Each person chooses whether or not they want to go through the dungeons again. Those who are actively seeking a chance are put on the high priority list. Those who would like another chance, but don't care if they're first in line are medium priority. Then you have low priority members who will go through if no one else fits the criteria."

He flipped the page again. *Emergency.* Only a few names were written on that page. "The people on the emergency list really don't want to go through, but if for whatever reason no one else is available, they'll step in. Anyone not on one of these lists refuses to go through at all."

"I see. And what do you recommend. Would Chouza be a good fit for our team? Or should we go with someone from the High Priority page?"

Balthazar closed the folder and set it aside. "Well, that's up to you. You said you want another strong fighter and Chouza is certainly that. I'm not entirely sure of your team composition to offer a full recommendation."

"You of course know about Jax and I. Kila's good with trap seeking and she uses daggers. Talia's our healer. She doesn't fight."

"At all?"

Amy shook her head. "No. She's bothered by the idea of hurting a living creature. To be honest, so am I."

Balthazar resumed stroking his beard. "But you do fight?"

"It's that or die, so yes."

"Hmm. And this Nolan?"

"He has arcane magick, but he was trained as a fighter by the royal blacksmith of Zadia. Of all of us, he's the best equipped in battle."

"So you need someone to round out your group and help protect Talia and yourself, mainly?"

Amy fidgeted with the pendant in her pocket, wondering if it were really a good idea to risk someone else's life. "Yes. Yes, we do."

"And you want it to be Chouza?"

"He wants it to be himself. If… If you don't think anyone else would be a better fit, then yes. I'd like it to be him."

Balthazar leaned back in his seat. "Very well. I will look through and see if anyone else fits your requirements and send them along in the next day or two. You've only just completed Death, so you should have the time."

"R-right. Thank you, sir."

"Balthazar waved her off. "Not a problem. That's what I'm here for."

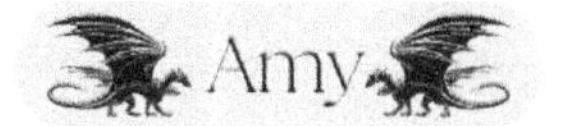

At Amy's second lesson with Inzo, he called for her to stop, training dummies standing in ashes around her. "You clearly do not have the motivation you need to master this technique." He gestured around her. "This is quite advanced, are you sure you wouldn't prefer to start with something easier? I can teach you how to maximize your flame's potential, or even how to expand it into a greater range. Those are much easier than this. You can build up to the other."

Amy flinched. "No! I have to be able to protect my allies. My magick may be powerful, but I'm useless if I can't use it because I can't control it."

Inzo studied her for a moment. "Very well. If you insist on continuing. Propugno!" Amy sensed the flow of magick from him, but couldn't tell what he'd done. "We're done with the training dummies. You will attack me now. And if you fail, it will be me who is hurt, not just an inanimate object."

Amy stepped back, horrified. "No! No, I won't do that!" She couldn't intentionally hurt someone. Especially someone who had been as helpful to her as Inzo.

"You will not hurt me. At least not badly. I have placed my own protection around myself, on top of our natural resistances."

Amy shook her head again. "I-I'm sorry. I can't." With that, she fled the training room.

Inzo stayed where he stood. "I will see you day after tomorrow, Little

Dragon."

Amy continued on without answering. Kukuri looked startled as Amy hurried out of the hallway. The gnome had slowly warmed up to Amy, though she remained far more friendly with Jax.

"Are you alright, Amy?"

Amy couldn't meet her eye. "I'm fine. See you later, Kukuri."

"Bye!"

She hurriedly pulled her disguise up as she left the library and suddenly found herself wishing Jax were there, but he'd gone with Nolan to the Fighting Pits to see his father. Despite herself, she missed his company, and the comfort she knew he would try to provide. Tired, and still fighting back tears, Amy hurried toward the manor.

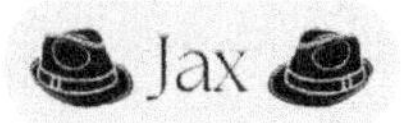

Jax groaned as Nolan was flattened. Again. Shane raised an eyebrow. "I know you said he's normally a pretty good fighter, but he's not shown it here. And I've seen plenty of his fights."

"I know. And I'm starting to question even that." He shook his head. "He's miserable. The girl he likes is dating someone else and he's drowning his sorrows in alcohol."

Nolan stumbled back to his feet, fists raised. Movement to Jax's left drew his attention and he spotted Chouza moving through the crowd.

The other man stopped next to Jax and gestured toward the ring. "Isn't he one of your and Amy's group?"

Jax pinched the bridge of his nose and lowered his head. "He is."

"What's wrong with him? Is he drunk?"

"He is." Jax sighed. "He was already pretty wasted when we got here, but then he just kept getting more from the bar. And since he's still upright…"

"Why is he fighting?"

"Because he's an idiot."

Chouza shook his head. "Is this your group, then? You and Amy, a drunkard, and a healer?"

"We have a monkeyfolk named Kila who has a sharp eye and is good with daggers. She's not here right now." Austin had taken Kila out for dinner. Again. It would have been amusing if it hadn't been taking such a toll on Nolan.

"Right. Amy mentioned her. She also mentioned that this guy was your primary fighter. This doesn't look very promising."

Jax hesitated, wondering if it was even worth trying to defend Nolan. "It's… complicated."

Chouza shook his head. "It's not complicated. If you're relying on someone who's drunk more often than not, you're going to get killed in those dungeons. They aren't a joke. You need someone who can hold their own. And he can't. Clearly."

"He's better when he's not drunk and has a sword…" Jax defended half-heartedly.

Chouza rubbed his face. "Just… consider finding another member who can fight. I'd hate to see any of you die so soon after starting." His words held a hint of a warning.

"I'm aware, Chouza. Trust me, I'm aware. Amy actually already recommended you."

Chouza blinked and glanced at him in surprise. "She did?"

Jax turned away from the fight, shaking his head. "She knew you wanted a chance. So she recommended you to Balthazar when she asked him to find us another member. Whether he considers you the best fit for our group is up to him."

Chouza relaxed slightly and nodded, turning to watch as Nolan got knocked from the ring. "Then I look forward to hearing from him."

When Jax and Nolan returned to the manor, Kila and Talia were talking companionably in the dining hall. Jax made sure Nolan had food before settling into his own seat, wondering if Inzo had kept Amy late. Nolan dropped into a seat as far from Kila as he could get and took an angry bite of food.

Talia glanced between them nervously, before attempting to continue their earlier conversation. "Anyway, where did he take you for dinner?"

Kila's eyes narrowed on Nolan, but she purposefully turned away from him. "A place called the Spotted Blue Badger. It's owned by a dwarf."

"Popped his cherry yet?" Nolan grunted.

Jax groaned, bracing for the coming fight.

Kila glared at Nolan. "No. And I don't plan to have sex with him until he's ready."

"I thought you didn't *do* feelings." Nolan shoved a forkful of his food into his mouth, glaring at Kila himself. "I thought you just fucked men and then left them."

"I never said that. I'm trying something new. Got a problem with it?"

"No, not at all." He stabbed a piece of meat and sawed it in half with a knife, glaring at Kila as he did so.

"What, would you have just taken me straight to bed, then?"

"Yep. No fanfare, no dinner. Just a good fuck. That's what you like, isn't it?"

"Can't I want more?" She snapped a carrot in half, biting a piece off viciously. "Everyone else can do it, why can't I?"

"Oh, so now you want it all, huh?"

"What's so wrong with that?!" Kila stood, slamming her chair back. "We're all going to die here anyway, so why can't I have some fun first? Huh?" She gestured at Talia. "Talia gets a hot guy and a stable relationship. Why can't I have that, too? Austin is kind and hot. What if I want to have the best of everything?" She stormed out of the dining hall, leaving Nolan staring after her helplessly.

Talia covered her face. "If you don't go after her, I swear to the gods…"

Nolan stood and rushed out, his steps fumbling and unsteady. Jax raised an eyebrow. "Are you sure him going after her is such a good idea?"

Talia sighed and shook her head. "Nolan really likes Kila. And she likes him. But she wants more than she's willing to admit and she thinks Austin is the way to get that. She's scared of the baggage Nolan carries. And he's hurt because she chose someone else when he's made it clear that he's interested."

"Ok, but that doesn't necessarily mean they're good for each other."

"No… It doesn't. But I think they're both going to be miserable until they try. At least then, they'll know." She looked away, wringing her fingers. "It doesn't help that I've been seeing Vallun more."

Jax shook his head. "Their problems aren't your fault... By the way, have you seen Amy?"

Talia shook her head. "I thought she was at her lessons with the teacher from the Wizards' Guild?"

"Well, yes. But Master Inzo generally makes sure to get done in time for us to be back for dinner. I think I might send a runner to the Wizards' Guild. Make sure she's okay."

After bidding Talia a quick goodbye, Jax hurried down the hall to the front door. Through Fredrikson's open office door, Jax heard Lillian's soft voice.

"Uncle, please just take the medicine."

"I said I don't want any!" A loud crash followed by a curse caused Jax to hurry forward. "Now look what you made me do."

"Uncle, here let me—"

"No! Just get out! Out I say!"

"Can I at least heal you?"

"No!"

The liquor cabinet behind Fredrikson's desk was shattered and a deep cut ran the length of his left arm. Lillian frowned and again attempted to reach for him, but the older man pushed her away.

She sighed and set a roll of bandages in front of him. "At least wrap it up before the blood gets everywhere?"

"Fine." He grabbed the roll and began wrapping the bandage clumsily around his arm. "Now get out."

"Uncle..."

"Out!"

Lillian stepped back and waved Jax from the room, carefully shutting the door behind them.

Jax raised an eyebrow. "What's that all about?"

"I'm not sure. Don't get me wrong, Uncle has gotten drunk plenty of times, but he's never been a belligerent drunk. And honestly, this has been going on for days now. He's never been on a binge this long."

Jax frowned, glancing at the door. *So much drama...* He shook his head. "I'm sorry, Lillian. Is there anything I can do to help?"

"I'm afraid not. We'll just have to wait him out, I suspect." She sighed. "I just worry about him. I know Austin is worried sick."

Jax nodded. "I can only imagine."

Lillian took a breath and straightened. "Anyway. I suppose you were headed to bed?"

"No, actually. I was going to send a runner to the Wizards' Guild. I haven't heard from Amy."

"Amy?" Lillian shook her head. "She returned hours ago. She went straight upstairs."

"What? Thank you, Lillian!"

"Of course. Is everything okay?"

"I don't know."

Hurrying into their suite, he found Amy curled up on the couch, papers with half-drawn images and tear stains scattered around her sleeping form. He froze, staring at her in shock. *She's been up here the whole time? And clearly upset.*

He stepped forward cautiously, pausing when she whimpered in her sleep. "Amy? Amy, it's Jax. It's alright."

Amy shifted, her face scrunching. "I'm sorry. So sorry."

The movement raised the side of her shirt just enough for Jax to spot deep scarring on her back. He gasped and knelt next to her, careful not to wake her. The scars were thick and clearly old. The skin stretched tight in some places, but bunched in others. *She must have received these before she was done growing. So as a child. What would cause scars— The fire that killed her family. She was in it.* She shifted and whimpered again.

Jax gently shook her. "Amy, it's alright. Wake up." She jerked upright, crying out. "Easy, Amy. It's alright. It's just me."

Amy panted, eyes darting around the room wildly before landing on Jax. "J-Jax?"

"Hey. It's alright. You're safe."

Amy let out a choked sob and quickly covered her mouth with a hand. "Sorry. I didn't mean to fall asleep out here."

"It's fine. Amy, what happened? You missed dinner and Lillian said you've been back for a while."

"I don't want to talk about it. Inzo just… I just—"

Jax's eyes narrowed. "Did he hurt you? Do something untoward?" He liked the Kushen man, but if he hurt Amy...

"No! Master Inzo has been nothing but kind." She picked at the hem of her shirt. "I just… Something he asked me to do bothered me is all."

"Are you going to elaborate?"

"I—" She paused, gnawing at her lip. "It's just… I'm trying to learn how to manipulate my magick around my allies. Allowing me to cast spells without hurting the ones who are with me."

"Well that sounds incredibly handy." Jax watched her with concern.

"It would be if I could figure it out. But right now all I'm doing is burning training dummy after training dummy. I can't seem to grasp it. And Inzo seems to think it's beyond my capabilities… at least, without a little extra motivation.``

"What do you mean?"

"He wants me to practice on *him*."

Jax's eyes widened. "Wouldn't that possibly kill him?"

"He says he has a spell that will prevent my fire from hurting him. At least, not badly…"

"But you're still uncomfortable with it," Jax finished for her. Based on what happened with her family, it didn't surprise him.

Amy nodded. "I don't *want* to hurt anyone. Bad enough having to fight things in these dungeons, but to intentionally hurt someone who isn't my enemy? It's just wrong."

"Have you told him that it bothers you?"

Amy looked away guiltily. "Well… I kind of ran when he suggested it."

"Amy, nothing will change if you don't *talk* to people," he chastised her gently. Amy didn't answer, still not looking at him. "Just think about it." Amy kept her head down and Jax sighed. "I'm sorry he upset you. And I'm sorry I wasn't here when you got back."

"It's… It's okay. You're right. I've been running from my problems for so long and now I can't do that. It's… hard." Without looking at him, she reached out and gripped his hand and Jax felt the smallest tremble to it. "Thank you for being my friend."

"Amy, it is my *honor* to be your friend. Trust me when I say that." He squeezed her hand lightly. "And I'm here if you want to talk. About anything. Anything at all. Whether past or present." He carefully avoided mentioning the scars he'd seen, but wanted Amy to know that she could talk to him about them if she needed to. No one should suffer through such a traumatic experience alone. The image of another girl left to suffer alone flashed through his mind, but he pushed it away, ignoring the pang in his heart.

"Thank you, Jax."

He smiled and settled next to her on the couch, gesturing to the drawings around her. "Why don't you show me what you've been working on?"

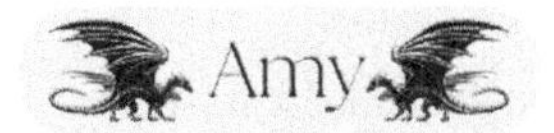

The next morning, Amy made her way to the dining hall, settling into a seat instead of grabbing an apple on her way out as she usually did. The night before, she'd found another bag in her room.

Payment for your services and a reward for a completed dungeon.

~Lillian

Inside, she'd found ten silver, plus an additional hundred gold. Amy had gaped at the money, tearing up at what would be enough to not only get new clothes and shoes, but also pay for the boat ticket to Aelish if she ever made it out of Lorencost. She'd tucked the silver into her coinpurse, but the gold she'd stashed in a separate purse that she shoved into her pack under the bed.

Soon after, Jax joined her. "Amy? Are we not going to watch the reset?"

"I think it's time we start trying to work together. You're right. I keep running from my problems and not talking to people. I want to change that." She looked down at the plate in front of her. On top of that, the gold she'd received made her even more determined to succeed, her goals more easily attainable. "I know the others probably won't listen to me, but I still need to try. I don't want to die because they hate me."

Jax slid into the seat across from her. "They don't hate you, Amy. They all just have things on their minds, too."

Talia smiled when she walked in and saw Amy. "Amy! You're here!"

Amy picked at her food uneasily. "Good morning, Talia. How are you this morning?"

"I'm good. Though Kila didn't come back to her room last night. I'm hoping that's not a bad thing."

Amy frowned, wondering about the implications of that. Just then, Kila herself walked in, looking exhausted and dejected. She got a plate and settled next to Talia.

Talia reached over to squeeze her hand. "Are you alright?"

"Nolan— He—" Kila stopped, fighting back tears.

"What did that idiot do?"

"He found me in the gardens last night. And he kissed me."

"He *kissed* you?" Talia rubbed her temples. "I told him to go *talk* to you, not kiss you!"

"Well, he was really drunk and he came out and found me, then made all these declarations before kissing me. I started to kiss him back, but... I-I told him that I couldn't. Not like that." Kila's eyes remained on her plate, not looking up. "Then I ran... I spent the night in the garden with Tsume."

Talia covered her face with one hand. "I'm so sorry."

Just then, Nolan himself stumbled in, clearly already drunk. "I was just coming to get a drink…" He lurched to a stop when he spotted Kila with the group. He pulled a bottle from beneath the bar and left the dining hall.

Amy took a deep breath. Time to start team building and take Jax's advice from the day before to heart. "Talia, would you get him a plate of food?"

Talia raised an eyebrow. "I can?"

Amy nodded and stood, jogging to catch up with Nolan as he lumbered toward the stairs, crashing into Lillian in the process. Lillian steadied him, even as her nose wrinkled. "Woah! Are you okay?"

"Fine," he slurred.

Amy gripped his arm. "I've got him. Could I get more of that stuff you gave him the first day?"

"Sure. There's some in my lab. I'll go grab it."

Nolan tried unsuccessfully to pull his arm from Amy's grasp.

"Lemme go."

"No."

"I just came to get more to drink. I don't wanna make a scene."

Jax approached and Nolan's movements slowed. "You're already making a scene. Let's just get you upstairs to your room."

Nolan grumbled and with Jax's help, Amy got him up to the suite he'd moved into when Kila started dating Austin. As soon as they entered his room, a replica of the one she and Jax shared, Amy wanted to vomit. Liquor bottles covered most surfaces and the room reeked of alcohol. Gagging, she and Jax lowered him onto the couch where he continued drinking the alcohol he'd gotten from the bar.

Sighing, Amy turned to Jax. "Could you go check on Talia and Kila?"

Jax glanced at Nolan, then back at her. "Are you sure you'll be okay with him here by yourself?"

Amy's nose wrinkled against the smell. "I'll be fine." With that, she began gathering the liquor bottles, tossing them into the wastebasket.

Nolan watched her through bleary eyes. "Normally I'm not opposed to having a pretty lady in my room, but right now I just want to be alone."

Amy ignored him, continuing to pick up the bottles. When there was a knock on the door, she walked over and opened it. "Thank you, Lillian."

Lillian glanced past her. "Do you need any help?"

Amy shook her head. "I've got it under control."

Just then a staff member approached. "Miss Talia said to bring this to you and apologize on her behalf, but she needed to remain with Miss Kila."

Amy nodded. "Thank you." She refocused on Lillian. "I think Kila and Talia could use some help, though. Kila wasn't looking well when she came in this morning."

"If you're sure." With one last glance past Amy, Lillian left.

Nolan took another long drink of liquor. "Who's that?"

"Here." She tugged the bottle from his hand and dropped the vial into it. "Drink this, then eat." She placed the plate of food on the end table next to him.

He reached half-heartedly for the bottle Amy held out of his reach. "Why?"

"Because you're drunk and you're going to be sick if you don't get some food in your stomach." She crossed her arms, keeping the liquor bottle well away from her face.

Nolan grumbled but drank the vial, shuddering as its effects ripped through his body. "I'm not hungry," he muttered much more coherently. "Kila must hate me." He looked down, unable to meet Amy's eye.

"You kissed her, knowing good and well that she's been dating Austin. Of course she's upset." She picked up the food and set it in his lap. "Eat." He started to protest again, but Amy shook her head. "No. You eat, I'll talk." Nolan stopped, shocked into silence. "You need to figure this out. Do you care for Kila? Then maybe you should consider the implications of that and tell her that instead of drinking yourself sick."

"Amy, please just leave me alone."

"No! We don't know when the next dungeon is going to open and right now you would be no good to us if it did. I don't want to die because you can't process your feelings for Kila!"

Nolan blinked in surprise as Amy stood up to him. "Lady Flame, you have no idea of my history. I didn't think I *could* love another. And yet..."

Amy didn't know anything of Nolan's history and she didn't care to delve into it just then, but his pain was obvious. "If you've loved once, why shouldn't you love again?" She sank onto one of the chairs across from him, setting the liquor out of his reach. "Look, I'll admit to knowing very little about relationships, or even friendships, but I do know that if you love someone, you need to tell them. After all, one or both of you could die in the next dungeon, and you'll forever regret not telling them you loved them one last time."

"You speak as if you know."

Amy shook her head, not willing to get into her own past at the moment. "Just think on what I said." She stood and grabbed the bottle again on her way to the door.

"Lady Flame, how is it that someone as lovely as you has never had a relationship? Surely you were highly sought after?"

Amy's mind strayed to all the 'suitors' her mother had proposed, though she'd never met them. For all she knew, Nolan could have been one of them. Yes, she had been sought after, but that had been a lifetime ago. Amy kept her back to Nolan as the memories played through her mind. "I never stayed in one place long enough."

"Why do I feel as if there's so much you aren't telling me?"

Amy hesitated in the doorway a moment. "Because there is." She closed the door behind her as she left.

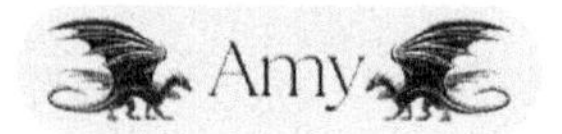

Amy

Amy sat picking at her lunch nervously, not paying attention to Kila and Talia's conversation. She still couldn't decide if she would be returning to the Wizards' Guild yet. She had spent the previous afternoon with Chouza and Kimi at the park, then he'd shown her around again.

Jax had returned that night exhausted and she'd left before he'd woken in the morning. Then he'd been gone to visit his father when she'd gotten back, so she'd yet to have a good chance to talk to him.

She relaxed slightly when Jax entered the dining hall, pulling the chair next to her out for him. He grinned and slid into the offered seat. "Amy! I missed you this morning."

"I decided to continue my usual routine. I want to work on our teamwork and all that, but I do still enjoy watching the reset."

"Of course. And no one can blame you for that," Jax assured her.

Talia paused her conversation with Kila and turned to Amy. "We're just glad you'll be around a bit more now."

Jax squeezed Amy's hand under the table. "Of course. What of you, Talia? I didn't see you here last night."

Talia's cheeks flushed. "I wasn't. Vallun took me on a date again and well… I stayed with him last night."

Jax raised an eyebrow. "Oh really? And how did that go?"

"Really well. I think… I might stay there more often. He asked me to start staying with him at night." Her cheeks reddened even more. "I really like him, so I… I think I'm going to take him up on it."

Kila gave her a small smile. "I'm happy for you, Talia. At least one of us is doing well in the love department."

"L-love?" Talia squeaked. "I-I don't know about love."

Amy quickly covered her mouth, trying to stifle a laugh. Jax's eyes darted to her as he tried to suppress his own grin.

Kila chuckled. "Of course. But at least it's a start."

"Right. Anyway, what are your plans today?" Amy asked.

Talia shrugged. "I have lessons with my new mentor at the Aristan temple."

Amy blinked, taken aback. "Mentor?"

"You and Jax aren't the only ones who sought out help. I know some about healing magick, but I thought it'd be best if I learned a little more. So on one of my trips to the temple, I asked if anyone there would teach me. I start my lessons with them today."

"I-I see. Good for you, then."

Kila lifted her hand. "And Vallun introduced me to one of the members of the Thieves' Guild to help me out."

Talia frowned. "Nolan's the only one who really hasn't sought out a teacher."

Jax raised an eyebrow. "At least we're all actually working on mastering our abilities. Maybe we'll stand a better chance in the next dungeon."

Hope bloomed in Amy's chest. "I certainly hope so."

Jax glanced around. "Speaking of; where *is* Nolan?"

Kila's lips pursed and she looked away. Talia sighed and squeezed her hand. "Nolan is in his room, pretty sick. Kila checked on him this morning wanting to talk about yesterday and he's not doing too well."

Amy sat forward. "What's wrong with him?"

Kila picked at a piece of meat on her plate, not looking up. "He's feverish and muttering something about a woman named Cassandra. And I'm pretty sure he vomited several times."

Jax frowned, tapping his chin. "Honestly? It sounds like he's detoxing."

Amy glanced over at him. "Detoxing?"

"He said yesterday that he'd quit drinking, right?"

Amy, Kila, and Talia all nodded. At dinner the night before, he'd again refused alcohol and had insisted that he'd quit drinking. Amy hadn't truly believed it but now…

"You think this is because of that?" Talia asked.

Jax shrugged. "You drink heavily everyday for years and your body becomes dependent on it. I suspect he's in a world of misery right now. But once he's on the other side, he'll be better for it. I hope."

Talia stirred her potatoes with her fork, her head down. "Lillian was checking on him when I went by. He says he wants to do better. *Be* better."

"I see. Let's hope it sticks." He turned to Amy. "Are you going to your lesson with Master Inzo today?"

Amy glanced at him from the corner of her eye. "Do you think I should?"

Jax gave her a reassuring smile. "I think you should. I'll go with you if you want me to."

"Thank you, Jax."

Once they reached the Wizards' Library, Amy hesitated outside, gnawing her lip.

Jax squeezed her hand. "It'll be alright, Amy. You don't have to do anything you're uncomfortable with."

Amy gripped his hand tightly, then, taking a calming breath, she stepped inside.

Inzo glanced up from his conversation with Kukuri and smiled when he saw her. "Little Dragon! I am glad you returned."

"I did. But I'm not comfortable with what you asked. I will keep practicing, but I won't use my magick against you."

Inzo gave her a warm smile. "Of course. Come." With that, he led her to the training room.

Jax squeezed her hand again. "See? I told you it'd be okay."

"Thank you, Jax. I'll see you after my lesson."

She continued practicing for several hours, growing more and more frustrated as she failed time after time. "You are growing impatient, Little Dragon."

Amy's eyes burned as she fought back tears. *How can I ever protect my companions if I can't even manage this one simple task.* "I *have* to figure it out," she whispered, all fight going out of her as she sank to the floor.

Inzo knelt next to her. "What is bothering you so much, Amy?"

Amy looked over as he used her name instead of the usual nickname. "I just… Fire is so destructive. It kills people and permanently maims others. I now have that destructive power, but I'm weak without it. And when my friends and allies are between me and the things we'll be fighting I'm useless to them."

"You should give yourself more credit. You have dragon blood in you. You are tougher than you realize."

Amy glanced at him in disbelief. "You really think that? Look at me! I'm small, I'm weak. One hit from a skeleton in the last dungeon knocked me out and almost killed me! I very nearly died in a pool of zombies. I don't stand a chance in these dungeons!" She buried her face in her hands. *What was I thinking, agreeing to this? Why did I think that I could do anything to help these people?*

"Are you sure about that?" He studied her intently. "Tell me, Amy, how long have you been traveling on your own? I presume your parents were not with you before you arrived here? Nor a husband? Sibling?"

Amy shook her head, a jolt of pain going through her at the mention of family. "No. I was alone. I've been alone for twelve years."

"And you are still young, so you must have been what, ten? Eleven?"

"Ten."

"So since you were ten years old, a child, you've kept yourself alive. *Without* magick. Tell me, does that sound weak to you?"

Amy started to argue, but stopped and actually *thought* about what he'd said. She had been a child— and a fairly coddled one at that. She'd survived against all odds from the accident that had killed her family and walked away. Maybe he had a point.

"Good. Now that you have regained some of your confidence, we will continue. But this time, *I* am your target."

Amy frowned and leaned away from him. "I told you, I'm not comfortable with that."

"I promise, you won't hurt me. Even if you do, it will be such minor burns that one spell from a healer will patch me right up. At least give it a try?" He stood and offered her a hand.

Amy hesitated, then let him pull her to her feet. "Fine. But at the first sign of injury, I'm stopping."

Inzo nodded his agreement and recast his spell. "Alright. Then let us resume." Amy hesitated, staring at Inzo as he stood in front of her. "You will not hurt me."

Amy drew on her magick, and cast the spell, fearing the sound of screams and the smell of burning flesh. But when the flames cleared, she saw Inzo standing unharmed, his clothing singed on the edge and his skin only slightly reddened, already fading right in front of her eyes.

He gestured down at himself. "Now, are you ready to truly commit? Sarcio." Amy gulped as his clothes repaired themselves and readied herself to cast her spell again, this time focusing on putting a protective barrier around him.

As dinner approached, she'd only had marginal success. She'd stopped searing his skin, but his clothing continued to be singed with each casting. She focused and cast the spell again, feeling an exponential increase on the pull from her magick. Sagging against a training dummy, she grinned when she saw that his clothing was unmarked and he was uninjured. "I did it!"

"You did, Little Dragon. I knew you could." Feeling the exhaustion hitting, Amy swayed, vision darkening momentarily. "You've used too much of your magick." He sighed, stepping forward to support her. "Do you have any left?" Amy tried to call on her magick, but her vision continued to fade and she could do little more than shake her head. "Little Dragon?" His tone grew more worried. "Why did you do this to yourself?" he murmured quietly. With that, her vision blackened and she collapsed.

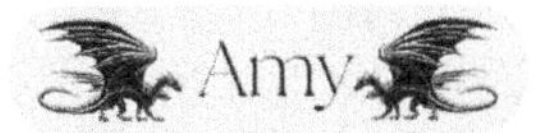

Amy's usual nightmares were muted and waking felt like trudging against a current. When she finally peeled her eyes open, she found herself in an unfamiliar room. The decorations were sparse and the bed was simple. Struggling to a sitting position, she tried to remember how she'd gotten there through her pounding head.

"You're finally awake!" Kukuri waved from a bench nearby, her feet swinging.

"Where am I?"

"A small room within the library. We keep them in good condition in case someone needs to sleep here. For example, when they completely drain their magick and push their bodies beyond what they're capable of handling." She grinned at Amy.

Amy's cheeks warmed. "Where's Master Inzo?"

"He returned to his home with his wife and children after bringing you here."

"Oh. I should head back. Jax and Talia are probably worried about me.".

Kukuri shook her head. "Don't worry. Jax checked on you before he left the library yesterday. He will have let your other friends know where you are."

Amy sighed in relief and stood. "What time is it?" she asked when her stomach growled. She felt the familiar tingle of Azurys curled around her navel in tattoo form.

"Mid-morning."

"Mid-morning! How did I sleep that long?"

"Using magick is physically exhausting to us as well as using our magickal energy. You aren't quite used to that yet so your body couldn't handle it," Kukuri shrugged. "It won't be as bad, the more you practice. But you did push yourself pretty hard yesterday."

Amy nodded. "I should head back... Thank you, Kukuri. Is there any chance I can get something to eat here before heading back to the manor? I'm hungry."

"Of course." Kukuri led her from the room and down a hallway.

Amy studied the walls around her, trying to find anything familiar. "Where are we? I don't recognize any of this."

"Well of course not. You've hardly seen anything of the library. Most of your time has been spent in the training room with Inzo. Not that it's a bad thing! This area is technically rarely used anyway. Usually just those who are training and over exert themselves stay here. It has a few small rooms, a kitchen, a washroom, and a few other necessities."

"Handy."

The two turned a corner and entered a small kitchen where a tall, blonde woman stood in front of a stove. Her eyes narrowed as she spotted Amy, but she refocused on the food without saying anything.

Kukuri hopped up onto a stool. "This is Jasmine. She's the resident cook/maid for the residential quarters."

Amy felt uneasy without her disguise, but gave a small wave. "Hi. I'm Amy."

"I know who you are. Everyone who works in the library knows of the demon-spawn sorceress studying under Master Inzo."

"Now, now, Jasmine. You know she's still a human, just with Awakened blood," Kukuri chided. "Just like you weren't really an elf."

Jasmine dumped the eggs onto a plate. "Yeah, I know. Either way, help yourself." She gestured to a small pile of bacon, eggs, and sausage.

Amy eagerly piled the food onto a plate, then glanced at the other two women. "Are you going to eat?"

Kukuri shrugged. "We've both already eaten. I just asked Jasmine to make something fresh."

"How did you know when I would wake up?"

Kukuri grinned. "Just one of my many talents."

Amy blinked, but shook her head. She never would truly understand the little gnome. She thanked Jasmine as the other woman left the room before quickly scarfing down the food.

"I should head back." Amy sighed, then she stood and stretched, grimacing as the scarring pulled against her shoulders. "Could you show me the way out?"

Kukuri led Amy back out into the main entryway of the library. "I'll see you tomorrow!"

"See you tomorrow." Amy waved and stepped out of the library. Her magick seemed sluggish and reluctant to listen to her, making her disguise even harder to summon.

She had almost reached the manor when she spotted a familiar figure. Unbidden, a smile rose to her lips. As if sensing her gaze, he turned and waved. The little girl on his shoulders did the same.

"Chouza and Kimi! How are you? Where are you headed?"

"Papa said we're gonna stay with the Ak-ams for a while."

Chouza chuckled and squeezed Kimi's leg. "Arkhams, Baby. And yes, we're going to stay with the Arkhams for a while. Assuming your group agrees."

Amy blinked and looked between them, finally noticing the bag slung over his shoulder. "Oh. Balthazar contacted you?"

"Yeah. I was told you're looking for a new member?"

"Yes. I took your advice and talked to the group. They agreed."

A small smile lifted Chouza's lips. "Thank you."

Amy chuckled. "Don't thank me. After all, we're asking you to—" She glanced at Kimi on his shoulders. "After all, this won't be an easy job," she corrected, not wanting to scare the little girl.

Chouza's smile dropped. "I know. Trust me, I know."

Jax met them at the bottom of the stairs as they entered the manor. "Amy! Are you feeling better?" He looked past her at Chouza, his brow furrowing. "Chouza?

"Much. Nothing a good night's sleep couldn't cure. Where are you off to?"

"I was going to do a bit of training before lunch. What about you?"

"I uh… Well, I met Chouza on my way back. Apparently he'll be joining us?"

"Sounds good to me." He nodded toward the stairs. "Why don't you go talk to Sir Arkham?"

"You don't think the rest of your group will want to talk to me first?"

Jax sighed. "I suppose you're right." He glanced at Amy. "Talia just got back. She's in the library with Kila. Nolan's in the training field. I was going to spar with Lucille."

Amy groaned internally. "I'll fetch Talia and Kila, then." She hurried into the library, distinctly aware of Chouza's eyes on her retreating form. When she stepped inside, she spotted Talia writing something in a journal, while Kila watched over her shoulder.

Talia glanced up and smiled when she saw Amy. "Amy! How are you feeling?"

"I'm well. It seems Balthazar has sent someone over to potentially join us. We were going to head out to the training field to see if we can all agree."

Kila scowled and crossed her arms. "Does it matter? You're just going to do what you want anyway."

Amy sighed. "Kila, I want us to work together as a group. That starts with us agreeing on whether Chouza's a good addition or not." Part of her hoped they would agree. The other hoped they wouldn't and he'd be sent away, where he was safe and Kimi wouldn't be at risk of losing her father.

Kila huffed and stood. "Fine. Where's he at?"

"He and Jax are headed out to the training field. Nolan's already out there."

Kila stomped past Amy. Talia chased after her, squeezing Amy's arm on her way by. "Sorry. She's just…"

"She doesn't like me. I get it. Let's just get this over with." Amy followed Kila out the back of the manor.

Chouza held Kimi's hand out in the training field. When Amy walked up, he smiled and gestured around him. "It's been a while since I've been out here."

Kimi pulled her hand free and ran to give Amy a hug. "Hi, Ms. Amy! Will you sit with me while Papa shows how strong he is?"

Amy chuckled and returned the hug. "Of course. I'd be happy to."

Chouza kissed Kimi's head and set the bag next to them. "I won't be long."

"Okay, Papa."

Amy settled onto the grass, stiffening as Kimi crawled into her lap. But her gaze quickly went to Nolan approaching Chouza. His skin had a sallow sheen to it, but at least he was upright.

He held out a hand. "I'm Nolan."

Chouza shook the offered hand. "I'm Chouza. Balthazar said you were looking for some help."

Nolan's eyes darted to Amy. "Lady Flame pointed out that we could really use some help. And she's right. I know you handle yourself well in the Pits, but would you be willing to spar and show us your skills with a weapon?"

"Of course." He grabbed a staff not unlike Amy's own from the wall of weapons. "Who am I sparring with?"

Nolan hesitated, then nodded toward the tutors standing nearby watching the exchange. "Lucille, if you don't mind. I'm not quite back up to my full strength."

Lucille tightened the band holding her brown hair back and stepped forward. The two faced off, Chouza with his staff and Lucille with a wooden sword. They each gave a short bow before Lucille made the first move, lunging forward with an arcing swing toward Chouza's middle. He shifted his hands, blocking the blow with the middle of the staff before sliding forward, using the right end to tap Lucille's shoulder.

She grunted and stepped back, circling Chouza. Chouza followed her movements, one hand near the end of the staff and the other closer to the middle. Not waiting for her to make the first move this time, he darted forward, the right side again going for Lucille's shoulder. She quickly blocked it with the sword, using both hands to hold him back.

He let her momentum swing the staff back, sliding his hands so that the left side again tapped her shoulder. Lucille's eyes narrowed and the two began to exchange blows faster than Amy could follow.

Kimi tucked her head into Amy's chest, letting out a whimper. "Is Papa gonna get hurt?"

Amy's arms tightened around her. "No, sweetie. Your papa is just practicing fighting. They're using wooden weapons so they won't hurt each other."

Kimi sniffled and kept her head under Amy's chin. Jax knelt next to them, watching the fight himself. "He's impressive," he whispered.

Amy's eyes followed Chouza as best she could. His body moved like a dancer, but in a much more deadly dance. She rested a hand on the back of Kimi's head, humming softly to drown out the thuds of wood colliding.

Finally, Chouza stood behind Lucille, the staff pulled tight against her throat. She tapped his thigh and Chouza released one side of the staff, letting it fall. The two gave a short bow to each other again before Chouza approached Nolan, breathing hard.

"I approve. Anyone have any objections?" Nolan's gaze traveled across Jax, Amy, Kila, and Talia, all of them shaking their heads. "Then welcome to the team, Chouza."

"Thanks." Chouza hurried over to Amy and reached for Kimi. "Is she alright?"

Amy helped Kimi to her feet and stood herself. "Just got a little frightened by the fighting is all."

Kimi lunged for Chouza, burying her face in his shoulder. "Are you hurt, Papa?"

"No, Baby. Papa's just fine. It's alright." He gave Amy an apologetic look. "I didn't even think about the fact that seeing the fighting would scare her. I assumed since she knows I fight in the Pits and I wouldn't get hurt, she'd be okay." He squeezed Kimi lightly. "I'm sorry, Baby."

"It's okay, Papa."

Jax dipped his head as he got to his feet. "I must say, that was impressive."

"Thanks."

Nolan followed Chouza over. "You'll make a great addition." He gave Amy a polite nod and she hurriedly returned it. "Might I inquire what your usual weapon is?"

"It's a double-bladed sword."

Nolan raised an eyebrow. "I look forward to seeing it in action, then. Why don't you go talk to Arkham?"

Chouza nodded. "Just let me find someone to watch Kimiko."

"I can watch her," Amy volunteered without a thought.

Chouza blinked and Jax raised an eyebrow. "Are you sure? As you saw the other day, she's a bit of a handful."

Kimi started to squirm, reassured that her father was okay. "Put me down, Papa! I want to play with Ms. Amy!"

Amy smiled and pulled her into her arms. "It's not a problem, Chouza. Go talk to Arkham. I've got Kimi." She set Kimi on the ground and offered her a hand. "What do you say we go play in the gardens?"

Kimi blinked up at her in confusion. "Gardens?"

Jax winked at Amy and knelt next to Kimi again. "Why, it's a magickal place where all sorts of flowers and trees grow. There's even fruit you can pick right from the branch."

Kimi's eyes widened. "Really?" She jumped up and down, tugging on Chouza's hand. "Can I go, Papa? Can I go? Pleeease?"

Chouza chuckled and nodded. "Of course, Baby. I'll be out in a little bit. And remember, Papa will look just a little different when you see him again, okay?"

"Right. Cause you'll be Awaited!"

"Awakened," Chouza corrected with a fond smile. "And yes, Baby."

"Oh yeah. Awakened." Kimi pulled on Amy's hand. "Can we go to the magick garden now?"

Amy chuckled and let her pull her along. "Alright. This way." She led Kimi through the hedge and into the gardens, Jax trailing after them.

He raised an eyebrow. "You volunteered for babysitting duty awfully quickly."

Amy shrugged. "I don't know. I just like Kimi. And she's not that much of a handful."

Jax eyed Kimi's tiny hand clutching Amy's. "So it would seem. I didn't know you were fond of kids."

"I've always had a soft spot for them." Not that she'd ever shown it while they traveled together. She'd steered clear of everyone then, but especially children. Seeing them reminded her of the brother she had lost.

"Right…" He shook his head and grinned as Kimi looked around in wonder at the garden.

"Well now, who's this?" Lillian asked, emerging from the trees.

Kimi blushed and ducked behind Amy's leg, peeking out from behind her. Amy chuckled and rested a hand on her head. "Lillian, this is Kimiko. Kimiko, this is Ms. Lillian. She's one of the Arkhams and one of my good friends."

Lillian smiled at Amy before kneeling. "Hi Kimiko. It's alright, you don't have to be afraid."

Kimi edged a little further behind Amy. "You're one of the Artums?"

Lillian chuckled. "Yes, I'm an *Arkham*. It's nice to meet you."

"My papa said he was gonna work for you."

Lillian glanced up at Amy with a raised eyebrow. "Oh really? Who's your papa?"

Amy stroked Kimi's hair soothingly, then scooped her into her arms. "Chouza Zhang?"

Lillian stood, brow furrowing. "Chouza? Wait, you mean this is little Kimi? Why, you were only a few weeks old the last time I saw you."

Kimi buried her face in Amy's chest and Amy gave her a light squeeze. "You know her?"

"Yes, of course. She was born here. I delivered her. Sad what happened to her mother, though." She held her hand out to Kimi. "It's alright, sweetie. You're safe here. Were you coming to play?"

Kimi gave a tiny nod, watching Lillian from beneath Amy's chin. "Mr. Fox-man said the gardens were magickal."

Jax chuckled at Kimi's nickname and Lillian's smile grew. "Of course they are. Come on."

Amy set Kimi back down and took her hand, following Lillian deeper into the garden. Jax fell into step on her other side. "Fox-man?"

Amy raised an eyebrow. "Well you do look like a fox."

"I suppose I do," Jax agreed. "I see you're still disguised."

Amy gnawed her lip. "I… I was just coming back from the library when I ran into them. I don't want to scare her."

"You can't disguise yourself all the time."

"I know…" Amy glanced down at Kimi as the little girl pulled her hand free and ran toward a fruit tree. "Careful, Kimi."

Kimi stopped and glanced back. "Can I pick a apple, Ms. Amy?"

Amy glanced at Lillian, waiting for her nod of approval. "Go ahead. Do you want some help?"

"I got this!" She ran up to one of the apple trees, pausing below one of the branches to look up at a piece of fruit. "Okay, I don't got this."

Amy chuckled and stepped forward, carefully lifting the little girl onto her shoulders. "Careful, Amy," Jax warned behind her. "She's almost as big as you are."

"Ha ha." She rolled her eyes and stepped closer to the tree so Kimi could reach an apple. "Got it?"

"Uh-huh!" Amy heard a snap as the apple broke off the branch and settled Kimi back onto the ground. She studied the apple critically. "Can I eat it?"

Lillian grabbed her own apple and held it up. "Yes of course."

Kimi studied it a moment longer before biting into it, the juice running down her chin. "This is yummy!" she said around the mouthful of food.

Amy chuckled and shook her head. "Don't talk with your mouth full."

Kimi quickly swallowed the piece of apple. "Sorry, Ms. Amy!"

"It's alright."

Amy watched Kimi as she finished the apple, then started digging in the dirt, chatting with Lillian about the different plants and insects she saw. *I could get used to this…*

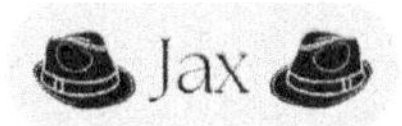

Jax smiled as he watched Amy interacting with Chouza's daughter. She seemed comfortable. And happy. The happiest he'd ever seen her. And Kimi clearly liked her. He chuckled when Kimi took off running, squealing for Amy to chase her and Amy obliged. The two looked so natural together. When Azurys appeared, Kimi was even more hypnotized, begging Amy to tell her how the tattoo form worked.

Lillian stepped up next to him. "She clearly likes her."

Jax nodded. "It would appear so. I'm happy for her."

"I don't think I've seen Amy smile this much since your group arrived here."

"I haven't seen her smile this much in the months I've known her."

A small crack drew Jax's attention to a catfolk approaching them, the fur across his face and hands a dark, ash gray. Jax recognized the clothing and the white hair atop his head. "Hello again, Chouza."

"Uh, hey. Looks like they're having fun." He scratched his cheek. "I hate the fur."

"It itches the first time, doesn't it?" Jax agreed with a chuckle. "And yes. They're having an absolute blast."

Amy glanced over and straightened, eyes locking on Chouza. Kimi followed her gaze and ducked behind Amy again. "Who's that?" Jax heard her ask.

Amy gently nudged her from behind her. "I do believe that's your papa."

Kimi blinked and looked between them. "Papa?"

"Hey, Baby."

Kimi's nose wrinkled. "Papa, you have fur!" Everyone laughed and Kimi looked perplexed. "What?"

"Nothing, Baby. Come here." Chouza held his arms open and Kimi ran to him.

"Ms. Amy helped me pick an apple, then Ms. Lillian told me what all the different flowers were!"

"Oh, really? Sounds like you were having fun."

"Uh-huh!"

Jax glanced at Amy who hadn't moved from where she stood. Chouza smiled over at her and she shook her head quickly. "Yes. We were having a lot of fun," she agreed, breaking from whatever trance she'd been in.

"Well, I hate to break up the party," Lillian said, "but it's about lunch.

Shall we head inside and eat?"

"Papa, I'm hungry!"

"Alright, Baby. Let's go eat."

The group trekked inside as Jax fell into step next to Amy, behind the others. "Kimi is quite adorable."

"Yes. And so well mannered."

"I've noticed. She seems to like you."

Amy chuckled. "And I like her."

He watched as her eyes strayed to Chouza again. *Interesting. Too bad I've never been able to get a reaction like that out of her.*

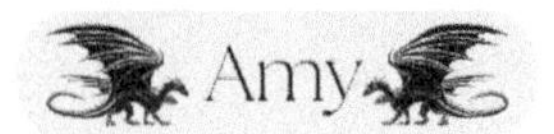

Amy walked between Jax and Kimi, trying not to stare at Chouza. His palms were clear of the thin ash-gray fur and his ears had shifted to the top of his head, twitching at every sound. When they stepped into the dining hall, she spotted Kila, Nolan, and Talia already at a table, Nolan's back to them.

They grabbed their plates and as Chouza pulled out a chair, Nolan scrambled back, nearly falling from his chair in his rush to stand. "What the hell?"

Jax blinked, looking between them. "What?"

"Am I fucking hallucinating?" He stared at Chouza, wide-eyed.

Chouza's fur bristled and he nudged Kimi behind him. "What's your problem?"

Nolan blinked, stepping back. "Chouza?"

"Yeah. What's your problem?" Chouza's fist clenched, his muscles tensed in preparation to fight.

"N-nothing."

Jax cracked up next to Amy and she jumped, staring at him wide-eyed. "Nolan's afraid of cats. And now we have a catfolk as part of the team."

Nolan glared at Jax. "I'm not afraid of cats! I just don't like them."

Amy chuckled and Kimi peeked around Chouza. "Why don't you like kitties?"

Nolan blinked, staring at the little girl. "I uh… I had one bite me when I was a kid. It was my sister's and it hated me. It'd bite me whenever I came near it. And it chased me." He righted his chair and slowly lowered himself into it.

"Oh. Well Papa won't bite you, will you Papa?"

Chouza chuckled and pulled a seat out for Kimi. "No, Kimiko. I won't bite him."

Jax shook with suppressed his laughter and Amy rolled her eyes at him, her own amusement barely contained.

Kila smiled at Kimi. "Hi. Is Chouza your papa?"

"Uh-huh. Why do you look like a monkey?"

Amy braced for Kila to snap at her, but the other woman simply laughed. "Because I'm a monkeyfolk."

"Oooh." Kimi stared at her wide-eyed.

Chouza set her plate in front of her. "Eat, Kimiko."

"Okay, Papa."

Kila smiled at Chouza. "She's adorable."

Chouza settled into his own seat, running a hand across Kimi's hair. "Thank you."

Kimi's eyes went to Talia next. "You're pretty."

"T-thank you."

Amy settled into her own seat on Kimi's other side, digging into her meal. As the others talked, she fought the urge to reach out and run her hand along Chouza's arm. *If his fur is as soft as a regular cat's, I bet having his arms around me would be heavenly.* She shook her head. *Where did that come from? And why is my heart pounding so loudly?*

"Amy? Are you alright?" Talia asked, studying her in concern.

"I'm fine! I uh… I'm just going to head to the library!" With that she stood quickly, stumbling over her seat in her haste.

Jax's brow furrowed. "Amy?"

"I'm fine!" She dumped her plate and hurried from the room, leaning against a wall outside to take deep calming breaths. Shaking her head, she resumed her path to the library, pushing the strange experience from her mind.

Amy hesitated at the entrance to the library, gnawing her lip. She still hadn't done any training with her staff. *It's time to change that.*

With that thought in mind, she left the manor and headed out into the training field, studying each of the training staves. Frowning, she picked one up and approached a training dummy. She tried to imitate how she'd seen Chouza holding it and ended up wacking herself in the thigh with it when she swung at the dummy.

She yelped and dropped the staff, scowling at it. Sighing, she picked it up, again trying to imitate Chouza's hold. And again, she wacked herself with it when she tried to hit the dummy. Several attempts later, she grabbed the end and swung it hard against the training dummy, knocking it over in her frustration. The impact jarred her arms and she dropped the staff again.

"That one's too big for you."

Amy jumped and whirled around to face Chouza. "What are you talking about?"

"That staff. It's too big for you." He walked over and studied the staves before grabbing one and walking over. "Here. Stand this up next to you."

Amy's brow furrowed, but she did as he said. The tip came to the middle of her head with the base on the ground. "Like this?"

"Yes. And that one's the perfect size. It should come to about your mouth, give or take an inch or two. Too long and it'll be unwieldy. Too short and you won't be able to grip it the right way. I can help teach you if you'd like?"

Amy cleared her throat, trying to work the lump from it. "S-sure. Where's Kimi?"

"Laying down for a nap. Meadow's keeping an ear out for her."

Amy relaxed slightly at the mention of the other caretaker for the guest suites. Meadow worked on the days June had off and of all the staff, she seemed the least bothered by Amy's heritage. "R-right. Okay."

Chouza gestured for her to face a new training dummy. "Alright. Take your stance." Amy glanced at him and slid her feet apart. "No, no. You're predominantly right-handed, right?"

Amy nodded. "Alright. Slide your right leg back some." He used his foot to tap her leg back a few inches. "Good. Now you're more balanced. You can't be knocked over as easily. Do you mind if I touch you?"

"S-sure," Amy squeaked, face heating even more.

Chouza gripped her shoulders, turning her body slightly. "Now, see. If you're hit from the front or the back, you won't get knocked off balance." He pressed the front of her left shoulder and she felt her weight settle back onto her right foot. "You already had a pretty good stance. Did you have any formal training?"

"A little. But I was young."

"Ah. " He smiled at her. "It's alright. You can relax. Like Kimiko said, I won't bite."

Amy flushed, her eyes settling on his lips as she imagined other things he could do with his mouth. "Of course not!" She cringed as her voice came out much higher than it should have.

Chouza chuckled. "Alright, now let's see what we can do with the staff." He grabbed a staff and settled into his own readied stance. "Your left hand should be about five to eight inches in from this end, depending on how long the staff is." He demonstrated where her hand should go, stepping forward to correct her grip before settling back into his own stance. "Your right hand should be closer to the middle, since that's the hand you're going to strike with." He slid his right hand down, gripping the staff loosely. "You use the left hand to balance and control the staff while the right hand generates momentum. Understand?"

Amy gnawed her lip, watching carefully as Chouza demonstrated the movement of the staff, stepping forward as he did so. "Now, to help follow through, you're going to step forward with the same leg. So if your right hand is going forward, your left leg will be your pivot point and your right leg will follow." He tapped his right leg. "Like this." He stepped forward again, swinging the right side of the staff at the same time as he stepped with his right leg.

"After you strike, you'll step back again, using the staff as a guard against counterattack." He demonstrated, keeping the staff raised in front of him as his right leg pivoted back again. "Now, of course, your left leg won't be completely still in an actual battle, but this gives you a good enough idea of how your legs and hands should move together."

"Right. Can I try?"

Chouza nodded and Amy slid her right hand into place, then stepped forward, knocking the staff into the side of the training dummy. The resounding thump sent a jolt through her hands, but not as painfully as it had before.

"Good!" He grinned at her and Amy couldn't deny the flutter of pleasure his praise caused. "Now, if you want to do two attacks back to back, you'll do your first attack," he waited as she mimicked his movements, "then your second one." After his first strike, he slid his hands down the staff until his right hand was close to the end and his left hand was in the center. "Then your right leg will become your pivot point." He stepped forward with his left leg, swinging the left side of the staff forward.

He faced her. "Swing at me and I'll show you how that would apply."

Amy's eyes widened. "I-I don't want to hurt you!"

Chouza chuckled. "Well I don't want you to swing full out. Just swing like you would if you were going to attack me."

Amy gulped, her eyes wide, but did as he said, swinging the right side of her staff forward. Chouza twisted his staff and blocked the blow.

"Now, I want you to block my blow." He carefully swung his staff forward and Amy imitated his block. "If your opponent blocks your blow, you have several options. See how you're holding against my staff?" Amy nodded and Chouza slid the staff down. "I can bring it down like this and pivot it up to jab directly into my opponent's face." He demonstrated and Amy jerked back, though he left plenty of room between them.

"Or—" he motioned for her to resume her position, "I can let their momentum power a follow-up strike, like this." He slid his hand down and while she pressed on the right side, blocking that blow, the left side swung around, catching her in the side. Again, his movements were slow and controlled, making sure it didn't hurt her.

"The other option, of course, is to simply retreat." He once again gestured for her to take her stance, blocking his blow. "If you want to retreat, you simply keep your own staff raised and step back on your pivot leg. Like this." He pivoted his right leg back and twisted to the left, letting Amy stumble forward.

She caught herself and regained her balance. "How did you learn all of this?"

Chouza shrugged. "Training. And lots and lots of practice."

"Right. Of course." She ducked her head.

"Do you want me to train you? I'd be happy to. Technically the staff isn't my primary weapon, but I've trained extensively with it. I'd be happy to pass it on."

"A-are you sure?

Chouza's eyes darkened. "You're my teammate now. I'll do anything I can to make sure you survive those dungeons."

Amy nodded. "Thank you, Chouza."

Chozua took a breath, smiling and clearing the darkness from his eyes. "Of course. Let's continue."

The next several hours passed until Amy could barely breathe and bruises covered her body. Even though Chouza had been careful not to hurt her, sometimes blows got through and connected more solidly than he planned. The trainers, Nolan, Kila, and Talia had come and gone, but they didn't interfere, leaving Amy to train with Chouza.

She dropped onto the ground, panting as she flopped back. Chouza stood over her, grinning. "You're doing well. You alright?"

"Fine. Just need— to remember— how to breathe."

Chouza chuckled and sat down next to her. "I think this is where we should call it for the day."

"I agree." She struggled up to rest on her elbows. "Why are you so composed?"

"You forget, I'm used to training for hours a day for the Pits. This was a light workout compared to what I'm used to."

"This— This was *light?*" She stared at him incredulously. "What do you normally do?"

"I don't think you want to know."

Amy's eyes widened. "Noted."

Chouza grinned at her. "I'm sure you'll get to witness it over the next few weeks. After all, we'll be working together for the foreseeable future."

Amy's cheeks heated. "Right."

Chouza studied her critically for a moment. "Do you stay disguised all the time? Even here?"

Amy shrugged, keeping her head down. "Not usually. I just didn't want to scare Kimi."

Chouza frowned. "You can't hide it forever. Wouldn't you rather her see you on your terms than by accident?"

"I know you're right, I just… I don't want to scare her."

Chouza chuckled. "Kids are more accepting than you give them credit for."

"I suppose so."

"Speaking of..." He rose to his feet, smiling toward the manor.

"Papa!"

Amy blinked and rolled over, watching as the little girl ran forward.

Meadow jogged behind her, her wispy brown hair escaping its bun. "Sorry Mr. Chouza. She was no longer content playing in the suite."

Chouza scooped the girl up. "It's alright. We're done anyway."

Kimi gave him a tight hug, then waved at Amy still on the ground. "Hi Ms. Amy! What are you doing down there?"

"I'm resting. You papa was helping me with my training."

"Oh."

Amy gnawed her lip for a second before sitting up. "Hey, Kimi. Come sit with me for a second."

Kimi squirmed and Chouza set her down. She hurried over and sat on the ground next to Amy. "What is it Ms. Amy?"

"You know how your papa changed forms after talking to Sir Arkham?"

"Uh-huh."

"Well… This… isn't my usual form."

"It's not?"

"N-no." Amy glanced at Chouza and he gave her an encouraging smile. "I disguise myself like this because people don't really like what I am usually."

Kimi's nose wrinkled in confusion. "Why not?"

"I'm what's called a… demonkin."

"What's a demonkid?"

Amy chuckled. "Demon*kin*. Would you like to see?"

Kimi straightened, her face brightening with excitement. "Yes, please!"

"Alright. Don't be scared, okay?" Amy glanced once more at Chouza before letting her disguise fall away.

Kimi stared at her with wide eyes. "Woah. You have horns! And a tail!"

"I do."

"Your skin is such a pretty color."

Chouza squatted next to her, kissing Kimi's cheek. "I agree." His smile made Amy's stomach flip-flop.

Amy flushed and Kimi giggled. "Will you play with me again, Ms. Amy?"

"Sure, Kimi. I'd be happy to."

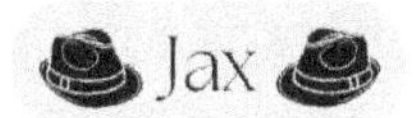

Jax rubbed his head as he walked into the dining hall. Inzo's lesson had been as brutal as usual, straining his mind in an attempt to focus on more than one consciousness at once. In the end, he'd managed one casting of a levitation spell while still focusing on Inzo's mind before his concentration had snapped, leaving him with a migraine.

Chouza and Kimi were seated with the group when he walked in, but Amy was nowhere to be seen. He frowned, grabbed his plate, and sat next to Chouza. "Evening. Where's Amy?"

Chouza chuckled. "I was training with her earlier and by the time dinner rolled around, she was so sore that she decided to go soak in a hot bath."

Jax raised an eyebrow. "Amy was training?"

Chouza nodded. "She definitely needs to practice, but there's potential there."

"Huh. Good for her." *Wish I could have seen that.*

Dinner passed in peace as conversation between the group flowed comfortably, aided by Kimi's occasional input.

After bidding everyone goodnight, he fell into step with Chouza.

"I'm not sure what the suite situation with Kila, Talia, and Nolan is at the moment. They started out together, then Nolan moved out. But with him and Kila together now, I'm not sure if he moved back in. You're of course welcome to join me and Amy in ours, or get one of your own." He smiled as Kimi snuggled into Chouza's arms.

Kimi's lip pooched out and she pulled back to look at her father. "I want to stay with Ms. Amy. I like her."

Chouza stroked her hair and pressed her back against his chest. "As long as it's okay with her. We won't encroach on her space without her permission."

"Papa, what does en- en-" Her face scrunched up as she tried to copy the word.

"Encroach?" Jax volunteered.

"Yeah. What does that mean?"

Chouza kissed the top of her head. "It means to invade. Or put yourself in without permission."

"Oh. And we don't do things like that, right, Papa?"

"That's right, Kimiko."

Jax watched the two, pleased with the interaction. Chouza seemed to be a good man and he was clearly teaching his daughter well. When they stepped into the suite, he spotted Amy in her nightdress seated at the table. *Nightmares of the Abyss* sat open in front of her, as well as a bunch of blank papers.

She glanced up with a smile but froze when she saw Chouza, quickly grabbing a blanket to wrap around herself. "Chouza!" she squeaked. "What are you doing here?"

"Would you mind if Kimiko and I roomed in here? If you'd rather, I can go to one of the other suites." He motioned back toward the door.

"No!" She cleared her throat as Jax gave her a funny look. "I mean, there's no need. There's two empty rooms so just help yourself."

Chouza nodded. "Thanks. Come on Kimiko, let's brush your teeth and get you to bed."

"Okay, Papa. Night night, Ms. Amy. Night night, Mr. Fox-man."

Jax smiled at the small girl. "Good night, little one."

"Night," Amy echoed.

Jax waited until the door to the washroom had closed before sliding into the seat across from Amy. "Are you alright, Amy?"

"I'm fine. Why wouldn't I be?"

"Well, you look like your cheeks are about to catch on fire."

Amy quickly reached up to cover her cheeks, glaring at Jax. "They do not!"

Jax chuckled. "Amy, do you like Chouza?"

"Of course I do!"

Jax rolled his eyes. "I don't mean like that. I mean, do you like him?"

"I don't know what you're talking about." She ducked her head, focusing on her work and giving Jax all the answer he needed.

A moment later, Chouza walked through and headed into the room next to Jax's. Amy's eyes never left him and Jax shook his head in amusement. *The girl is absolutely enamored. Shame. I would have liked a chance, but if he makes her happy, then what can I do?*

"So what are you working on?" Chouza asked when he returned quite a while later, gesturing to the book and paper in front of Amy.

Amy didn't answer and Jax nudged her gently. "Amy?"

"Huh?"

"Are you alright? You keep spacing out." He smirked. "Are you still weakened from last night?"

Amy cleared her throat. "Ummm… Yes, that's probably it."

Chouza looked between them, frowning. "What happened last night?"

Jax again waited for Amy to answer, but she just stared at Chouza. "She used up too much of her magick in training yesterday and ended up having to stay at the Wizards' Guild overnight. It seems she's not fully recovered."

"Oh. I shouldn't have pushed you so hard earlier. Maybe you should rest?"

"Right! I think I'll do that!" Amy scrambled to her feet. "Good night!" She tried to gather her materials, but a few pens clattered to the floor. Chouza leaned down to help her pick them up, leaving their faces inches apart. Amy's face reddened and she jumped backward. "S-sorry!" She bolted into her room, leaving Chouza standing with an ink pen in his hand.

Chouza glanced between Jax and the closed door, perplexed. "Did I do something?"

Jax bit back laughter. "No, Chouza. Just Amy being Amy. I'm off to bed myself. Goodnight."

Choua stared blankly at Amy's door. "Night."

16

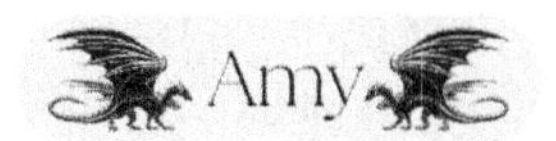

Amy

That night, instead of her usual nightmares, dreams of Chouza tantalized her. She jerked awake when she heard her door open.

"Papa?"

Amy rubbed the sleep from her face. "Kimi?"

"I want my papa."

Amy climbed from the bed and knelt next to Kimi. "Oh, sweetie. Come here."

Kimi hurried forward and buried her face in Amy's neck. "I had a bad dream."

Amy scooped her up and squeezed her lightly. "I'm so sorry, honey. Here, I'll take you to your papa." She carried Kimi out of her room and to the room next to hers, hesitating at the door before knocking lightly. "Chouza? Chouza, Kimi's looking for you."

A moment later, the door opened to Chouza in only a pair of loose-fitting pants. "Amy? Kimiko, what's wrong?"

Kimi lunged out of Amy's arms and into Chouza's. "Papa, I had a bad dream and woke up and you weren't there and I was scared."

"It's okay, Baby. I'm here now." He glanced at Amy. "I'm sorry. Did she wake you?"

Amy smiled sadly at Kimi and shook her head. "It's alright. She came into my room looking for you."

Kimi buried her face in Chouza's chest, sniffling lightly. "Can I sleep with you,Papa?"

"Of course, Baby. Thank you, Amy."

"It's not a problem." Amy stroked Kimi's hair. "I know what it's like to wake up scared and alone. It's not a feeling I would wish on anyone, but especially not such a precious child as Kimi."

Chouza studied her for a moment before nodding. "Thank you. Good night, Amy."

"Good night."

Chouza stepped back and shut the door, murmuring calming words to Kimi as Amy returned to her own room, heart fluttering.

After that, Amy struggled to fall back asleep. Every time she closed her eyes, Chouza's bare chest rose to her mind.

Finally, near her usual wake time, she gave up and made her way downstairs. Jax raised an eyebrow when he joined her by the front door. "You look like you didn't sleep last night."

Amy shrugged. "Kimi woke me up early this morning. She had a bad dream and was looking for Chouza. I guess she got confused in the middle of the night as to which room was his."

"Poor dear. Is she alright?"

Amy nodded. "It seems so. I took her to him and he calmed her down." Unbidden, heat rose to her cheeks as she again remembered Chouza's bare chest.

Jax smirked. "Something else happen?"

"What? N-no!"

Jax chuckled. "If you say so. Let me grab some breakfast and we can go."

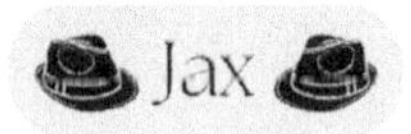

When Jax and Amy returned to the manor, Amy led the way up the stairs and to their suite. Jax nearly ran into her when she froze in the doorway.

"Amy?" He leaned around her, trying to see what had caused her to freeze.

In the suite, Chouza was doing one-armed pushups with Kimi sitting on his back. She grinned when she saw Amy and Jax. "Hi Ms. Amy! Hi

Mr. Fox-man! Papa's doing his morning exercises!"

Chouza glanced up at Kimi's words. "Oh. Amy. Jax. Hop off, Kimiko."

Kimi bounced off Chouza's back and ran to Amy. "Hi, Ms. Amy."

"H-hi Kimi."

Chouza stood and Jax studied his bare chest appreciatively, admiring the way his muscles bunched under the thin, sweat-slicked gray fur. He glanced at Amy, chuckling at the flush spreading from her neck up to her cheeks. *It seems I'm not the only one that finds him attractive.*

"Where have you two been?"

Amy's eyes were wide as she stared at Chouza, mouth opening and shutting, but no words emerging.

Jax nudged her. "He asked where we've been."

"U-uh. We were watching the hot man— I mean touching the reset— I mean watching the reset!" Her face flushed a deep red.

Kimi giggled. "Ms. Amy, you're funny!"

Jax snorted. "Yes, Amy. Absolutely *hilarious.*"

Amy glared at Jax, face still bright red. "Very funny, Jax."

I don't think I've ever seen anyone crushing that hard. His gaze returned to Chouza, once again admiring his features. *Though I can't really fault her, even if he's not quite my type.*

Chouza grabbed a towel, wiping it across his face. "So you went to watch the reset, then?"

Amy kept her eyes averted from Chouza. "Yes. We did. We do every morning."

Kimi tugged on Amy's hand. "Kind of like how Papa does his exercises every morning!"

Jax raised an eyebrow. "Oh, so you do this *every* morning"

Chouza set the towel aside and took a drink of water from a glass on the table. "Yeah. Usually right after breakfast. Kimiko helps me out."

"Yeah! I'm his helper!"

Amy smiled down at the little girl. "That's very sweet of you, Kimi."

Chouza set the drink aside and sat down on the floor. "Kimiko, time for sit ups."

"Okay, Papa!" The little girl ran over and sat down on Chouza's feet as he began lifting his chest to his knees, then resting back onto the floor. "One! Two! Three!"

Amy focused on Chouza again, her mouth a slight 'o' as she watched him. Jax glanced at her from the corner of his eye. *If I didn't know any better, I'd think he was showing off.*

Jax tapped Amy's shoulder. "Amy, were you going to grab your drawing supplies?"

"What? Oh, right! Right, I was going to get those. Which means I need to go to my room. Which is over there. Behind Chouza." She gulped. "I'll uh. I'll just go do that." She edged into the sitting room, eyes locked on Chouza and Kimi.

Jax placed a hand over his mouth, straining to keep his laughter contained as he watched Amy enter her room. *By the gods, she's adorable.*

A moment later, she re-emerged clutching her sketch pad and the bag containing all of her pencils. Chouza paused in his work-out and smiled over at her. "See you later, Amy. Jax."

"Y-yeah. See you later, Chouza," she squeaked, hurrying away. "Bye, Kimi."

"Later, Chouza. Kimi." Jax followed her out as Kimi called her own goodbye from inside the room. He waited until they reached the stairs before smirking at her. "And here I didn't think you could get any redder."

"I don't know what you're talking about," Amy mumbled, ducking her head.

"I'm sure you don't." He mellowed slightly and glanced over. "You know, Amy. It's alright if you find him attractive. That's not a bad thing."

Amy squeezed her sketchbook tighter to herself. "I don't know what's wrong with me."

"Wrong with you?" Jax stared at her shock. "Amy, there's nothing *wrong* with you. Chouza is a very attractive man. I'd be more worried if you *weren't* attracted to him."

"But I can't focus when he's around. All I want is to touch him!" She covered her face with one hand. "I want *him* to touch *me*. And hold me. I *never* want that!"

"Amy? Have you never had a crush before?"

Amy lowered her eyes. "I guess not."

Jax squeezed her hand. "It's alright, Amy. It's natural to be attracted to other people. It isn't *wrong*."

Amy glanced at him sharply. "But I can't focus when he's around!"

Jax gave her a soft smile. "It's alright, Amy. Maybe you should talk to him about it. After all, he could feel the same way."

Amy's cheeks reddened again. "I can't talk to him about that! He might think I'm daft or something. Especially after what happened at the Pits."

"Amy. I promise you, Chouza doesn't think you're daft. If I were to guess, I'd say he thought the exact opposite." Despite his words, Jax couldn't help but wonder what she meant about something happening at the Pits.

She glanced at him from beneath her lashes. "You think so?"

"I can almost guarantee it."

"Mister Jax, Miss Amy."

Jax squeezed Amy's hand again before turning to the staff member that had addressed them, a young blond man named Colin. "Yes?"

"Sir Austin wishes to see you in his forge. He says your weapons are ready."

Amy's eyes widened. "Really?"

"Yes, ma'am."

Jax raised an eyebrow. "Let's go see, then, shall we?"

The two exited the manor. Far ahead of them, Nolan and Kila were already entering the froge.

"Wait up!" Talia called from behind them. Jax and Amy paused, waiting for her to catch up before they continued. "So new weapons, huh?"

Jax smiled reassuringly at her when he heard the uncertainty in her voice. "It would seem so."

She ducked her head, twisting her hands nervously. "I still don't know if I can actually use it."

Amy squeezed her hand before quickly releasing her. "It will be fine. With Chouza joining us, you and I can stay back. You don't have to lift a weapon if you don't want to."

Talia's hands relaxed and she sighed. "I feel bad relying on others to fight for me, but the idea of hurting living creatures…"

"It's abhorrent," Amy agreed, voice bitter.

Talia rubbed her arm. "The last dungeon was okay. Those creatures were already dead and brought back by unnatural means. But that's not going to be the case going forward, is it?"

Jax shook his head. "No. I don't suppose it will be. It's alright, though, Talia. You don't have to change your morals. We'll take care of you as best we can."

Talia's fingers traced the holy symbol around her neck. "I know."

Nolan and Kila were already examining their weapons carefully as Austin explained their features when Jax, Talia, and Amy entered the forge. "The blades are reinforced with magick, so they're unlikely to break even under the greatest strain."

Nolan lifted his longsword to the light, turning it to study the edge. "I must say, your craftsmanship is remarkable."

"Thank you. I take great pride in my work." He gestured to the table where Jax's new rapier, Amy's staff, and Talia's spear lay. "Why don't you go ahead and try yours out? They're reinforced for now, but as you wield them, they'll start attuning to your inherent magick, allowing them to grow in power as you learn your abilities."

Jax lifted the rapier, testing the balance and grip. "Well, it's no Shinzo, but it is quite comfortable in my hand. Thank you Sir Austin."

Austin frowned. "Please, just Austin. I never liked that title and I hope to never end up next in line to take Uncle's position."

"Indeed." Jax watched as Amy hovered her trembling hand over the staff before taking a deep breath and lifting the deep red wood from the table. Immediately, flames licked along its length. "Amy!"

"It's alright. It won't hurt me." She ran her hand along the staff and the flames flicked out wherever she touched, leaving just the ends alight. "Thank you, Austin."

Austin dipped his head. "It's my pleasure. Good luck, Amy."

Jax raised an eyebrow at their interaction as he fastened the sheath to his new blade onto his belt. The door behind him opened and Chouza stepped in wearing a pale blue tunic. "Sorry. Had to get Meadow to watch Kimiko."

"Not a problem, Chouza. Your blade is hanging over there." Austin nodded toward a wall of weapons and Jax followed his gaze. On that wall, miscellaneous weapons that didn't fit anywhere else were displayed: swords with rings, nine-section whips, poleaxes, etcetera, and on one side, what looked to be two longswords joined at the hilt.

Chouza grinned and lifted the blades from the wall. "Impeccable as always, Austin. I assume it's been sharpened recently?"

"Each weapon gets checked at least once a week for rust. Yours was sharpened as soon as we heard you were joining us," Austin assured him.

"Good to hear." Chouza gripped the swords with his left hand facing down and his right hand facing up, then twisted them. With a click, the two pieces separated, leaving him with dual longswords. "Even the separating mechanism still works wonderfully."

"I take great pride in my work."

Nolan sheathed his own blade and stepped forward. "Perhaps now we can get a true demonstration of your talents, Chouza?"

"Happy to." Chouza clicked the blades back together and settled the hilt on his shoulder.

Jax glanced at Amy and nearly laughed aloud at the awe on her face. He touched her hand gently and she jumped. "What?"

"Want to watch a demonstration?"

Her eyes darted to Chouza, Nolan, and Kila leaving the forge. "S-sure."

Out in the training field, Chouza settled into a readied stance, his right hand facing up near the guard of one blade, his left hand facing down near the guard of the other right at shoulder-length apart. He faced one of the training dummies and spun the blade around him, his hands and shoulders moving quickly in a pattern Jax had no hope of following. Electricity arced around the blades as they spun.

Without warning, he lunged forward, one of the blades swinging down to dig into the training dummy's right shoulder. In the same motion, he followed through and the other blade swung in behind it, hitting the head. He pivoted and repeated the action, one side of his sword hitting the left side and then the second blade following through.

Charred lines stretched from the base of the dummy across the grass where the electricity had entered the ground.

Everyone stared at Chouza in shock as he once again spun the blades before settling it back on his shoulder, the electricity dissipating. Suddenly, his wiry muscles made more sense. He needed to be able to move quickly with the blade to use it to its full potential, but he also needed the strength to deliver debilitating blows with it.

He grinned. "Satisfactory?"

Nolan cleared his throat, blinking rapidly. "T-that's quite satisfactory. But the true test will be combat. I'll withhold full judgment until we've entered the next dungeon."

Chouza chuckled. "Of course." He walked back to Jax and Amy.

Again, Amy was just staring in awe when Jax bumped her hip with his. "What did you think?"

"Amazing," she breathed before blinking and snapping her jaw shut. "Uh. Great. It was great."

Jax covered his mouth quickly, hiding his laughter behind coughing.

"Are you alright, Jax?" Chouza asked as he stopped in front of them.

"Just fine. Just a bit of dust in the air. Isn't there, Amy?"

"What?"

"I said there's a bit of dust in the air, isn't there? After all, you must have tasted it with the amount of time you stood with your mouth open."

Amy's coral skin flushed a deep red and she ducked her head. "I don't know what you're talking about!"

"I'm sure. Come on, it's about lunch. Let's go eat. You'll be joining us, Chouza?"

"Yeah. Just let me drop my sword off in my room and pick up Kimiko."

Jax studied the blades appreciatively as they walked, the hilt resting on Chouza's shoulder. "I must say, this seems highly impractical."

Chouza chuckled. "It is, to an extent. Normally, I carry it in dual hilts just for travel. But if I know I'm going into combat, I like to keep them connected like this."

"It's certainly a unique blade."

Chouza shrugged. "My mother brought hers from Calionisia. It's fairly common there. She taught me and when I arrived here, Austin studied the mechanisms and replicated them. He even made a few improvements like reinforcing the connecting point and adding magick."

"That's quite interesting. I look forward to seeing what you can do with it in battle. I'll just be sure not to stand too close." Jax chuckled. "After all. It appears it could be just as dangerous to someone standing too close."

"That's probably a wise decision," Chouza agreed.

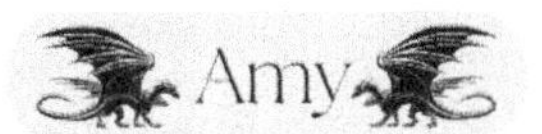

Amy rubbed her face, trying to wipe the memory of Chouza's bare chest from her mind. She hadn't expected to see him when she stepped into the sitting room that morning and had barely been able to formulate any words during lunch. Relief filled her when she realized she could head to her lesson with Inzo.

I still feel like something is wrong with me. Or maybe… Maybe Jax is right. I do really like Chouza. A lot. But a crush? I can't imagine him feeling the same way. He has a daughter for gods' sake!

Far quicker than she anticipated, she arrived in front of the Wizards' Library. She waved to Kukuri as she passed the counter and made her way to the training room. Inside, she found Inzo sitting on one of the benches.

"Ah, Amy! Have you fully recovered?"

Amy quickly took stock of her magick pool and her own body, nodding confidently. "Yes, Master. Yesterday's rest has completely rejuvenated me."

"Good. Then perhaps you would like to tell me about that scarring on your back?" His face and voice remained gentle.

Amy flinched back. "W-what do you mean?"

"The deep burn scars on your back. Would you care to tell me how you came by them?"

Amy quickly shook her head. "How? How do you know about those? I'm always so careful!"

"Yes, but when you overdid it the other day, your tunic shifted while I was carrying you." He stood and approached her. "Little Dragon, what happened to you? Those are from far before you got here."

"I-I don't want to talk about it." She took a step back, wanting to flee again.

"It is why you are so afraid of your fire, isn't it?" At Amy's stiff nod, he gestured her forward. "It's alright, child. I won't pressure you. But why didn't you tell me before? I could have helped you overcome it."

Amy shook her head again. "It's not something I want to talk about. I just want to learn how to control my fire so that I won't ever hurt anyone else."

"I understand, Young Dragon. But sometimes you need to make allowances for yourself. And sometimes your past is far more important to your future. If you don't wish to tell me, I will not push you. But I am here to listen if you are willing to talk."

Amy gnawed at her lip, clutching at her shirt. "My family died in a fire. I… I was the only one to survive."

Inzo stepped forward and wrapped his arms around her. "I am sorry, Little Dragon. And to suffer in silence for so long…" Her stiff body slowly relaxed as she tucked her head under his chin. "But you are not alone now, little one. I will certainly be more careful with how I teach you. Triggering your trauma will not help you." He pulled back and held her at arms' length. "Let us continue."

"Wait, can I ask a question?"

"Of course."

"Why was so much of my magickal energy depleted when I cast the spell the other night? I should have been able to do it a few more times before I ran out, but it felt like so much of my magick was dumped into that one spell."

Inzo nodded. "I wondered if you would notice that. It is good that you have such a strong connection to your magick. It did take more because you had to use extra magick to place the barrier around me. And that magick was expended when it did its job. Does that make sense?"

Amy frowned, nodding. "Will it always take that much out of me? I'm not sure how practical that is if I can only do it a time or two before

I pass out."

"It won't always be that way, no. The more you practice, the less magick will have to go into the barrier, allowing you to more efficiently use it. It will always drain you a little more than just casting the spell would, but eventually, you will be able to spread the barrier so thin, you will barely notice it."

Amy sighed in relief. "Alright. Then let's get to it."

"Are you alright if we continue the way we did it before? With me as your target? As you have seen, I am not in danger."

Amy gnawed her lip a moment before nodding. "That's fine. As long as I won't hurt you."

Inzo quickly cast his spell and the two resumed, Inzo coaching her on how to thin the barrier without breaking it.

She had successfully protected him twice, but the drain on her magick had been severe, causing her to sway each time. After the second time, Inzo shook his head. "That's enough for today."

Amy sank down onto a nearby bench. "Does everyone struggle this much?"

"No," Inzo said, and Amy's heart dropped. "Usually it takes them even longer. And most of them have been using magick for a much longer period as well."

Amy looked up in surprise. "Wait, you mean—"

"You have come further in the four lessons I've been teaching you than most pupils do in months or even years of training. Admittedly, I usually only do weekly lessons with them, but even so." He smiled, the skin around his eyes crinkling. "Be proud of yourself, Amy. You are doing impressively well."

Amy returned his smile, then pushed to her feet. "I should head back. If I leave now, I'll be able to join the others for dinner." She hesitated, realizing she knew very little about the Kushen man outside of his dragon type. "Unless… perhaps you would like to join me for dinner at a tavern? I would love to visit with you over a meal."

Inzo shook his head. "Alas, I can not. My wife is home preparing our own dinner and I promised the kids a story tonight. Perhaps some other time."

"You have kids?" She remembered Kukuri mentioning something about that the day before, but had been too exhausted to think about asking.

Inzo's face lit up. "Aye. A three year old little girl named Aleah and a ten month old boy named Yugo. They are my pride and joy."

"They sound lovely. I won't keep you from them any longer. Thank you and goodnight, Master Inzo."

"Goodnight, Little Dragon." He stood and they walked out of the library together. He turned right, deeper within the Wizards' Guild, whereas she went left to head back to the manor.

When she arrived at the manor, she spotted Jax, Chouza, and Kimi on their way to the dining hall. Frowning, she remained just out of sight, not wanting them to see her yet. The sight of Chouza once more sent a thrill through her body, her hands itching to touch him. She waited silently as they left her sight before making her way upstairs, asking a passing staff member to prepare a plate for her and apologize to the group, citing exhaustion. She wouldn't be able to do that the next day since she didn't have a lesson, but she would certainly use that excuse for now.

She froze at a knock on the suite door. "Lady Flame?"

Amy hesitated a moment before opening the door. "Nolan?"

"Hello, Lady Flame. I know you said you were tired, but do you have a moment?"

Amy sighed and stepped back into the room, gesturing him in. "What do you need?"

Nolan followed her in, glancing around appreciatively. "Something occurred to me."

Amy's eyes narrowed, her palms growing slick. "And that is?"

"I knew you seemed familiar. And the way you talk, it's much too proper for you to be the commoner you pose as."

"What are you talking about?"

Nolan faced her straight on. "You're Amelia Pruitt, aren't you?"

Amy's heart stopped. "I-I don't know what you're talking about." She backed toward her bedroom door.

"You are, aren't you? The lost heir to the Pruitt family fortune?"

"I-I…" She straightened and gritted her teeth. "So what if I am? I'm just another traveler here."

Nolan blinked. "Well yes, I suppose so."

"Are you going to take me back there if we break the curse? Get the reward for me going to jail?"

Nolan's brow furrowed. "Going to jail— Lady Flame, why would you go to jail?"

Amy's arms wrapped tightly around herself as she fought to block out the memories of screams filling her ears and smoke clogging her nose. "I killed my family! It was my fault!".

Nolan shook his head. "No, you didn't."

"What?" The horror faded and she stared at Nolan, her heart skipping a beat.

Nolan gestured to the couches and Amy hesitantly followed him. "Someone by the name of Ryder Cross has been the caretaker of the estate for the last ten years, but for the last two, the second-born, Damien Pruitt, has been in charge."

Amy's eyes widened. "D-Damien? He's alive?"

Nolan nodded. "He was paralyzed from the waist down in the accident, but he's very much alive." He shook his head. "Did you not know?"

"N-no! They told me he was dead!"

"He's not dead, Amy."

Amy shook her head. "W-why would they tell me he was dead, then?"

"I don't know."

Her mind raced as she contemplated what he'd told her. *Is he lying to me? But why would he lie? What does he have to gain? If he convinced me to go back with him, it'd be easy to turn me in and get the gold for my reward.*

She jumped to her feet, backing away from him. "You're tricking me!"

"I'm not—"

"No! You're tricking me! They told me he was dead. You just want to get me back there so you can get your reward and get in the King's good graces!"

Nolan flinched and his face hardened. "Think what you will." He stood and approached the door. "Good night, Amy."

Once a plate was brought to her, she ate quickly, then slipped into her room, her mind in turmoil. *He has to be lying. If he's not and Damien is alive, then I abandoned him when he needed me most and the doctors lied to me. No. He's lying. He's just trying to trick me into going back with him. That's all.* She curled up on the bed, biting her knuckles to keep from sobbing. *I can't even go check. To go back to Zadia now, I'd lose so much time if he is lying. I could get caught. But if I don't go check and Damien is alive, I'd never forgive myself.*

A knock on her door some time later startled her.

"Amy? Are you still up?" Jax called through. Amy remained quiet, hoping he would just go away. "Amy?"

"Y-yeah. I'm here."

"Can I come in?"

Amy sat up and wrapped a blanket around herself. "Go ahead."

The door cracked open and Jax stepped inside. He frowned as he settled at the foot of the bed. "Are you alright?"

Amy rested her chin on her knees. "I don't know."

"What's wrong?"

Amy bit her lip. "Y-you know who I am, right?"

Jax's brow furrowed. "You mean that you're Amelia Pruitt? I'm aware. Why?"

"Nolan recognized me."

"Is that bad?"

"I-I don't know. He tried to tell me my brother was alive. But he can't be alive, can he? He died! I know he did!" Tears welled in her eyes and she wiped angrily at her face. "He's lying. He's just trying to get me back there so that he can get the reward. Right?"

Jax edged closer to her and reached over to take her hand. "So wait, you… you had a sibling?"

Amy gripped his hand tightly, choking back tears. "A little brother. He was a few years younger than me. My father was teaching me to take over so they tried to keep him out of the public eye. They wanted him to have a fairly normal childhood."

Jax stroked her hand gently, studying their clasped hands

contemplatively. “How do you know for sure that he died?”

Amy’s grip on her legs tightened and she buried her face between her knees. “The doctors told me. They said I was the only one that survived.”

“I see.”

“I want to believe Nolan. I miss my brother so much. I do. But if he is alive, I *abandoned* him. Our parents were dead, he needed me, and I left. I abandoned him.” A sob escaped her throat and Jax wrapped her in a loose hug. “What kind of sister would I be if I abandoned my own brother after our parents died and our home burned down?”

“A sister that didn’t know any better. You were told he was dead. You wouldn’t have been able to know if he was or not.” He paused, squeezing her shoulder gently. “Besides, if he were alive, surely they would have told you in the time you were recovering?”

Amy gnawed her lip, shifting uneasily as she wondered if her leaving too soon had stopped her from learning that her brother had survived. “I— P-probably.”

Jax pulled back slightly to look down at her, his head cocked. “Amy… Just how long were you in recovery?”

Amy pulled away from him, ducking her head. “A week,” she whispered. “I ran away after a week.” Jax’s eyes widened, but Amy continued, unable to stop the torrent of words. “It was my fault! They were trying to find who did it and they were going to arrest them. I-I panicked! I didn’t know what to do, so I ran!” Her body trembled as she blurted the words, rocking back and forth on the bed.

Jax gently rested his hand on her leg. “Hey. Hey, it’s okay. But what do you mean it was your fault? What could you have done that could have possibly put you at fault for any of this?”

Amy fought back another sob, struggling to breathe. “Our tutor’s lab was in the basement. He canceled our lesson for the day, but I went down anyway. I-I knocked into a table and something fell and then everything exploded.”

Jax gently gripped her shoulder. “Amy? Amy, look at me. You’re safe. It’s just me here.” She tore her gaze up to meet his. “Everything will be okay.”

Immediately, her body stilled and she was able to take a deep breath again. She took a few breaths and closed her eyes, leaning her head against his shoulder. "Thank you, Jax."

Jax wrapped his arm around her shoulder again, resting his head against hers. "It's what friends are for, right?" She sniffled and nodded. "I promise, Amy, I'll always be here for you. I'll always be your friend."

"And I'll always be yours." She stayed where she was, listening to his heart beating. "What do I do? What if Nolan's telling the truth?"

"I… I honestly don't know about your brother. I'm not that knowledgeable in the business circuit, but the only name I've heard related to the Pruitt trading company outside of your own was someone with the last name of Cross."

"That's my father's cousin Ryder. I-I think he took over after my family died."

"I see." He rubbed her shoulder gently. "Well like I said, I've only heard his name associated with your family's business so if your brother is alive, he's either being hidden behind your cousin, or it's possible that Nolan *might* be lying. But I don't know either one for sure. Though at the same time, how would Nolan know you had a brother? You said your family kept him out of the public eye, right?"

Amy shrugged. "Other noble families knew of him. He attended a few balls with us and other things like that. It's not completely impossible that Nolan's father knew his name."

"Well even with that said, why would Nolan think to mention your brother at all?"

Amy pressed closer to Jax. "I-I don't know. To lure me back? After all, if my brother were alive, of course I'd go. It'd be an easy way to get me back there. To get the reward."

"Maybe. But why specifically mention your brother? If he truly wanted to trick you, then surely he would have tried to make it even more enticing? Said the rest of your family was alive as well?" He shook his head. "But again, I don't know anything for sure. But to me, Nolan doesn't seem like the type to lie to get what he wants. Not really."

Amy's mind raced at Jax's words. *Why would he only talk about Damien? I mean, obviously if he mentioned my father was alive, that wouldn't make sense. He would be running the business, not Ryder. But my mother, maybe? Why just Damien? And he knew his name. He could be taking the opportunity, but who's to say we'll even make it out? What's to gain from this now?*

"If you want, maybe once we leave here, we can try to find out together?"

Amy jumped at his words, pulled from her thoughts. "W-what?"

"Well, after we're free from here? If you wanted at least, I can help you find out about him. If he is… dead, or maybe he really is alive."

Amy gnawed her lip, his heartbeat helping to keep her grounded. "It's taken me twelve years to get from Zadia to here. I'll never make it out if I go back now…"

"That was twelve years by yourself, though. Many of them as a child. Maybe together we can half that. I'm willing to travel that distance to help you get the closure you need. One way or the other."

Amy closed her eyes, relaxing into Jax's arms. "Okay. Thank you, Jax."

"As I said before: Anything for a friend."

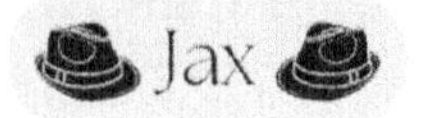

Jax studied his hands as he walked back from breakfast with his father. He coudln't explain what happened the day before. Amy had been distraught and he only wanted to calm her. Then, he'd felt his magick release and Amy was calm again. *Was that my doing?*

When he stepped into the manor, Nolan and Kila were disappearing down the hall to the back door. Pushing his musings aside, he hurried forward. "Nolan, could I have a word?"

Nolan slowed and kissed Kila on the cheek. "Go ahead. I'll catch up." Kila scowled, but continued walking, leaving him to wait for Jax. "What can I help you with?"

"I talked with Amy last night. She said that you know who she is."

Nolan's arms crossed. "I do."

"Did you mean what you said? About her brother?"

"That he's alive?"

"Yes."

Nolan sighed. "Yes, Jax. I meant what I said. Amy's brother is alive and well. He started taking over the family business about two years ago."

Jax's eyes narrowed. "Then why was Amy told that he was dead? According to her, she was told that her entire family was dead after the accident."

Nolan threw his hands up. "How would I know? Because they were jerks? All I know is her brother took over and they're still looking for her, but she's presumed dead at this point."

Jax raised his hands placatingly. "I'm not meaning to upset anyone. Just… Amy was telling me about what happened. I just wanted to hear both sides for myself. Amy can be a bit emotional when it comes to her past."

Nolan scoffed. "You've got that right. Is that all you needed?"

"Yes… I suppose that's all." He turned away but paused. "Actually, one more thing. Knowing this information, what do you plan to do with it? Do you plan on doing what Amy fears and turning her in for the reward? Or…" He gestured vaguely around them.

Nolan snorted. "You mean if we survive this hellhole?"

"Yes. Let's assume we do. What do you plan to do with that information afterward?"

Nolan gave an exasperated huff. "I don't know? Nothing? What *should I do?* Look, if you want to ask me something, just ask. Don't beat around the bush."

Jax rubbed his face. "Basically what I just said. Do you plan on turning Amy in?"

"Turning her in *where?* They're trying to find her because she's missing! If she doesn't want to be found, then who am I to judge?"

Jax's eyes narrowed. "What exactly is the reward *for?*"

"She disappeared right after Lord Charles and Lady Annette were killed. She was badly injured, but just up and disappeared in the middle of the night. Most people assume she's dead, but a few of them refused to give up."

"So it's not a warrant? It's simply a search and retrieve?"

Nolan shook his head, brow furrowed. "A warrant? Why in all of Zeaggatha would it be a warrant?"

Jax sighed. "Because of a guilt-ridden little girl who misunderstood her situation."

"What are you talking about?"

Jax met Nolan's eye. "I want your word that nothing of this conversation will reach the ears of the others. This is *Amy's* past we're talking about. No one else's. I don't want anyone pressuring her into revealing details she's not comfortable with."

"Yeah, sure. Whatever."

"Amy put the blame of her family's death entirely on herself. She's been running all these years because she thought they wanted to arrest her."

Nolan stepped back. "What? No. They caught the man responsible for the explosion. She was just as much a victim as the rest of her family."

Jax's ears perked up. "What?"

Nolan shrugged. "Not many details were released to the public. Just that the alchemist whose lab had exploded had been arrested and later hanged. I mean, there were rumors, but nothing concrete."

"I-I see. And no one knows why it was the alchemist charged? Everything I had heard said it was just an accident."

Nolan shook his head. "No, it definitely wasn't an accident. I do know there were explosive reagents in that lab. Something beyond what a private tutor should have. He was hanged for murder and treason. Beyond that we weren't given any details. It was a pretty big deal amongst the upper class for years."

"Obviously… Thank you, Nolan. You've given me quite a lot of information. I won't keep you any longer. I'm sure Kila's already agitated enough at me for interrupting your morning."

Nolan nodded. "Right. Well, have a good day." He followed Kila, leaving Jax to contemplate his words.

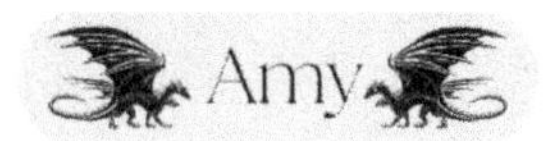

Amy perched on a rooftop with Jax as they waited for the reset to start. The previous day had passed surprisingly uneventfully. She had gotten up after Kimi woke her again and watched the reset with Jax, then had lunch with the group, and while Jax had his lesson with Inzo, she'd trained a bit more with Chouza. Each time he'd touched her, heat had spread through her and she wanted nothing more than to have his arms around her. She still didn't know what to think about it.

Nolan hadn't looked at her the entire time. She'd almost apologized on several occasions, but the fear that he would use it to manipulate her kept her from saying anything. Even still, she wondered if he'd told her the truth. Her heart wanted to believe him, but her mind said it was impossible.

Even as Amy carried on a conversation with Jax, she could tell his mind was elsewhere. She gently touched his arm. "Hey, what's up?"

"Hmm?"

"It's obvious something's on your mind."

Jax gave a self-deprecating chuckle. "Yes, I suppose it is." He hesitated and she watched him curiously. "I… spoke to Nolan yesterday."

Amy stiffened. "About what?"

"I wanted to know what information he had and what he planned to do with it."

Amy's eyes widened and filled with tears. "What? Why would you do that?"

"I was worried about you. Please, just hear me out."

"It wasn't your place to talk to him." She looked away from him, watching as the reset began. "Vide." The world around her grayed as signs of magick coated each person, giving them a pale glow. Fascinated, she watched them racing around her, leaving silver trails behind.

A pulsing ripple of pitch black magick spread from further in town, then another, and another. About a mile in the direction the ripples came from, a deep gray tower stretched into the clouds.

Jax followed her gaze. "What *is* that?"

"I'm not sure."

Hurriedly jumping from the rooftop, she followed the ripples to the park she and Chouza had taken Kimi to. The ripples seemed to originate from the fountain in the center, but the tower itself had disappeared. As she got closer and closer to the fountain, an invisible force, like a strong wind forced her steps to slow until she couldn't get any closer.

Jax braced himself behind her. "I don't see anything now. But I'm sure I saw some kind of building here earlier."

Amy nodded. "I saw it, too. Did you use a spell to watch the magick?"

"Yeah." The resistance from the ripples stopped and Jax stumbled into her, knocking them both to the ground. "Sorry."

"It's fine." She stood and brushed the dirt from her hands as Jax turned in a circle, studying their surroundings. A grassy field surrounded the fountain with a ring of trees even further off. Nearby, an old, rickety gardening shack broke up the field.

"We're in the Great Park."

"Yeah. We brought Kimi here." The ethereal quality faded from the few people in the park as they resumed their daily activities.

The fountain stretched at least fifty feet from edge to edge. Stones circled the shallow pond and large koi fish swam inside. In the center, a pillar stood with a large winged figure atop it. Larger than a human, its features hinted at beauty, though an otherworldliness made her want to avert her eyes.

Frowning, she studied the rest of the fountain, indulging the natural instinct to look away from the statue. No magickal energy radiated from either the statue or the fountain itself, leaving no indication of the tower appearing there. Not only that, but the tower had been much larger than the fountain. It didn't add up. She allowed the spell to dissipate and color returned around her.

Jax followed behind her, circling the fountain curiously. "I wonder where it came from. Or where it went."

"I don't know. But I think we should talk to the Arkhams about it. Maybe they know something."

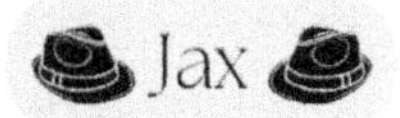

Jax frowned as Amy deftly dodged Fredkrikson's swing, hurrying past him once he'd moved out of the way. Fredrikson watched her go, guilt lining his face. Jax sighed and shook his head, following after Amy. She paused at the bottom of the stairs, then continued around them to the hallway behind.

Jax hesitated, glancing between the stairs and Amy. He had assumed they would talk to Arkham. "Where are we going?"

"Lillian is almost always out in the gardens at this time of day. I'm going to talk to her."

"How do you know that?"

"She told me."

"What?"

"One morning when I was out in the gardens, she told me she spends her mornings out there because it lets her be close to nature."

"Oh." He trailed after her, once again wondering about the secrets that surrounded her.

Once they stepped out of the manor, Azurys peeled from her tattoo form and Amy reached down to scratch her. "Could you find Lillian for me?"

The little cat mewed and took off into the underbrush while Amy waited.

Jax looked between them. "Aren't you going to follow her?"

"Not until she's found Lillian."

Jax raised his hands in surrender. "Alright, then. Don't elaborate."

Amy sighed. "I told you before that I can sense her emotions. So when she's satisfied, I'll know she's found Lillian."

"Oh." Jax covered his face, suddenly feeling very dumb. "Sorry."

Amy shrugged and resumed her study of the surrounding gardens. "Speaking of." She started down a path and Jax hurriedly followed after her.

Lillian's voice filtered through the trees as they followed the winding path. "Is Amy looking for me?"

Azurys meowed.

"Oh. She and Jax?"

Another meow.

"Are they okay?" Amy rounded the corner and Lillian stepped forward. "Is everything alright, Amy?"

"Everything is fine. We were just wondering if you knew anything about the tower that appeared in the center of town?"

"Tower? What tower?"

Jax's eyes darted between Lillian and Azurys, who sat nearby with her tail curled over her paws. *Was she talking to Azurys? And understanding her?* He cleared his throat and refocused on the conversation. "It appeared over the fountain in the Great Park?"

Confusion colored Lillian's face. "Fountain?"

Amy sighed. "I guess that answers that question."

"Sorry. I don't remember there being a fountain there before the war. You could maybe ask Father? If it was built recently, he'll have a record of it."

"Alright. Thank you, Lillian."

"Sorry. I do wish I could be of more help."

"Lillian." Lillian and Amy both turned to look at Jax questioningly. "Were you talking to Azurys just before we got here?"

Lillian nodded. "Yes, of course."

"O-of course? That's news to me!" He gestured at Azurys. "How was I supposed to know you could talk to animals?"

Lillian chuckled. "Sorry, Jax. I'm a druid and my link with Tsume has helped me learn to understand felines specifically pretty efficiently. Other animals I have to use a spell to understand."

Jax pinched the bridge of his nose. "I swear, the more I learn, the more I realize how little I know."

Amy chuckled. "It's magick, Jax. I've learned that if I lower my expectations of how much I actually understand, the new stuff isn't quite so overwhelming."

Lillian smiled sympathetically at him. "Sometimes I forget that all of you didn't grow up with magick as part of your daily lives. For me, some of my earliest memories are of my mother flying with us. Or of my father healing our cuts with his magick. It's always just existed for us. It's… strange to think of it not being commonplace."

"It's alright, Lillian. The outside world lacks much of what makes this city so magickal. And magick itself is only one of them." Jax glanced at Amy in surprise at her words. She seemed almost… wistful.

Lillian squeezed Amy's hand. "Like I said, you should talk to my father about that fountain. He should know what you're referencing."

"Alright. Thank you, Lillian."

After bidding Lillian goodbye, Jax and Amy followed Azurys back through the winding path to the manor. He stole glances at Amy whenever he could, still trying to figure out the secrets she kept hidden and how to continue their earlier conversation. When they reached the hedge between the garden and training field, Amy stopped, staring out onto the field.

Following her gaze, Jax spotted Chouza warming up, arms stretched out to his sides as he did lunges. Even from a distance, Jax could see the muscles rippling beneath the thin fur of his chest.

He glanced back at Amy again, nudging her gently when she remained stock-still. "Amy. Are you coming?"

"W-what?" She jumped and shook her head quickly. "Yes. I'm coming." She gave Chouza one last glance before following Jax.

"Amy, are you ever going to talk to him?"

"I talk to him all the time."

Jax sighed, shaking his head. "I swear, you would be frightened of a rabbit if it so much as looked at you wrong."

Amy glared at him and he chuckled, leading the way up the stairs and to Arkham's office. Talia met them at the second floor landing. She waved and hurried to catch up with them. "Where are you two headed?"

Amy smiled at the other woman. "Talking to Arkham. How are you this morning?"

Talia shrugged. "Doing well. I spent the night at Vallun's again. He wants me to move in with him."

Jax frowned. "Already? You've only been dating for a week!"

Talia fidgeted with her fingers, not quite meeting Jax and Amy's eyes. "I know. And I know it's probably rushing things, but… we don't know if we're going to survive these next dungeons and well… I want to spend time with him while I can. And if things don't work out, well, it's not like I can't move back in here."

Amy stepped forward to wrap Talia in a tight hug. "It's alright, Talia. You don't have to explain yourself to us." She pulled back and held Talia at arms' length. "Does he treat you well?" Jax stared at her in shock, never expecting to see her initiate such close contact with anyone.

Talia's cheeks flushed. "So well. He makes me breakfast most mornings and calls me 'angel'. He's so sweet."

"Then that's all that matters to us," Amy assured her. "If you're happy and he treats you well, then we're happy for you. Right, Jax?"

Jax blinked, pulled from his shock by her words. "Right. You're happy, we're happy."

Talia smiled shyly. "Thank you. Both of you. It's nice that someone at least supports me." She glanced back toward the suites again, her face falling.

Amy pulled her into another hug. "Sorry, Talia." She stepped back. "Where are you headed now?"

"Umm… I'm not actually sure," Talia admitted. "I didn't really have a destination in mind. You said you're headed to talk to Arkham?"

Jax nodded. "We found something this morning that we wanted to talk to him about."

"Not the Sins again, I hope?"

Amy shook her head. "No. Something else. Do you want to come?"

"Sure." Talia followed Amy and Jax up the stairs where Amy paused before knocking on the door frame.

Arkham looked up from the paperwork on his desk. "Amy? Come in."

Jax saw Amy swallow hard before stepping inside. "Sorry to bother you, sir, but something happened that we think you should know about, if you don't already."

"Have you encountered the Sins again?"

"N-no." Amy glanced at Jax and he placed his hand on her shoulder. "We were near the Great Park and we noticed a tower appear over the fountain there during the reset. It disappeared quickly, though."

Arkham's eyes narrowed. "A tower?"

Jax rested a hand on Amy's shoulder and took over. "Yes, sir. We were watching the magick underlying the reset and noticed it resonated from the center of the city. When we followed it, we found the fountain in the Great Park."

"There was also some kind of force keeping us from getting too close to the fountain once the tower disappeared," Amy added.

"I see. And you all saw this?"

Talia shook her head. "I wasn't there. I just met them here a few minutes ago."

"But both of you did?"

"Yes, sir."

Arkham frowned. "I know nothing of a tower that appears within the Great Park. Nor do I remember a fountain in that location. Can you describe it?"

Jax nodded. "It was a dark gray, almost black. I only caught a glimpse of it, but I couldn't tell just how tall it was. I know it was massive."

"As far as I could tell there were no windows, either," Amy volunteered. "But it looked old. Very old."

Arkham drummed his fingers on the desk for a moment. "I believe I will send my men to check on it. Thank you for bringing it to my attention."

"Yes, sir."

"Is there anything else?"

"No, sir."

"Very well. You are dismissed."

Amy quickly retreated from the room and Jax hurried after her. "Hey. Are you alright?"

"I'm fine," she assured him, but her nervous glance over her shoulder betrayed her.

Jax sighed and followed her to the stairs. Talia settled into step next to them. "So a tower in the Great Park?"

"Yes. Though I have no idea where it came from or where it went."

"Should we ask people in the city? I could talk to Vallun."

Amy glanced over at her, gnawing her lip lightly. "That might be a good idea. I have my lesson with Master Inzo this afternoon, so I'll talk to Balthazar about it. With his census, if anyone would know about it, he would. Though we don't want to scare anyone so maybe keep it kind of quiet until Arkham knows more."

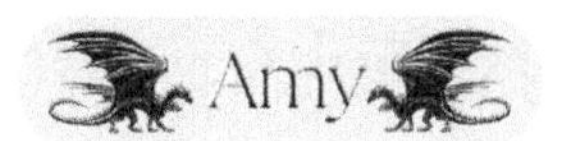

"Good afternoon, Young Dragon."

Amy smiled at Inzo's words and hurried forward. "Good afternoon, Master."

Inzo returned her smile, the skin around his eyes crinkling. "You did well last lesson. Are you ready to get started?"

"Actually, could I ask a question first?"

"Of course."

"You know the fountain in the center of the Great Park?"

Inzo nodded. "Yes. My children love to play in the field next to it. Why?"

"Do you know anything about a tower that appears over it during the reset?"

Inzo's brow furrowed as he contemplated what she'd asked. "Tower?"

Amy sighed. *If Jax hadn't seen it too, I would really think I'd imagined it.* "Yes. At the beginning of the reset a tower appeared over that fountain. Jax and I only caught a glimpse of it this morning, but I'm *sure* I saw it."

Inzo studied her. "Come." He left the room and Amy followed in confusion until he stopped and knocked on Balthazar's office.

"Enter!"

Inzo pushed the door open and waved Amy in. "Amy has some information I think you would find interesting."

Balthazar looked at Amy expectantly. She glanced at Inzo, then repeated what she'd told him.

Balthazar's frown grew at her words. "In the sixty years I've been here, I've never seen this tower, nor has anyone I've talked to mentioned it. You're sure you've seen this?"

"Yes! It was there, I swear! Jax saw it, too! You can ask him." The more they questioned her, the more irritated she grew. She knew what she'd seen.

Balthazar raised his hand. "We believe you. Could you show us where it was?"

"I suppose." She led them from the office and towards the front of the library.

Jax looked up from where he was reading on a couch in the entryway, his gaze going between her and Balthazar. "Amy? Did you already talk to him?"

Amy ducked her head. "Sorry. I know you wanted to join us, but I mentioned it to Master Inzo and he wanted me to tell Balthazar."

Jax stood and set the book aside. "It's alright, Amy. I understand. Where are you headed?"

Balthazar cleared his throat where he stood near the door. "She was just going to show us what she was referencing. You've seen it, too?"

"Yes, sir. I was with her this morning."

"Hmmm. Come along if you wish."

Jax glanced at Amy and she nodded gratefully. Once they reached the park Amy led them to the fountain. "It was here. Though much larger than the fountain is."

Balthazar stepped forward. "Sentio." Amy's brow furrowed at the unfamiliar word, but she didn't comment, simply watching Balthazar circle the fountain.

Jax followed after him. "It only appeared in the first few minutes. After that, it disappeared. And we couldn't get close."

Inzo remained near Amy. "Come, while they're doing this, we're going to continue training"

Amy looked around apprehensively. People wandered the park, some picnicking on the hill nearby, a guy tossing a ball back and forth with two kids. "But there are people here."

Inzo led her to a quiet hill nearby. "Yes. So we won't be practicing your magick. We will be attempting to unlock your claws." He lifted a hand and it shimmered, blue scales covering his forearm as his nails lengthened into claws.

Amy blinked. "O-oh. But I can't do that."

"You will be able to eventually. Maybe not yet, but we will try. Close your eyes. Now, I want you to picture a dragon. A red one to be exact."

Amy did as he said, conjuring up an image of a red dragon. One that looked remarkably like the one on Lady Arkham's back in the portrait Lillian had shown her the day after she'd arrived.

"Do you have it?" Inzo asked, and Amy nodded. "Good. Now focus on its claws specifically. Imagine how the scales must feel. How the fingers elongate to a sharp point. Then, funnel some of your magick into your hands, letting it transform them."

Amy tried to do as he said, but nothing happened and she opened her eyes, shaking her head. "I'm sorry, Master. I don't know if I can do that."

"It is alright. Try again?"

Amy attempted it again, but no matter what she tried, nothing happened. And even more, the sounds around her distracted her— the kids shrieking in excitement, the parents calling to them, the water trickling in the fountain— all of it combined into a cacophony of noise that she struggled to tune out. She shook her head. "I'm sorry, Master."

Inzo studied her and she watched as the blue faded from his skin and his nails blunted once more. "You are an odd one, Little Dragon."

"Sorry, Master."

"You need not apologize. It is simply a fact. Much of your capabilities defy the norm. You have no claws, or at least have not unlocked them yet, even though that is normally the first thing unlocked; you have a familiar, even though that is unheard of for a Dragon-Blood; you are a demon-spawn, which again is unheard of. You are certainly unique."

"Demonkin."

"What?"

Amy lifted her chin. "We're called demonkin. I don't want to be called a demon-spawn anymore."

"Of course."

Amy's brow furrowed. "It's unheard of for a demonkin to be a Dragon-Blood?"

"After I began training you, Balthazar and I started going through the records. All of what he had, as well as notes from back before the curse even hit. I've found no mention of a cross-blood." At Amy's confused look, he explained. "There are many different magickal creatures that can produce sorcerers, as well as create half-breeds, such as demonkin. There's devil-spawn, celestials, jynn-descended, etcetera. But usually if one of them shows inherent magickal powers, it corresponds with their ancestry. You, however, are a demonkin with draconic heritage. I'm not sure if it is because you were originally human and the Awakening brought forth the other blood or if you are just a unique case, but I can find no record of anyone existing like you."

Amy watched Jax and Balthazar talking near the fountain,

contemplating what Inzo had said. "I'm not the only Dragon-Blood to have a familiar."

"Oh?"

"Lady Arkham, Lillian's mother, had a familiar named Zeke."

"Lady Arkham was a Dragon-Blood?" Inzo frowned. "How did you discover this?"

"There are paintings of her in the manor with similar tattoos." She gestured to the tattoos on the backs of her hands. "And Lillian told me about her familiar when she met Azurys." At her name, the little cat's ears pricked, though she didn't look up from intently watching the fish within the fountain.

Inzo gave her a nod. "I do remember her portrait now. I never put much stock in the tattoos I could see as they were much larger than a normal sorcerer mark."

"Mine are as well."

Inzo looked at her in surprise. "I had assumed they were just on the backs of your hands, though even that would be odd. How far do they spread?"

"They wrap around my arms and cover the upper half of my back. After the last dungeon, they spread across here, as well." She traced a line beneath her breasts.

"I have read about tattoo-covered sorcerers, but I've never met one. Though I suppose I have now." He gave her a smile. "Do not worry, Little Dragon, there is nothing wrong. It just means that there are very few like you."

Amy sighed, glancing away. *Of course I can't just be normal.* "So then you must have a sorcerer tattoo as well?"

Inzo turned his back to her, letting the shoulder of his cloak and shirt fall to the side. On the back of his left shoulder, a blue dragon wreathed in lighting snarled at her. Though as the book had said, it was only about the size of the palm of his hand.

"So does that mean you use electricity?"

Inzo pulled his clothing back into place. "Correct Little Dragon. I am an electric blue."

"Balthazar! What are you doing out here?" A dark-haired woman approached where Balthazar took notes near the fountain. Jax stood next to him, occasionally pointing something out.

Balthazar looked up as she approached. "Felicia! How are you doing?"

"I'm well, Balthazar. I thought the days of you leaving the Wizards' Guild were gone?"

"I was just doing some research. I may be old, but I'm not helpless just yet."

The woman laughed. "So what are you researching now?"

"Just seeing if there was anything magickal here."

"I've never seen anything. What makes you think there is?"

"A tip I received. Though I'd have to agree with you that there isn't." He nodded toward where Inzo and Amy stood. "I'm sure you remember Master Inzo. And perhaps you would like to meet his newest pupil?"

Felicia made her way over to them. "Hello again, Master Inzo!" As she approached, Amy realized she was probably not much older than she and Jax, mid-twenties at most. Then she offered a hand to Amy. "Hi! I'm Felicia! If Master Inzo is training you, you're in good hands. He was my teacher a few years ago."

Amy shook the offered hand. "Oh. Are you a Dragon-Blood, then?"

"No, no. I'm a wind elemental sorceress." She grinned and lifted her hair to show Amy the wispy cloud tattooed on the back of her neck.

Inzo chuckled. "If I only taught Dragon-Bloods I'd have no pupils."

Felicia's eyes sharpened as she looked back at Amy. "You're a dragon sorceress?"

Amy's eyes flicked to Inzo nervously before she looked back at Felicia. "Yes. A red dragon."

Felicia studied her, but Inzo stepped forward, drawing her attention again. "I was just working on some combat training with Amy here in the park. Had to make sure Balthazar didn't collapse on the way here, didn't I?"

Balthazar muttered something about uncivilized youngsters, but Felicia just laughed. "Of course. Well, it was good seeing you again. And nice to meet you!" She waved to Balthazar as she left.

Amy gave a small sigh of relief before turning back to Inzo. "So you don't just teach Dragon-Bloods?"

Inzo shook his head. "Of course not. In fact you're only the third Dragon-Blood I've taught." She caught a flash of pain on his face, but he quickly hid it. "I teach whatever sorcerer comes to me for help. There's several other teachers within the Wizards' Guild and we try to pair pupils with a teacher from the same bloodline, but it doesn't always work out that way, hence me teaching an air elemental."

"Oh. So do you have students other than me and Jax right now, then?"

"I do. Five others in fact. I teach them in the mornings."

"Oh. Am I cutting into your instruction time for other students?"

"The current adventuring party takes precedence so I am willing to give you two as much time as you need." He lowered himself to sit on the ground, seemingly content to take a break from training for the time being.

She glanced once more at Jax and Balthazar before settling into the grass next to him. "These other people you teach, who are they?"

"Residents from the city. Just because magick has died out in the outside world doesn't mean it has here. In fact, I generally have two to three new students a year. The other teachers get about the same. They each get a lesson a week for about two years. By then, they're at least confident enough to handle themselves. Then the adventuring parties have the occasional sorcerer as well. Those get the majority of our attention."

"So that's just sorcerers. What about those with studied magick?"

Inzo waved a hand. "That is beyond me. There are other teachers for them. If you are curious you could ask Balthazar."

"Ask me what?" Balthazar asked and he and Jax walked up.

Amy scrambled to her feet. "I was just asking about the other teachers for non-sorcerers."

"Ah. Yes, I actually have several wizards who teach students who want to learn magick, but show no blood magick."

Jax raised an eyebrow. "Maybe Nolan should do that."

Amy hadn't seen Nolan use magick much. *It might be a good idea to help him learn.*

Balthazar shrugged and tucked the book he'd been writing in into a bag. "It certainly wouldn't hurt for him to get some formal training if he has shown an aptitude for studied magick."

Inzo lifted himself to his feet. "Well, shall we head back?"

Balthazar nodded and the group began the trek back to the Wizards' Guild. "Unfortunately, Amy, I couldn't find anything to indicate that the fountain is anything but what it appears."

Amy shook her head. "I know what I saw."

"And I believe you. Which is why I would like to meet you here in the morning."

"That's fine." She indicated where she and Jax stopped that morning. "I'll meet you there?"

"Very well."

The four returned to the Wizards' Guild in companionable conversation. Having spent most of the afternoon traversing the town, Inzo spent the rest of their lesson reviewing the history of Dragon-Bloods and dragons themselves.

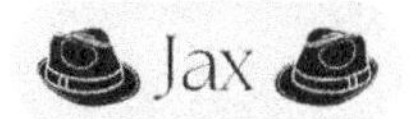

By the time Jax and Amy returned to the manor that evening, Chouza, Kimi, Nolan, and Kila had already settled in for dinner.

Kimi's eyes lit up when she saw them. "Ms. Amy! Come sit with me!"

Amy's eyes darted to Chouza, but she nodded and settled in next to the small girl. "Hi, Kimi. How was your day?"

"It was great!" Kimi began to describe her day of playing in the gardens and with the toys one of the staff had delivered to their suite as Amy listened patiently to her, a fond smile on her face.

Jax raised an eyebrow at the interaction but didn't call her on it, simply happy to see her happy. He still felt guilty about going behind her back before. "Have you been training any with your magick recently?" he asked Nolan.

Nolan shrugged. "I've been working with Gerald between combat practice and working with Austin in the forge."

"I figured. There's full teachers at the Wizards' Guild if you're interested. Not just the teacher Amy and I are learning from, but actual studied magick casters as well." He shrugged. "I just thought I'd mention it to you."

Nolan tapped his forefinger against the glass of tea in his hand repeatedly. "I may consider it. If nothing else, I wouldn't mind seeing this Wizards' Guild."

Kila huffed, stabbing a piece of steak on her plate viciously. "Sure. All of you can just go galavanting around the magick place. Sounds like an absolute blast."

Nolan nudged her gently and she growled before storming away from the table. Nolan sighed and shook his head. "Sorry about her. So you two are doing well on your magick training, then?"

Jax raised an eyebrow, surprised by Nolan's attempt to stop Kila. "Pretty well, yes. We can show you where it is tomorrow if you'd like."

"I may actually take you up on that. I'm struggling to figure out more than just the basics and I imagine having a teacher more suited to my style would help with that. Gerald seems to focus more on general magick, which is great, but I want to learn more about how to use it to enhance my fighting. Specifically how to use it in tandem with my sword."

"Very well. I have my next lesson tomorrow. You can join me. Will you be coming, Amy?"

Amy glanced between them nervously. "Umm. I was actually going to train with Chouza again. If— if you don't mind."

Chouza smiled down at her. "Of course not."

Nolan raised an eyebrow. "You're training her?"

Chouza shrugged. "She uses a staff which is what I was trained with. It makes sense for me to teach her."

"Good. We don't want another incident like what happened in Death." With that, he stood. "I'm going to go talk to Kila. Maybe I can calm her down."

Amy ducked her head and Jax fought back a groan. *Well it was going good…*

Chouza cleared his throat lightly. "So, training at the Wizards' Guild, huh?"

Amy flushed, glancing up at him through her lashes and Jax struggled to keep from laughing. "Um, yeah, actually."

"I never really understood all that magick stuff. What are you working on?"

"I'm trying to learn how to manipulate my magick around my allies so that I can hurt enemies without hurting them."

His eyebrows rose. "Wait. You can do that?"

"Not very well. But I'm working on it! And yes, it is definitely possible."

"Huh. Well that will be handy. It would be nice not to worry about scorched fur." Amy flinched and Jax could see the guilt on his face. "Sorry. Didn't mean to upset you."

Amy just shook her head. "I'm heading up to bed."

Kimi tugged on Amy's sleeve. "Ms. Amy, will you read me a bedtime story tonight?"

"I—" She glanced at Chouza helplessly.

"You don't have to."

Amy glanced between them before her face softened. "I'd be happy to."

Kimi squealed in delight and jumped to her feet, tugging Amy's hand until she followed after her. "I want you to read the one about the prince that got turned into a frog!"

Amy chuckled and trailed along after her. "Oh I know that one."

Jax watched her go. "Kimi seems to like her."

"She adores her," Chouza agreed, watching Amy and Kimi's retreating forms with a smile. "I'm happy, though. She doesn't have a maternal figure around and I hate that."

Jax raised an eyebrow. "You like her, too, don't you?"

Chouza chuckled, rubbing at the back of his neck sheepishly. "I suppose I do. But Kimiko loves her and that's the most important thing."

"Yes, I suppose it is."

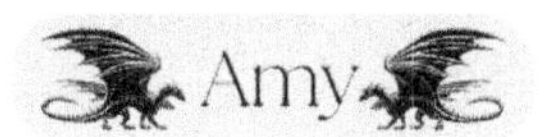

"Goodnight, Kimi." Amy smiled and quietly slipped from the room with Chouza, surprised to see Jax seated on the couch with a book.

He glanced up when the door closed and set the book aside. "You get her to sleep alright?"

"She passed out less than five minutes in." Amy chuckled. "Poor thing was tired."

"Must have had quite the eventful day."

Chouza shrugged. "Nothing out of the ordinary. Just a lot to do here."

Jax stood and stretched. "Yes, I suppose there is."

They visited for a bit before each of them disappeared into their own rooms. Only a moment passed before there was a light knock.

She opened the door and sighed. "Hi, Jax."

Jax leaned against the frame. "Do you think you could bear to pick up the conversation from earlier?"

Amy ducked her head, fiddling with her hands. "I-I guess…"

Jax followed her into the room and settled onto the bed next to her. "I'm sorry I talked to Nolan without your permission, but there's apparently much more to the story than either one of us thought there was. For one thing, he doesn't appear to be lying about your brother."

Amy's head jerked up. "You mean he really is alive?"

"From what I'm able to read off Nolan, I think it's quite likely your brother is alive. He doesn't seem to be talking in terms of rumors or hearsay, but actual facts."

Amy's hand covered her mouth. "H-he's alive?"

"It… would seem so. There's also other news I learned from him as well."

Amy's eyes widened. "There's more?"

Jax sighed. "Quite a bit."

Amy leaned forward, grabbing his arm. "What else?"

Jax rubbed his neck, remaining quiet for a moment. "You know how you said there were people looking for you?" Amy recoiled, but Jax continued. "Apparently it's not for what you assumed."

Amy's brow furrowed. "What do you mean?"

"They weren't coming after you with a warrant. There's no warrant at all. The only people looking for you are those looking out of concern for your safety, not wanting you arrested."

"I-I don't understand."

"I don't believe your accident was an accident." Jax's expression remained gentle as he watched her. "According to Nolan, the alchemist that tutored you was arrested for treason and murder."

"Mr. Duncan? But why?"

"Apparently there were explosive regents in that lab. Stuff that a private tutor shouldn't have had. And certainly not in a lab that children had access to."

"Oh… But it was still my fault… The table?" She fought back tears, staring up at Jax.

He opened his arms in invitation. She hesitated a moment before leaning into him. "I don't know, Amy. No one knows exactly what happened that day. But if I were to guess, he always meant to hurt you and your family. That's probably why he canceled your lesson that day, so that he wouldn't be there."

"But why?"

Jax gently rubbed her arm. "Maybe because of your father? He could have been hired by a competitor to scare your father away from a deal? I don't know. But whatever the case, it wasn't your fault."

Amy's hand covered her mouth as she fought back sobs. Twelve years of pent up guilt and fear bubbled to the surface. "I abandoned my brother… How could I do that to him?" Unable to stop herself, tears flooded down her cheeks.

Jax's arm tightened around her. "You didn't know any better. You were scared and in pain and they told you he'd died. You are not to blame here. Not in the least."

He continued to hold her as sobs wracked her body, until finally, she'd exhausted herself. "Thank you, Jax."

He continued to gently rub her arm. "It's not a problem, Amy. I'll always be here for you."

She sniffled before turning to wrap her arms fully around him, burying her face in his chest. "I owe you so much."

Jax stiffened a moment before returning the hug, holding her tightly. "You don't owe me anything, Amy. You're my friend and that means I'll do whatever I can to help you. And when all of this is over, I'll help you get back to Olkbus to see your brother if that's what you want."

"I do. If…" Amy's voice cracked. "If he'll see me, that's what I want."

"Then we need to break this curse and get out of here. Get some rest, Amy. We have a lot of work ahead of us still."

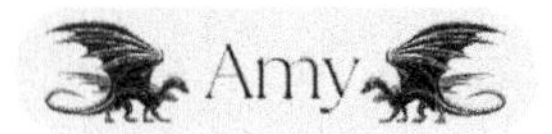

The next morning, Amy met Jax by the front door before dawn. With a curt greeting, the two made their way through the mostly deserted streets to the park. Balthazar was already studying the fountain, the tip of his staff glowing with light magick. He looked up as they approached and met them about a hundred yards from the fountain.

Amy gestured to it. "Find anything new?"

Balthazar shook his head. "Unfortunately, no."

Amy had expected the answer, but it was still disheartening. She led the two of them over to where she'd noticed the gardening shed the day before, studying it critically. Despite its rickety appearance, the shed seemed in good repair and well used. Pleased, she climbed up to perch on top, her feet dangling off the front. Jax raised an eyebrow but followed her up while Balthazar chose to remain on the ground.

A few minutes passed and Amy recast her spell, watching as the world around her grayed. Suddenly, a pulse of energy pushed from the fountain, pressing Amy back, nearly knocking Jax off the roof, and causing Balthazar to stumble.

The tower appeared in front of them, much larger than the fountain itself. The smokey gray stone walls stretched high above them, with no windows or doors anywhere in sight. The square tower enclosed the entire fountain and cast an eerie shadow on the land beneath it. Amy shivered, her instincts screaming at her to run in the other direction. A single rune glowed brightly on the side facing her and she quickly pulled a piece of paper from her bag and copied it down.

Less than five minutes passed before the tower disappeared, leaving no indication that it had ever existed. Still, the same force kept them from moving any closer than their current position.

Beneath them, Balthazar blocked the wind with his arm, his eyes narrowed. "Well, you certainly weren't lying. I've never seen anything like it."

Jax helped Amy down from the roof before addressing him. "Surely *someone* must have noticed it by now?"

Balthazar shook his head. "I've seen no record of it anywhere. Nor has anyone I've talked to noticed it."

Amy frowned. "So it's something new?"

Balthaza drummed his fingers on his staff. "Perhaps, though what would trigger it to start appearing now?"

"I'm not sure." She held the paper she'd drawn the rune on out to him. "Do you know what this means?"

Balthzar shook his head. "I noticed that, too, though I've never seen anything like it. Would you mind if I took that with me?"

Amy passed him the page. "If you happen to figure out what it means, could you let me know?"

"Of course." With that, Balthazar went one way while Amy and Jax went another, the ripples of magick pulsing through them.

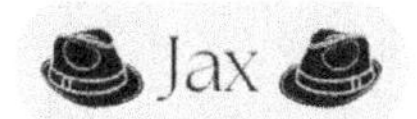

Jax glanced at Nolan as they approached the Wizards' Guild. "I'm glad you decided to come. Balthazar will likely get you a teacher perfectly suited to your magick style."

"I certainly hope so. I've been trained as a soldier, but magick has never even been a factor before. If I'm to best utilize it in battle, I need someone who knows how to do that." His eyes narrowed as they turned down the dead-end alleyway. "Jax?"

"Relax. It's a hidden entrance." He pressed his disc to the wall and stepped through the archway. "They want to protect the magickal items in here so they make it hard to get in."

Nolan studied the wall critically as he followed Jax through. "I see." His demeanor lifted, however, as they passed the merchant stalls. "Do we have time to stop? I would love to see what kind of magickal equipment they have."

Jax shook his head. "Sorry. If I'm to introduce you to Balthazar and still get to my lesson on time, we need to keep going. You can come back afterward, though. It's not like you have to stay while I'm with Master Inzo."

"True."

Once they reached the library, Jax took a breath and carefully replicated the words he'd heard Amy and Roxuh use to get them in. *I really need to learn this language.*

Nolan raised an eyebrow but followed him through. "Secret language, too?"

Jax nodded. "It's apparently the language of dragons. Those statues out front guard the library from anyone who would use the knowledge within the library for harm."

"Handy that." He stopped and stared up at the vaulted ceiling, mouth agape. "Now I don't know much about magick, but I'm almost certain this building wasn't this big."

Jax chuckled. "You're right. They've expanded it internally with magick. There's a lot magick can do, Nolan. You just have to be open to learning it." With a grin, Jax led him forward. "Kukuri? Where are you?"

The little blue-haired gnome jogged down the hallway. "Jax? What are you doing here? Shouldn't you be heading to your lesson?"

Nolan's eyes widened. "You're a gnome!"

"Yes, Captain Obvious. And you're a celestial. Now that we've got that out of the way..." She turned back to Jax expectantly.

Jax quickly covered his mouth, trying not to laugh at Nolan's flabbergasted expression. "I was going to introduce Nolan here to Balthazar. He's looking for a teacher."

"Oh, well why didn't you say so?" She grinned at Nolan. "Come right this way! Now off with you, Jax. You don't want to keep Inzo waiting."

Jax chuckled. "Have fun."

Nolan blinked. "Er. Right."

Inzo stood from the bench when Jax stepped inside. "Hello, Jax. Are you ready to get started?"

"Yes, sir." Clucking in the corner drew his attention and he raised an eyebrow. "Ummm… Sir? Why are there chickens here?"

"Those are so that you can practice seeking out multiple consciousnesses at once. Admittedly, they aren't the smartest creatures in the world, but I'm sure they will suffice."

Jax studied the half-dozen chickens. "Right…"

"First I want you to see if you can sense more than one at a time."

"Okay." Jax closed his eyes, casting his mind toward the chickens. He easily found the first, barely a spark compared to Inzo's usual blaze, and attempted to keep it within range as he sought out the next, once again finding the tiny spark. "I've got two." The strain to focus on the two already had a bead of sweat forming on his forehead.

"Good, good. See if you can get three."

Jax gritted his teeth, his mind straining to expand past the second. The chickens moved about their pen, making it even harder to keep ahold of the first two. His focus snapped and he dropped to his knees, gripping his head as a migraine pulsed behind his eyes.

"Easy." Inzo offered him a glass of water. "Did you get the third?"

"N-no. Two was the best I could do."

"Okay. We'll start there for the time being. Take a moment to rest, then try again."

"Yes, Master."

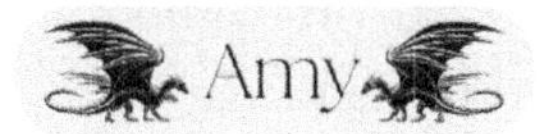

Amy followed Chouza back into the manor, her arms and legs sore. He had been teaching her more about her staff and how to use it to block attacks, deeming that more important for her to learn than how to actually fight with it since protecting herself meant staying in the fight longer to use her strongest asset: magick. She agreed, but it didn't make it any easier.

Chouza glanced over at her in concern. "Sorry about that last blow."

Amy shrugged. "It's alright. It was my fault for not moving quick enough." She'd been watching the way his muscles flexed and hadn't moved quickly enough to block a blow to her left thigh. A bruise had already formed and it throbbed painfully whenever she took a step. She tried, unsuccessfully, to hide her limp.

"Still. Might want to get Lillian to check on it. Just in case."

"Uh-huh." She spotted Jax with his head down on the table, ears drooping. Talia was nowhere to be seen and Kila sat next to Nolan, his arm looped tightly around her. "Jax? Are you alright?"

His ears flicked, but he didn't lift his head. "My brain hurts."

"Rough day at lessons?"

"Chickens."

Amy blinked and glanced at Chouza who looked just as baffled.

He pulled a seat out for Kimi and glanced at Jax. "I'm sorry, did you say chickens?"

"He wanted me to use my magick to seek out chickens." Jax groaned and sat up. "The bloody poultry barely have a consciousness to seek out, much less focus on."

Amy raised an eyebrow. "Well, that's… interesting."

"Annoying is more like it. They move constantly and then I have to adjust my consciousness to keep focusing on theirs and then it's an even bigger strain. And then he wanted me to do that all while I tried to cast my telekinesis spell!" Jax threw his hands up in defeat and dropped his head back to the table with a groan. "Bloody chickens."

Amy suppressed a smile. "I'm sorry, Jax."

He groaned and waved her off without lifting his head. "At least I don't have to go back for a couple of days."

Amy chuckled. "No, you don't have to go back for a bit." She turned to Nolan hesitantly. "Did you find a teacher?"

"I spoke with Balthazar. He's quite the… interesting character, isn't he?"

Amy chuckled. "He certainly is."

Nolan hummed agreement. "But anyway, yeah. He said he had someone in mind and sent a messenger to them. Said to come back tomorrow evening."

"I guess you'll be coming with me, then?" Amy gnawed her lip and glanced down at her plate, not entirely convinced she liked the idea of him infringing on her and Jax's walk to the Wizards' Guild.

"Appears so." He set his fork down. "That reminds me. I want everyone here in the morning."

Jax shifted his head enough to see Nolan without lifting it from the table. "Why?"

"Because it's time we start practicing as a team. We're all learning our abilities separately, now we need to learn to apply them together." He squeezed Kila's side before releasing her and sitting forward, his elbows resting on the table. "No offense, Chouza, but your blade especially concerns me."

"It's a valid concern. But I only use it the way I showed you when none of my allies are nearby. In any other situation, I use it as two swords."

"Good to know." He faced Amy and Jax. "We need to work on placement and how we work together. So after you watch the reset in the morning, could you please return here?"

"Uh, yeah. Sure," Amy agreed

Jax pressed himself up, resting his cheek on his fist. "I'll let my father know I won't be meeting him tomorrow, then."

"Good. Then let's get some training in."

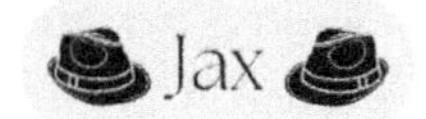

Jax frowned as he overlooked the park with Amy. Their usual quiet perch was now surrounded by people whispering and waiting anxiously.

"Seems word has spread." Amy's eyes narrowed and her hand fidgetted in her pocket.

"Yeah," he agreed. "People have noticed." He still wondered what changed for it to start appearing.

The sun peeked over the horizon and immediately the original citizens entered their usual reversal. The ash gray tower appeared over the fountain, encompassing the entire thing. Gasps and cries of fear echoed around them. Even those not using magick could see the tower.

Amy took a few minutes to start sketching it out and Jax alternated studying the tower himself and watching her. Once again, her eye for detail was exquisite.

The tower winked out of existence and the people around them slowly dispersed. A few eyed Amy on their way by and he intentionally put himself between them. Try as she might to keep her heritage hidden, rumors traveled fast amongst the guilds and the suspicion in their eyes left no doubt in his mind that they knew what she was.

When they entered the manor and asked about Nolan and the others, a staff member directed them to the training fields. Talia shifted uneasily next to Kila, who spun her dagger between her fingers, looking bored.

Kila bumped her shoulder against Talia's. "It's okay, Talia. Sometimes we have to do things we don't want to do. If it's for your own safety, don't you want to try?"

Talia sighed. "Of course I do."

Nolan grabbed a training sword from the rack of weapons. "Not only that, but we need to see how we work with our new member."

Chouza nodded approval as he stretched nearby. He smiled when he saw Amy and Jax. "Morning."

"Morning," Amy mumbled, cheeks heating. Jax bit back a smirk, amused by the shyness from Amy.

Nolan cleared his throat, pulling their attention back to him. "Alright, let's get started." He gestured Kila forward. "Alright, Kila, I want you to put your weapons down and fall backward, trusting that I will catch you."

Kila raised an eyebrow, one hand on her hip. "And why would I do that?"

"It's an exercise that they had us do back in Olkbus. If one member of a line falls, the entire unit does. We have to trust that if we stumble, the people next to us will cover us until we regain our footing."

"No." Amy's words were barely a whisper as she took a step back.

Jax's eyes darted to her. *This isn't going to end well.*

Talia stepped in front of her. "Come on. If I have to, you have to. You can always just watch."

Amy shook her head, her eyes wide and skin pale. "People don't touch me unless I want them to. This... This is not one of those occasions. I will run drills all day if that's what you all think will get us to survive the dungeons, but I will not do this."

Kila shrugged and turned her back to Nolan, doing as he directed. He stepped back, letting her fall flat on the ground. "And *that* is what our group is like right now," Nolan said, looking directly at where Amy stood gaping at Kila. "This is the first lesson. Our weapons and magick are useless if we do not know one hundred and ten percent that we can trust our teammates to be there when we need them most. Amy, thank you for proving my point."

Talia rushed forward, forgetting about Amy for the moment. "Kila! Are you alright?"

Kila sat up, glaring at Nolan. "I'm fine. Let me guess, that's what we're like now, but if I were to do it again, you'd catch me?"

Nolan nodded. "Exactly. I failed all of you in the last dungeon. My addiction nearly cost me my relationship with Kila as well as Amy her life." He offered his hand to Kila and pulled her to her feet once she took it. "That's the other lesson. When someone falls, we help them up. I forgot those lessons and I'm apologizing. Now I'm asking you to trust me again. Amy? Throw your weapon away and trust me to catch you." He waved her forward.

Amy backed away again, shaking her head. "No. Not happening."

"There has to be some similar exercise? Where she doesn't have to be touched?" Talia suggested.

Kila shook her head. "That's not the point."

"Amy stop!" Nolan commanded, and Amy's steps faltered. "What are you so afraid of?" He quickly closed the distance to grab Amy's wrist. "We need to work on this."

Amy's entire body trembled, her eyes wide. "Let me go! I told you, people don't touch me!"

"If you want to build trust, this is not the way to do it!" Jax tried to intervene, but Kila blocked his path.

She stood between them, her arms crossed. "Nope. You're going to let them work this out."

"What? No!" He tried to step around Kila again, but she moved quickly.

Nolan kept his grip on Amy. "I need you to trust me."

Amy struggled in his grasp, trying to rip her arm free. "Let go of me!" Chouza took a step toward them, his face angry and Jax shoved past Kila, but it was too late. Amy finally pulled herself free and backed away. "If you wanted to gain my trust by this show, you've failed! I don't trust anyone!" She bolted.

"Amy, if we don't work this out, we'll die!" Nolan called after her.

Jax froze, torn between chasing after Amy and staying to chastise Nolan. "What the hell, Nolan? She's uncomfortable enough as it is! Why did you have to do that to her?"

Nolan crossed his arms. "She needs to learn to trust us. And that means putting herself in uncomfortable situations."

Chouza hurried after Amy and Jax glared at Nolan. "Uncomfortable? You call that uncomfortable? She was close to panicking! You haven't built teamwork here. In fact, you've probably just driven her further away!" He rushed after Chouza. "Idiot!"

"It's no wonder Amy is so jumpy. She can't even feel safe in the manor," Chouza growled.

Jax shook his head sadly. "Amy's always been jumpy. But no, the way Nolan and Kila treat her doesn't make it any easier."

Chouza huffed, his fists clenched. "Either way, we should find her."

"I agree. Make sure she's okay. Let's split up. She can't have gotten far, right?"

"I certainly hope not…"

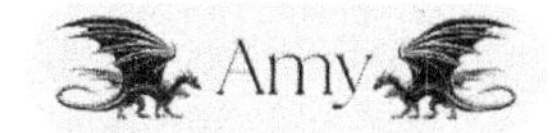

Amy rested her chin on her knees, absently watching the people moving about the street below her. She'd found a hidden nook on a rooftop and settled in, letting her racing heart slow and tears fall in privacy. She rubbed at the wrist Nolan had gripped absently, wincing as she brushed a sore spot. Azurys curled up against her back, purring.

Several hours passed in relative peace until she saw familiar gray fur approaching. She sighed but made no move to hide.

Chouza stopped and looked up at her, one hand shielding his eyes from the midmorning sun. "Do you do this often?"

Amy edged further back into the small bit of remaining shadow. "Do what?"

"Sit on rooftops."

Amy shrugged. "It lets me see all around while staying out of the crowd."

Chouza looked around at the aforementioned crowd. "I guess it does." He waited silently for Amy to say something. When she didn't he stepped closer to the building. "Are you alright?"

Amy gritted her teeth and looked away. "I'm fine."

"Amy, would you like somewhere to stay for a few days? Away from the manor?" Amy's eyes darted to him, suspicious but hopeful. When she didn't answer, he continued. "I still have my apartment if you want it."

Amy blinked. "Why?"

"I may not be a genius, but as I said before, I *am* observant. You clearly struggle being around other people. And Nolan doesn't understand that others might have a past that affects how they interact. I just thought you'd like a place to have some solitude if you wanted it. You *can* say no, though."

"No, why are you helping me?"

Chouza blinked, confusion coloring his features. "Why wouldn't I?"

"You don't know me. I'm no one to you." It hurt to say, but she couldn't understand why he kept offering to help her.

"Maybe. But you're still my teammate. And you seem like a nice enough girl. I also know that the dungeons take their toll on even the strongest person. To go into the next dungeon, you need to be at your best. And you aren't right now. I don't want you to die because of it. Plus, Kimiko really likes you."

She slowly slid from the roof to where Chouza stood waiting. "Thanks," she said quietly, careful to keep a short distance between them. Azurys followed her down, hopping from crate to crate until she reached the ground.

"It's no problem." He gestured for her to walk with him, heading in the general direction of the Fighting Pits.

Amy watched him from the corner of her eye as they walked in silence. Everything about him just drew her closer, even as she struggled to stay a reasonable distance away.

"Where are we going, anyway?"

"An apartment complex run by an old traveler's wife. Older travelers try to look out for the newer ones and she does so by keeping an apartment complex available for any who need a home. I found this place soon after I quit the dungeons."

"Oh. Well, that's nice at least."

Eventually, they reached another tall building with a sign out front labeled Evergreen Apartments. Chouza opened the door and waved Amy inside. The interior was nice, but not overly fancy. A portly older woman sitting behind a desk looked up when they entered, squinting as she tried to make out who they were.

Chouza smiled at her. "Hey, Glinda."

"Chouza? Is that you, boy?" Glinda's face lit up when Chouza nodded. "Well, I wouldn't have pegged you as a catfolk."

Chouza scratched his cheek with a sheepish grin. "Yeah, well, it's a form I'm not particularly fond of."

How could he not like it? The fur is probably soft and warm and the way his muscles move beneath his skin... He's beautiful.

Glinda gave him a fond smile. "Well what can I do for you? Have you decided to move back into your apartment? Where's little Kimi?"

"Kimiko's back at the Arkhams' manor still. I was hoping my companion here could use the apartment for a few days." He shifted enough for Glinda to see Amy huddled behind him, not liking the attention drawn to her. "Could she get a spare key to my apartment?"

"Your companion? Is she quitting the dungeons, then? She's a human."

Before Amy could answer, Chouza shook his head. "She's simply uncomfortable in her new form and prefers to keep herself in this one. She struggles with crowds and the manor has become difficult for her to remain in." Amy blinked in surprise. He hadn't told a single lie, but he made it sound as if she simply wanted a vacation.

"Of course, dear." She smiled kindly at Amy. "Such a young little thing. Come." She waved Amy forward, then leaned down to dig something from beneath the counter. Amy's eyes darted to Chouza and he nodded. When she approached, Glinda set a key on the counter in front of her. "There's always two keys to each apartment. Luckily, Chouza never needed the second."

"T-thank you." Amy took the key and slipped back behind Chouza.

"No problem, dear. I look forward to seeing you around here."

Chouza thanked Glinda and led Amy toward a stairwell to the left of the front desk. "Come on, I'll show you where it is." Amy gave Glinda a small wave before following after him, her arms wrapped tightly around herself and her head down. "You really don't do well in social situations, do you?"

Amy shook her head. "I don't like people looking at me, especially when I'm already uncomfortable."

"I've noticed."

Amy glanced at him from the corner of her eye. "You didn't tell her what I was."

Chouza's face softened. "Why should I? What I said was the truth. You are uncomfortable in that form, there's no need to make you feel worse about it."

"Thank you. Again. For all of this." She gestured around them.

"It's not a problem, Amy. I understand the need to get away from everything. From the pressure. For me, it's the Pits. You don't have that, so the least I can offer is a place to have some solitude. It's not as if Kimiko and I are using it right now anyway." They continued up another flight of stairs. "Though I do apologize for the long walk," he added with a chuckle. "My apartment is on the third floor."

Amy shrugged, rubbing her arms against the slight chill. "It doesn't bother me."

Chouza slid his overshirt off, holding it out to her. "It gets cold up here."

"Oh." Amy hesitantly took the shirt, draping it over her own shoulders. She took a deep breath and the smell of sandalwood and chocolate washed over her. Her eyes closed and she smiled as she breathed it in. The scent was so him that she couldn't help the flash of heat that washed through her. "Thank you."

Chouza quickly shook his head, but not before Amy thought she saw a flash of *something* in his eyes. "No problem."

Eventually, they reached the third floor and he stopped in front of the last door on the left. "Here we are. Apartment 313." He unlocked the door and pushed it open. "It's not much, but it's comfortable."

A small sitting room with an adjoining kitchen was immediately visible to her right as she walked in. A table sat low to the floor with four cushions around it in the corner. In the sitting room directly in front of her, two low couches framed a deep gray rug with a coffee table between them. In all, the entire apartment was no larger than the suites in the Arkhams' manor. Two doors led to the left and another led to a room off the kitchen.

"It's perfect," she breathed in awe.

"I'm glad you like it. The kitchen should still have some food in it, stuff that stays good for a while. One bedroom and the washroom are right through there," he said, gesturing to the doors on their left. He pointed to the door next to the kitchen. "Kimiko's room is through there."

"Thank you. I'll restock anything I use."

Chouza shrugged. "Don't worry about it."

Multiple paintings hung on the walls of the sitting room—one with a field of pale blue flowers, one a mountain range cloaked in fog, and the third a path through a bamboo forest—but she paused at a portrait of Chouza and a tall brown-haired woman cradling a tiny baby. "Is that…?"

"Kimiko's mother, Khiran. Yeah."

"I see where Kimi gets her height."

Chouza chuckled sadly. "Yes well, I guess I'll leave you be."

"You don't have to leave, you know." The quiet words slipped out before Amy could stop herself.

"Are you sure? I know you wanted solitude and I don't want to intrude on that."

"You don't bother me like the others do."

Chouza's smile was breathtaking. "I'm glad. But I need to get back to Kimiko. I've already been gone much longer than I'd planned."

"Oh."

Chouza hesitated with a hand on the door. "If you'd like, I could bring her back here and make lunch for you? Then if you still want the company, she can take her nap here. I'm sure she'd appreciate being back in her own bed."

Amy's heart lifted and she smiled tentatively at him. "Ok."

"Alright. Then I'll see you in a bit. I need to let Jax know I found you. He was helping me look."

Amy gnawed her lip, ducking her head. "You didn't have to look for me, you know."

Chouza started to reach for her, but hesitated and dropped his arms. "Yes, I did. What Nolan did wasn't okay."

"He just wants us to be a team," she defended half-heartedly, once again rubbing at the sore wrist. A faint bruise had already formed.

Chouza carefully reached forward, giving her ample opportunity to pull away. He took her hand and studied the bruise. "No. He wants to be in control. And anyone who doesn't fit his ideals, he tries to change. That's not how this should work."

Heat spread through her from the point where their hands touched up her neck and into her cheeks. "Sorry."

"You have nothing to apologize for." He released her hand and stepped back, clearing his throat. "A-anyway. I'll go get Kimiko and then come back."

Amy ducked her head to hide the blush. "Right. Just please don't tell the others where I am?"

"Of course."

"Jax can know. I don't mind if he comes to see me."

Chouza gave her a small smile. "Alright. I'll let him know. Do you want him to come back with me?" Amy bit her lip a moment, then nodded. "Okay. Then we'll be back in a bit."

"Okay."

Amy sighed in relief as the door closed and took a moment to study her new surroundings again, moving on to the rooms to her left. The first one opened to a bedroom dominated by a large bed with pale gray sheets. A double-bladed sword like the one Austin made for Chouza hung on the wall next to an armoire. Peeking inside, she spotted several more of the overshirts like the one she clutched tightly around herself in various shades of blue, gray, green, and brown, as well as plain cotton shirts.

Feeling guilty about snooping, she closed the armoire and stepped back out of the room. The second door led to a small, modest washroom with a privy and a basin for washing. She didn't see a tub, but assumed the apartment complex had a communal bath. Gray and light blue dominated the color scheme for the entire apartment.

Checking the third room, she chuckled at the bright pink decor. The small bed had pink sheets, a pink rug covered part of the floor, and pink curtains covered the window. A well-worn stuffed cat slouched on the pillow. A shelf to her right had a few bins with toys spilling out from them, as if Kimi had left mid-play.

She closed the door and stepped back into the kitchen, opening the curtains in the sitting room to look out over the busy street. Azurys curled up on the back of one of the couches, her tail twitching just in front of her eyes as she watched Amy. Sighing, Amy wandered the apartment aimlessly as she waited anxiously for Chouza to return.

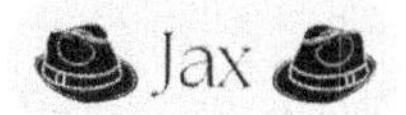

Jax paced in front of the manor, occasionally glancing toward the gate to the city. He had given up searching for Amy over an hour before, but there was still no sign of Chouza.

Finally, he spotted Chouza coming up the path. "Did you find her?"

He nodded, glancing around quickly. "She's alright. I took her back to my apartment so that she could have some time to herself."

Jax sighed in relief. "How is she?"

"She was pretty shaken up and I could tell she'd been crying." His face hardened. "And Nolan left a bruise, but otherwise she seems okay now."

Jax's fur bristled. "That ass was holding her hard enough to leave a bruise?" He glanced back at the manor. "I swear to the gods I'll kill him."

Chouza grunted. "Trust me, I'm with you there." He shook his head. "But that won't help Amy. I'm getting Kimiko and heading back over there. She said she'd like it if you came to visit, too."

"I wouldn't mind seeing that she's safe with my own eyes. As long as she's certain that's what she wants."

"It seemed that way. Just let me get Kimiko."

"Right."

By the time Chouza returned with Kimi in tow, Jax had calmed and was leaning against the porch railing. "Hi, Kimi."

"Hi, Mr. Fox-man!"

Chouza chuckled and squeezed her hand. "I keep trying to tell her your name is Jax, but she insists on using Fox-man instead."

Kimi tugged on his hand. "It sounds cool!"

Jax swished his tails and grinned. "I'm quite inclined to agree with you."

Kimi giggled and Chouza just shook his head, waving for Jax to follow him. "Come on. I'll show you where she is."

"Are we going to see Ms. Amy?"

"Yes, Baby. Ms. Amy had a bad experience this morning so she's staying at our apartment." Chouza stopped and knelt in front of Kimi. "But you can't tell the other adults, okay? She's scared and wants to stay where she's safe."

"Is Ms. Amy in trouble?"

Chouza glanced at Jax before placing a hand on each of Kimi's shoulders. "She's not in trouble, no. But Ms. Amy has a hard time with people and one of our teammates doesn't understand that. He did something that really upset Ms. Amy and she just needs a place to feel safe for a while, okay?"

Kimi's lip pooched out and her brow furrowed. "Okay, Papa. But we can still go see her, right?"

"Of course, Baby. As long as she's okay with us being there." He stood and offered Kimi a hand, which she took gleefully.

"Can I draw Ms. Amy a picture while we're there?"

Jax chuckled and offered Kimi his hand as well. "I'm sure she'd love that."

"Okay! Hey Papa, do you think Edgar is there?"

Jax raised an eyebrow. "Edgar?"

Chouza chuckled. "It's her little stuffed cat. I thought I packed it for her, but she can't find it and she's upset. I told her I'd check the apartment, but I hadn't made it out there yet."

"Edgar helps me sleep."

"I see." Jax squeezed her little hand. "Then let's hope he's waiting for you at home, then."

Jax followed Chouza through the streets, into the Northeast District, and past the Pits to a modest apartment complex. Chouza glanced up at one of the windows on the third floor and Jax followed his gaze to where Amy stood half-hidden behind a curtain.

She was already waiting for them in the doorway of apartment 313 when they reached the top of the stairs.

"Ms. Amy!"

Kimi ran forward and Amy leaned down to scoop her up, burying her face in her hair. "Hi, sweetie. How are you?"

"I missed you."

Amy squeezed her a little tighter. "I missed you, too." She lifted her eyes to Jax and Chouza. "Hey."

Jax sighed in relief; she looked better. "Hey."

She set Kimi down and stepped back into the apartment, waiting until everyone had stepped inside before closing the door. Kimi immediately ran for what Jax assumed was her room and he heard a squeal of delight.

"Papa, Papa, he's here!" She came running back with a fuzzy but worn, dark gray stuffed cat clutched in her arms. She bounced up and down and lifted it to show it to Chouza. "Look, Papa! Edgar is here!"

Amy chuckled. "Edgar?"

"He's my kitty!" Kimi clutched him to her again and spun in a circle. "I missed you, Edgar!"

Chouza ruffled her hair and chuckled. "Well now that we know where he is, we'll be sure to take him back to the manor with us."

"Okay, Papa!"

Chouza chuckled and ruffled her hair. "I'll start lunch. Would you like some tea?"

"That sounds lovely, thank you." Jax settled onto one of the low sofas across from Amy. "You cook?"

Chouza glanced at Kimi with a sad smile. "It's been just me and Kimiko for almost four years. I had to learn to cook to feed her."

"That makes sense."

Kimi scrambled up next to Amy, scratching Azurys. "Hi, kitty!"

Azurys meowed and pressed her head into Kimi's hand, causing the little girl to giggle before plopping into Amy's lap. Azurys stretched and jumped down to join her. Amy wrapped her arms around the both of them, resting her chin on the top of Kimi's head.

Jax chuckled lightly before refocusing on Amy. "How are you?"

Amy shrugged. "I'm better now."

He tried to subtly study her wrist, but she hid it under her other arm. "He bruised you."

"It's fine, Jax."

"No, it's not fine!" Jax lowered his voice. "It's not fine at all. He never should have pushed you like that, much less left a mark."

Amy's arms tightened around Kimi and she ducked her head. "Please just drop it, Jax."

Jax wanted to protest, but seeing how small and frail she looked caused him to pause. "Alright. I'll drop it. But I won't stand for this again."

"It won't happen again. I'll just have to try harder."

Chouza dropped the pot onto the stove with a clatter and crossed his arms. "No. No, *you* don't have to try harder. *He* needs to try harder to understand that not everyone is the same. What happened was *not* your fault. *You* have nothing to apologize for."

Jax blinked in surprise at the man's passion but quickly cleared his throat. "He's right, Amy. Triggering someone else's trauma is never okay. And then to hurt you because of it? Nolan was the one in the wrong here. Not you."

Tears welled in Amy's eyes as she looked between them. "Y-you're sure?"

Chouza walked over and knelt in front of her, carefully taking her hand. "I'm absolutely certain. Hurting someone because they're afraid is never okay."

Kimi nuzzled against Amy. "I'm sorry you were scared, Ms. Amy."

A few tears escaped Amy's eyes and she sniffed, quickly reaching up to wipe them away. "It's okay, Kimi. I'm better now that you, your papa, and Jax are here."

Kimi beamed up at her and Amy kissed her forehead. Chouza squeezed her hand gently before standing. "Here, the tea is almost ready." He pulled four glasses down from a cabinet and dropped some leaves into them, then poured the boiling water over them. Jax got up and helped him carry the four cups to the sitting room.

Chouza set a smaller cup in front of Kimi. "Let yours cool for a minute, okay Baby?"

"Okay, Papa. Can I go color in my room now?"

"Of course."

Kimi wiggled down from Amy's lap and skipped off to her room as Chouza returned to the kitchen. Azurys rubbed along Amy's leg before following Kimi. Amy cradled the cup of hot tea between her hands, watching the steam rising from it.

Jax set his cup aside and settled onto the couch next to her. "Are you planning to stay here long?"

Amy shrugged, but didn't look up from the cup. "Probably no more than a day or two. Just long enough to get some space. I need…" She glanced at Jax before returning to her study of the cup. "I've been on my own since… since my parents died. I'm not used to having so many people around constantly. And to not be able to leave if things get… difficult. Whenever someone questioned too much, or pushed too much, I'd just leave. Head for the next town. I can't do that here. I'm trying, but..."

"But that many years of habits is hard to retrain," Jax finished for her. "That was what? Twelve years ago?"

Amy's breath hitched. "Almost thirteen now…"

Jax closed his eyes, trying to keep the sadness from overwhelming him. *She's still so young. She was just a child then. To think she's been carrying all of this guilt and sadness for so long...* He finally opened his eyes again and reached over to cautiously take her hand, giving her ample opportunity to pull away. When she didn't, he closed his hands around hers and smiled gently at her. "I'm sorry, Amy."

"Lunch is ready," Chouza called from the table.

Amy jumped and some of the tea sloshed over her hands and his. "Oh gods! I'm so sorry, Jax! I didn't— I'm sorry!"

"Hey, hey! It's okay! Chouza, do you have a towel we can use?"

"Yeah, of course." Chouza tossed them a hand towel. Amy was shaking like a leaf and looked like she wanted to cry as she tried to dry Jax's hands and her own.

Jax took the towel from her and grabbed her hands. "Amy! Amy, it's okay, I promise."

"I'm sorry. I didn't mean to."

Chouza joined them at the couch and took one of Amy's hands. "It's okay. It was just an accident."

Amy kept her head ducked as tears dripped onto her and Chouza's clasped hands. "I'm sorry."

Chouza sighed and wrapped his arms around her, holding her against him. She stiffened but then relaxed into him as he stroked her hair.

Jax watched with a sad smile. "It's alright. I'm not hurt. My fur protected me from most of the heat. I'm more worried about you."

Amy pulled back from Chouza and looked down at her hands, completely clear of any indication of a burn. "I-I'm fine."

Jax's eyes widened. The tea had been hot and even through his fur, he knew his hands were scalded. But Amy's hands looked completely fine. "Well. That's good, at least."

"Yeah." She shook her head buried her face in Chouza's chest.

He gave her a light squeeze. "Come on, lunch is ready." He stood and offered Amy a hand up, which she hesitantly took. "Kimiko! Lunch is ready!"

The door to Kimi's room opened and the girl ran to the table, plopping down on her cushion. "What are we having, Papa?"

Chouza chuckled. "Just some fried rice. Not much was left here so I had to make do with what we had."

Amy stared at the plate of rice, carrots, and peas. "It looks great, Chouza. Thank you."

Chouza smiled at her and settled onto the cushion next to Kimi, leaving the one next to Amy for Jax. She hesitantly picked the mug of tea back up and took a slow sip, her muscles visibly loosening.

Chouza chuckled and took a drink of his own tea. "Relaxing, isn't it?"

"Very."

"Lillian gave it to me after I had trouble… coping with what happened in the dungeons." He glanced at Kimi and Jax saw pain twist his face before he continued. "I've used it sparingly since then."

Jax cocked his head. "How long have you been here?"

Chouza reached over to run his thumb across Kimi's cheek. "Since a few weeks before she was born. So right at four years now."

Amy set her mug down and lifted her chopsticks. "That's a long time to be stuck in the same town."

Chouza shrugged. "Maybe. It was hard the first few years, but it's a big city and there's plenty to do. Add in good friends and family and things could be worse. Some people have been here much longer."

"I suppose so," Jax agreed. But still, he could see the regret and sadness on Chouza's face as he looked at his daughter.

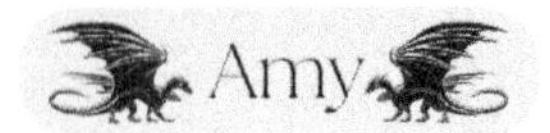

As lunch neared its end, Amy frowned and picked at her food. Jax took her hand. "What's wrong?"

"I'm supposed to have my lesson with Master Inzo today."

Chouza set his plate aside and took another drink of his tea. "Are you going?"

Amy ducked her head as guilt filled her. "Honestly? I don't want to."

"Then don't."

Amy turned to Jax in surprise. "What?"

"Don't." He shrugged. "If you don't want to go, then don't. How about I trade with you? I'll go today and you can go tomorrow instead?"

"Are you sure that would be okay?"

"I don't think Master Inzo would mind." He squeezed her hand. "He cares about you. If you need a day to rest, he's not going to complain."

"I… I suppose so. Thank you, Jax."

Jax chuckled. "Don't thank me. I'm getting an extra day of lessons out of the deal."

Amy smiled and shook her head. "I suppose so."

Jax set his plate aside and stood. "I do need to get going if I'm going to make it, though. Just let me know if you need anything, okay? You can send a runner to the manor at any time and tell them your location isn't to be revealed. The Thieves' Guild won't break that confidentiality."

"Okay. Thank you, Jax."

Jax searched her face before slowly leaning in to hug her. "It's not a problem, Amy." He pulled back and smiled. "Do you mind if I come back in the morning to see you?"

"Of course not. I'll look forward to it."

"Okay. I'll see you tomorrow, then."

After Jax left, Chouza lifted Kimi into his arms. "Alright, Kimiko. It's naptime."

"But Papa, I want to play with—" her words were cut off by a large yawn, "Ms. Amy."

Amy brushed a piece of hair from Kimi's face. "Don't worry, Kimi. I'll still be here when you wake up."

"Promise?"

"I promise."

Kimi nuzzled into Chouza's shoulder and yawned again. "Okay."

Chouza chuckled and carried her to her room. Once again, Azurys trotted after them and Amy shook her head. She quietly gathered the dishes from lunch and brought some water in to begin washing them. She had just set the last mug aside when Chouza stepped out of Kimi's room, gently closing the door behind him.

Amy followed him over to the couches and sat down across from him. "This place is amazing. You and Kimi live here by yourself?"

Chouza nodded. "I'm glad you like it. Occasionally I'll have a friend from the Pits visit, but for the most part, yeah, it's just us."

"It sounds wonderful."

"It is. The only disadvantage is the long walk up the stairs. It was annoying at first, but I started to consider it a fair trade-off for my love of chocolate." He chuckled. "After all, it helps me stay in shape."

"I can barely even remember the taste of chocolate. It's so expensive I could never afford to get it myself. And the ice cream was sweeter than I remember regular chocolate being."

Chouza stood, moving to a cabinet in the kitchen where he pulled out a bag. "Lucky for you, I kept some here. I took most of it with me, but I left this little bit here." He held the open bag in front of her. "Here."

Amy stared at him in shock. "I-I can't take that. It's not cheap and I don't want to eat what little bit you have."

Chouza shrugged. "Between my pay at the Pits and the bonus from the Arkhams, I have plenty of silver to buy more if I want. Go ahead."

Amy hesitated before pulling out a piece of chocolate, turning it in her hands for a moment. Chouza pulled one out as well, popping it into his mouth before making a sound of appreciation. More heat rushed through Amy at the sound and to hide her embarrassment, she popped her own chocolate into her mouth. Immediately, her eyes closed as the flavor washed over her tongue, a moan of pleasure escaping her. She had forgotten how much she loved it.

When her eyes opened again, Chouza blinked and quickly looked away, but Amy thought she saw her own heat reflected in his eyes. He cleared his throat and gestured to the bag sitting between them. "Go ahead and have another."

"I can't. Really."

Chouza rolled his eyes. "Stop worrying. I don't mind."

Amy only hesitated a second before taking the offer, this time able to suppress the moan that wanted to escape. She rolled the bitter-sweet morsel in her mouth, letting it melt and coat her tongue as she watched Chouza grab another piece as well, giving her a smile.

Once the chocolate in her mouth had completely melted, Amy lowered her head, watching him through her lashes. "I still don't understand why you're being so nice to me."

"You're a nice girl, you deserve to have someone be nice to you."

"I wish everyone thought that way." She looked away, studying the picture of the bamboo forest on the wall. "Nolan thinks I'm a thief and a liar. Or at least he used to. I'm not sure if he still does." Chouza let out a huff of annoyance. "I mean, he has a good reason, I suppose." She contemplated for a moment before pulling the pendant from her pocket, letting the light reflect off of it. "He's convinced I stole this from his room."

"That's a pretty necklace."

"It belonged to Arkham's son."

He raised an eyebrow. "The one who defeated the demon lord?"

"Yeah. As we were entering the town we came across this merchant who had it with him in a pretty box. Nolan and Kila basically threatened him to get it because of the way he acted when Jax wanted to know how much it cost. I picked it up to look at it, then put it back. Nolan took the box and that was the end of it, I thought. That night, I found the pendant in my pocket. I've not been able to get rid of it since."

"You've tried?"

Amy nodded. "Nolan even chucked it out the window. It was still back in my pocket by the next morning." She turned the pendant in her hands, studying the now familiar features, including the same rune she'd seen on the tower on the back. "The Arkhams still don't know I have it. Arkham was so suspicious of my new form that he would never believe that I didn't steal it or have some evil intention for it. I need to prove myself to him first. That I'm not like the Sins."

"You already have." Amy looked over at Chouza in surprise. "I've not encountered all of the Sins, but I've heard enough stories to know that if Nolan had pulled that stunt on one of them, he would have likely been no more than a corpse." Amy gave him a half-hearted smile but looked away. "You're a good person, Amy. Your blood isn't going to change that."

"I hope not." She tucked the pendant back into her pocket.

He studied her silently again. "You have a decent group, you know. If you could all just work together. Jax especially cares about you. After you took off, he chewed Nolan out on your behalf."

"I know. Jax is a good friend. He's always been the voice of reason."

"And Talia as well, I imagine. Seems like you need them both with the chaos of your group."

"We really do. We can't stop fighting amongst ourselves long enough to make a plan and it could have gotten us killed in the last dungeon."

"Yeah, Jax filled me in on what happened in there." He gestured at the bag again. "You can have another piece if you want it."

Amy immediately took the offer, reveling in the treat she'd been denied for so long. "If you aren't careful, I might eat all of it before I leave." The teasing surprised her, but she found herself relaxing around him, much more at ease than usual.

He grinned. "A worthy sacrifice. You know, you don't have to keep that disguise up here."

Amy wrapped his shirt tighter around herself. "It's just become second nature to maintain the magick by now."

"I bet. But you don't have to if you don't want to. I don't mind and I'm sure it drains you to keep it up."

Amy watched him silently for a moment before releasing the tether of magick, letting it sink back into her magick pool. Chouza glanced over as her form shimmered and gave her a reassuring smile. After a moment, he stood and made his way to the window.

Amy followed him, gazing out over the street. "You have a nice view." Sparks crackled through her where her arm just barely brushed against his.

Chouza pinned the curtain back and looked out over the street. "It's not the tallest building in the city, but it does warrant a good view."

"Yes, it does. Thank you, Chouza. Again."

"I don't want anything to happen to you because your teammates pick on you. That's not fair to anyone."

Amy smiled shyly up at him. "I appreciate it."

He cautiously took her hand. "You deserve so much more than what you've gotten. Just know that."

The warmth of his hand wrapped around hers felt so *right*. "I wish I could believe that."

Chouza gently placed a finger under her chin. "You do deserve it. And I'll keep telling you that until you believe it."

Amy flushed, heat rushing through her body as the desire to lift onto her toes and kiss him entered her mind. "Thank you, Chouza."

"Believe me, it is absolutely my pleasure."

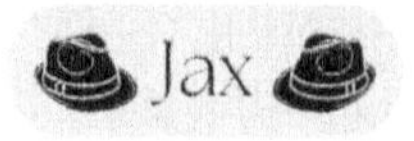

Jax hurried toward the Wizards' Guild, frowning when he spotted Nolan waiting for him by the alleyway. "Nolan? What are you doing here?"

"I have my lesson with my new teacher. I thought today was Amy's day?"

"It's supposed to be. But what happened earlier shook her enough that she didn't feel like she was in the right headspace for a lesson."

Nolan's eyes narrowed. "I never saw her return to the manor."

Jax entered the alley, not looking at Nolan. "She didn't."

Nolan fell into step next to him. "So where is she?"

"No offense, Nolan, but that's none of your business. She's safe and that's all that concerns you."

"She's a teammate, we should know where—"

"No. You lost all rights to knowing where she was when you gripped her wrist hard enough to leave a mark. She'll come back when she's ready."

"She shouldn't have left in the first place, we—"

Jax whirled on him with his teeth bared. "No! You don't get to dictate what we do. You may know combat, but you know *nothing* about us or our pasts. So get off your high horse and come on." He pressed the disc to the wall and stepped through, leaving Nolan to follow or not.

To his disappointment, Nolan followed. "We need to learn to work together."

"And part of that means learning boundaries."

Nolan crossed his arms. "No, it means pushing yourself out of your comfort level. We're going to die in those dungeons if we can't work together."

Jax stopped and took a deep breath, resisting the urge to punch Nolan. "No. Triggering Amy's trauma gets you *nowhere.* She. Isn't. Like. You. So stop trying to make her like you.

Nolan glared at Jax. "You think Amy's the only one with trauma? Try watching the woman you love killed right in front of you. Try being whipped to near death because you spoke out against her marriage to someone else. Then tell me about trauma."

Jax stepped back, eyes widening. "T-that doesn't—"

"We all have trauma, Jax. That doesn't make us any less likely to die if we don't work together now." He stalked toward the library, leaving Jax speechless in the street.

Yes… We do all have trauma. An image of a young girl with messy blonde hair and a missing eye flashed through his mind before he shoved it away and hurried after Nolan. *The difference is, not all of us use it as an excuse to abuse others.*

When they reached the library, Nolan waited for Jax to get them in, then followed him inside. Kukuri grinned when she saw them. "Jax! Why don't you show Nolan the training room?"

"Of course." Jax gestured for Nolan to follow him, still musing over what he had told him. The revelation made Nolan's drinking problem make more sense, but it still didn't ease Jax's anger at his treatment of Amy. He led Nolan down the hall and stepped into the large training room.

A brown-haired man Jax didn't recognize sat next to Inzo. They both stood when Nolan and Jax entered and the unfamiliar man stepped forward. "Which one of you is Nolan?" he asked brusquely.

Nolan offered a hand. "That would be me."

He took the offered hand and shook it firmly, his stocky frame larger than Nolan's. "My name is Daryl. But you may call me Mr. Holman."

Nolan nodded. "Yes, sir. And you can teach me?"

Daryl drew his sword. "Acidum Mundi." Acid coated his blade. "Satisfied?"

"You can teach me to do that?"

"And much more."

"Good." He waved to Jax. "See you later."

"Yeah. Later." He watched Nolan and Daryl move to the far side of the room before turning to Inzo.

"Today is Amy's lesson. Where is she?"

Jax hesitated. He hadn't considered what he would tell Inzo. "We traded."

"I did not agree to this."

Jax glanced over at Nolan, debating on how much to tell the man. "She's… not in a good place for a lesson today. Please, Master Inzo. Will you just teach me and let Amy come tomorrow?"

Inzo's eyes narrowed as he followed Jax's gaze. "Is Little Dragon okay?"

"Physically, yes. Just a bit traumatized. She needs rest."

Inzo's hand twitched, but otherwise he didn't react. "Very well. We will pick up with you, then."

"Thank you, Master."

"I do not have the chickens today, so we're going to focus on your telekinetic abilities instead."

"What do you mean?"

He picked up one of the stones nearby and held it on his open palm. "I want you to see how many of those you can lift at a time."

Jax groaned. "Yes, sir."

By the end of Jax's session, his pounding head made his vision blurry.

Inzo guided him to one of the benches. "You did well."

"If by well you mean horribly."

"You managed to get ten off the ground almost every time. That's impressive."

Jax gripped his head and dropped into the seat. "Off the ground. That was it. I couldn't do anything else with them."

Inzo settled next to him. "It takes practice, young Jax. You won't get all of it at once."

Jax sighed and leaned his head back against the wall. "I know, Master. I do. It's just so frustrating."

"I know. But you are doing well. And though I know little about your magick type, I would say you are progressing rapidly." He rested a hand on Jax's shoulder. "Only a little over a week ago, you could barely lift a single object. Now you can lift ten. That is progress."

Jax gave him a grateful smile. "Thank you, Master Inzo." He stood as Nolan walked toward them. "Nolan. Your session is done?"

Nolan rubbed his eyes and yawned. "Yes. Is this why you and Amy are always so tired after your lessons?"

Inzo studied him curiously. "Using magick is tiring. But like any other muscle, it grows stronger with exercise."

"Good to know." He ran his hand down his face before dropping his arm to his side. "Are you ready to head back?"

Jax rubbed his temple again. "Yeah, sure. Let's go." He gave Inzo a short bow. "I'll see you in a couple of days, Master Inzo."

"I will see you soon, Jax."

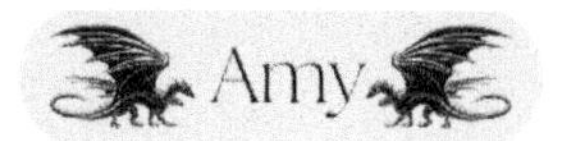

The time with Chouza passed in peaceful companionship until Kimi woke up. Then, she spent time playing with the young girl and Azurys. After dinner, Chouza pulled the curtain aside again to look outside. "It's getting late. We should head back to the manor."

Kimi's lip pooched out. "Awww. But, Papa! I want to stay with Ms. Amy and Azuweez!"

Chouza chuckled. "I know, Baby. But Ms. Amy came here to get some peace and quiet. We've already invaded that long enough. You can play with them tomorrow. Why don't you go get Edgar?"

"Oh, alright." Kimi huffed and trudged to her room.

Amy joined Chouza at the window. "You don't have to leave, you know. It's your apartment."

"We'll stay if you want us to, but I want you to get the chance for some privacy. It's up to you."

Amy didn't respond right away, gnawing her lower lip as she thought about what he'd said. *I came here for privacy, but now I desperately want him to stay. What is it about him that suppresses all of my usual aversions? I want nothing more than to lean against him and feel him wrap his arm around me.*

Chouza carefully touched her hand. "I don't mind either way."

"The problem is, I don't know what I want," she whispered. "I did want privacy, but you're so easy to talk to. I enjoy being around you." She dropped her gaze to the ground.

"I'm glad. And the feeling is mutual." She could feel his eyes on her as he waited for her to decide. The realization that he wouldn't do anything she didn't want him to filled her with gratitude.

"I think… that you should go back to the manor." If he stayed, she wouldn't be able to resist the urge to be near him and she wasn't quite ready to explore what that meant yet. Chouza nodded and stepped away. "Before you go, though, can I do something?"

"Sure. What's up?"

"Can I touch you?" Her face heated, but she pressed on. "Ever since I met you, I've wondered if your muscles were as hard as they looked," she mumbled quickly, looking down at her feet.

Chouza was silent and Amy worried she'd offended him, but then he held out one of his hands. Cautiously, she placed hers in it, marveling at the warmth he radiated. He placed her hand on his chest before letting his fall away, leaving her to explore the hard planes of his muscles through his shirt without interference.

Unconsciously, her other hand lifted to rest on his chest as well, tracing the lines of his chest down to his abs, then back up. They were soft, but firm, seemingly a contradiction, but still perfect. Her eyes followed her hands up, then further to meet his eyes. She could see barely veiled amusement and also something she recognized, but couldn't name. She jumped and pulled her hands back. "T-thanks," she squeaked, stepping back out of reach.

Chouza smiled. "No problem. Now unless there's anything else you want to see if it's as hard as it looks, I should go." His face blanched. "That came out wrong."

Amy giggled, then slapped a hand over her mouth. "I'm good." She started to shrug the shirt off her shoulders, disappointed as the scent of sandalwood went with it.

Chouza shook his head. "Keep it. You need it more than I do."

"It's getting colder outside. I'll be fine."

Chouza held up an arm, cutting off her protests. "In case you haven't noticed, I have a built in fur coat. I'm much more equipped for this weather than you are." He carefully draped it back across her shoulders.

"Arlight. If you're sure." Silently she inhaled the intoxicating scent again.

"I'm sure." He pulled the curtain back over the window. "Kimiko! Come on!"

"I'm trying to find Edgar! He's hiding!"

Chouza chuckled and rolled his eyes. "There's a small market one street over if you want any fresh food. No one will bother you here as most of them know I'm at the manor, so you should have all the privacy you want." Amy nodded, pulling her disguise back up as Chouza reached for the door.

Amy hesitated in the doorway as Chouza stepped into the hall.

"Thanks again for this."

"I'm happy to help. Ask Glinda if you need anything. And don't be afraid to ask any of the neighbors if you need help. Just tell them you're a friend of mine and they'll do what they can. I won't tell the others you're here so they won't come find you. Jax, Kimiko, and I will come by tomorrow to check in on you if you don't mind."

"I'd like that."

Kimi hurried up to Amy and wrapped her in a tight hug. "Bye, Ms. Amy! Love you!"

Amy's jaw dropped. "I-I love you, too, Kimi."

"I hope you feel safe soon and can come back!" She held the little cat up. "Say bye-bye, Edgar!"

Amy couldn't help the small smile that lifted her lips. "Bye Kimi, bye Edgar."

Kimi gingerly hugged Azurys as well. "Bye, kitty. See you tomorrow."

Azurys meowed and licked Kimi's cheek, causing the girl to giggle.

Amy chuckled and glanced up at Chouza, a blush spreading across her cheeks. "I'll see you tomorrow."

"See you tomorrow." He gave her a wave and started down the hall. Amy fought against the urge to call him back. *I'm getting what I wanted, aren't I? So why am I so disappointed?* When he reached the stairwell, he waved at her one more time before lifting Kimi onto his shoulders and disappearing from sight. Amy returned the wave, then stepped back into the room and shut the door, taking a shuddering breath.

Attempting to distract herself from the desire to chase after him, she gathered their dishes from dinner, washing and drying them before returning them to their homes.

Inside the bedroom, she opened the armoire, hesitantly pulline one of his shirts off a hanger. Slipping into the washroom, she cleaned up and stripped down before pulling his shirt over her head. It hung to her knees and covered her hands, proving to be a perfect night dress.

Azurys hopped up onto the bed and curled up on one of the pillows, her jaws stretched in a yawn.

"I hope Chouza doesn't mind cat hair." The irony of her words struck Amy and she started giggling uncontrollably.

Climbing into the bed, she snuggled under the sheets, his scent surrounding her and overwhelming her senses. She pulled the covers up and immediately succumbed to sleep, nightmare-free for the first time in a long time.

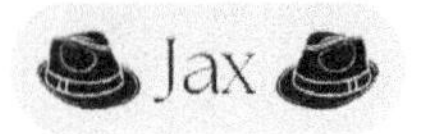

A man dangled from chains in front of Jax, sharp hooks speared through his wrists and ankles holding him upright. He screamed in agony as the dark-haired man with sunken eyes used the chains to make him dance. "See, Jackie? Cause them pain and they'll do anything for you. Isn't his dancing *fabulous?*"

The image shifted to a woman strapped to a table. The dark-haired man stood over her with a Cheshire dagger. "If you use a white-hot blade, it stops the bleeding as you cut." To demonstrate, he pressed the tip of the dagger into the joint at her wrist. Her screams nearly drowned out the sizzle of burning flesh.

The smell made Jax's stomach roll and he squeezed his eyes shut, not wanting to watch any more of the torture Gallund inflicted. He screamed as the dagger entered his side, struggling against the ropes binding him to the chair. "Uh uh uh, Jackie. You know better. Never close your eyes. I want you to watch. I want you to *learn.*"

Again, the image shifted. Moans filled the air as Gallund wheeled in what used to be a human. "Did you know, Jackie, that a person can survive about three days without their skin? Some can go longer, but most don't last more than a day or so. The shock of having it removed usually kills them." Again, Jax's stomach rolled. "Come now, Jackie. You need to learn if you're ever to take my place."

Jax tried to fight against the bindings, but when he looked up again, he froze. A messy-haired girl was strapped to a chair in front of him. Her left eye had already been gouged out, and her right arm and left leg were gone.

Her remaining eye was wide as she stared at Jax in terror. "Please. Please don't hurt me!"

Gallund placed the Cheshire dagger in Jax's hand. "Now, Jackie. It's time for your graduation. Kill her. But make sure it's painful. I want to hear her scream." He untied the ropes binding Jax to the chair.

The girl flailed. "No! Please, no!"

Jax stood and took a step toward her. "No." His hand moved of its own accord, running the blade gently across her cheek. "No, I don't want to!" He pressed harder and a thin line opened, blood running down her cheek and onto his blade.

The girl whimpered, straining to pull her head back. Gallund grabbed her hair, pinning her in place. "Go on, Jackie. Have some fun."

Jax's hand drew back, even as his mind begged him to stop, and stabbed the blade into her stomach. She screamed and he pulled the blade back again, stabbing it into her again, over and over.

"Jax! Jax stop!" The image wavered as a voice that didn't belong pierced it, and Jax froze.

"Go on, Jackie, finish the job." Gallund released her hair and she slumped forward, tears streaking her face.

"Jax! It's just a nightmare! Wake up!"

Jax turned, trying to place the voice. "A nightmare?"

"No. This is real, Jackie. *You* are the new Gallund. You will kill her and you will take my place." Gallund's sinister smile twisted his face. "You are the new Gallund."

"No!" Jax flailed the dagger, trying to shove Gallund away from him. It changed to a giant sword as he tried to keep Gallund at bay. "No! No, I'm not you!"

"Jax! Jax stop!"

Finally, the image shattered and Jax struggled against a strong force holding him still. The dark gray of Chouza's fur filled his vision as the larger man pinned him from behind. Jax gasped. "I'm sorry. I'm so sorry."

Chouza's grip loosened slightly. "Jax? Are you back with us?"

"Papa? Has Mr. Fox-man stopped being scary?"

Chouza released Jax and stepped toward the door. "Kimiko, go back to your room. I'll be there in a minute."

Kimi whimpered but backed away. Jax gripped his head and dropped to his knees, the memories rushing through it as he continued to mutter apologies.

"A-are you okay?"

Jax took a few deep breaths, trying to push the memories away. "I'm fine, Chouza. What time is it?"

"Uh... I'm not sure. Still somewhere in the middle of the night?"

"Okay."

"Is there anything I can do? Get you a glass of water? Send someone in to clean up in here?"

Jax's eyes ranged across the furniture he'd destroyed with the summoned blade. "Just— just go. Please." He coudln't look at Chouza as he tried to still the shaking in his body.

"Are you sure?"

"Yes. Thank you for waking me. I'm sorry I frightened Kimi."

"Alright. Good night, Jax."

"Good night."

Once he heard the door shut behind Chouza, Jax sat back against the wall, his head thudding against it. After a moment, he struggled to his feet and stepped out onto the balcony, letting the night air cool his sweat-drenched body. *Gaige...* The messy-haired girl's face flickered in his mind again. *I hope you're well...*

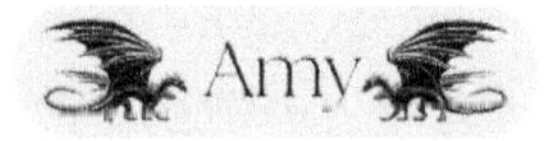

The next morning, Amy watched the reset from the window in Chouza's sitting room, still clad in his shirt. She had slept better the night before than she had in as long as she could remember.

As she watched, the few people on the street slowed, then reversed; once more, the reset had begun. It wasn't until it had already started that Amy remembered the tower. *I wonder if anyone else will go see it.* Eventually, a tabby cat trotted toward the building, unaffected by the reset.

A few minutes later, Amy stiffened at a knock on the door. She cautiously approached it, wishing for a window to look through. "Who is it?"

"It's Lillian."

Amy blinked in surprise at the familiar voice, before opening the door, clutching Chouza's shirt tightly around her. "Lillian? What are you doing here?"

"Checking on you. Can I come in?" She eyed Chouza's shirt with a raised eyebrow and Amy flushed.

Amy stepped backward into the sitting room, allowing Lillian to follow her in. "How did you find out where I was?"

"Chouza told me." Amy looked away, his betrayal hurting more than she'd expected. "He knew I was worried about you. Talia told me what happened and when you hadn't returned by dark I was about to go searching for you myself. When I saw him and Kimi returning, I asked if he knew where you were. Then I may have threatened to sick Tsume on him if he didn't tell me."

Amy's jaw dropped. *Poor Chouza! No wonder he told her.*

"Anyway, once he told me you were safe and where you were, I knew you'd be okay for the night. But I thought you'd want these." She pulled a bag off her shoulder, offering it to Amy.

Amy took it and opened the top, reaching in to pull out a set of clean clothing, undergarments, food, and other necessities. "You brought all this for me?"

"Look, I'm not sure what has happened to you before, but I do know that you deserve the chance to go through the dungeons if you want to. If you need to stay here to do that, then I'll do what I can to help."

Amy stared at her in surprise. "Do you help everyone this much?"

Lillian hesitated, looking around at her surroundings. "No. I mean, I used to." She sighed. "The first fifty years or so, I did everything I could to help people. Became… emotionally attached to each group that went through. With each person that died, I tried to avoid that attachment. It became too painful so I stuck to just providing potions to help them that way."

Amy glanced at the bag sitting next to her. "So why me?"

"I don't know," Lillian admitted. "But I find myself… drawn to you. I want to protect you and help you as much as I can. It's silly, really, but I almost feel as if you're family."

"Oh." Amy stared at Lillian, shocked speechless. *Family? What if she feels this way because I have the pendant? Can Lillian sense that her brother is nearby?* A flash of guilt caused her to look away. She wanted more than ever to show Lillian the pendant, to beg for forgiveness for not telling her earlier, but some part of her demanded that she remain silent.

"Like I said, I just thought you could use those things. By the way, I went by the park and the fountain on the way here," she added. "You said it appeared right at the beginning of the reset, right?"

Amy's brow furrowed. "Did you not see it?"

"I was there as soon as the reset started and I didn't see anything. I'm sorry, Amy, but are you sure you weren't imagining it?"

Amy frowned. "I'm absolutely sure because Jax and Balthazar saw it when they went with me."

"Hmmm. I wonder why it didn't appear today, then." Lillian shook her head. "Either way, Father says another dungeon will be opening soon. How much longer do you intend to stay?"

Amy hesitated. "I think just one more night. I've had a chance to calm down and get a good night's sleep so I think just the one night will be more than enough for me to handle being around the others again."

Lillian stood. "Okay. I'll keep your location secret. I hope you get the peace you're looking for."

"Thanks for the clothes." Amy sighed, following Lillian to the door. "I guess I'll see you tomorrow?"

Lillian nodded. "I'll see you tomorrow." With that, she slipped from the apartment and down the hallway, shifting into the tabby cat Amy had seen before.

Amy closed the door and hurried to the bedroom, pulling the pendant from her pocket to study it. *Is this the reason Lillian feels a kinship with me? Am I unintentionally manipulating her into helping me more than she would have normally?*

"*No.*" Amy jumped as the familiar voice entered her mind. "*It's more than that. She does not know I am here...*"

Amy stared down at the pendant. "Are you sure?"

"*Yes.*"

"How? How can you be sure?"

Devon didn't respond again and after a moment, Amy placed the pendant back in her pocket. She returned to the bag Lillian had brought and carried it to the bedroom, laying everything out: a new tunic, pants, undergarments, food, even a few books, far more than should have fit in the small bag. *A bottomless bag. Just bigger than the other one.*

Azurys purred from where she still laid on the pillow. She grinned at the cat as she changed into the clean outfit. "Are you just going to sleep there all day?"

Azurys leapt down from the bed, trotting past Amy into the sitting room.

Amy rolled her eyes and carefully folded Chouza's shirt, placing it on her pillow. After dressing, she followed Azurys back into the sitting room. Pulling out one of the books Lillian had given her, she curled onto a cushion, intending to spend the morning reading. She'd barely gotten settled, however, before another knock on the door startled her. Assuming Chouza, Kimi, and Jax had arrived, she hurried over and opened the door.

Instead, Talia sighed with relief. "Amy!"

Amy stepped back. "Talia? What are you— How did you—" She shook her head. "Hi, Talia."

"I'm sorry. I was just so worried when I heard that you'd quit! You *haven't* quit, have you?"

Amy glanced behind her at a tall, blond-haired man. "No, I haven't." Unease filled her when she realized she hadn't used her disguise.

Talia seemed to notice her gaze. "Oh, sorry. Amy, this is Vallun. Vallun, this is Amy."

He offered a hand. "Nice to meet you."

Amy shook his hand quickly before wrapping her arms tightly around herself.

Talia squeezed Vallun's arm. "Can you give us a moment?"

"I'll be nearby if you need me." Vallun kissed Talia's head, and walked away down the hall.

Talia smiled after him before turning back to Amy. "Can I come in?"

Amy nodded and Talia stepped in, pulling the door shut behind her. She let the silence linger for a moment before clearing her throat. "I'm sorry if you didn't want company." Amy's gaze stayed on the floor; she didn't really want to talk to the other woman. "It's just… I was at Vallun's house this morning when one of his members—he's the leader of the Thieves' Guild, by the way—came by to report that the red-headed woman from the current group was quitting. She'd been seen getting an apartment here. I just *knew* it had to be you. You haven't really quit, have you?" she asked desperately. "I mean, after what Nolan did, I'd understand if you did, but…" she trailed off, staring at Amy hopefully.

Amy stayed silent for a moment, surprised by the outpouring of words. "No, I'm not quitting. I just… I needed a few days away from everything. Peace and quiet where I wasn't constantly near other people."

"Oh. Well, I can understand that. Yesterday must have been hard for you. I'm sorry it ended up that way. Don't worry, I won't tell anyone where you are. Just promise you'll come back soon, alright? We need you."

"I won't put Chouza out by staying here much longer. I'll be back in the morning, I promise."

Talia smiled at her. "Alright. And you know, if I ever do anything to upset or hurt you, just let me know. You can talk to me."

"I'm not really upset with anyone anymore. I'll admit, I was at Nolan, but it's true that his training makes it hard to consider the individual instead of the unit. Not everyone is like that. I'll… try to get used to it."

Talia gave her another smile before opening the door. "I'll see you in the morning, then, Amy. Rest well." With that, she slipped from the apartment and joined Vallun and Chouza further down the hall.

Chouza looked over as Talia left the apartment, frowning until his eyes met Amy's. His resulting smile made her own grin spring to her face. He gave Vallun a nod, had a few terse words with Talia, then continued toward her, Kimi skipping along next to him.

"Ms. Amy!"

The little girl rushed forward and Amy scoped her up. "Hi, sweetie!" Her eyes lifted to Chouza. "Hey."

"Hey. Sorry about that. I didn't think about the fact that one of the Thieves' Guild would report to their boss. Or that Talia would be with him when they did."

Amy shrugged, waving him into the apartment. "It's alright."

"And sorry about Lillian, too. I wasn't going to tell her, I swear!"

Amy chuckled, settling onto the couch where Kimi tucked her head under Amy's chin. "It's fine, Chouza. Hard not to give the woman what she wants, especially when she threatens you with a lion."

Chouza smiled. "Alright. I just know you wanted some peace and quiet and with two visitors already this morning, and now us, I guess you aren't really getting it."

Amy shrugged. "Honestly, Lillian just brought me a few things and Talia didn't stay long. And well, like I said yesterday, you two don't bother me like the others do."

"I'm glad you don't mind my company." Chouza shook his head. "I meant to grab a few things from your room for you. I can't believe I forgot. And of course all of my clothes would be too big."

Amy blushed. His shirt had worked perfectly the night before. "It's fine. She brought me some spare clothes and a few other necessities."

Chouza raised an eyebrow as he saw the heat spreading across her cheeks. "Something I said?"

Amy just shook her head, then grinned. "Oh, by the way. I hope you don't mind cat hair." She scratched Azurys's ears.

"Ha ha. Very funny." Beneath the sarcasm, Amy heard the amusement.

"No, really. She slept on one of your pillows last night so I thought I'd warn you that there may be cat hair."

Chouza shrugged. "It's fine. Not like I'll be back here for a while. Did you sleep well at least? Even if you've had a lot of company this morning? No nightmares?"

Amy nodded. "Yes. I slept without nightmares for the first time in… well, years."

He gave her a funny look at the word 'years,' but made no comment on it. “Glad you did. Seems Fear is about to open.”

“Lillian said a dungeon was about to open. She didn’t mention it was Fear.” Amy sat forward, shifting Kimi. “I thought there was no way to tell which one it was?”

“Well, from rumors I’ve heard from other adventurers, in the nights leading up to Fear opening, participants have nightmares about their greatest fears. Let’s just say no one at the manor got a good night’s sleep last night.”

Amy’s eyes widened and she wrapped her arms tighter around Kimi. “I’m so sorry. You could have stayed here! You didn’t have to leave!”

“I’m fine, Amy. Really.”

Kimi buried her face in Amy’s chest. “Mr. Fox-man scared me.”

“Kimiko!”

Amy glanced between Chouza and Kimi. “What happened with Jax?”

Chouza sighed. “He didn’t want me to tell you.”

“Chouza, where’s Jax? What happened? Is he okay?”

“He’s… alright now. But when I finally got into his room this morning, there was a greatsword pointed at me.”

Amy frowned. That didn’t sound like Jax. He’d never been one for brute force, preferring speed and precision. Whatever nightmare he’d had must have really messed with him. She sat Kimi on the couch next to her and stood.

“Amy?”

“I’m coming back with you.” She entered the bedroom and grabbed the bag Lillian had brought.

He followed after her, waiting in the doorway. “Are you sure? I thought you would stay at least another night?”

Amy paused with the bag in her hand. “Jax is the first person who was content to spend time with me without pushing boundaries. Honestly, he’s the first person I’d even consider a friend. He was there for me, so now I need to be there for him.”

“I’m sure he’ll appreciate that.”

She gazed longingly at the shirt folded atop the pillow. She wanted nothing more than to curl back up in it and get another night of uninterrupted sleep, but Jax had stood by her when the others had tormented her. He'd been there when she found out about her brother. He needed her now and she wouldn't let him down.

"Come on, Azurys." Amy quickly pulled her disguise up as the little cat hopped off the back of the couch and trotted toward her with a meow.

Chouza took Kimi's hand and led them out of the apartment, locking the door behind them. As they reached the bottom floor, she approached the desk where Glinda sat.

"Well, hello, dear. How are you doing this morning?"

Amy returned the kind woman's smile. "I'm doing well. I just wanted to return this." She set the key on the desk, but the older woman just shook her head, glancing behind her to Chouza.

"Leaving already? Seems Chouza here is rather fond of you. Why don't you keep that for now? I would love to see you around again."

"Glinda!" Chouza coughed from behind her. Amy looked between them. "Go ahead and keep it, Amy. Like I said, the place is yours for however long you want it."

"Well... Alright," Amy conceded, sliding it back into her bag. She had no intention of using it any time soon, but it *would* be nice to have a place to escape to if she absolutely needed it. And only Chouza, Jax, Lillian, and Talia knew where it was.

"That's a good dear. I'll see you later." Glinda smiled at her before turning back to her paperwork.

Bemused, Amy followed Chouza from the building. He rubbed the back of his neck sheepishly once they got outside. "Sorry about that."

"It's quite alright." Amy chuckled. "She seems like a kind woman."

Chouza chuckled. "She definitely is. Though she has entirely too much interest in my personal life." Amy raised an eyebrow, glancing over at him. "She seems to think that I'm lonely up there by myself. I keep telling her I'm fine, but she's convinced I need a wife and Kimiko needs a mother."

Amy's cheeks heated. Hopefully, Glinda didn't get the wrong idea. *Would that be so bad?* She quickly shook the thought away. *Where did that come from?*

Realizing she'd been quiet for too long and Chouza was looking at her expectantly, she forced a laugh. "Yeah. Seems like a handy thing to have." She flushed again. "That came out wrong. I mean you probably are lonely. I mean— I'm sure you're not— you could probably have anyone— I think—" she finally stopped, looking down at her feet as she walked. "Sorry," she muttered. Azurys rubbed against her leg.

Chouza just laughed. "You're fine, Amy."

They continued on in companionable silence— at least on Chouza's part. Even Kimi stayed uncharacteristically quiet. Azurys moved to trot next to the little girl, lifting her mood.

Finally, they reached the manor, dodging Fredrikson's cane. "I almost gotcha that time."

"Sure, Old Man," Chouza retorted good-naturedly.

"Ooh, gettin' sassy there, Kitty Boy?"

Amy watched the exchange silently, still bitter about his words from before. "Have you seen Jax?"

Fredrikson's eyes turned to her. "Foxy? Last I saw he was in the dining hall, but that was this morning. Why you lookin' for him, Girly?"

"I just need to talk to him."

"He certainly looked pretty rough when I saw him at breakfast. Might do him some good to talk with someone."

Amy thought for a moment. "I bet he's in the library. Thank you, sir."

"Not a problem, Girly." He ambled into his office near the front door, leaving Chouza to trail after her.

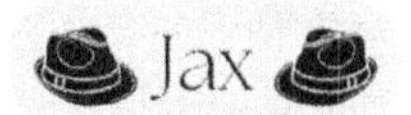

Jax stared at the book in his hand. He'd been unwilling to risk sleeping again and spent the morning in the library, hoping to distract his mind through reading. Unfortunately, he'd been unable to focus and when breakfast arrived, he'd barely read even a page. Afterward, he'd returned there, content in the solitude it offered.

You are me. I didn't fail.

Jax gritted his teeth. Gallund had been quiet lately, but his dream had stirred him up again. *No. No, I'm not.* Thankfully, he hadn't demanded blood. Yet.

"Jax?"

Jax's head jerked up at Amy's voice. "Amy? What are you doing here?" He straightened, quickly running his fingers through his hair in an attempt to comb it.

Amy settled onto the bench next to him. "Jax? Are you alright?" Chouza led Kimi deeper into the library, giving them a measure of privacy.

He forced a smile. "Why wouldn't I be? Just struggling to get into this book. It's rather dull."

"Jax…"

"I'm fine, really."

"No, you aren't." She touched his hand and he flinched. "Oh, Jax. What happened?"

Jax tried to laugh it off, but his face fell. "You're already dealing with so much. I don't want to burden you even more with my problems."

"You're my friend. Your problems aren't a burden. Please, Jax."

Jax couldn't help the warmth that spread through him at her calling him a friend, even as his ears drooped.

"I'm guessing Chouza told you what happened?"

"Some. Kimi let it slip."

Guilt flooded Jax and his head dropped into his hand. "I scared the poor girl, didn't I?"

"A little."

Jax shook his head. "At least she wasn't with Chouza."

Amy took his hand, squeezing it lightly. "What happened?"

"I nearly ran him through."

"But you didn't."

"No…" Jax sighed and glanced at where Chouza had Kimi deeper in the library. "Apparently everyone was affected."

Amy followed his gaze. "I understand if you don't want to talk about it."

Jax hesitated, studying Amy. His head sagged and his ears flattened. "My mom died when I was young. About thirteen. She was sick and we were too poor to pay the temple for the medicine she needed. Once she died, there was nothing left for me in that town, so I left, looking for my father.

"Anyway, about five or six years back, a group of us were hired for a job. Turned out to be a setup and everyone but me was killed. I was captured by a serial killer who wanted to turn me into his protege. He tortured and killed people in front of me." Jax shuddered, trying to keep the images of Gallund's work at bay and ignore his voice. "He was trying to brainwash me. Turn me into him." He lifted his shirt slightly to let Amy see the deep scars on his stomach and sides, still carefully concealing the mass of scarring just over his heart. "If I dared to look away or close my eyes, he'd stab me with a dagger, always careful to make sure it didn't kill me.

"Eventually I escaped, though I sometimes question if he didn't succeed in corrupting me, even just a little. That's what my nightmares were about last night." He finally focused back on her face. "That he had succeeded." He stopped, unable to mention the girl meant to be his graduation. "I've fought so hard against it... When Chouza finally woke me, I was trashing my room."

Amy leaned forward to wrap her arms around him. "I'm so sorry, Jax."

Cautiously, he returned the hug. "I-it's alright, Amy."

Amy lingered for a moment before pulling back, looking down at her hands. "You told me before that if I ever wanted to talk, I could talk to you, right?"

Jax nodded and his brow furrowed. "Yes, of course."

"Well, the same goes the other way. I'm here if you ever want to talk."

"Thank you, Amy."

She smiled gently at him, then watched Chouza following Kimi through the shelves, the little girl's chatter echoing in the quiet library. "I suppose I should stop hiding..."

"No one will pressure you into telling them about that. It's personal to you."

"Yes... But you've shared your story. One that was personal to you. So... I think it's only fair you know mine. *All* of mine."

Jax's squeezed her hand. "If you're sure."

Amy returned the squeeze and stood. "Come on. Chouza?"

The other man appeared around a bookshelf. "Yeah?"

Jax could see the tension in Amy's body. "Would it be okay if Kimi went to play with Lillian? I wanted to talk to you and Jax and... I don't want to scare her."

"Yeah, of course. Just let me walk her out to the gardens."

"If you're okay with it, Azurys can take her."

Chouza's brow furrowed. "Really?"

"She's more than she appears." She scratched Azurys's ears. "Azurys, lead Kimi out to Lillian please." She took Kimi's hand. "Make sure you stay with her, okay?"

Kimi bounced on the balls of her feet. "Okay! See you later, Papa!"

"Be good, Kimiko!"

"I will!" She took off after Azurys.

Amy rubbed her face. "Come on. I'd rather be in the privacy of our suite."

The men glanced at each other and followed Amy out of the library. Jax glanced over at Chouza as they climbed the stairs. "Sorry about the sword."

Chouza shrugged. "I wasn't hurt. You should see if Lillian has something that could help you sleep tonight. She can do some amazing things with her herbs."

Jax considered his words, relief filling him. "I think I'll do that."

Ahead of them, Amy kept her head down, her shoulders hunched. Once they reached the suite, she stopped in the center of the room. "Lock the door." Jax soundlessly obeyed.

Amy kept her back to the two men, who glanced at each other again in confusion at her actions. "You want to know what I'm most afraid of?" Not waiting for an answer, she reached around, slowly pulling the back of her shirt up to reveal burns that stretched down from her shoulders, disappearing into her waistband. With sick horror, Jax realized he'd only seen a small portion of them before. "Myself."

"Yourself? Amy, what *are* those?" Chouza asked.

"Burns," Jax answered for her, studying them. "From when your family died."

"What?" Chouza looked between them, shocked.

Amy lowered her shirt, keeping her back to them and looking away. "Does the name Pruitt mean anything to you?"

"Well yes," Chouza answered. "Everyone knows the Pruitts. They were nobility and the main trading family in all of Zadia. In all of Sciena, really. At least until…" he trailed off and Jax knew he'd realized the implication. His voice softened as he continued. "Until their manor burned down around a decade ago…"

"A fire that was started in the alchemy lab in the basement. I… I'm still not entirely sure what to believe." She turned back around to face them. "I was there. The manor burned to the ground with all of us inside. I bumped a table and everything exploded. For more than half my life, I've lived a lie created by my fear and guilt. I don't… I'm not sure about anything anymore."

"Amy…" Chouza stepped closer to her.

"You had to have been close to the blast. Close to the start of the fire…" Jax paused. "You're most afraid of yourself… of fire. Amy, how did you survive?"

"The blast threw me into a stone hallway where I was mostly protected from the flames and the rubble of the collapsing manor. But it also trapped me there. For several days" She made her way to the table and sank down onto the bench.

Chouza slid in next to her, hesitating as if he wanted to wrap an arm around her. "The first time you'd slept without nightmares in years…" Chouza quoted. "That's what your nightmares are about, aren't they?"

"When I woke up in the hospital they told me that I was the only one that survived… Nolan… Nolan said my brother was alive. He said that he was in a wheelchair, but alive. I left him. I didn't know."

Chouza gently placed an arm around her, pulling her to him. Amy stiffened at first, then succumbed, turning to bury her face in his chest. Chouza gently stroked her back, murmuring consoling words.

"How long did it take you to recover? Surely they could have healed more than this?"

"There were some temple healers that probably could have healed me more, I just left before they were done."

"You left?" Chouza pulled away enough to look down at her. "Amy, as severe as those burns had to have been… To leave before they were fully healed could have killed you!"

Amy flinched and looked away. "I know that now. At the time, I just wanted to get away. They were asking questions that I couldn't answer. They were trying to figure out what had started the fire… They'd called in the local baron and were going to arrest whoever had done it for the deaths of three nobles, as well as the staff."

Chouza squeezed her arm. "Amy, even if it were your fault, it was an accident. They wouldn't have arrested you. They would have just sent you to live with a family member."

"Maybe… but I still had nothing left there to live for. Or at least that's what I thought. So I stole some loose fitting clothes and my staff, and I ran." She pulled her necklace from her blouse. "This was the only thing that I had on me that survived the fire. It was my mother's."

Jax reached over to take her hand. "It's why Nolan made you so nervous. He's from the capital of Zadia, Olkbus, like you."

A few tears trailed down Amy's cheeks. "I knew that if anyone were to recognize me and take me back there, it would be him. He and his father had worked with my father many times. We'd even attended the same balls from time to time. While I don't look like I did back then, I favor my mother strongly. I knew that if he took the time to think about it, he'd recognize me."

"It makes sense. The heir to the Pruitt fortune would be highly sought."

Chouza gently rubbed her arm. "They must have been weak healers for your back to have scarred that badly."

Amy shrugged. "I suppose if I'd stayed longer than a week, it wouldn't have been so bad, but their questions were getting more and more pointed. I was afraid they were about to figure it out."

"A week! Amy, how are you even alive? How were you able to move?"

Jax squeezed Amy's hand. "Easy, Chouza." He wanted nothing more than to calm her and again, he felt some of his magick flow from him and into Amy.

Amy's trembling eased. "It's alright, Jax," she whispered. She took a deep breath. "After I left, I disguised myself as a boy and got a job with a caravan not employed by my family, trying to put as much distance between me and Olkbus as I could. I don't even remember what I did to keep the wounds covered. Those first few months are just a blur of constant agony. I was hired to help tend the livestock. The man that hired me was… unkind to say the least. He'd grab me and yank me around, shove me, beat me if I didn't do what I was told quickly enough. And it all hurt. His touch was agony on the wounds."

Jax squeezed her hand again. "That's why you hate being touched so much…"

Amy nodded, looking down at their joined hands. "I tried so hard to keep him happy, to avoid contact, because the burns hurt so bad. And he was just the first of many who treated me that way. But I didn't have much of a choice. The longer I stayed in Zadia, the more likely I would be recognized. Once I finally made it out of Zadia, I was able to be pickier about who I worked for. If they touched me, I ran. It didn't matter at that point. It made travel slower, but it did make my pain more bearable, if only just a little.

"I had… a friend for a while. She was nice to me. We bunked together, ate together. Did everything together. But when she found out who I was, she insisted I go back. When I refused, she tried to report me to the caravan head. I know she was just desperate for money like me, but… I had to run again."

Jax smiled sympathetically. "It's why you've had so much trouble letting us be your friends, isn't it? Why you never truly opened up to me back when we traveled with the caravan?"

"Letting someone close just opened me up to disappointment. I couldn't take that chance. Especially not with how much I paid to be in that caravan."

Jax studied her sympathetically. He knew the feeling of running from one's past. He understood the guilt of causing others pain. "Thank you for telling us. I'm sorry for your loss and your pain."

"Thank you." She buried her face into Chouza's chest again. The larger man carefully wrapped his arms around her, resting his chin on her head.

Jax watched her sadly for a moment before standing. "I think I'll go see Lillian about those herbs."

"She's with Azurys, Kimi, and Tsume in the garden," Amy said without moving.

"Thank you, Amy. I'll see you later."

"See you later."

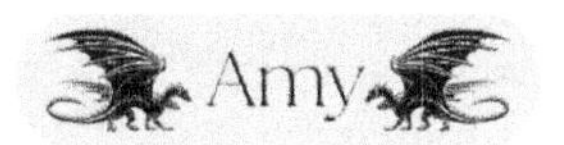

"Didn't you have your lesson with Inzo today?" Chouza asked after a while. Amy jumped, snapping awake from where she'd been half-asleep, the accident that killed her family playing over and over in her mind.

"Sorry. I didn't mean to startle you."

"It's fine. What was the question?"

"Did you have your lesson with Inzo today?"

"Yeah, after lunch."

"Well, it's lunch now. Do you want to head down?" Amy hesitated, and Chouza squeezed her shoulder. "We can stay up here if you want to."

Amy shook her head. "No. Let's go." She pulled away from Chouza, suppressing a sigh of disappointment as she stood. He followed her wordlessly to the dining hall where they settled in next to Talia.

The other woman smiled when she saw Amy. "Hey, Amy! I thought you weren't coming back until tomorrow?"

"I wasn't planning on it."

"Papa!" Kimi ran toward them, Azurys following on her heels. Amy moved over, letting the little girl sit between them.

Lillian waved and went to get her own food. Chouza chuckled. "Did you have fun?"

"Uh-huh!" Kimi took a large bite of food as she tried to tell Chouza and Amy about playing with Tsume and Azurys.

Chouza tapped her chin. "Finish your food."

"Sorry, Papa!"

Amy glanced around, worried when she didn't see Jax with Lillian and Kimi. "Have you seen Jax?" she asked Lillian as she walked by on the way to her own table.

Lilillian paused. "He was heading out of the manor when we were coming in. He mentioned going to the temple."

Amy relaxed slightly. "Oh. Okay. Thank you."

"Not a problem, Amy. And it's good to see you back." She gave Amy a gentle smile before joining the rest of her family at the head table.

Talia set her fork aside with a sigh. "So have they filled you in on what's been going on?" Amy nodded. "You didn't have any nightmares, did you?"

Amy cocked her head. "How did you know?"

"Because you weren't here. I didn't have any either and I wasn't here. The other four did. It must be limited to the manor." She lowered her voice, eyes darting to where Nolan and Kila sat a few chairs away. "I'm sorry about this morning."

"Why?"

"I just… I guess it makes sense that the other people here in town would take an interest in what was happening. Apparently, one of them spotted you getting the apartment there and told Vallun. I was there with him when they reported in. I should have left you alone, I know."

"It's fine." Amy looked away uneasily. *Now that I'm thinking about it, it does bother me how quickly word of me 'quitting' has gotten around.*

She jumped when Chouza touched her arm. "Are you coming back here after your lesson? Or going back to where you stayed last night?"

"I'll come back here."

"Are you sure?"

"I'm sure. My place is here. I committed to these dungeons and I can't take off every time I get upset." She knew that returning to the manor meant returning to her nightmares, but she'd dealt with it for so many years that nothing the dungeon could throw at her would be worse than what she'd already seen.

"I should probably get going," she added, glancing at the clock near the door. "I'll see you all tonight."

With that, she stood and took off for the Wizards' Guild. When she arrived, she found Inzo waiting in the training room and some of the tension eased from her body.

"Hello, Little Dragon. How are you today?"

Amy slipped easily into the draconic language. "Much better than yesterday, but… Fear will be opening soon."

"You are sure it is Fear?"

Amy nodded. "It seems that the group at the manor had nightmares last night."

"The group at the manor. Were there some who were not?"

Amy shifted uneasily. "Yes. Talia was with her partner Vallun and I…" she paused, trying to figure out what to say.

"I had heard rumors one of you had quit. The red-haired woman? I assumed it was you, and yet here you are. Were those rumors wrong?"

Amy shook her head. Of course he had heard. "Something

happened at the manor yesterday and I... I needed some time away. The new member of our group, Chouza, offered me the use of his apartment." She looked down at her feet. "Apparently a member of the Thieves' Guild saw me and reported that I'd quit..."

"There are some who are eager for another chance at the dungeons. Any chance that a member has quit is viewed as an opportunity." Inzo sighed, pain twisting his face. "They seem to forget why they quit in the first place."

"Master? Why did you quit?"

He settled onto one of the benches nearby, and Amy followed, sitting next to him. "I stumbled into this town about eighteen years ago. My magick had unlocked years before so I was overconfident and headstrong.

"My best friend was pulled into the town with me, a woman by the name of Shiva. We had been traveling along the western coast of Kush, heading toward the southern nations in hopes of finding adventure. When we appeared in the forest, we made our way here, where Arkham made the same offer to us as he did to you. We agreed and went through the Awakening process. I was a monkeyfolk and Shiva was an earthkin with an affinity for the sword, though that was no surprise to me.

"We then proceeded to seek out others within the town to help us. When the first dungeon opened, we went in with confidence. When we met little trouble in that dungeon, it gave us a sense of imperviousness. We went into Judgment next and Lust used her power to turn Shiva against us. She... she nearly killed our allies, but in the end we were able to prevail, though only just."

Amy remained silent as Inzo talked, seeing how much talking about his friend and what had happened in the dungeons hurt. It was no surprise that so few people talked of the dungeons and their experience when many were hurt and killed within them.

"When we returned to the manor and Shiva learned of what had transpired, she blamed herself. When the next dungeon opened, we were more cautious. This time we entered Calamity. At one point, we entered an area that had no magick, a beautiful forested area that seemed peaceful.

"Wolves attacked us and our healer, Turo, was desperately trying to pull me away from a wolf that was attempting to kill me." He leaned down and rolled his pant leg up to reveal faint scarring along his calf. "While we were distracted, the rest of the wolves descended on Shiva and our other ally, a dwarven spellcaster named Kent. They never stood a chance and I watched as they were torn apart in front of me, unable to do anything. Turo tried to help, but he was no match for the wolves on his own and eventually we surrendered.

"We returned to the Arkham manor beaten and battered, Shiva and Kent nowhere to be seen." He finally met Amy's gaze again. "So many people here in this town have similar stories, mine is not unique. Some are more gruesome than others, but almost all involve a friend's death. They seem to forget that in their eagerness to return there."

"I'm so sorry, Master. I didn't realize…"

"It is fine, Little Dragon. You deserve to understand what you have agreed to risk. Even if you survive, there is a good chance one of your friends may die."

Amy flinched, thinking of the people back in the manor. *Who will we lose? Talia? Jax?* She cringed away from the thought of Chouza dying in front of her. She didn't want any of them to die.

"After we surrendered, neither of us wanted to enter the dungeons again, not to mention we would have had to start over if we did. I returned here and, after my mentor died, I took on the training of new sorcerers, focusing on Dragon-Bloods. I found out sometime later that Turo had killed himself, his guilt at being unable to save Shiva and Kent becoming too much for him to bear."

Amy couldn't help the tears at Inzo's words. How did he survive such a loss? How did anyone survive such losses? Inzo reached up to wipe away a tear from her cheek. "Do not cry for me, Little Dragon. I am strong and while Turo, Kent, and especially Shiva will forever weigh on my mind, they also solidified my resolve to help those who followed me. In the ten years I have been teaching, I have taught many students, both those who have attempted the dungeons and those who were born here in the town and wanted to learn magick just for the sake of mastering their blood."

"But to have witnessed that? And to then be stuck here? I can't imagine," Amy whispered.

"Unfortunately, you may not have to imagine. I've heard bad things about Fear. And from what you have said, it certainly sounds as if that is where you are headed next."

Amy gulped. "What can you tell me about it?"

"You will face many common fears within it, but you will also face your own greatest fears. Pride is not magickally inclined, so you shouldn't need to fear his interference, only his taunts. Unfortunately, there is not much more I can tell you than that."

Amy had suspected as much. "Thank you for telling me all of this, Master."

"Of course. Anything that helps you break this curse is worth it. While I'm not sure that I would leave here if it was broken, I do know that these deaths need to stop. And the only way to do that is for the dungeons to no longer exist."

She'd seen enough of what happened within the town to know that he was right.

He stood and gestured for her to do the same. "Now. Shall we get to work? Amy jumped to her feet and moved to stand near him, resuming her training.

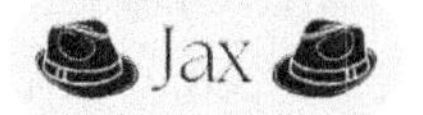

Jax stared up at Bielia's temple. A stone statue depicting a curvy woman with her arms lifted toward a full moon and roses curling around her legs dominated the front. Inside, tapestries hung along the walls, depicting the woman in different roles. One showed her holding a baby to her breast; another showed her stomach round with child; a third showed her lounging on a bed, men and women surrounding her, their hands caressing her body; a fourth showed her dancing. In all of them, roses and the full moon appeared somewhere.

At the altar stood a statue of Bielia surrounded by children. Water poured from a pitcher in Bielia's hands into the hands of the children. A table in front of it held an offering plate, as well as a handful of green and reddish-orange candles.

Clerics in similarly colored robes moved about, greeting other visitors and leading them to rooms in the back. Other scantily-clad members lounged on cushions, talking or reading.

Ignoring the other people for a moment, Jax approached the altar, kneeling in front of it. He tilted his head back, staring into the face of the goddess. *What do I do? I fought so hard to rid myself of Gallund's influence and yet… His bloodlust took hold. How can I be sure his influence is truly gone? How can I keep from hurting everyone? Talia, Chouza, Amy…*

And why would you want to do that? Bloodshed is glorious.

Jax tried to ignore Gallund's words, letting the image of Amy curled into Chouza's side fill his mind. *I knew something had to have happened for her to end up here on her own, but that… A week. By the gods how did she survive? She should have died judging by those scars. So why didn't she?*

He sighed and ducked his head. *Bielia… if you're listening, please help me. Help me protect Amy. Especially from myself. She's powerful, there's no doubt, but she's still so frail. Please give her a chance to grow into the person I know she can be. And please… watch over Gaige, wherever she is, in this life or the next.*

You should have spilled her blood while you could…

He stood and dropped a few silver into the offering plate. A soft pair of hands ran across his shoulders and down to his chest. "I don't think I've seen you around here," a sultry voice purred.

Jax raised an eyebrow and glanced over his shoulder. "I'm new."

"You must be working for the Arkhams." The fair-skinned woman with raven hair stepped back, letting him turn to face her. "You look troubled. Maybe I can help?" A dark green off-the-shoulder gown hugged her curves, the orange-red trim cutting into a deep 'v' between her breasts and down to her stomach. The hem of the skirt ended just above the floor and the entire thing seemed to defy gravity.

He let his gaze travel along her curves. "Oh?"

"My name is Elina. I'm a cleric here. Perhaps a massage would help to soothe away your troubles?"

"You know, that sounds lovely, my lady. And perhaps some extra tension released at the end?" One thing that never changed in the Bielia temples: they rarely denied a request for sex.

A pleased smile spread across her lips. "I would be honored." She led him down a hallway to the left of the altar and past several doorways. Moans echoed from a few of the rooms they passed.

She stopped in front of another door and opened it. "Welcome to my room."

Jax stepped into the luxurious bedroom. A massage table sat against one wall and a bath sank into the floor near the other, but a large bed dominated the center of the room, almost as large as the ones in the Arkham Manor.

She gestured to the massage table. "Why don't you undress and get comfortable?"

Jax nodded and did as she said, watching her lay a sheet across the table and set a tub of lotion next to it. When he had fully undressed, he climbed up onto the table, tucking his arms under his head.

Elina dipped her fingers into the lotion and spread it across her hands, then began massaging his back. Jax couldn't help but moan in pleasure. She worked in silence for a few minutes, rubbing the knots in the muscles along his back.

"Care to tell me about your troubles?"

Jax hesitated, debating on how much to tell her. "A dungeon is set to open soon."

"I see. And you're afraid?"

Jaw winced as her fingers grazed a scar. "Of the dungeon? Yes. But also… We're going into Fear. And a side-effect of that is nightmares plaguing us in the days leading up to it."

"Ah. That explains why you look so tired."

Jax closed his eyes, letting himself get lost in Elina's hands. "Yes. I found out after I woke that my nightmares caused me to draw a blade on one of my companions in the middle of the night. Had he not pinned me…"

Elina worked further down his body, massaging his lower back and butt. "Did you speak with Lillian? She has an herbal draught that may help with that."

"Yes. She gave me something to take tonight so that I can have a dreamless sleep." He stayed silent for a moment, his body responding to the way her hands moved across his skin. "It doesn't help my worry over the dungeon to come, however. For myself and my companion."

"Just one of your companions?"

"We talked some today about what we may face in the dungeon. Most of their fears seemed pretty benign. One fears nothingness, one heights, another clowns—"

"Clowns?"

"Don't ask. He's a strange man. Honestly, I hope he's chased by a whole hoard of them. It would serve him right." He sighed. "I'm not sure about one of them, but my other companion, my friend…. She's afraid of herself. Her family died in a fire when she was young. And she's a fire Dragon-Blood. Her greatest fear is also her greatest power."

"I see. That must be difficult for her."

"It is."

"And what of you? What is *your* greatest fear?"

"Honestly.... Myself as well."

"And why is that?

Jax rolled himself over on the table and Elina's hands paused in their massage. She ran her fingers across the scars on his stomach and Jax watched her face, waiting for the disgust or pity that they usually elicited. "Gruesome, aren't they?"

To his surprise, she showed no sign of disgust, only sadness, her hand lingering over the mutilation on his chest. "These aren't from the dungeons."

"No. They're from my past."

Elina resumed the massage, starting with his chest and moving down his stomach. "So then do these have something to do with your fear of yourself?"

Jax tilted his head back, eyes traveling across one of the beams on the ceiling. "I... I was meant to take the place of a very, very bad man. He tried to corrupt me. And I fear that he succeeded, to an extent." Again, the image of Gaige flashed before his eyes. "I escaped, but... sometimes I wonder if I truly did."

"You're working for the Arkhams, that's all the commendation I need."

Jax's brow furrowed. "Does that mean you've worked for them?"

Elina's hands paused. "I have."

"I take it things didn't go well?"

"No... Me and three of my friends tried it and well... We failed on the second dungeon." She started massaging his legs. "We were young and dumb."

"How did you end up here?"

"I was born here."

"Really?"

"Yes. Second generation, actually. My father was a traveler, but my mother was born here." Pain twisted her face. "He attempted the dungeons again when I was young and died. My mother wasn't too happy when I decided to go through them myself."

Jax reached down to grab her hand. "I'm sorry for your loss."

"Thank you." Her hands began to trail his body, much more sensually than before. "Did you still want that extra release of tension?"

Jax moaned as her hands caressed his body. "Most definitely."

"Then perhaps we should move to the bed?"

Jax reached up to pull her lips to his, their mouths moving together in a heated kiss. "I think that sounds like a lovely idea."

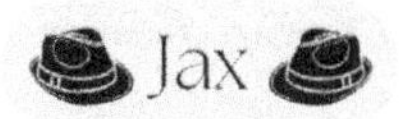

Jax stirred awake sometime later, groaning as his body fought against it. A gentle hand ran across his bare chest. "Feeling better?"

He peeled an eye open, studying the beautiful woman still lying naked next to him. "Much, actually. Though I didn't mean to fall asleep after."

She shrugged. "You needed it. And we see our clients for however long they require. It doesn't matter if all you required was sleep."

He lifted himself onto his elbows, eyes again trailing across her flawless skin. "What time is it, anyway?"

She shrugged, lying back so that he could get a clearer view. "Almost dinner. Getting hungry?"

"A bit." He leaned forward, trailing kisses along her jaw. "But I might let that wait for a bit."

She sighed in pleasure and tilted her head back, giving him access to her neck and collar. "Is that so?"

"It's been a while since I've been with anyone. I may have forgotten how much I enjoy it." He nudged her legs apart. "So long as you're agreeable, of course."

"Do I look unagreeable?"

"Not at all. By the way, have you ever been with a foxfolk?"

"Not to my knowledge."

"Want to try it now?"

Her eyes sharpened with interest. "Now that's an offer I can't refuse."

Jax's form shivered and he grinned down at her. "What do you think?"

She reached up to run her fingers through the fur of his cheek. "You're silver."

"I am."

"You're beautiful."

"Mmm. Thank you." He resumed trailing kisses along her body and she shivered. "Everything okay?"

"The fur tickles a bit. But not in a bad way."

"Oh?"

"Not bad at all. Shall we test it out?" Her hands went further down his body and he smirked. "Seems as if *he's* eager."

"Indeed." He latched his lips with hers and once more joined their bodies.

When they finally separated, he laid back and Elina rested her head against his chest. He gently stroked her hair, staring up at the ceiling. "Can I ask a question?"

Elina shifted to look at his face. "Of course."

"You didn't use a guard. Why?"

"Because your blood is Awakened."

He propped his head up with his arm. "Well, yes. But what does that have to do with anything?"

Elina chuckled. "Well it's not highly advertised, but one of the side-effects is that no one with Awakened blood can have a child. At all. It renders you sterile."

Jax cocked his head. "Really?"

"It does. Of course, that doesn't protect you from all the other risks of having sex, diseases and all, but at least an unwanted pregnancy is avoided. Here at the temple, we closely monitor to make sure we aren't spreading anything. Once Arkham dilutes your blood, you go back to normal. It's a temporary side-effect, so most people don't talk about it. Many don't even notice."

"Fascinating." He stroked her back, relaxing in the silence for a while. "Thank you. This has helped more than you realize."

"It's an honor. We all want to help the current group as much as possible. And you looked so lost and hurt. It didn't look like an expression that belonged on your face. Though any of us that have tried the dungeons have been there."

"You said you tried two?"

Elina sighed, laying back so that they were side-by-side. "Growing up, my mother was certain that the dungeons could not be completed. That there was no point and we should just make the best of the life we had. She… wasn't the same after my father died, and I pretty much raised myself. When I was eighteen, I decided to prove her wrong. She was livid, but there wasn't much she could do to stop me. My friend Tommy agreed. He wanted to attempt them, too. We were both born here. We both wanted to see what the outside world was like. So we convinced our other friends, two siblings named Tegan and Lorelei, to help us."

She gave a dry chuckle and shook her head. "We were all so young and dumb. Lorelei and I were eighteen. Tegan was only seventeen. Tommy was the oldest at nineteen. And we all had very little training. I knew a little bit of healing magick. Tommy was a wiz with a sword. Tegan and Lorelei used blood magick. We probably would have been a pretty good team if we'd had a little more training.

"One of the times no new travelers entered the city, word went out that Arkham needed a group of volunteers. Even just someone to complete the first dungeon and then quit in the second, preventing innocent bystanders from being pulled through. With some convincing, we talked Tegan and Lorelei into volunteering with us."

She sat up and turned her back to Jax. "We went in with an overinflated sense of confidence and it nearly killed us. We were swarmed early on by skeletons in Death, but my healing magick was effective and we made it out, defeating the sinspawn at the end. Lorelei and Tegan wanted to quit right then, but Tommy didn't… And his enthusiasm and confidence were enough to convince me that we should keep trying, so I helped him talk the other two into it, too.

"So when the next dungeon opened, we went in again. Into Time. About halfway through, we were turned into children and…" She choked a bit and tilted her head back. "We were fighting, using weapons that were far too big for us in armor that dragged the ground. It was brutal. Lorelei fell. I… I couldn't save her. Tegan surrendered and immediately disappeared. Tommy kept fighting, though. He refused to give up, even though I begged him to. I… I didn't want to fight anymore. Lorelei may have been Tegan's sister but she was my best friend.

"So I surrendered and returned to the Arkhams' manor. Tegan immediately started yelling at me, blaming me for Lorelei's death. I tried arguing with them, but it was true. I helped Tommy talk them into joining us. We were so busy arguing that we almost didn't notice the Gate close. But Lillian did. Tommy was badly wounded and bleeding out. Lillian only barely saved him.

"It didn't matter, though. A week later, I went to check on him because I hadn't heard from him in a few days and found him hanging in his apartment. His guilt over Lorelei's death drove him to suicide. And I lost Tegan as a friend. They blamed me for losing their sister and Tommy's death only solidified it for them. I've tried reaching out a few times since then, but I'm always ignored. I heard from their mother that Tegan's working for the Cranes out in the fields. But that's about all I know."

Jax stared at her back, shocked. "I-I'm so sorry."

Elina shrugged, her back still to him. "My story is far from unique. Even if someone leaves the dungeons, it doesn't always mean they survive." She faced him again. "Sorry. I guess that was a bit more than you asked for, isn't it?"

"No. Thank you for telling me. I appreciate that bit of insight." He reached up to tug her back into his arms. "You can surrender in the dungeons?"

Elina snuggled back into his side. "In most of them, yes. The only one I've heard of that you can't is Disease. Gluttony won't let you. The only catch is that if you surrender, you start over. So if your entire team quits, you have to start from Death again. At least one person in your team has to keep going, no matter what."

"Good to know." He kissed her head. "Thank you for telling me."

"It's fine. We all want to help as much as we can."

"Yes, but it has to be hard." He ran his hand through her long, black hair. "How long ago was that?"

"Five years… Almost six now…."

Jax's eyes closed. *Around the same time Gallund had me. Seems nowhere is truly safe…* He sighed and ran his hand down her back, smirking at the soft moan it elicited from her. "I should probably head back to the manor."

"Probably." She lifted herself up so that her hair formed a curtain, blocking them off from the rest of the world. "I'll be here again tomorrow afternoon if you wish to come back."

"That sounds lovely." He reached up to tangle his fingers into her hair, pulling her into a kiss. "I look forward to it."

She ran her hands across his chest. "As do I."

Grudgingly, Jax climbed from the bed and let his form shift back to human. Elina's eyes roamed his body and he remained still for a moment, letting her get her fill before getting dressed. "Thank you again, my lady. Today has eased much of my tension."

Elina pulled the gown back up and over her shoulders, settling it into place with practiced ease. "It was my pleasure. You're a skilled lover."

"That's quite a compliment coming from a cleric of Bielia. Especially one so lovely as yourself." He cupped the back of her neck with his hand, pulling her into another kiss. It had been a while since he'd taken a lover and the reminder of how much he enjoyed it made him reluctant to let go.

She leaned into the kiss before pulling back with a chuckle. "Go. You've been here most of the day and I'm sure your companions are worried about you."

Mention of his companions brought his mind back to Amy. She likely would worry if he didn't get back soon. "Yes. I suppose they are. Thank you, my dear. And I do hope to see you tomorrow." He gave her a short bow, kissing the back of her hand. "Until next time."

Elina flushed and smiled at him. "Until next time."

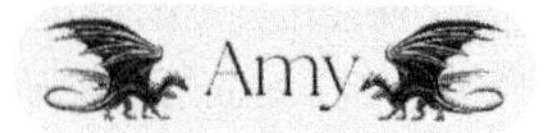

Flames surrounded Amy and screams echoed around her. She tried to step forward, to find whoever was screaming, but her feet refused to obey. She tried to free herself, only to be greeted by the sight of her own body engulfed in flames. She gasped, expecting to feel the familiar pain, but instead, she simply felt *power.*

The flames devouring the building around her, her childhood home, were originating from her. She was burning it down. And she was enjoying it. Horror filled her, even as she reveled in the power flowing through her.

"Sister!" She jumped at the familiar voice, whirling in search of Damien. "Sister, help me!"

"Amelia!" a new voice called. Amy's heart clenched at her mother's voice. "Amelia, why are you doing this? Please! Please, stop!"

"I'm not! I swear, I'm not!" Amy sobbed, even as more flames pulsed from her body, feeding the fires around her. "I'm so sorry!"

"Amy!" Chouza's face swam in front of her, the flames greedily licking around him, desperate to suck him into their embrace as well.

"No! No, run! You can't stay here!" she whimpered, cringing away from him.

Something grabbed her shoulder, stopping her from moving back. "Amy, it's alright! It's just a bad dream! Wake up!"

She struggled against the bonds holding her in place, trying to keep him from getting any closer. She didn't want to hurt him. She didn't want to hurt anyone.

"Amy!"

Amy was wrenched from the dream by the smell of burning flesh. Chouza's arms wrapped tightly around her, one hand in her hair keeping her firmly against him as sobs wracked her body.

He gently stroked her back with his other hand. "It's alright."

Amy sobbed for several moments, letting Chouza hold her until finally she could compose herself enough to pull back. As she did, she realized Chouza must have rushed into the room without bothering to add more clothing, as he sat in front of her with nothing more than a pair of loose-fitting pants on.

Bold scorch marks crossed his chest and arms, burning the fur away and leaving the skin underneath angry and blistered. "It's alright, Amy. It's worse than it look."

Amy's hands covered her mouth. "W-what happened?"

"It doesn't matter. Are you alright?"

Amy shook her head, then really studied the burns. The marks across his chest perfectly matched a smaller humanoid body. His forearms and hands were much worse than his biceps as if… As if being used to hold whatever had burned him. "I-it was me, wasn't it? I burned you?"

Chouza frowned but nodded. "You were locked in your nightmare. Heat was pouring off you and I didn't know how else to get you out of it."

Amy glanced down at her sheets, marred by thick scorch marks. "I'm so sorry. There must be something I can do. What time is it? Maybe Lillian can help?" Her voice rose with her distress.

"It's alright, Amy. It's the middle of the night, I doubt Lillian is awake."

"We can't just leave them untreated!"

"Hey, it's alright," Chouza insisted, reaching up to wipe a tear from Amy's cheek with the back of his finger.

Amy jerked back and shook her head. "There's an infirmary here. There must be burn cream in there!" She jumped from the bed, but Chouza remained where he was, his face twisted in pain as he attempted to get up. Azurys hopped up next to him, resting her head on his knee.

"I think I'll wait here." He forced a smile and Amy's heart twisted.

She swallowed hard and rushed from the suite and down the stairs. Six beds, separated by curtains, greeted her as she walked into the infirmary. Cabinets lined the far wall and she opened one after the other in search of any kind of medicine to help Chouza. All were labeled, but with herbal names that made no sense to her.

"Come on, come on! There has to be burn cream here somewhere!"

"Can I help you?" a voice asked from the doorway. Amy whirled around, spotting the medic, Sydney. She reached over and lit a lantern, eyes narrowing as she saw Amy.

"I-I need burn cream," Amy explained, glancing back at the open cabinet.

Sydney approached the cabinet, closing the one in front of Amy and opening the furthest one to the left. "How bad is the burn?"

"There are blisters."

Sydney pulled out a tube of oil labeled "Calendula Blend" and held it out to Amy.

She took it quickly, then hesitated. "H-how do I use it?" She couldn't risk making Chouza worse.

Sydney raised an eyebrow. "Perhaps you would like me to take a look?"

Amy nodded emphatically and hurried from the room, leading the medic and her bag full of medical necessities back to the bedroom.

Chouza remained where she had left him, studying one of his hands. He looked up as they entered and quickly straightened, unable to hide the cringe at the movement. Sydney expertly studied the burns before beginning to pull different items from her bag. Amy pressed her back against the wall near the door, trying not to cry.

About thirty minutes later, Sydney stepped back. Chouza's hands, arms, and chest were loosely wrapped in bandages and a strong herbal scent filled the room. "The bandages are there to make sure you don't get anything in the burns. When you get up in the morning, you'll need to leave them off for a while to let them breathe. I did some basic magick to heal most of the surface wounds, but I only have minor healing abilities. Lady Lillian would be able to heal it more." She glanced at Amy again as she left and Amy could see the accusation in her eyes.

Amy ducked her head, guilt filling her. *I hurt him. I don't know how, but I hurt him. How could I? Oh gods… Kimi. What if she had come in?*

"Amy, It's okay. I'm fine."

"You should get Lillian to check those first thing in the morning," she whispered, not looking at him.

"Amy…" The bed shifted as he stood, stepping toward her.

Unable to face him, she shook her head, turning to flee the room. She had hurt someone she cared about. Even if she wasn't responsible for her parents' deaths, she was still dangerous to those around her.

"Amy, wait!" Amy didn't stop as she rushed down the stairs and out of the manor, weaving deep into the gardens in an attempt to lose herself to the sound of night. Azurys raced after her.

Finally convinced no one would find her, she sank down against a magnolia tree, letting the pent-up sobs escape. Azurys nuzzled Amy's hand, purring. "It's alright, Azurys. I'm okay." The words sounded hollow, even to her own ears. Unwilling to allow herself to fall asleep again, she sat picking at the grass next to her, weaving it into a small basket as she waited for dawn to arrive.

Several hours later, a twig snapping caused Amy to jump and look up, a whole mess of tiny baskets scattered around her. Most of the grass around her had been picked down to the ground, though she hadn't even realized she'd done it.

Lillian stepped through the greenery, glancing around the small clearing in confusion. "Amy? What are you doing out here?" Tsume stood just behind her and Amy suspected the lion had led Lillian to her.

Amy pressed her back against the tree, cringing away from Lillian. "I— I— You should check on Chouza."

"What? Why?" She stepped forward but stopped when Amy whimpered and tried to scramble back, crushing a few of the baskets under her feet. Lillian's eyes widened as she took in the sheer number of them. "Amy? How long have you been out here?"

"A few hours. Please, just go check on Chouza?" She couldn't stop the crack from her voice as she fought back tears. "Please, he's hurt and needs healing."

"Hurt? Amy, what happened?" Lillian pressed, concern creasing her face.

"Please just go help him. He should be in his room."

Lillian finally relented, turning to disappear back the way she had come. Amy sniffled and wrapped her arms around her legs, resting her chin on her knees. Another hour passed before Lillian reappeared.

"Alright, Chouza's fine. I healed him up, though the treatment Sydney did last night would have had him healed in a few days on its own."

"That's good."

Lillian settled onto the ground next to Amy, ignoring her attempt to cringe away. "Chouza told me what happened. It's not your fault, Amy."

Amy shook her head. "I hurt him."

"Because your elemental aura awoke." She reached over to take Amy's hand, but Amy jerked away.

"My what?"

"Your elemental aura. My mother had hers perfectly mastered by the time I was born, but I've heard a few stories about scorched suspects." She grinned, but the smile faded when Amy simply looked away. "Amy, it was an accident. It's not like you did it on purpose."

Amy sighed. "I've had nightmares for years. I didn't think the ones from Fear would be that much worse than what I usually experience. Chouza must have heard me and came into my room to try and calm me. I-I burned him before I woke up. I didn't know I was doing it! I don't even know how I did it!"

"It's your dragon blood. You have an elemental aura that you'll eventually be able to control, though for now, it will likely only activate in times of great fear or pain. Chouza's okay. He's not upset with you."

Amy just shook her head again, fighting to keep from crying. "It's not okay. I hurt him! And it could have been so much worse!" The air around her started to warm again as her fear rose to the surface.

"Easy, Amy. It's alright. You didn't get much sleep last night, did you?" Amy shook her head and Lillian stood and disappeared into the surrounding greenery again, leaving Amy alone.

A few minutes later, Lillian returned, holding out a vial of freshly ground herbs suspended in some sort of fluid. "Here."

Amy hesitantly took it, turning it over in her hands. "What's this?"

"It's a weaker version of the same thing I gave Jax yesterday. Make sure you're in your bed before you take it as it should take effect almost immediately."

Amy glanced at it warily. "What does it do?"

"It will help you sleep." Amy started to protest, but Lillian shook her head. "Without dreams."

Amy hesitated, then nodded. "Thank you, Lillian."

"It's my pleasure, Amy. And please remember, you can always come to me, even if it's the middle of the night."

"I'll keep that in mind." Amy made her way back inside and up the stairs to her room. She hesitated at the door to her suite, afraid of running into Jax or Chouza, but after another glance at the vial in her hand, she went inside. To her relief, the doors to Chouza and Jax's rooms were closed and the room was empty.

The door to her room hung from its hinges, the lock broken from where Chouza had forced his way in. She ran her fingers over it and sighed. Knowing she couldn't do anything at the moment, she slipped into her room, propped the door shut as best she could, and climbed into the bed. After one last glance at the vial, she downed the liquid and slid under new sheets. With the sound of Azurys's purrs in her ears, she sank quickly into a deep, dreamless sleep.

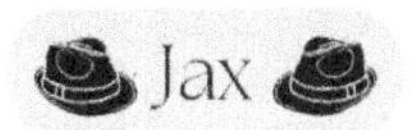

Waking after using Lillian's medicine felt like wading through quicksand and Jax groaned as he woke. After a moment, he sat up and rubbed his face. Light peeked through the curtains and he frowned, pulling a pair of pants on to step out onto the balcony.

It's already morning. I wonder if Amy went to the tower without me.

Jax quickly dressed and stepped out into the suite, freezing at the sight of Amy's door propped shut, the hinges nearly ripped from the wall. He knocked on her door but didn't hear a response. Carefully pushing the door open, he found Amy curled beneath her sheets, her body tense, but her face relaxed in sleep. Bold scorch marks marred the headboard behind her.

He glanced back at the clock in the main room. *It's nearly eight. She never sleeps this late…* Unwilling to wake her, he pulled the door back shut and headed downstairs. Chouza, Kimi, Nolan, Talia, and Kila were all already seated at the table in the dining hall.

Jax grabbed his food and settled into the seat next to Chouza. "Morning."

Everyone muttered their greetings, all of them with bags under their eyes. Except for Kimi, who grinned when she saw him. "Morning, Mr. Fox-man!"

"Hi, Kimi. Did you sleep well?"

"Uh-huh! You didn't wake me up this time!"

Jax gave her a sheepish smile. "That's good." He leaned closer to Chouza and lowered his voice. "What happened with Amy? Why's her door broken?"

Chouza frowned and matched his tone. "Her nightmares. She ended up burning me on accident last night. Something Lillian called her elemental aura awoke." He shook his head. "The on-staff nurse did some basic healing, then Amy took off. I tried to chase after her, but…" He sighed. "I couldn't. So I waited in the sitting room, but she never came back.

"Eventually Lillian came in and woke me, healed me the rest of the way up, and then sent me back to bed. I wanted to go find Amy, but she promised that Amy was fine and she'd take care of her. When Kimiko woke me, I peeked in and Amy was back in bed, so I guess Lillian kept her promise."

Jax's eyes widened in shock. *This isn't going to do well for Amy's mental state. Poor girl can't catch a break.*

He stiffened as one of the staff members approached the table. "Excuse me. Lord Arkham said that a dungeon has opened."

Jax scowled. "Now?"

"Sorry."

Nolan set his fork aside. "Someone will need to wake Lady Flame."

Loathe to let Nolan anywhere near Amy, Jax stood. "I'll do it."

Chouza grabbed his arm, stopping him. "No. Let her sleep."

"But—"

"The dungeon doesn't have to be entered the moment it's opened. According to Arkham, it can stay open for up to twenty-four hours. Amy can finish resting."

"Even so, we shouldn't leave it open that long," Nolan argued.

Kila nodded. "We should get this over with as soon as possible."

"No," Chouza growled. "I don't know much about magick, but I do know it's physically exhausting. And Amy is already exhausted. You wake her now and she won't be at her best. That's not what you want from your *team*."

Nolan met his gaze for a moment before nodding. "Very well. If you're certain it can wait, we'll give her a bit more time to rest." He addressed the staff member. "Please let Sir Arkham know we need a few hours."

The man bowed and quickly hurried away. Kila scowled and crossed her arms. "I still think the sooner we get it over with, the better."

Nolan shook his head. "In this case, I believe Chouza is right. My instructor mentioned something similar. That lack of sleep is a spellcaster's worst enemy. If Lady Flame had as rough of a night as I heard, it stands to reason that she didn't get the sleep necessary for her magick. We can go in once she wakes."

Kila snorted and Jax slowly sank back into his seat, looking between them. "So I'm not waking Amy?"

Chouza speared another piece of sausage and shook his head. "No. Let her rest."

"Right…" Relief filled him. *At least she'll get a little more sleep.*

Chouza sighed and set his fork aside. "Come on, Kimiko. Let's head up to the suite and I'll play with you for a bit before I have to go work."

Kimi jumped to her feet and followed Chouza to dump her plate. Jax glanced once more at the others before following.

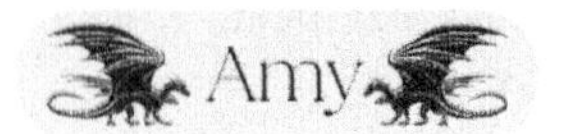

Amy stared at the scorch marks on the headboard of the bed. Azurys licked the back of her hand and she absently scratched her ears. She didn't want to face the others. And she certainly didn't want to face Chouza. She'd hurt him and she had no control over it. *What if it's worse next time?*

Rubbing her face, she stepped out onto the balcony, letting the cool air clear her head. High above her, the sun cast deep shadows across the gardens in front of her. *What do I do? What if Kimi had come in last night? I can't bear the thought of hurting her… Or Chouza again. Why did he have to come in? He could have left me be. It's not like I don't already deal with nightmares…*

Her stomach grumbled and she reluctantly stepped back inside. She dressed quickly and pulled the door open, immediately freezing. Jax sat on the floor with Kimi and Chouza watched from a nearby couch. They both looked up when the door opened.

Jax's eyes immediately found her. "Hey, Amy."

Kimi followed his gaze and jumped to her feet, racing toward her. "Ms. Amy!"

Amy's stomach dropped and she raised her hands, stepping back. "N-no, Kimi. Stay back please."

Hurt crossed Kimi's face. "But… I want a hug, Ms. Amy."

"I know, I just…" She hugged her arms tightly together, her heart pounding.

"It's alright, Kimiko." Chouza knelt next to the little girl. "You remember how I said sometimes people don't want affection?"

"Uh-huh. Sometimes people don't want hugs," Kimi recited. "And that's okay. It's their choice."

"Exactly. And right now, Ms. Amy doesn't want a hug. So we'll respect that, okay?" He glanced over at Amy, a small smile lifting his lips. "She had a bad dream and didn't sleep well."

Kimi's lip pooched out and her head dropped. "Okay… But can I give you a hug later, Ms. Amy?"

Chouza took her hand. "That's not nice, Kimiko. Give her time, she just woke up."

"Okay, Papa."

Just then, Azurys darted from Amy's room and circled Kimi. The little girl squealed and followed Azurys back to Jax, sitting down with her tail curled over her paws.

Jax waited until Kimi followed suit before focusing back on Amy still hesitating in the doorway. "Breakfast is over, but there should still be something in there. Why don't you go grab some food and bring it back here? We received word that a dungeon has opened."

"W-what? Now?"

Jax nodded. "I'm sorry, Amy."

She shook her head and quickly hurried from the suite. Downstairs in the dining hall, she stood in front of the platters of cheese and bread. Her stomach rolled at the thought of trying to eat any of it.

Two staff members whispered at a table, their eyes darting toward her. With a sick sense of realization, Amy knew word of what happened had spread through the manor. Unwilling to stay there any longer, she grabbed an apple and hurried back to the suite. She hesitated at the doorway, but more whispering staff members prompted her to slip inside.

Jax gave her a sympathetic smile when he saw her. "Too nervous to eat?"

Amy glanced at the apple and sank onto the couch furthest from Chouza. "Yeah…" She pulled her feet up under her and watched as Kimi and Jax built a tower of blocks. Occasionally, Azurys batted one of the blocks closer to Kimi with her paw.

"Hey, Jax. Do you think you could take Kimiko to her room for a minute so I can talk to Amy?"

Amy's eyes widened at Chouza's words. *Why? Does he not think Kimi's safe around me? I mean, she's not, but…* The thought hurt and Amy ducked her head, looking away.

"Yeah, of course. Come on, Kimi. How about we play a round of Go Fish?"

"Okay!" The girl bounced to her feet and followed Jax to her room. Azurys darted after them, slipping throught the door just before it closed.

Chouza waited until the door closed before moving to Amy's couch. "We need to talk."

"No, we don't."

"Amy…"

Amy sighed. "I'm sorry about this morning."

"It's alright. I'm not upset."

Amy's head jerked up. "Not upset? I hurt you! You should be livid! You shouldn't want me anywhere near Kimi! You shouldn't even want me in the same *room* as your daughter!"

"Maybe. But I'm not. What happened was an accident. You didn't do it on purpose. With practice, you can control it, just like everything else." Amy shook her head, tears welling in her eyes. "Amy, I'm not upset with you. And I trust you no less with Kimiko now than I did yesterday."

"What if I hurt you again? What if I hurt Kimi?"

"We'll figure that out if it becomes an issue. But you won't hurt Kimiko. I know you won't. Do you want to know how I know?" Tears ran freely down her cheeks. "I know because you love that girl and would never let anything happen to her, not even yourself. You aren't a danger to us,. Everything will be okay."

He opened his arms and Amy crawled over to him, curling into his side. The thick smell of healing herbs filled her nose as he wrapped his arms around her and Amy marveled at how right it felt to be held by him.

Eventually, her tears slowed and she relaxed against him. "I'm sorry," she whispered.

"You have absolutely nothing to be sorry for." He used a finger to tilt her chin so that she met his gaze. "You had a nightmare and your body reacted in a way that you had no control over. Lillian healed me and I'm fine now. You have a teacher, right? Maybe after the dungeon, you can talk to him about it. He'll be able to help you."

"R-right." Heat spread through her cheeks with the realization of how close his lips were to hers. Hers felt dry and she quickly licked them, her breath hitching slightly.

Chouza's eyes darted to her lips and he inched closer. His hand moved from her chin to her cheek, cupping it gently. Slowly, he leaned forward until their lips connected.

Immediately, a jolt went through Amy and she jerked back, gasping. She reached up to touch her tingling lips. "W-was that supposed to happen?"

"S-sorry. I shouldn't have— I didn't mean—" Chouza's own eyes were wide. "I'm sorry if I pushed a boundary I shouldn't have."

Amy reached up to place a finger to his lips. "I'm not upset. But that… that feeling? Was that supposed to happen?"

"N-no. I've never had it happen before." He rubbed his face. "I'm so sorry, Amy. I didn't mean to take advantage of the situation like that."

"Take advantage?" She frowned. "What do you mean?"

"You were vulnerable and I kissed you. I'm sorry. I shouldn't have taken advantage of you to satisfy my own desire." He shook his head. "I'm so sorry—"

Amy leaned forward to press her lips to his again, the jolt spreading from their lips to settle in her stomach. Chouza stiffened in surprise at first, but quickly placed a hand on the back of her neck, tilting her head to deepen the kiss. Heat spread through her and her arms went around his neck, her fingers tangling into his hair.

She moaned, turning to face him more as he ran his tongue across her lips. When they parted, his tongue darted into her mouth, dancing with hers. She melted into him, moaning in pleasure as one of his hands gently gripped the back of her neck and the other went to her hip.

The door to Kimi's room burst open. "Papa, Papa! I beat Mr. Foxman at a card game!"

Amy jerked backward. In her lust-filled haze, she'd moved to straddle Chouza's waist, her arms wrapped around him. She scrambled off his lap, blushing deeply. Jax followed Kimi out, raising an eyebrow at her position. "Well. Good talk?"

Chouza cleared his throat. "T-that's great, Kimiko."

"Ms. Amy? Why were you in Papa's lap?"

"Uh…" She glanced at Chouza, but he was at just as much of a loss for words.

Jax chuckled. "Well, you know how it makes you feel better to sit in your papa's lap?"

"Uh-huh."

"Well, your papa was just comforting Ms. Amy. That's all."

"Oh. Okay! Do you feel better now, Ms. Amy?"

Amy cleared her throat. "Um. Yes, sweetie. Much."

"Can I have a hug now?"

"Kimiko," Chouza warned.

"Yes, Kimi. Come here." Amy opened her arms and Kimi immediately clambered up into her lap with a happy squeal. She smiled over Kimi's head at Chouza, a faint blush still coloring her cheeks.

Chouza returned the smile and reached over to squeeze Amy's leg. A knock on the door caused Amy to jump.

Nolan's voice filtered through the door. "Is Lady Flame awake?"

Jax scowled and his ears flattened. "Yes, she is."

"Then we need to get this over with. We'll meet in Sir Arkham's office in one hour."

Amy's grip tightened on Kimi as the little girl looked between the adults in the room. "Does that mean you have to go work now, Papa?"

"Unfortunately. Tell Ms. Amy and Mr. Jax bye. You're going to stay with Ms. Lillian while I'm working."

Kimi pouted and snuggled deeper into Amy's lap. "I don't wanna."

Chouza sighed. "I know, Baby. I do. But we have to do this, okay? This is what Papa signed up for."

Kimi buried her face in Amy's chest. "Will you stay, Ms. Amy?"

"I can't, Kimi. I have to go, too."

"Okay." Her tiny arms wrapped around Amy's stomach. "Be careful,

Ms. Amy. I love you."

"I love you, too, Kimi. I'll see you soon, okay?"

"Okay..." She climbed off Amy's lap and ran to give Jax a hug. "Bye, Mr. Fox-man."

He squeezed her gently. "Bye, Kimi."

"Alright, Kimiko. Come on. Let's go find Ms. Lillian, okay? I'll be back in a bit to get my armor on," he told Jax and Amy.

Amy watched him go, blinking when Jax bumped her shoulder with his. "Good talk?"

Amy flushed. "He just... He was holding me and then our lips were so close and... It felt so right, Jax. He was warm. And comfortable."

"I'm happy for you. Really." He squeezed her hand. "Chouza seems like a really good guy. And he's raising Kimi well."

"He is." She ducked her head. "He was afraid he was taking advantage of me."

Jax chuckled. "What?"

"When he kissed me? There was this spark. Jolt." She shook her head. "I don't know. Anyway, it surprised me so I pulled away. And he thought I didn't like it. So he was apologizing for taking advantage of me."

"Was he?"

Amy's brow furrowed. "What? No! Definitely not!"

Jax smirked. "So you wanted it just as badly as he did?"

"Well yes, I—" She glared at Jax. "You were baiting me!"

Jax laughed and she popped his arm, but that only made him laugh harder. "Hey! No hitting!"

Amy attempted to continue glaring at him, but eventually relented, laughing with him. "Okay, yes, Jax. I do like him. A lot. And he, apparently, likes me. Though I still don't quite understand why."

Jax pulled her into a loose hug. "Because you're amazing, Amy. You're strong, beautiful, powerful. Chouza sees it. I see it. You just need to let yourself see it."

Amy blushed but returned the hug. "Thank you, Jax."

"It's not a problem, Amy." He pulled back and took her hands into his. "And I mean this honestly. If you need *anything*, you tell me, okay? If you want relationship advice? Just ask. I'm here for you. If you want help with the juicy bits," he wiggled his eyebrows suggestively, "you come to me and I will make sure to help you out."

Amy popped his arm again. "Jax!" He cracked up and Amy couldn't help but smile. "Thank you. Really. And I'll keep that in mind."

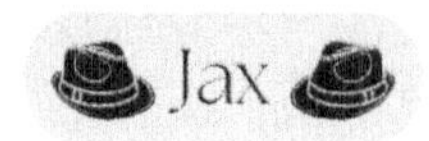

"Just tighten that buckle there."

Amy did as Jax told her. "Good?"

"Perfect. Thank you for the help, Amy. I can get it on by myself, but it's much easier with help."

Amy stepped back as Jax belted his new rapier onto his side. "No problem."

He adjusted it until it was comfortable. "Are you going to change?

"Yeah. I'll meet you in Arkham's office."

"Alright." He pulled her into a gentle hug, then stepped back and held her at arms' length. "And Amy, no matter what happens in this dungeon, remember that you *aren't* alone. We care about you. A lot. You have friends now. Don't let your fear make you doubt that, okay?"

"I'll try. But the same goes for you, too. You're my friend. My first real friend. I don't want to lose you in there."

Jax wrapped her in another hug. "Thank you, Amy. I'm honored."

Amy clung tightly to him and Jax could feel the lines of her scarring through her shirt. "Just be careful, okay?" she whispered.

"I will if you will."

Amy pulled away and took a deep breath. "I need to change. I'll see you in Arkham's office."

Jax took the fedora from his head and settled it onto the pillow of his bed. He coudln't risk losing the last gift his mother had given him.

He made his way out of the suite and up to Arkham's office. Inside, Nolan and Kila waited impatiently. "Where's Amy and Chouza?"

Jax struggled not to roll his eyes at Nolan's demanding tone. "Chouza had to take Kimi to Lillian and Amy is getting changed. They'll be here in a minute."

Kila huffed impatiently. A few minutes later, Talia joined them, quickly followed by Amy and Chouza. "About time you showed up," Kila grumbled.

Chouza's eyes narrowed, but he just held out a bag. "Here. Lillian sent along a bag of healing potions. There's six for each of us."

Arkham waited silently until they had distributed them. "Is everyone ready?"

They glanced at each other nervously and nodded. Arkham pressed his hand to the door and it clicked open. Once everyone had stepped onto the platform, he closed the gate and activated the lever.

Amy tucked herself into the space between Jax and Chouza with a nervous glance around, gripping Jax's hand tightly. He gave it a light squeeze. "It'll be okay." The knuckles of her other hand turned white with the strength of her grip on her staff.

Chouza wrapped an arm around her waist and she leaned into him. "We're here. Don't worry."

Once they reached the large open area of the basement, Arkham led them to the stone archway that housed the Gate, the pale glow brightening as he placed his hand on it. "I'm sure you've figured out by now that you'll be going into Fear." Everyone shifted uneasily. "This one will test you mentally. You'll face your own greatest fears in this dungeon. You may be separated, so take that into account. Be careful and we will see you when you return."

"Alright, same order," Nolan commanded. "Chouza, once we get inside you'll be bringing up the rear to protect the spell casters in the center. In the meantime, come with me." He quickly cupped Kila's cheek. "See you on the other side. I love you."

Chouza hesitated a moment before pressing his lips to Amy's quickly. She gasped in surprise, but he'd already passed through the Gate with Nolan. Kila blinked in shock at Nolan's words, mouth gaping as she stared at the gate.

Jax squeezed Amy's hand again. "Remember. No matter what, you aren't alone." He stepped forward. "Ready, Kila?"

"Y-yeah. Let's go."

With one last glance at Amy standing next to Talia, he and Kila stepped through the Gate.

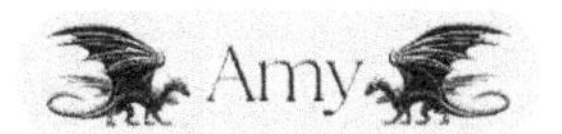

Only those too blinded by pride, dare to claim they have no fear."

Amy shuddered as the words echoed through her mind, the deep voice giving it a threatening air. When the bright flash of light cleared, she rubbed her eyes, trying to adjust to her new environment. A white hallway stretched in both directions, with no distinguishing features in either direction.

Damien waved from about ten feet away, his mousy brown hair ruffled and uneven. He looked just like she remembered him, with a round face, freckles across his nose, and clothes covered in dirt from playing. "You know Sister, I'm *glad* you abandoned me. Or killed me." He shrugged. "Either way, it achieved the same result. After all, who could bear the shame of a sister who hurts everyone she cares about?"

Amy gasped and with a sob tried to step forward, but her feet felt rooted in place. "I'm sorry! Please, I'm so sorry!"

Damien shook his head and walked away, disappearing around a curve in the hallway. Amy collapsed to her knees, sobbing. Through the haze of grief, she realized the rest of the group hadn't appeared with her. Wiping the tears from her eyes, she looked around.

Clearly, that wasn't my brother. That was how he looked when I last saw him. If he is alive, he'd be a man by now, not just a child. It was a figment of my mind. Of my fear. This is part of the dungeon. It's okay. I'm okay. I'm not alone. The others are in here somewhere, too. I'm not alone.

The thought bolstered her, even if it didn't do much to calm her racing heart. She struggled to her feet and studied the hallways more critically. The white marble walls stretched ahead of her, beckoning her forward. Even with her ability to see in the dark, she knew the hallway was perfectly light, even without a discernible light source; the forest green cloak on her shoulders and coral of her skin hadn't faded to gray.

Gathering her nerves, she started forward, looking around her apprehensively. Eventually, the hallway ended and an archway to her left opened into another one.

Jax leaned against the opposite wall, his fedora resting haphazardly off one ear. "Well, hello Amy."

"Jax! Are you alright? What's going on?" She tried to step forward, but couldn't move again.

Jax smirked. "Did you really think I was your friend? Why would I want to be your friend? You destroy everything you touch. You hurt everyone you care about. Seems to me that being your friend would be a death sentence."

Hurt flooded Amy as she stared at him. "W-what? Jax, why?"

He walked away and tears welled in her eyes as she once more tried was once again unable to chase him. He followed the curved hallway further and further until he disappeared from sight. Amy stumbled forward as whatever held her in place released her. She ran toward where she had last seen him, but there was no sign of her friend.

If Damien wasn't real, maybe that Jax wasn't real. The real Jax would never say anything like that. He promised he was my friend. And he wasn't wearing his fedora when we came in. That wasn't real. It can't be real. Still, a few sobs escaped her. *It wasn't real.*

She took a deep breath and glanced back the way she had come, but ultimately decided to follow the fake Jax. After several twists and turns, dead ends, and double-backs, Amy realized she'd traveled deep within a maze. *Being lost and being alone. Two common fears.* A pit settled in her stomach.

She suspected the others were doing the same thing as she wandered through the corridors. Eventually, she pulled a piece of chalk from her bag, marking her path and then marking an 'x' if she had to double back due to a dead end.

After rounding another curve, Lillian sat on the floor, leaning against Tsume. "Well, Amy. It's about time you made it this far. You're such a disappointment. I don't know why my mother had any interest in you. You're a danger to my family. My home. What if you'd burned the entire manor down? Or used my lab to explode it like you did your own home?"

"Lillian… Please… Please, stop."

Lillian smirked and gracefully lifted herself to her feet. Tsume knelt and allowed Lillian to climb onto her back. "Do us a favor and just die in here. It'd be better for everyone." Tsume loped away.

Amy gritted her teeth and continued forward, trying not to let the words of the people she had seen stop her. The curves grew more and more pronounced the further she traveled, the hallways getting shorter and more frequent. She rounded another curve and found Chouza standing with Kimi. Immediately, her legs locked.

She covered her ears and shook her head. "I don't want to hear! I don't want to know!"

Chouza smirked and his words still reached her clearly. "Did you really think I cared about you? Or that I'd ever forgive you for what you did? You could have killed me. You could have killed Kimi. I could never forgive you for that. I only pity you."

Amy's heart clenched and she tried to step forward, though her feet remained rooted to the spot. "I'm so sorry," she whimpered.

Kimi stuck her tongue out at her. "You're just a mean person! You're trying to take my Papa away from me and replace my mama!"

The harsh words from the usually sweet little girl caused something to harden in Amy. She dropped her hands from her ears and lifted her chin. "You aren't real. I know you aren't. The real Kimi loves me. And I love her. You aren't real!"

Instead of walking away, the image of Chouza and Kimi shattered. A door materialized in the wall behind where they had stood. Determined, Amy gripped the knob and pressed it open.

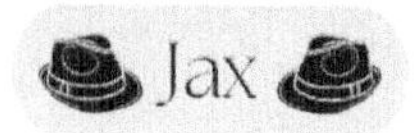

Jax

Jax glanced around the white marbled halls apprehensively. *Fear… What do you have in store for me?*

He froze when he saw his mother and father. His father wrapped an arm around his mother's waist and kissed her cheek. She smiled, then raised an eyebrow at Jax. "You know, I'm glad I died before you became such a monster. Abandoning someone who needs you. Murdering people. Such a bad person."

"No," Jax whispered, staring at them with wide eyes.

His father dropped his arm and took his wife's hand. "Why did you have to come find me? I'd made a life here. I was happy. I prefer the image of you I'd built up in my mind, not the monster you've become."

Jax gasped. "What? Father, no!"

They walked away, leaving Jax to stare after them, unable to move. Once they disappeared around the curve, he stumbled forward. *What the hell was that? My mother is dead. My father is back in Lorencost. There's no way… They weren't real. They're figments of my fear. They wouldn't really say that.*

Taking a deep breath, he glanced in either direction, then went the opposite direction of his parents, only to be blocked by a dead end. Sighing, he retraced his steps, following the hallway around.

Several turns later, the curves grew more pronounced. He stepped through an archway and a familiar figure caught his eye. "Oh thank the gods. Amy!"

She raised an eyebrow. "Hello, Jax. Come to kill me now?"

Jax stumbled to a halt. "W-what?"

"Gallund did well with you. Shall I be your next victim? Just die in here. Leave the rest of us alone." She walked away, leaving Jax staring after her.

No. No, that wasn't her. That couldn't be her. She'd never say something like that. Plus, I never told her Gallund's name. Right? He racked his brain, trying to remember the conversation he'd had with her the day before. *No. I'm certain I never told her his name. That wasn't really her. It's just Fear. Just. Fear.*

He shuddered, again going the opposite direction the fake Amy had taken. Several twists and turns later, the hallways had started to straighten out again. *Assuming I'm meant to be heading toward the center... I believe I'm going the wrong way.* He pulled a piece of chalk from his bag and marked the direction he was going.

He turned around and attempted to find his way back to where he had encountered Amy, but quickly found himself thoroughly lost.

"This is getting boring. Just follow the path."

Jax froze, recognizing the deep voice from when they entered the dungeon. Bright red droplets resembling blood appeared on the floor. With one last glance around, he followed it along, careful to avoid stepping in it.

The droplets passed under an archway, then continued to the left. He paused for a moment to study the path to the right.

"It's about time you showed up."

Jax froze, his back to the speaker. "No."

"What? Did you think you could just abandon me and I wouldn't find you?"

He slowly turned, facing the messy-haired girl that haunted his dreams. Her missing limbs had been replaced with shadowy versions of themselves. "I'm sorry, Gaige. I couldn't stay. Gallund's influence—"

"Oh no, you don't understand." A harsh smirk twisted her face. "I simply wanted to thank you. After all, you would have killed me if you'd stayed. Of course, I had no chance of surviving on my own anyway, but death by starvation is better than death by the blade of someone you trust, right?"

Jax choked slightly and dropped to his knees. "I'm so sorry. Please, I'm so sorry."

She walked away, leaving him rooted to the spot. The trail of blood-spots followed her steps. A pained sob ripped from his throat. *She wasn't real. She wasn't real. She wasn't real. She. Wasn't. Real.* He repeated the mantra over and over, trying to convince himself. Logically, he knew it couldn't be her. But still, the words played on his fears.

After a few deep breaths and another reminder that it couldn't be the real Gaige, he pulled himself to his feet, following the trail of blood forward. After what felt like forever, he rubbed his face. "This is ridiculous."

He followed the blood drops around a sharp curve and stumbled to a halt. A figure he'd hoped to never see again leaned against the wall. "Well hello there, Jackie."

Jax tried to step back, but once more his feet were rooted to the ground. "No. No, you're dead."

"I am, all thanks to you. You were such a *fine* student. And you've done so well. A few more lessons and you'll be a perfect masterpiece."

Jax shook his head. "No. You aren't real. You're dead. I killed you. You're dead. This is my fear. You aren't real!"

Gallund smirked as his image shattered and a doorway materialized in the wall behind him. Jax took several shaky breaths, trying to ignore the trembling in his body. Hoping the doorway meant an end to the maze, he stepped forward and turned the knob.

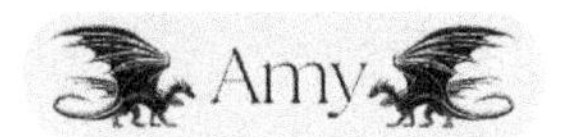

Amy stepped through the doorway into a large central chamber. Six doors circled the room with Kila and Nolan sitting in the center.

Kila glanced over when the door opened and rolled her eyes. "Great. The traitor showed up."

Nolan squeezed her arm. "Kila. Hey, Lady Flame." Kila huffed and turned away.

Amy's eyes ran across the other doors in the room. "Hey, Nolan. Good to see you, too, Kila. How long have you been here?"

Kila grunted and laid back on the floor. "A little bit. You took forever." She shook her head. "Don't bother. They're all locked and even I can't open them. I came through that one." She pointed to the one opposite Amy's.

Nolan jerked his head at a separate door. "And I came through that one."

"So then the others will likely come through those." She glanced at the three remaining doors, trying to ignore the slight tremble in her hands. Kila grunted in agreement, but just leaned back on her elbows, staring at the marble ceiling.

Eventually, another door opened and Talia stumbled in, looking around wild-eyed. Kila jumped to her feet. "Talia, are you alright?".

"Kila!" Talia raced forward, throwing herself into the other woman's arms.

Kila held her tightly. "It's alright. You aren't alone anymore."

"Are you alright, Talia?" Amy asked.

"I-I'm okay now." A faint shake to her voice betrayed her.

Just then, another door opened and Chouza stepped through, looking around. Amy took a step back, the last person who confronted her in the maze flashing through her mind.

Chouza spotted her and hesitated. "Amy?"

Amy gnawed her lip. "You're real, right? It's the real you? Not the you this dungeon conjured up?"

"You saw me?" Chouza strode forward, wrapping her into a hug. "Whatever he said, just know it's not true. It's just your fear." He buried his face in her hair. "I saw you. And Khiran."

Amy returned his embrace, pressing her face into his chest. "I'm sorry. I'm so sorry." She pulled back and peered up at his face. "Did you go through a maze?" He nodded. "That's what I thought. From what I can gauge, the maze was meant to represent being alone, which is one of Talia's fears. Though I doubt it's her biggest fear as we've only just started."

"Makes sense. Are you alright?"

"I'm... better now." She glanced around at the gathered parties. Nolan had one arm wrapped around Kila as she held Talia tightly to her. She frowned. "Jax still isn't here."

Chouza's arms tightened around her. "I'm sure he's fine."

"I hope so."

"Did everyone see people they knew?" Nolan asked. Amy couldn't help the quick glance at Chouza as she saw his lips tighten into a thin line.

Kila settled back onto the floor. "Yeah."

Amy glanced around at everyone nodding. All of them had people who they cared about and cared about them. Unbidden, her eyes went to

Chouza. He leaned in to kiss her forehead. "It wasn't true. Remember that."

She tucked her head under his chin. "I know. And whatever I said, it wasn't true either, okay? Or what Khiran or Kimi said."

He pulled her closer. "Thank you."

She kept her eye on the only door that hadn't opened yet. *Come on Jax. Where are you?*

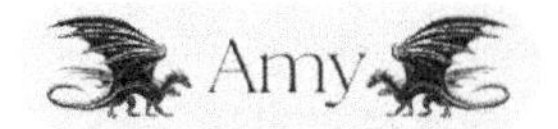

Finally, the door to the round chamber opened and Jax stumbled through. Immediately, Amy scrambled to her feet. "Jax?"

"N-no! Stay back for a moment. Are you real?"

Amy raised her hands. "I'm real, Jax. Those people just played on your fears." She took a few cautious steps forward. "They weren't real. Whatever they said wasn't true."

Jax's breathing slowed slightly and he stepped forward, pulling her into a tight hug. He buried his face into her neck. "I'm sorry. So sorry."

Amy quickly returned the hug. "Easy, Jax. It's alright. You're alright. We aren't alone, remember?"

He clung tightly to her. "Thank you, Amy."

She rubbed his back. "It's alright, Jax. You aren't alone. Whatever they said wasn't true."

"Finally," the same deep voice as before boomed. "I thought you would never arrive. Time to move to the next level."

"Oh not this guy agai—" Jax's words cut off as the room around them and the floor disappeared, leaving them all to plummet downwards.

Amy screamed and clung to Jax. Screams and cries of terror echoed around her as they plummeted straight down. She squeezed her eyes shut until she felt herself stop moving. Peeking her eyes open, she found herself suspended just over a body of water. With a gasp, she plopped into it.

She quickly swam back to the surface while Kila propped herself under Talia. "Now where are we?"

Chouza broke the surface next to her, holding onto Nolan. "Not sure. But fur— and water— do not mix." He grunted as he tried to keep the heavily armored man afloat.

Nolan coughed out a mouthful of water. "We need to find a way out of this!"

Amy scanned the solid domed walls around them. "I don't see any visible way out. I can try to swim downwards to see if there's something down there?"

Nolan nodded to her. "Do that. Jax, can you see if you can spot an illusionary wall? The sooner we get out of here the better."

Jax sputtered and sank beneath the water. Amy quickly helped him back to the surface and propped him up.

Once Jax caught his breath, he rubbed his eyes. "There's magick everywhere. So much that it hurts to look at. But at a quick glance, there's nothing discernibly different about any of them."

Amy tread water, her eyes roaming the walls. "Then it's probably down there. Drowning. Another fitting fear I suppose."

Once she had assured herself that Jax was okay, she took a deep breath and dove down through smooth water. But as she got deeper, a current pulled at her. She let it pull her along, conserving some of her strength. In the center, a whirlpool formed, funneling into a hole large enough for her to easily pass through.

The stone walls from above extended all the way down to the solid stone floor. The only visible way out was the whirlpool. She fought against the current until she reached the calmer waters. Finally reaching the surface, she took a few gasping breaths.

Nearby, Chouza struggled to keep Nolan afloat. "Are you alright?"

"I'm fine! The water funnels out at the bottom, but I have no idea where it goes. And if I go in, there's no getting back out."

Nolan gritted his teeth, scanning the walls and ceiling again. "It doesn't look like we have much of a choice. Lead the way, Amy."

"Alright. Pair up with someone who can swim well. Our best bet will be to swim straight down, then let the current pull us in. Don't fight it, that will only sap your strength."

Jax's eyes widened and darted around their surroundings. "We're really letting ourselves be pulled deeper into the water? What if there's no way out? What if we all drown?"

"The dungeons are always beatable. Pride wouldn't put a room with no exit." Amy propped herself under one of Jax's arms. "And I'll be with you the whole time, okay?" Jax gave a sharp nod and Amy addressed to the others. "Everyone ready? Take a deep breath and follow me."

She filled her lungs as much as she could and pulled away from Jax, taking his hand and guiding him down. She glanced back long enough to ensure the others were following before heading straight into the whirlpool.

Instead of fighting against it, she kicked straight into the center, trying to keep them stable and heading in the right direction. Next to her, Jax's eyes bulged in fear. *Just hang in there, Jax. It'll be okay.* She squeezed his hand tightly and let the current pull her through the hole.

The tunnel took a sharp turn and Amy kicked to the surface, pulling Jax with her. The rushing water pulled them along and Jax surfaced, coughing. The tunnel twisted and turned, the rapids dragging them along.

Amy struggled to keep her grip on Jax. "Don't let go!"

Jax's grip tightened as he barely avoided getting pulled under again. "I'm trying not to!"

Suddenly, the tunnel beneath them disappeared and they plummeted downwards again, splashing down into a deep underground lake. She pulled Jax to the surface again, coughing as water filled her lungs.

Not far away, the murky water lapped against a stone shore. "The edge is that way, go!"

Jax coughed out several mouthfuls of water before trying to follow her gaze. "Where? It's pitch black in here!"

"Of course it is." She gave Jax a gentle shove in the direction of the shore. "Just keep swimming that way. I don't see the others."

Jax reluctantly released her hand and swam in the direction she'd indicated. She scanned the lake surface. Near where the tunnel poured into the lake, she saw Kila and Talia struggling and swam to them.

"Where's Chouza and Nolan?"

"I don't know! I can't see a bloody thing!" Kila shouted.

Talia tried to tread water, even as Kila helped keep her afloat. "I-I don't know! They went in just ahead of us."

Amy gritted her teeth, searching the surface of the water. "They must still be underwater. Talia, the edge is that way. Kila can guide you."

Talia's eyes were wide as she looked the way Amy had pointed. "What about you? Where's Jax?"

"Already there. I'm going to see if I can find the others."

"Please hurry!" Kila begged. "Nolan won't be able to swim with all that armor on!"

"I know." Amy pushed them in the direction of the land and took a deep breath, diving into the water. The stone walls extended deep down and Amy swam along them, trying to spot her other two allies.

Finally, she found Chouza and Nolan struggling beneath the water, about halfway down. Nolan hung upside down, his foot stuck in the crumbling stone wall. Chouza tried to move the stones out of the way, but couldn't see them.

Amy hurried forward, grabbing Chouza's hand. He flailed against her, but she took carefully touched his cheek and he stilled, letting her guide him to where he needed to grip. A few seconds later, he propped himself under one of Nolan's arms and Amy took the other, both of them propelling Nolan to the surface.

Once they broke the surface, Nolan and Chouza both coughed, choking out mouthfuls of water. After a particularly violent coughing fit, Nolan took a shaky breath. "Thank you," he rasped.

"We don't leave teammates behind." Amy scanned their surroundings as the men caught their breath. "Come on. The shore is this way."

With Chouza's help, she led Nolan to where Jax, Kila, and Talia had hopefully already gotten out of the water. To her relief, she spotted Jax standing right at the edge. Behind him, Talia held Kila tightly, following Jax's gaze.

She said something to Kila, who took a blind step forward. Finally, Amy's feet brushed solid ground and she sloshed out of the water. The clank of metal on stone echoed around them as Nolan followed after her.

"Nolan?" Kila took another cautious step.

"It's alright, Love. I'm here." Kila raced forward and stumbled into Nolan's arms.

Chouza's hand reached out and Amy took it. "Are you alright?"

"Better now that we're all on land." She gazed around them. "Has anyone cast a light spell yet?"

Jax crossed his arms. "I tried. Unfortunately, it does no good."

Amy's brow furrowed. "So what fear is this, then?"

Nolan held a shaking Kila to him tightly. "Darkness."

"Right." She scanned her surroundings. "So there's three of us that can see. And three that can't."

Jax stepped closer to her. "Do you see a way out?"

"Not really." She studied the water line, but it ended at sheer rock faces in either direction. The stone floor beneath them continued as far as she could see away from the water. "But my guess would be that way."

Jax raised an eyebrow. "You know, I'd feel a bit more confident if I knew what 'that way' was."

"Right. Sorry. Directly away from the water. Unless we're meant to get back in?"

"Let's not," Jax said quickly.

"Right." Nolan pulled one of his boots off and dumped water from it, then repeated the process. "I'm with the fox. Either way, we need to get moving."

Jax scowled. "Alright, Nolan. Care to lead the way since Kila can't see and Talia and Amy are both spellcasters?"

"Fine." He dug into his bag and pulled a rope out. "Here. Everyone hold onto this. Amy, Talia, you two will have to keep an eye on Kila, Jax, and Chouza. Make sure they don't get lost."

Jax crossed his arms. "We're hardly going to wander off in the dark."

Nolan grunted and handed Kila the rope. "We'll see."

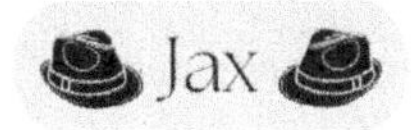

I hate this. Darkness stretched in all directions, with only the sounds of breathing, the clinking of metal, and shuffling feet ahead of and behind Jax. Finally, the faint outline of the people in front of him started to come into focus.

His ears perked. "Is it just me, or is it getting lighter?"

Kila nodded emphatically. "I can see a little bit now."

The wide tunnel narrowed and the light grew brighter. Eventually, the tunnel turned into a hallway that ended in a narrow archway.

"Finally. Something different," Nolan muttered. He gathered the rope back and gestured Kila forward. "You good to take the lead now?"

"Of course," Kila said, the shake in her voice betraying her. She stepped through the archway and Nolan followed. Talia hurried forward, but Amy hesitated. The archway led to a narrow tunnel that left no room for Jax to pass her.

He reached forward to squeeze her hand and she jumped at the contact. "Are you alright, Amy?"

"F-fine." She edged forward into the new tunnel.

Jax glanced at Chouza worriedly before following. As they walked, the ceiling of the tunnel lowered and the walls started to narrow until Chouza and Nolan's shoulders were brushing the sides and they had to duck their heads.

Ahead of him, Amy's breathing grew uneven, her grip on her staff turning her knuckles white. The ceiling continued to lower, until all but Amy were hunched forward, trying to avoid hitting their heads. He could hear Chouza's sword dragging the floor behind him, the whine of metal on stone grating his ears.

Amy stopped and took a step back, stumbling into Jax. He caught her, feeling her entire body shaking. "Amy? What's wrong?"

"N-nothing." She took a small step forward, but then immediately pedaled backward again. "I… I'm fine. I can do this. I'm fine," she muttered under her breath, barely loud enough for Jax to hear.

Unaware of Amy's pause, Kila, Nolan, and Talia continued forward, the gap between the two groups growing wider. Jax reached forward to rest a hand on her shoulder, frowning when she jumped. "It's alright Amy. Chouza and I are here with you. Just focus on us."

"Y-you're behind me, though." She turned to where she could see him. "I don't like small spaces."

"I understand."

"You can still hear us, right?" Chouza asked from behind him.

"Y-yes."

Jax took her hand and squeezed it gently. "Like you said, this dungeon is meant to be beatable. That means there's an end to this tunnel. You won't get trapped in here. And we'll be right behind you."

She gnawed her lip and gave a short nod before facing the steadily shortening tunnel. She crept forward again, ducking her head to avoid the low ceiling. Far ahead of them, Nolan, Kila, and Talia had stopped.

Kila knelt in front of a tiny tunnel. "We're going to have to crawl from here out and it's going to be a tight fit."

Nolan turned sideways to get more room for his armor, his bent knees resting against one wall and his back leaning against the other. "Do you see an end to it?"

"Not really. Do you want me to go check?"

Nolan tapped his thumb against his sword hilt, glancing back at the rest of the group as he contemplated. "No. We don't want to get separated in here again. We just have to trust that there's a way out. Because if not, I don't think we're coming back this way."

Amy pressed back against Jax and he winced as she knocked his head against the ceiling. "Easy, Amy."

She shook her head, trying to press further back. The temperature in the tunnel rose. "I'm not going in there."

He carefully reached around to grip her hand in the tight quarters. "Amy. You can quit. You can give up now and leave the dungeon. You don't have to continue."

"I-I know."

"If you do decide to quit, none of us would think any less of you for it," Chouza assured her.

"I'm guessing this is your fear?" Kila asked from ahead of them. Jax readied himself to defend Amy against her, but instead of the snarky comment he expected, she grunted. "Like you said. There's got to be a way out. Just take your time." Jax heard the sound of shuffling as first Kila, then Nolan, and finally Talia started crawling down the dirt tunnel.

Amy knelt in front of it. "Remember, Amy. We're right behind you. And if it ever becomes too much for you, you can quit."

"R-right." She slowly crawled forward and with one last worried glance back at Chouza, Jax followed.

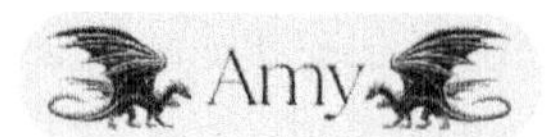

Amy's heart raced as she crawled through the tiny tunnel. It had been what felt like hours since Jax and Chouza had convinced her to enter it with no end in sight. "Jax?"

"I'm here, Amy. It's alright." His voice came from just behind her and the knowledge that he was close helped to reassure her.

"Okay. Chouza?"

"I'm here, too, Amy."

Amy sighed in relief at his voice. "H-how much longer do you think this will go on?"

"Actually, I think it's opening up," Kila called from ahead of them.

Amy's head lifted, knocking against the ceiling and she gasped. She dropped to the floor of the tunnel and covered her head. She tried to pull her knees to her chest, but the confines of the tunnel didn't let her move. The temperature around her rose. *Not again. I'm trapped. Fire. Burning.* Her pulse raced in her ears and she whimpered.

"Amy! Amy, it's okay! You're okay!" Jax's voice echoed to her as if from far away.

"If you can get her moving, it opens up right here."

"Amy, did you hear Kila? It opens up. You can get out of here. You aren't trapped!"

"Amy, it's okay. We're here, remember."

A hand gripped her leg and immediately a sense of calm washed through her. "We know you're scared, Amy." She uncovered her head enough to peer back at Jax. "We know. But we're here. And you can get out of this. Just ahead of you, the tunnel opens up. You can get out of here. All you have to do is keep moving."

"P-promise?"

"I promise, Amy." He squeezed her leg gently and released her. "Just go a little at a time. We're right behind you."

Amy gnawed her lip. "O-okay."

"That's it, Amy," Chouza encouraged as she rolled back onto her stomach and pressed herself up onto her hands and knees. "A little at a time."

Ahead of her, Talia peered back at her. "Come on, Amy. The exit is right here."

Amy hurried forward, gasping as the tunnel suddenly opened into a wide cavern. Nolan blocked her path. "Easy. You don't want to go any further."

Amy froze, standing on the edge of a high cliff. Jax crawled out of the tunnel behind her and stood, trying unsuccessfully to brush the mud from his fur and clothes. "Well, that was fun."

Chouza grunted and followed him out, reaching back to pull his sword from behind him. "Are you alright, Amy?"

Amy pressed herself against his chest, ignoring the mud that squished between them. "Thank you. Both of you."

"Of course." He wrapped his arms gently around her, rolling his shoulders with a grimace. "We promised that you wouldn't be alone." His body stiffened. "Please tell me that cliff doesn't just drop straight off."

"Unfortunately it does," Nolan confirmed. "The path continues along the edge of this cliff for as far as I can see."

Chouza's arms tightened around her. "Of course it does."

Jax glanced between him and the cliff. "Oh right. Heights were your fear."

Chouza cleared his throat. "Y-yeah."

Amy squeezed his waist. "We'll be okay, Chouza."

"I know."

Nolan stepped aside, gesturing for Kila to take the lead. "Alright, Kila. Lead the way."

Kila started down the narrow path. On their right, a stone cliff stretched out of sight. On their left, the stone dropped straight down. Far beneath them, spikes of stone pointed straight up and across the ravine, a second cliff towered high above them.

Amy edged aside. "Go ahead, Jax."

"You're sure?"

"Yeah."

Jax slipped past her and Amy took Chouza's hand. "It's alright. I'll stay with you."

"Right. Thanks, Amy."

She followed after Jax, gripping her staff with one hand, and Chouza's hand with the other. He kept a tight grip on her, his other hand holding his sword. They continued along the path until far ahead of them, a rope bridge extended across to the second cliff.

Chouza's grip tightened on her hand. "You've got to be kidding me."

Jax hesitated in front of her. "Even I don't like the look of that."

Kila followed the edge of the cliff around and stopped on a small ledge in front of the bridge. "There's no other way. We have to cross."

Chouza's eyes darted toward the spikes at the bottom of the ravine. "Is that thing even safe?"

Nolan plucked one of the ropes where it fastened to a wooden anchor and frowned. "I mean, we have to assume it is? Otherwise, we wouldn't be able to cross. They seem to be in good repair. Kila, take it slow."

Kila edged forward on the rope bridge, testing each board carefully before placing her weight on it. She made it halfway across before the beating of wings reached Amy's ears. She stiffened and tried to follow the sound.

Jax glanced over at her. "Amy?"

"Something's coming. I can hear it."

Jax's ears flicked before his eyes widened. "I can, too. Nolan—"

"I heard you. Land or air?"

"Air."

"Right. Kila! Get across, now! Whatever's coming you don't want to be—"

He cut off as Kila screamed in terror. The bridge shook and groaned as a large, winged creature hit it from underneath. Kila flew through the air, only barely managing to grasp the rope on the side to keep herself from falling into the void below.

"Kila!" Nolan stepped forward, but Jax grabbed his arm. "There's more! Look!"

Two more of the beasts lifted into the air in front of the rest of the group. Gray skin stretched taut over gaunt ribs. "What are these?" Amy gasped.

Talia pressed back against the wall, eyes wide. "Lower-level demons called tytos. I've read about them, but I've never seen one. Watch out for their acid breath!"

One of the tytos in front of them hissed. Acid dripped from a mouthful of long, sharp teeth.

Nolan lifted his sword in front of him. "Noted!"

On the bridge, Kila swung her leg forward and looped it into one of the ropes on the side of the bridge, using it to twist herself back onto the planks in the middle. The first tyto followed, its cloven feet landing on the thin wood. The board beneath it snapped and it beat its wings to regain its balance, towering several feet over Kila.

Nolan glanced quickly at Talia. "Anything else you know about them?"

"Uh… They don't like lightning. They're slow on foot, but quick in the air. They don't see very well, but their hearing is amazing."

The tyto lunged forward, its teeth snapping inches from Nolan's head. The second tyto reared back and acid sprayed toward Amy, Jax, and Chouza. Chouza grabbed Amy and pulled her back the way they had come, while Jax jumped forward onto the small platform where Nolan and Talia already stood.

Chouza teetered on the edge of the cliff for a moment before Amy yanked him back. The rock where they had been standing started dissolving, the acid eating through it. She edged further away from it. "Let's not get hit by that."

Chouza twisted the handle of his sword, separating it into two blades. "Agreed. Amy, get back."

Amy glanced around her. "Where? There's nowhere for me to go!" Again, the word that had popped into her head when she discovered the new tattoo came to mind.

Chouza growled. "Yeah, I know. Just… try to be careful, okay?"

"I can do that." She gnawed her lip. "Tutela!" Immediately, a shimmer covered her chest and arms. She gasped and studied the armor her magick had created, feeling it slowly pulling on her magick.

Across from them, Jax and Nolan were already battling the other tyto, Nolan deftly blocking the sharp claws swinging at him. "Jax! Help Kila!"

Jax glanced reluctantly at Amy before darting out onto the bridge. Amy pressed helplessly against the wall, trying to stay out of the way of Chouza's swords. The tyto's teeth gnashed against his left arm, the thick padding of the armor thankfully protecting him. The sword in his right hand crackled with electricity as he stabbed into the creature's gut.

Amy gritted her teeth, calling up all of the training Inzo had given her. Her magick rippled and flowed, ready to do her bidding. She carefully molded it around him then lifted her hand. Before she could cast a spell, however, the tyto on Chouza shrieked in pain and released him. He swung his sword in a wide arc and sliced off its head. It plummeted backward, back into the void.

Another angry shriek drew her attention to the bridge. Jax and Kila had managed to draw the third tyto across to the platform on the other side. With more room to work with, they were able to pin it between them and Jax's rapier slid under its arm into the soft flesh there. The second tyto dropped over the side of the cliff.

Nolan stabbed his sword into the third tyto's chest and yanked it back, letting the lifeless body plummet backward. "Anyone hurt?"

Jax glanced down at himself and shook his head. "Surprisingly, no. I thought that would have gone a lot worse."

Amy turned to check on Chouza and gasped. The piece of armor where the tyto had bitten was dissolving. He struggled with the buckles of his gauntlet, trying to undo it without touching his arm to anything else. "Talia! How do you get rid of the acid?"

"It should just wash off!"

Amy pulled the waterskin from her bag and dumped it onto his arm, using her other hand to try and wash it off. She gritted her teeth as pain erupted in her palm, the acid already starting to eat at her skin. When she had no water left, she stopped, watching the armor warily.

Chouza panted for a moment, watching as well. To Amy's relief, nothing else seemed to be dissolving. She stared at her palm. The acid had left angry red blisters and her shirt had been eaten away several inches up her arm, revealing her tattoo.

Chouza reached forward and cradled her hand. "We should get Talia to look at this."

"R-right." She turned back toward the platform and froze. The acid from the initial attack had eaten through the walkway, leaving a several-foot gap between them and the platform Talia and Nolan were on. Even as they watched, the stone along the edges started to crumble. "We're going to have to jump."

Chouza shook his head. "There's no way."

Amy gnawed her lip. "Unfortunately, I don't think we have any other choice. Do you want to go first, or do you want me to?"

Chouza's jaw clenched as he looked between her and the ever-widening gap. "You go ahead. Talia needs to look at your hand."

"You sure?"

"Yeah. Go." He took several steps back. "Get a running jump."

Amy bit her lip and followed him. On the other side, Nolan looped one arm around the post that anchored the bridge and held the other out toher. "I'll catch you. Come on, you can do it, Amy."

Amy took a few deep breaths and ran forward, leaping across the gap. Her foot landed too close to the edge and the crumbling stone caused her to lose her footing, but Nolan grabbed her arm and hauled her up. "You alright?"

"I'm good. Thanks, Nolan."

He gave her a nod. "Go get checked out. Come on, Chouza. Your turn."

Amy backed up out of the way but didn't go to Talia yet. "Come on, Chouza. If I can make it, you can."

Chouza took a few deep breaths, then shook his head and followed Amy's steps. Like her, his foot hit the crumbling edge and he stumbled, but Nolan grabbed one of his arms and Amy lunged forward to grab the other.

She bit back a hiss of pain as her injured hand protested the contact with his arm and helped Nolan pull him up onto the platform. Chouza pulled her into a tight hug and Amy could feel his heart pounding against her ear.

Nolan gave them a moment before clearing his throat. "Lady Flame, you should really let Talia look at your hand."

She flushed and pulled back from Chouza. "Right."

Talia studied her palm critically. A quick healing spell later and the blisters had faded to just an angry red mark. "This is the best I can do for now. The deeper damage will need to be looked at by Lillian. Until then…" She pulled bandages from a kit and wrapped them around Amy's hand. "Just try not to get anything into it."

"Okay. Thank you, Talia."

"We're lucky it was just a few lower-class tytos. Usually, when they're around, there's a grand tyto as well. Those things will melt skin from bone with their breath alone."

"Lucky indeed." A loud thumping drew her attention and she peered over the edge. What she'd originally thought was a large rockface far below them shifted and leathery wings unfurled. "Talia… How big were those grand tytos?"

"About the size of houses." Her brow furrowed. "Why?"

Dread filled her. "Run." She shoved Talia toward the bridge. "We have to get across that bridge. Now!"

"But—"

"No buts! That grand tyto you mentioned? It's down there, and it's on its way."

Nolan followed her gaze and sheathed his sword. "Two at a time. I'm not sure how strong this bridge is and I don't want it snapping under too much weight. Amy, Talia, you two go first."

Amy shook her head. "You go with Talia. We need strong fighters on both sides. I'll stay with Chouza."

Talia crept forward, keeping a close eye on her footing. Nolan started to protest but snapped his mouth shut. "You're right. As soon as we're across, you two follow."

"We will. Go!" Nolan stepped out onto the bridge behind Talia.

Chouza shook his head. "I can't do this, Amy."

She gripped his hand. "Chouza, I know you're scared. And I'm so sorry that we have to rush. But if we stay here, we will die. Kimi will be left without a father. You either have to quit or cross, okay? I'll be right there with you."

Chouza's jaw clenched as the thumping beneath them grew louder. "I know! I know. Just—"

"I'll be right with you the whole time."

"Alright, Amy!" Nolan called from the other side. "You and Chouza come on across!"

She waved to let him know she'd heard and took Chouza's hand, carefully stepping backward onto the bridge. "Just focus on me. Just watch me. Okay?" He nodded tersely and Amy led him out onto the bridge. "Just don't look down."

She glanced over the edge and her heart started to pound as the large maw of the grand tyto opened beneath them. A roar echoed around them, shaking the canyon walls. Chouza stumbled and Amy squeezed his hand.

"You're almost here!" Jax called from behind them.

The grand tyto's wings beat as it lunged upwards, its jaws closing around the center of the rope bridge. It snapped and Amy felt herself falling. She slammed against the side of the rock wall, one hand holding Chouza's, the other gripping her staff. Nolan held the other end, suspending them over the deep ravine.

"Don't. Let. Go," Nolan gritted out. Amy bit back a cry of pain as her shoulders strained to hold Chouza's weight and her hand protested the grip on her staff. "Jax, get a rope down to him, now!"

Amy felt her left shoulder pop and couldn't resist crying out, losing her grip on the staff.

"Amy!" Jax cried.

She jerked to a stop again, one edge of Chouza's sword perilously close to her face as he caught her around the waist, his other hand holding a rope. "Pull us up," he called.

His grip on her waist slipped and she did her best to hold onto him, pain radiating from her entire left arm

Slowly, Nolan, Jax, Kila, and Talia managed to pull them up. The grand tyto lunged upwards again, barely missing their feet. Another roar echoed around them before Amy heard a deep breath.

Talia's eyes widened. "Run! Now!" She took off down the ledge, Nolan and Kila just behind her.

Jax followed but slowed when Amy couldn't keep up. "Are you alright?"

"I-I think my shoulder is dislocated." She bit her lip, struggling to see through the tears.

Chouza passed his blade to Jax. "Carry this!" He scooped Amy into his arms, careful to not jostle her injured shoulder. She started to protest, but the sound of acid spraying below them caused her stomach to drop.

Jax took off with Chouza just behind him. The path ended at a wall and turned sharply to the left into a new cavern. Talia, Nolan, and Kila stood near the center, panting. The first bit of acid hit the wall behind them and the rock face began to dissolve.

Talia hurried forward. "Amy? Are you alright?"

Jax shook his head. "Her shoulder dislocated when she was holding Chouza up."

Chouza carefully set her back on her feet, catching her when she swayed. "Easy."

Talia hovered a hand over her shoulder. "It's definitely dislocated and some of the muscles are torn as well. This is beyond what I can heal. The best I can do is set it and bind it so you aren't hurting it any worse."

Amy gritted her teeth and took short, panting breaths. "Do what you can, please."

"Right. This is going to hurt." Talia lifted Amy's arm, rotating it slightly. A slight pop accompanied a sharp pain as the ball popped back into the socket. Heat flared from Amy and she gasped. Talia pulled another roll of bandages from her bag and tucked Amy's arm against her chest, winding the bandage under her arm and up and around the back of her neck to form a makeshift sling.

Chouza took his sword back from Jax. "Thanks. Are you alright, Amy?"

"B-better now." She wiped at her face, thankful that her injured hand

and shoulder were on the same side.

Nolan gazed around them as he offered Amy her staff back. "Let's take a moment to rest. This place looks safe enough for now. Jax, you and Kila keep watch."

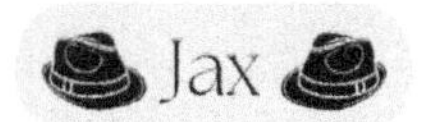

29

Jax

Jax watched Amy with concern as she sat next to Chouza on the floor. He offered her his waterskin and she took a small sip before passing it back, her skin sallow and sickly. *I think she's in a lot more pain than she's willing to admit.*

"Where did you learn the trick for the magick armor?" The armor had long since disappeared, but Jax couldn't help his curiosity.

Amy shrugged with her uninjured shoulder. "It came to mind when I discovered my new tattoo just after the last dungeon. I just never tested it out."

"Why not?"

Amy ducked her head. "I was afraid it was something dangerous."

Jax frowned, but before he could protest, he heard the sound of shuffling feet from a nearby hallway. He and Kila had checked it before allowing Amy to rest, but it had stretched quite a ways ahead of them and neither felt comfortable straying too far from the rest of the group.

"We have company." He tightened his grip on his rapier as Chouza helped Amy to her feet. Immediately, she recast the spell, the glimmering armor coating her torso.

A dozen white-faced clowns shuffled down the hallway. The fool's hats on their heads ended in snapping snakes. Each of them held a knife that dripped blood, a sadistic grin twisting their face in a mockery of joy.

Nolan paled and slammed his helmet back onto his head. "You know, I don't like clowns, but this takes it to a whole other level."

Kila took a hurried step backward. "Are we supposed to fight these things or go around them?"

"Do you see a way around?"

"Not really. We could probably just rush past them, but I'm not sure that's in our best interest." Jax's eyes darted to Amy. *She, especially, I don't think would make it.*

Amy winced as she lifted a hand. "Ignis!" Flames poured from her palm, charring the skin of the leading clowns. She stepped behind Chouza, retching. His brow furrowed until he realized the problem. *These creatures are alive! Not undead like the last dungeon. This must be horrible for her.*

Chouza planted himself in front of her, spinning his blades quickly before lunging forward to decapitate the first clown. Kila darted toward a second one and Jax joined her, the two working in sync to drop it.

Nolan took a stumbling step backward, his sword gripped in both hands and raised in front of him. One of the clowns impaled itself on his blade and slid forward to let the snakes snap at Nolan's face.

Jax darted forward, but to his surprise, Amy pulled an ornate dagger from Chouza's waist and sliced the snakes in half. Nolan's eyes widened as blood splattered him. Determination hardened Amy's face as she lifted the dagger in front of her, her other arm still wrapped tightly in the sling.

Dread filled Jax. *She can't use her staff with only one hand.* Two more of the clowns leaped toward him and Kila, and he found himself unable to keep track of Amy anymore. One of the clowns swung its dagger at him and he jumped back, knocking into Kila.

She stumbled and missed her throw, her dagger flying harmlessly past a clown. "There's too many of them! We can't fight all of them!"

Chouza's blade pierced the clown approaching Jax. "Yes, we can! Stay together! Don't let them separate us. Keep Amy and Talia behind us!"

Kila and Jax stood on either side of Nolan. Amy stepped up next to Jax, the dagger still gripped tightly in her hand, but he placed an arm out. "It's alright, Amy. We can handle this."

She hesitated, but to his relief stepped back next to Talia. "Just be careful."

"We will."

Nolan lunged forward and stabbed his blade through one clown's heart, then pulled back and sliced through a second's stomach. Jax and Kila darted forward, Kila jamming her dagger under one's chin as Jax stabbed his rapier through another's throat.

Chouza again clicked his blades apart, the double longswords swinging not quite in unison so that just after the first hit, the second reached its mark as well. Only a few minutes later, the group stood in front of a pile of corpses.

Chouza flicked the blood from his blades and clicked them back together before turning to wrap Amy in a hug. "You stole my dagger."

"I don't have one of my own."

He kissed her head and took the dagger from her, sheathing it back on his belt before removing the sheath and adding it to hers. "Well, now you do."

"But—"

He rested his forehead against hers. "No buts. It was an oversight to not make sure you had one before entering. We'll get you a new one when we get out of here. For now, you need a weapon you can use."

She nodded hesitantly.

Nolan leaned against the wall on the opposite side of the chamber, his face hidden beneath his helmet still. "This is sweet and all, but maybe we should go? I'd rather not face another one of these monstrosities."

Amy flushed. "Right. Let's go." She picked her staff up and with Chouza's help, strapped it to her back.

Nolan straightened and after Talia finished checking each of them over, gestured for Kila to take the lead. Jax fell into step next to Amy as they started down the hallway. "Are you alright?"

She ducked her head and looked away from him. "I'm fine."

"No, you aren't. That's the first time you've had to use your fire on a living thing, isn't it?" He reached over to take her uninjured hand.

"I used it on Wrath, remember? And Master Inzo."

"Yes, but that wasn't a conscious decision and he ate it anyway. And you knew it wouldn't hurt Master Inzo." He squeezed her hand lightly. "This is different."

She sighed and her shoulders hunched slightly. "I hate the smell of burning skin. And knowing that I'm intentionally hurting someone…"

"It reminds you of what happened to your family, doesn't it?" She gave a sharp nod and he squeezed her hand again. "Just remember, this is different. This is about survival."

"I know. But still…"

"It's still hard. I'd be more worried if it wasn't. Amy I—" His words cut off as they once again plummeted downwards. Amy's hand ripped free from his and he hit the ground hard.

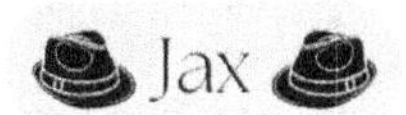

Jax groaned as he slowly returned to consciousness. His head pounded from the impact with the ground and his mouth felt like cotton.

"Oh, Jackie." Jax's blood ran cold. "It's so good to see you taking such a liking to being the new Gallund. And your technique has improved *so* much."

Jax peeled his eyes open and his stomach dropped. Kila, Nolan, and Chouza all lay in front of him, multiple limbs missing and throats cut. Something warm ran down his arm and he looked down to see Talia's lifeless body held against him, a knife in his hand having just slit her throat.

Gallund gripped Amy's hair in his fist and she flailed, trying to pull herself free as tears streamed down her face. "So tell me, Jackie. Do you want her next? Or would you rather have one of them?"

He gestured to Jax's right and Jax followed the movement, horror filling him, even as a grin spread across his face. Mutilated bodies stretched as far as he could see: his parents, the Arkhams, Elina, random people he'd seen around Lorencost, and right up front, Gaige.

She glared at him through her one remaining eye. "You didn't kill me last time. But then you left me to die. Why don't you just finish it this time? Finish it!"

No! No, no, no! Even as his mind screamed at him to stop, he let Talia's body drop to the ground and stepped toward Gaige, lifting the Cheshire dagger. Gallund grinned. "Ooh, good choice. She's been waiting for this for *years*."

"Jax!" Talia's voice echoed around him and he frowned.

Gallund's twisted grin stretched even wider. "Go on, Jackie."

Jax took another step forward, but Talia's voice again echoed to him. "Jax! It's not real! It's just the dungeon!"

He stumbled as something shook his body and he glanced back at the dead Talia on the ground. Shaking his head, he took another step. Gaige lifted her chin to meet his eye. "Alright, Jax. It's time to wake up."

Jax felt like he'd been punched in the gut. He rolled to his side and vomited. Talia jumped out of the way. "Jax? Are you here now?"

"Y-yeah. I'm okay." Jax looked around him at the white marbled walls and floor. The bodies had all disappeared and the rest of the group seemed intact. Nolan held Kila tightly, while Chouza gently stroked Amy's cheeks, murmuring quiet words. Her eyes were squeezed shut as she whimpered.

Nolan took a step toward Chouza. "Wake her up."

"I'm trying."

Nolan strode forward, pulled the gauntlet from his hand, and slapped Amy's cheek.

Hard.

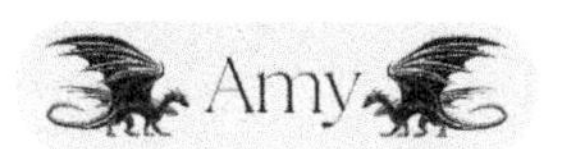

Flames roared around Amy. Screams of agony filled the air and she whirled, trying to find the source.

"Amelia!"

"Amelia, stop this!"

"Amy! Big sis, why are you doing this?"

Her parents' and brother's voices had no distinguishable source. She trudged through the ash settling around her, the sitting room of her childhood home burning down around her.

She stepped into a hallway and found the charred remains of her brother. She screamed and turned away, smoke choking clogging her throat. Behind her, Jax stood with flames licking at his body. She stumbled back and tripped over Damien, landing on the floor.

Jax's face twisted in pain. "Why are you doing this, Amy? Are you going to kill us all?"

"No! No, this isn't real. It can't be real!" She scrambled to her feet and tried to run. Rounding the corner, she ran straight into her parents. Angry red blisters covered their skin, and flames ate away at their clothing and hair.

Her mother reached forward to caress her cheek. "You will kill all of them, just like you did us."

A sob ripped from Amy's throat and she pulled away, running for the front door. She grabbed the knob and screamed in pain as the heat burned her hand. Whirling, she saw Chouza holding Kimi. She pressed back against the door.

"No. No no no. This isn't real. It isn't real."

Chouza pulled Kimi tighter against him as flames covered their bodies. Kimi sobbed into his shoulder as Chouza glared at Amy. "It's okay Kimi. It'll be over soon. You won't be in pain much longer."

"Get her out! Save her! Please!" Amy begged.

"How can I save her from you? You will kill us all." The manor around them disappeared. Behind Chouza, flames licked at everyone Amy knew or cared about: her parents, her brother, Jax, Talia, Kila, Nolan, the Arkhams, Inzo, Balthazar, Kukuri, Kraven. All of them screaming in pain.

"You did this."

Amy raised her hands to cover her face, only to realize the flames were pulsing from her body.

"Amy!"

The distant voice didn't connect with the scene around her.

"Amy! It's not real!" Chouza's face shifted slightly from twisted anger to gentle care. "Amy, I'm here. It's not real. You're safe. We're all safe." Kimi disappeared and Chouza stepped forward, arms outstretched. "I'm here, Amy."

Suddenly, pain exploded across her left cheek and the flames around her flared higher. Chozua cried out and the world around her disappeared.

"What the hell, Nolan!"

Amy gasped and sat up. Jax knelt next to her, watching something else. She followed his gaze. Nolan had a bruise forming on his cheek as he glared at Chouza. Blisters covered his right hand and scorch marks blackened the front of Chouza's armor.

"We needed to snap her out of it!"

"By slapping her?" Chouza's fists clenched. "I was working on it! You saw me working on it!"

Nolan slid the gauntlet back on his hand, wincing. "It was taking too long."

"Taking too— By what standard? Why did it matter how long it took?"

Amy whimpered and Jax glanced down at her. "Chouza!"

Chouza glared at Nolan a moment longer before turning, his face softening when he saw Amy. "Hey."

She pressed back against Jax, eyes tracing the scorch marks on Chouza's armor. "I did it again. I hurt you."

"I'm fine, Amy."

She shook her head. "No. No, you aren't fine!"

Talia hurried forward, closed her eyes, and pressed her hand to his chest. "Actually, the burns are fairly superficial. Even I can heal this." She used another healing spell and some of the stiffness in Chouza's posture eased.

"Thank you, Talia." He stepped closer to Amy and showed her his hands. "See. I'm fine."

"It's alright, Amy." Jax squeezed her shoulder gently. "We're all okay."

Amy's trembling eased and she struggled to her feet. Jax helped pull her up, careful to avoid her injured shoulder. A set of double doors that Amy hadn't noticed at the opposite end of the room creaked open and Amy drew the dagger from her waist.

Two creatures with shaggy reddish-blond fur stepped into the room. Thick manes framed their faces as they prowled forward on two legs.

Amy stepped closer to Jax and Chouza. "Pride's sinspawn. We need to be very careful not to get bitten this time."

The two pridespawn stopped just inside the door. "If you will follow us, our master wishes to see you." The gravelly voice reminded Amy of

Tsume's growl.

Nolan lifted his sword. "Your master?"

"Yes," the second one said.

Kila narrowed her eyes. "How do we know you won't just attack the moment we get close?"

"We are not sneaky thieves. We fight with honor."

Jax's nose wrinkled. "Ouch."

Nolan straightened and relaxed his grip on his sword. "Very well." He lowered his voice. "Either way, keep on your guard. Amy, Talia, you two stay near the middle."

Kila and Nolan led the way, followed by Talia, Amy, and finally Chouza and Jax. Amy sheathed her dagger and took a deep breath. *Let's hope this isn't a huge mistake.*

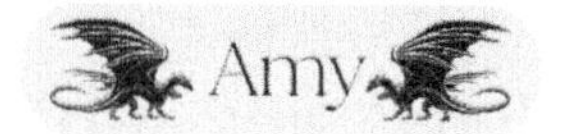

Pain radiated from Amy's shoulder as they followed the sinspawn. Jax glanced at her every few seconds and she knew he was worried about her.

The two pride sinspawn led them through the double doors and down an ornate hallway. Tapestries of a demonkin man with a square jaw, reddish-orange skin, and black horns that arched high above his head lined the walls.

"Conceited much?" Jax muttered. Amy gave him a sharp look. "Sorry."

The hallway abruptly opened into a large, ornate chamber where the same demonkin they had seen in the tapestries lounged on a throne up on a high platform. Two more pridespawn stood on either side of him, holding platters with drinks and food on them.

"It's about time you six made it here. I thought you never would." He cracked his neck and stood, strutting down the stairs.

Nolan lifted his sword. "You must be Pride."

"Indeed. And you're an idiot afraid of clowns. I quite enjoyed what my dungeon did with that." He gestured around him. "You see, the moment you step foot inside my dungeon, it feeds off of your fears and then enhances them, gives them a face, a challenge. And I get to watch as your spirit breaks."

He stopped at the bottom of the stairs. "And then if you do succeed, you face what frightens you the most. Your past." His eyes ranged over

Amy, Jax, and Kila. "Your future." He smirked at Talia. He glanced at Chouza before refocusing on Nolan. "Or even your present."

Amy glared at him. "You take pleasure in other people's pain?"

"But of course." He sidled forward and Chouza and Jax immediately stepped in front of Amy. "Aww. Big, powerful protectors for the little fire dragon." He smirked. "I'd like a new challenge. You see, I've been here for three hundred years, watching as my dungeon tormented people. Then if they made it past those fears, they get dumped in that same room you just did. Up until now, my sinspawn have fought them. But I'm bored of that. Today, you will fight me."

Talia gasped and Amy stiffened. *We weren't even able to touch the last two Sins we met. What chance do we have against this one?*

Pride dropped into a crouch and raised a hand in a 'come and get me' motion.

Talia shook her head. "He's got to be kidding, right?"

Chouza kept one arm raised in front of Amy, the other gripping his sword tightly. "I don't think he is."

Nolan's eyes narrowed. "Our best bet is to all attack at once and overwhelm him. Even then, this will be a hard fight. Kila, Jax, try to get around behind him. Chouza, you and I will head in straight on. He doesn't seem to be using any weapons so try to keep him from hitting your head. Just let him go for center of mass and focus your attention on hitting him. Let's just hope our armor can take the hit."

"Don't underestimate a skilled fighter's blows with just his fists."

"I'm aware, Chouza. But I also know that we need to consider this very carefully. We don't—"

"Oh, come on." Pride rolled his neck. "Are you just going to stand there talking or are we going to fight?" He smirked. "Fine, if you won't come to me, I'll come to you."

He darted forward and Nolan barely had time to lift his sword before Pride ducked under it and used his leg to sweep Nolan's feet out from under him. The clang of metal echoed around them as he fell flat on his back.

Pride immediately grabbed Chouza's arm, turning and slinging him around and past him. He pivoted again and slammed the heel of his foot directly into Kila's stomach, doubling her over.

Amy gaped as the man moved almost too fast for her to follow.

Blood trickled from Pride's nose and Amy recognized one of Jax's mental attacks. Before he could land another blow, she stepped forward and raised a hand, flames pouring past Jax to hit their opponent. When her flames cleared, Pride appeared to be uninjured.

Chouza's spun around him again, blocking Pride from getting too close. The Sin raised an eyebrow. "You think that will stop me?"

Kila darted in to stab a dagger into his side. "No, but it will distract you."

He reached down to grab her wrist and yanked the dagger out, slinging her across the room like she weighed no more than a doll. Acid coated Nolan's blade as he rolled to his feet and charged forward.

Pride slid past his arm and hit the outside of his elbow with his palm and Amy heard a sickening crack. Then, he spun and his elbow caught Nolan in the side of the head. Nolan cried out in pain as his right arm hung at his side.

Talia immediately hurried forward, channeling healing magick to all of them, but the serious injuries were too much for her to handle. Jax darted in, his new rapier in one hand and a dagger of force in the other, using the rapier to distract so that he could try to drive the dagger into Pride.

The Sin slid out of the way and grabbed Jax by the back of the neck, throwing him past him. Amy cast another fire spell, heat pouring off of it as it hit Pride full force. When the flames cleared, much of Pride's skin had blistered. He growled and turned to Amy, but Chouza darted forward, his blade slicing across Pride's back.

Pride whirled and drove his foot into Chouza's chest, slinging him back. He slammed into the wall and slid down.

Amy shrieked and raced toward him. "Chouza!"

Pride laughed and whirled to dodge another blow from Kila. Nolan tried to slice across his stomach with the blade in his other hand, but Pride grabbed his wrist and slung him past him, dancing around their blades like it was some kind of game.

Talia frantically tried to heal the steadily increasing number of wounds as Pride broke bones and snapped joints. Nolan charged forward again and Pride drove his fist straight into Nolan's chest, crumpling the metal and dropping the man inside.

Kila screamed and darted forward, daggers swinging wildly. Pride's eyes narrowed as he blocked each blow. Taking advantage of the distraction, Jax drove his rapier into Pride's side, but the Sin just planted his palm into Jax's chest, knocking him to the ground.

Amy hurried over to him and helped him to his feet. "We're helpless against him!"

Jax grunted, his hand on his chest. "I know. But if we quit, we start over."

Dismay filled her. "What? You said we could quit!"

"I said *you* could quit. But if we fail or we all quit, we start over. Nolan and Chouza are out." Kila flew past them and collapsed to the ground. "And so is Kila. Talia's doing her best, but I don't see a way out of this. And I'm afraid if we quit now, they won't come back with us."

Pride's eyes turned to them and a smirk crossed his face. Amy raised her one uninjured hand, her eyes narrowed. "That isn't an option, then. Ignis!" Flame, hotter than any she'd produced before, poured from her palm and hit Pride head-on. He shrieked in pain and dropped to a knee.

"Good job!" Jax darted forward, his rapier at the ready, but Pride stood again, glaring past him at Amy.

"You'll pay for that." His skin had burned and blistered away, blood pouring from his chest and face. He stepped toward Jax, but Amy bathed him in flames.

Amy dropped to a knee behind him. "That's it, Jax! I can't do it again!"

"Then we need to finish this."

Amy watched in horror as Pride fixed his sights on her. Chouza struggled to his feet and planted himself in front of her. "I'm not out of this fight yet."

"Chouza, he'll kill you! Quit! Go back to Kimi! Please!"

He shook his head. "I won't let him kill you."

She whimpered as Pride charged forward. For a short time, Chouza expertly fended off blows. Pride, however, clearly outmatched him and with a few quick jabs had Chouza on the defensive. Jax maneuvered himself to stand beside Chouza, blocking Pride's path to Amy. With a sickening crunch Pride's fist connected with Chouza's shoulder and his arm went limp.

Gritting his teeth, Chouza passed her his sword and raised his other arm to begin returning punches blow-for-blow. Even as he started to falter, he kept himself between Pride and Amy, protecting her with his own body. Jax drove his dagger into Pride, but the Sin didn't seem to care, simply flicking Jax away like an annoying gnat. Talia attempted to jump forward to heal Chouza, but Pride blocked her movements, keeping between the healer and Chouza.

Jax glanced behind them to where Amy knelt, panting. "Amy! Do you have one more in you?"

"I can try." She reluctantly dropped Chouza's sword and struggled to her feet, once more focusing on the reserves of her magick. She raised her palm, directing the flames at Pride and guiding them around her allies. Unfortunately, she had to spread her magick too thin, and in the process of protecting her friends, she couldn't conjure the stronger flames and they brushed harmlessly off of Pride. Her stomach twisted when she spotted the singed fur on Chouza and Jax.

She didn't have the chance to worry long, as Pride once again glared at her. He stepped forward again and with a few more quick jabs, Chouza dropped to the floor, blood trickling from the corner of his mouth.

"No!" Amy screamed. She tried to step forward, but her vision spotted. *I used too much magick.*

Jax darted forward, attempting to do battle against the demonkin who was so clearly stronger than all of them combined. Proving that, Pride delivered a few quick blows to Jax and the foxfolk dropped as well.

Amy stared around them in horror as four of the six of them were unconscious, or maybe even dead. Another wave of healing left Talia, attempting to save them, but it was not enough to wake them. Amy drew her dagger. She knew she didn't have a chance, but she had to keep him away from the others or else he would kill them in front of her and she couldn't bear to see that.

A sadistic grin spread across his face as he saw her challenging him.

"You're no fighter," he taunted. "You're just a little spell caster. What are you going to do that they couldn't?"

Amy didn't let herself think. She stepped forward and raised her palm, letting flames wash over him again. Her chest clenched and she swayed on her feet, coughing up a mouthful of blood. He growled in pain and anger.

"All right, that has to stop!" He lunged forward, slinging fists in her direction. She managed to dodge the first two thanks to Chouza's training, but the third connected hard with her already injured shoulder, causing her to stumble and her newly discovered armor to shatter. She saw the grin of triumph on his face as he reared back to deliver another punch, one that she knew she wouldn't be able to dodge. Before it could connect, however, a form appeared in front of her—that of a red-skinned demonkin.

Bradley caught Pride's fist in his hand, stopping the blow from connecting. "Now, now, now, Bassie. You know the rules."

"You know we aren't supposed to touch the adventuring party," Whittaker said from Pride's other side. Amy blinked, confused by the sudden appearance of two of the other Sins, even as she struggled to stay conscious.

Pride glared past him at Amy. Her legs went out from under her and she dropped to her knees. "They're gnats!"

"Perhaps," Whitaker said, his voice as emotionless as ever. "But that doesn't change Pandium's orders. If they die in the dungeon, it's unfortunate, but oh well. We are not to attack them."

Pride growled again. "Why shouldn't I kill them?"

Just then, an ear-splitting shriek echoed through the chamber, and Amy stared in horror as Bradley stood with Pride's severed arm in his hand.

"That's why," Bradley sneered. "You know the orders, so you need to follow them. Otherwise, we won't be the worst thing you deal with."

Amy crawled over to Chouza, pressing her ear to his chest. To her relief, she could still feel his heart beating. She slumped back, darkness crowding her vision. "What about us? We… we finished the dungeon, what happens now?"

Bradley glanced behind him, raising an eyebrow as if he had forgotten she was there. But underneath the feigned disinterest, she thought she spotted a tinge of something else. Maybe regret. Or worry. "Oh, right. You guys are still here. You can go. Congratulations, you completed the dungeon." With that, he raised his other hand and snapped. A flash of white light enveloped them and Amy's vision blacked.

Amy's story continues in *Charred by Disease*

Thank you for reading *Scorched by Fear*.

Please consider leaving a review to support the author, publisher, and future works.

For updates on new releases, follow the author and publisher on Twitter.
@kthrynwtkns
@PhoenixQuinnPub

About the Author

A.K. Watkins

Adam and Kathryn Watkins live in small town Arkansas with their three kids, two dogs, and five cats. When not writing, they enjoy playing Pathfinder and gaming online.

Made in the USA
Monee, IL
22 October 2022